BORN
OF FIRE

BORN
OF FIRE

S H E R R I L Y N
K E N Y O N

St. Martin's Paperbacks

BORN OF FIRE

Copyright © 2009 by Sherrilyn Kenyon.
Excerpt from *Born of Ice* copyright © 2009 by Sherrilyn Kenyon.

Cover photograph © Shirley Green

For information address St. Martin's Press, 175 Fifth Avenue, New York, NY 10010.

ISBN: 978-1-61523-731-9

Printed in the United States of America

*For all the ebook authors out there, past, present
and future. Let's hear it for fighting the good fight.*

*To Bonnee and Silke for giving me a chance
when no one else would.*

*To everyone out there who is and was a fan
of the futuristic genre
and to the writers who originally built it.*

*And as always, to my family, friends, and fans
for always being there when I need you. You guys rock!*

AUTHOR'S NOTE

The title of this book was chosen not just because it described the hero and heroine and their backgrounds, but because this story was the phoenix of my career.

In the early 1990s, I sold six books in one year and then for four years, I couldn't give away Alpo to a dog kennel. Even though I'd made bestseller lists and won awards, my writing career tanked.

Part of the reason was that the paranormal/futuristic market of the early 1990s dried up, and we early pioneers lost our contracts and were left to find new paths.

Even though I tried numerous other genres and finished several books, no publisher would take them. In fact, it was while chasing that dream that I wrote what is called the ultimate "marketable" book that had all the elements of the hottest trends of the mid-1990s in it. There was no reason for it not to sell.

That book garnered me the worst rejection of my career. The infamous: "No one at this publishing house will ever be interested in developing this author. Do not submit her work to us again." Yes, it was a kick in the teeth, but to this day I am grateful to that editor because she forever changed my course as an author, and

I know I wouldn't have the career that I have today had she not written those words to my agent.

And we definitely wouldn't have this book.

It was that rejection that made me decide that I didn't want to succeed by trying to play by other people's "rules." Being the good Southern Celt that I am, I lifted my chin and said out loud, "If I'm going to fail, then it will be on my terms, while writing the books I want to write and it will be by listening to no one but my characters."

That very afternoon, I sat down and started writing *Born of Fire*. I knew it would never sell. No one would touch a futuristic, and the paranormals were quickly going extinct. But I didn't care.

Syn and Shahara were burning inside me, and this was the only story I could tell. I wrote it, never expecting it to see the light of day.

Ironically, it ended up being the very first ebook that a New York published author sold. Dreams-Unlimited was one of the original ebook publishers who didn't last long enough to see the ebook market really take off. We sold next to no copies of this book, yet I will always be grateful to Silke and Bonnee for their enthusiasm for this book and these characters. You guys were great.

And for those who have read *Born of Night*, you may notice that the time line is a bit off in this book. That was a conscious decision on my part.

Originally, *Born of Night* was published by another house, and my agent at the time told me to make sure we took out anything that made these two books appear related to keep me out of trouble with the original house. So as I rewrote *Born of Fire* for Dreams-Unlimited, I purposely deviated from *Born of Night*'s history and time line. In the original *Born of Fire*, Nykyrian was renamed Alexei and was an aristocrat who'd eloped.

While putting the two stories back together as a real series, I realized that the overlapping storylines still worked, but that they wouldn't mesh 100%, and for that I beg your understanding as a reader. Matching up the time lines would have interfered and broken up the action sequences in both books, as well as some of their motivations. In order to be true to the characters and their story, I decided to let the time line stand.

I hope you enjoy this latest foray into the Ichidian Universe.

Hugs, always.

PROLOGUE

"They're going to kill me, Shay. I need your help."

Haunted, Shahara Dagan replayed her sister's desperate voice mail message over and over again as she sat alone at her kitchen counter.

She'd stupidly thought it'd been a joke. What with Tessa's flair for exaggeration and her melodrama, as well as the number of times she'd cried her death was imminent over nothing more than a hangnail, how was she supposed to know that this time the cry for help had been real?

Shahara wanted to scream, to curse, to tear her house apart—to do anything other than wait for the loaners who would return and finish off her sister.

Dammit, Tess, at least go to loaners I can make suffer when they hurt you.

But no. Her sister had gone to "legitimate," government-backed loaners who could take whatever steps they needed to to collect their funds.

Even kill the debtor as an example to others.

She growled in frustration. How many more times would Tessa borrow money from scum to invest in stupid schemes or just throw away on gambling? And how many more times would Tessa run to her when the balance came due?

Like she could just snap her fingers and get it.

But then she'd trained her sister from an early age that she would always make everything okay. Whatever Tessa asked, she gave.

No questions asked.

Shahara hung her head in her hands. Never once in the past had Tessa been hurt. And she cursed herself that she hadn't been quicker this time. She'd gathered as much as she could as fast as she could, but it hadn't been enough.

There never seemed to be enough.

She sighed in disgust.

Why hadn't Tessa come to her sooner? Maybe then she could have sold something to pay off her sister's latest debt.

She gave a bitter laugh as she looked around the threadbare furniture she'd recovered from landfills and her rundown, one-room, economy condo. Sell what? Thanks to her siblings, she didn't own anything of real value. Not even her rusty, dilapidated fighter would bring enough money from an auction to pay half of what Tessa owed.

"I swear, Tess, one day *I'm* going to kill you."

If only their father hadn't been such a dreamer, maybe then he could have left them something more than a mountain of debts that she still, fifteen years later, hadn't paid the full balance on.

If only Tessa hadn't inherited their father's useless idealism.

If only—

The landlink buzzed.

Shahara stared at it, her throat tightening to the

point she couldn't breathe. It had to be the doctor. She'd been waiting half the night for this call and now she was too terrified to answer.

Please don't let Tessa be dead . . .

She should never have left the hospital, but after waiting alone for three hours, she couldn't stand it any longer. Too many memories of her mother's final days had tormented her. Closing her eyes, she tried to blot out the images of whispered conversations from dispassionate health-care workers. The smell of antiseptics. Their collective curled lips as they looked down on her family for not having enough money to pay for treatments.

Most of all the sight of the doctor covering her mother's lifeless body with a sheet. His emotionless tone still rang in her ears. "Too bad you didn't bring her in sooner. We might have saved her if we'd had more time."

And more money.

Her father hadn't been able to afford a lengthy hospital stay or even the medications her mother had needed. Poverty had crippled her mother, then killed her. Too many members of her family had died and she couldn't stand to lose Tessa, too.

I'll do anything to get the money. Please, just let her live.

With a shaking hand, she opened the channel. The screen brightened to show her the doctor staring at her with dark, unsympathetic eyes. Shahara's stomach twisted into a cold lump of fear and, for a moment, she thought she'd be sick as she waited for news she didn't want to hear.

"Seax Dagan," he said, addressing her with her professional title, "your sister is out of surgery and in recovery. She'll be fine . . . in time, but the voucher she used for the hospital cost was returned with a denial. I'm afraid without proper medical attention, your sister won't last for more than a few hours."

Shahara closed her eyes, relief washing over her.

Tessa would make it.

"Fria Dagan, did you hear me?" he asked, reverting to the ordinary form of address for a woman—and a term letting her know that he thought she wasn't worthy of the title seax. After all, a seax worth her salt wouldn't be impoverished.

If only the bastard knew the truth. It wasn't her lack of skills that kept her poor, it was her family obligations, and unlike others of her ilk, she would never abandon her family.

Even if they were stupid when it came to money . . .

"We're going to have to turn her out unless we can get a valid voucher."

The knot in her stomach twisted even harder and she clenched her fists. Shahara was so tired of being poor, so tired of the people who looked down their snobby noses at her and demanded their money as if all she had to do was grab it off the nearest shelf. People who had no idea just how precious every credit was.

Every bead of sweat came with a hefty price tag . . .

She opened her eyes and forced her anger and hatred aside. "I heard you, Doctor. I'll get the money for you in cash. If you'll give me three days."

His sympathetic stare turned to doubt. She'd seen that look too many times in her life and she despised it.

She added coldly, "I'll sign over the deed to my ship as collateral."

He nodded. "Very well. We'll keep her here for the duration." He cut the transmission.

Wanting to flip off the doctor for his condescension, she stared at the blank screen. "You're lucky I'm almost a lady."

For the briefest instant, she considered asking her brother, Caillen, or sister, Kasen, for the money, but she knew they didn't possess it any more than she did.

Because of Kasen's necessary medical treatments and meds, she was always behind on her debts and asking Shahara and Caillen for money.

Caillen, like her, would have plenty if Kasen and Tess could ever learn to manage theirs. And if he wasn't helping her make the payments on their father's leftover debts.

Shahara sighed. Even if she asked, her brother and sister would have to borrow it, and the type of people they ran with were even worse than the ones after Tessa. The last thing she wanted was to see them hurt.

Family.

It was all she'd had growing up an orphan on the streets. It was all anyone could ever depend on. After the death of their parents, she and her siblings had pulled together to survive. They watched one another's backs. Now Tessa needed her and nothing and no one would keep her from saving her sister's life.

No matter what, she couldn't afford to let Caillen know what'd happened. Reckless and hotheaded to the extreme, he'd go after those responsible, and she couldn't stand the thought of him lying next to Tessa in the hospital.

Or worse, being arrested for it.

Not to mention, *that* was the last thing they could afford.

She was the oldest and it was her responsibility to settle this.

With a determined hand, she pulled her holstered blaster across the counter, clutching it until her knuckles blanched. Maybe she didn't have the best occupation in the universe, but it kept her fed.

Her stomach rumbled a denial.

I don't need to hear it from you, too. Everyone wanted to give her attitude today.

Grabbing her weapon, she stood up and moved to her bedroom in the corner, where she could change out of her only dress and into her work clothes. She pulled her tight, black battlesuit on, the armor creaking as she fastened the front and collar. It was old and out of fashion, but Armstitch cost way too much.

One day, though, she'd have the money to go buy another.

One day . . .

Yeah, you've been saying that for years.

Ignoring the inner voice she was sure was there only to aggravate her, she stared at herself in the chipped, broken mirror. Her hollow, golden eyes were dull and ringed with dark circles from a night spent worrying over her sister.

She touched her face, seeing so much of her mother on the outside, but knowing the similarity went no deeper. All she'd ever wanted was to be the same kind, loving, gentle woman her mother had been.

She wasn't.

Unlike her mother, she didn't believe in the innate goodness of others. Growing up responsible for the welfare of three younger siblings had taught her early on the necessity of having a hard edge.

Life was harsh and people were worthless and mean to their bitter cores. They only used and betrayed. *That* was the only code she believed in.

Trisa. That's what Caillen called her. She was just like the small, spiked animal that shot its poisoned quills at its enemies. Better to strike first than be victimized.

Besides, she refused to make apologies. She'd always done what she had to, to keep her family together and safe. And no one, absolutely no one, would ever jeopardize what she'd struggled so hard to maintain.

Her soul charged by her conviction, she pulled her small reserve blaster out of its box and checked the charge level before fastening it inside her right boot. Then she strapped the other blaster to her right hip and slid her daggers into the custom sheaths that were hidden throughout her clothes.

It was time to do business.

She walked the two feet to the kitchen where her father's old laptop rested on her counter.

There were only two legal ways for an uneducated woman to get the kind of money she needed—prostitution and bounty hunting. She refused to sell her body, and at least as a free-tracer, she was able to uphold her oath as a seax while she cleaned some of the filth from the cities. The same type of filth that fed off people like Tessa.

Those who tried to feed off her.

With that thought in mind, she brought up her computer and typed in her tracer's code. The outstanding bounty sheets refreshed. Eager to get on with the hunt, she looked over the worst criminals in existence—rapists, murderers, pedophiles, terrorists, and those who were all four combined.

Shahara flipped through them quickly, scanning for an appropriate target whose bounty could pay off most of what she owed.

All of a sudden she found it.

Her blood began to race with the thrill of a seriously high-profile target who'd just been reattached to the list.

"C.I. Syn wanted dead by the Gourish president for the kidnaping, rape, and suspected murder of his daughter Kiara Zamir. Wanted alive," for three times the Gourish bounty, which was staggering, "by the Ritadarion government for filching, murder, treason, and prison escape." The amount being offered for him by the Ritadarions would pay off Tessa's debts, the hospital bill, the liens on her ship, and she'd have a little left over to live on for awhile.

Provided her sister behaved.

Not to mention, she wouldn't have to decapitate him for the Ritadarions. She shuddered as she read over the death contract. President Zamir wanted Syn delivered alive and while she didn't mind killing a criminal, she never wanted to dissect one to collect her bounty.

Gah, what had Syn done to Kiara Zamir to warrant that kind of hatred?

"You *are* an evil bastard . . ."

Neither dead nor alive would be easy—which was why the bounty on him was so high.

Shahara bit her lip in indecision. Syn's name was more than well known and more than well feared. He'd made his reputation for being the best computer hacker and file filch in the known universe. And before he'd left his mid-teens he'd been imprisoned by the Ritadarions.

Twice.

Rumors of his cruelty circulated within the small group of tracers she associated with. To her knowledge, no other free-tracer had ever tried to bring him in, which in and of itself spoke volumes about his dangerous reputation.

Bound-tracers who were sent in after him almost never returned.

The tiny handful of ones lucky enough to live through an encounter with him were never fully intact.

It didn't matter. She pushed her doubt and uncertainty away. She'd never failed a mission before. Tessa's life depended on her success and she wouldn't fail this time.

Signing her name on the screen and swiping her index finger imprint, she accepted the contract.

CHAPTER 1

Hell had many interpretations. Syn knew that better than anyone. In his life, he'd managed to live through most of the common variations and discover a multitude of new ones.

Why was it every time he thought he had life tamed, the treacherous beast turned around and bit him on the ass?

Cocking his head, he detected the sound of footsteps on the wet pavement behind him as he walked toward the bay where he'd docked his fighter. Anger scorched him. He slid his hand closer to his concealed weapons. He'd been stalked enough times in his life to recognize the sound of someone trailing him while trying to remain inconspicuous.

Tonight, he just wasn't in the mood to deal with it.

Streetlights glinted against the drying puddles that splashed beneath his boots. Steam hissed an escape from boilers and chimneys, adding an eeriness to the otherwise quiet night.

Unless he missed his guess, which he never did, six men were behind him. Only Syn and the six of them walked down the street at this late hour—another factor that told him whoever it was wanted one thing—

Him.

"Come get some," he muttered, unable to find an ounce of patience for anyone stupid enough to try and kill him. What little patience he possessed had ended hours ago.

You just made a bad mistake, boys. I definitely wouldn't want to be you.

'Cause tonight, he wanted blood without being particular as to whom he took it from. They were definitely in the wrong place at the wrong time.

Never attack a target who was already pissed off at someone else and at the universe in general—someone who was aching for a fight and a whipping boy. It never went well for the antagonists.

During the past two days, he'd been buffeted by a steady stream of absolute bullshit aggravations. The highlight of which was the new bounty being offered for his head that had brought out every needy freetracer and assassin within striking distance.

It's so good to be me . . .

Earlier that day, he'd been attacked by a group of assassins and had his precious fighter damaged in the process. But the absolute *best . . .*

His best friend, Nykyrian Quiakides, had not only slept with the woman Syn was accused of raping and murdering, but had gone into hiding with her, thus guaranteeing that Syn's head would be the price for their screwed-up and doomed relationship.

At present, life was just too disgusting for words and he really was tired of dealing with it.

Not once in the last two days had he been able to even nap, and sleep dep always made him edgier than normal—and shortened the fuse on an already notoriously hot temper.

Syn pulled the safety off his blaster and slid his hand over the rough, bone grip.

Tonight, his stalkers would learn a valuable lesson about angry Rits who didn't get enough sleep.

With a quick turn, he headed into an alley on his right. It was time he put a stop to this crap and got some serious sleep time.

Taking cover in a small, shadowy alcove, he tried to ignore the foul stench of the decaying garbage that lined the alleyway behind him. He'd grown up in filthy alleys like this one, with the stench of the street lulling him to sleep at night. He clenched his teeth in rage, the smell and memories doing nothing to improve his foul mood.

He may have been conceived in the gutter. He refused to die in one.

The steps drew closer. He tightened his grip in anticipation.

"Should we go in after him, or wait till he comes back out?"

He rolled his eyes at that puss of a comment. The speaker had been male with a slight Trioson lilt to his voice. Heat simmered in Syn's blood as he prepared himself for the coming fight.

"You go in and see if it dead-ends. He might've already escaped us."

"Me?" the voice cracked.

"Just do it!"

A grimy, middle-aged human male stumbled into the alley like someone had shoved him. Unlike his own eyes, which saw better at night than in the day, Syn knew the short, fat man would have to wait a few minutes before his eyes adjusted to the pitch darkness.

A smile curved his lips. How would the fat, little

rodent react when he learned only three feet separated them?

"Looks good for your funeral, huh?" Syn taunted.

The man jerked around, trying to focus his eyes at the darkened alcove shielding Syn.

As the man reached for his blaster, Syn caught his arm. He jerked the weapon from the man's hip and tossed it across the alley into a Dumpster where it landed with an echoing clatter.

"Durrin!" the man shouted, his voice shaking.

Syn shoved the man away from him and turned to face a dark, Partini male who led the four other humans toward him.

An ugly, orange-fleshed humanoid, Durrin towered several feet over him. The snarl that twisted his thin, yellow lips would have sent most men to their knees in quaking fear. But Syn recognized scare tactics when he saw them, and there wasn't much left in life that frightened him.

Still, it wasn't often someone dwarfed Syn's height and he found that fact a *bit* disturbing.

"C.I. Syn," the Partini rasped in a deep accent. "You're being remanded into Gourish custody . . . dead."

'Cause let's face it, dead was just easier.

Or so they thought.

Syn barely had time to dodge the large knife aimed for his throat. Partinie had an aversion for blasters, but then, their dagger and knife abilities were such that it didn't put them at any disadvantage.

What the idiot didn't know was that Syn had grown up in prison where you either learned to handle a knife . . .

Or you died.

Syn *tsk*ed as the alien pulled back for another strike. "You missed with me so close? What? You failed your assassin training classes?" He shook his head. "Did you even bother to show up? Or are you just that incompetent?" He added a little distance between himself and the assassin's black, poison-coated knife. One scratch from that and he would die. Quickly.

And most painfully.

He scoffed at the Partini. "I feel I should warn you, I'm in a *really* bad mood."

The short man returned to the side of the others while they stood back with the stupid assumption that Syn was going down under the Partini's blade.

They'd learn.

"You'll be in a worse mood when we haul you in dead!"

Syn grimaced in pain at a comment so stupid it didn't even rate a snotty comeback.

What drugs were they taking? He hadn't survived this long on the street to have these dumbasses kill him now.

The Partini lunged.

Syn easily sidestepped him and kicked him into the wall so hard that he recoiled off it and slammed into the Dumpster. The alien landed in a heap on the ground.

"Next?"

The others rushed forward to attack. Syn stomped the heel of his boot against the ground, releasing the blade in the toe and whirled to catch the first one who reached him in the neck. His attacker dropped to the street, screaming from the wound.

The next one tried to shoot him. Syn dodged the blast and the laser cut into another member of their group who died so fast, he didn't even make a sound. Catching the guy who'd fired at him by the wrist, Syn used the blaster to shoot another assassin before he chopped him in the throat and knocked him to the ground.

There were only two left. The Partini and the fat human weasel who'd entered the alley first. The human whipped out his blaster to aim at his head.

Bored with them, Syn pulled out his own blaster and shot the human in the hand that was holding his blaster. His weapon forgotten as it clattered to the ground, the coward dropped to the filthy street, whining like a babe.

Syn turned around to face the Partini who'd now regained his footing. Double-checking the condition of the others, Syn saw that three humans were still alive, but out of commission.

The other two were still dead.

Good.

Syn watched the Partini closely as the alien lunged for him. He caught the alien's wrist before the knife could make contact with his skin.

The Partini tried to pull loose, but Syn held fast with one hand. "Tell me," he asked snidely, "what smells like shit and screams like a girl?"

He shot the Partini in the knee.

The Partini screamed like a woman meeting her long-lost best friend as he crumpled to the street, his poisoned knife falling on the concrete with a metallic clink.

Syn kicked the knife into the darkness, out of the assassin's reach. "That's right. *You.*"

The Partini glared at him. "A blaster against a knife isn't fair."

He approached him slowly. "No shit . . . and so goes

my incentive to fight fairly. You want fair, play with kids. You wanna come at me, make out a will."

Looking down at the gaping wound in the Partini's leg, he arched his brow at the scaly bone that protruded. "I never knew Partinie had articulated bones. *Very* interesting. I wonder what the rest of your skeleton looks like."

Fear flickered deep in the alien's eyes.

Syn slid the plate back on his blaster and checked the charge level. Satisfied it would fire several more rounds, he released the plate and let it snap loudly back into place. That should make them piss their pants.

Those who were still alive anyway. The others had already done that.

He stared coldly at the assassins. "I suggest you recant your contract on me first thing after you have your knee tended. The next time you come at me, the authorities will have to run a DNA scan to identify your remains."

The Partini glared at him with hatred, but Syn recognized the fear that underlay the hate. He'd made his point. These assassins would never again bother him.

Satisfied, he glanced back at the human who was still whimpering. The man had managed to tie a ragged scarf around his injured hand and watched him as if he expected Syn to kill them.

He probably should, but he wasn't *quite* that cold-blooded.

At least not tonight.

"There's a hospital two blocks down on your right. I suggest you use it." He left them to tend their injuries.

No good deed goes unpunished.

No doubt he'd live to regret his mercy tonight as he

regretted any time he'd ever been nice to someone. It always came back to bite him on the ass.

So be it.

Tired of the endless wave of assassins and tracers who forever sought him, he headed to the landing bay down the street and climbed aboard his sleek, black fighter, which still had burn marks on the paint from his earlier attack. With any luck, he just might make it through the next few hours without someone else trying to kill him.

He doubted it.

"Of all the time to run out of whisky . . ." Figured his flask would be empty.

But one thing stood certain, the next time someone came at him, he wasn't going to be as nice. He was tired of being blamed for crimes he hadn't committed— tired of fighting for a life that didn't seem worth the effort.

Basically, he was just tired, period.

Yeah, well, it's penance for all the crimes you did commit and got away with.

That was always a possibility.

Of course, his worst crime had been surviving a life that should have killed him before he learned to walk . . .

You think you're so special, don't you? You and those arrogant eyes just like your mother's. But you're nothing, boy. You're from my genes, cut from the same cloth as me. Just. Like. Me. So don't be thinking you're better 'cause you're not. We're shit and that's all we'll ever be. At least I know how to make money. You can't even take a hit without crying like your sister. Worthless bastard.

Syn could still see the look of hatred on his father's

face. Feel the blow of his fist whenever Syn made the mistake of getting too close to him.

Yeah, the old fart was right. In the end, he *was* worthless.

Not wanting to go there, he checked his coordinates.

It didn't take long to reach his nearby home planet of Kildara. Unfortunately, the mid-afternoon sun hung high on his city, its bright, glaring rays making his light-sensitive Ritadarion eyes water in protest.

He hated the day, the heat, the noise—the light that hid none of the street's ugliness.

Even though he lived in the best district of Broma, all he had to do was travel three blocks over and he'd see enough homeless, impoverished people to twist his stomach raw. He'd done his best to forget his past, but it just didn't seem possible. Every time he thought he'd managed to bury that shit so deep it could never rise up, something or someone always brought it back to him with sharp, crisp brutality.

Disgusted, he entered his oversized apartment. He had too many other problems to deal with and he was really too tired to think.

He shrugged his jacket off and tossed it over his black leather sofa before picking up the remote to lower the blinds against the bright sunlight.

He leaned his head against the cool, metal slats and sighed. Never in his life had he been more repulsed. Nykyrian was in love with Kiara Zamir and her father was out to crucify them.

Why wouldn't Nykyrian listen to him and return her before it was too late? What kind of fool with a price on his head fell in love with a princess from a planet that wanted him dead?

Syn rubbed at the sudden throb in his temples,

repulsed by his friend's devotion to a woman who would be the death of them all.

What an idiot. Women were treacherous. All of them. And Kiara had already shown her true colors. The moment she'd seen them for what they were—what their pasts had made them—she'd vomited and cursed them, just like everyone else.

Lying *harita*.

But then, having been stupid enough once to think that a woman could see through his past to the person he'd become, he understood Nykyrian's idiocy better than he wanted to.

Yet it was all a lie. No one escaped their past. No matter how hard they tried.

Men were blind fools and women weakened the soul and stole the heart. Then when they had both in their possession, they stomped them into the ground.

Bitches.

Unable to stand it, he went to his bar and grabbed a glass and a bottle of the strongest whisky he had. As he poured it, his gaze fell to the stuffed animal and photo frame of his son.

Paden . . .

He winced in misery as bitter memories tore through him.

Mara, listen to me. I'm not my father. I would never *hurt you.*

No, you're worse than your father. At least he stayed in the gutter where he belonged. You . . . you made me believe the lies you told. That you were decent and respectable. You said your father was a businessman. You bastard! His wife had raked him with a sneer so filled with hatred that it was forever branded in his memory. *How could I have ever let you into my life?*

I would never hurt you or Paden. Please, listen to me.

She'd slapped him so hard, the blow had split his lip. If anyone else had dared that, he'd have cut them in half. But like a pathetic nothing, he'd taken it from her.

Get out! I've already called the enforcers to arrest you. If I ever see you again, so help me, I'll shoot you myself!

This from the woman he'd lived to make happy. The woman he'd given everything to. His heart. His soul. His life.

In the end, it didn't matter that he'd treated her like royalty and would have sold his soul for a single rose to make her smile. Mara had betrayed him and taken everything he'd ever cared about for no other reason than his father had been a first-rank bastard and Syn, rather than lying down and dying, had fought to make a better life for himself.

It had never mattered to him that he was shit to the world. He was used to that. It was the day he'd become shit to his wife and son that had ruined him.

All he'd ever wanted was for one person to not blame him for his parentage. One woman who could look at him like he was a man and not a monster out to hurt her.

Then he'd asked the dumbest, most pathetic question of his life. *Did you ever love me . . . even a little?*

How could anyone love something like you? You're a liar, a thief and a convict. All I wanted was your money. If only I'd known the truth about you . . . you disgust me. Get out!

Yeah, there was no such thing as love. It was a myth made up by assholes who only wanted to sell stories and rings people couldn't afford to gullible fools.

He didn't understand love in any fashion. The gods

knew, he'd never seen it in his life. It was as elusive to him as sleep.

His fury dying at the last thought, he grabbed his son's frame, the stuffed toy, and his bottle, and skirted around the edge of his two facing sofas.

Stifling a yawn, he headed to his bedroom in back.

Later, he'd beat sense into Nykyrian. Right now, all he wanted was a good eight solid hours of oblivious rest.

You know it's not safe here.

Yeah, his apartment had been seriously compromised, but damn it, he wasn't going to be run out of his home for anything. If they came for him here, they'd learn . . .

And if they killed him, really, who would care?

Without disrobing or removing his blaster, he threw himself face down on the light, feather mattress that heaved under his weight. He clutched his soft, feathered pillow under his head, and sighed in deep contentment before he rolled over onto his back. A few hours of this and he'd be as good as new.

He leaned up to shove Paden's frame and toy into his nightstand, then took a deep swig of whisky straight from the bottle and set it aside.

Lying back on his bed, he closed his eyes.

Gah, nothing felt better than this . . .

Just as he started to doze, he heard a sharp click from the main room that sounded like someone had deactivated his alarm system and opened his front door.

Senses alert, he tensed, forcing himself to lie still and listen. When he heard nothing more, he wondered if he'd imagined the sound. Hell, it was probably nothing more than a hallucination brought on by sleep dep—or overworked nerves—that heard assassins coming at him from every shadow.

Of course the alcohol didn't help, ei

The muffled, padded sound of bo
hardwood floor barely reached his ears.
inary about that. Someone was defini
through his flat.

Damn . . . Would he ever get another
sleep?

Clenching his teeth, Syn slid his blaster
leather holster. Only one thing made hi
furious—unknown people in his home. He did
into other people's homes and, dammit, he e
the same courtesy.

Well, whoever they were, they were about to r
a memorable lesson in manners.

Syn rose from the bed and crept to his door,
blaster gripped tightly in his hand. He flattened him
against the wall and pushed the control to slide t
door open.

Nothing.

Frowning in confusion, he looked around the main
room from the safety of his partially concealed position behind the wall. There wasn't so much as a shadow
in the dim light of his apartment.

Syn scoffed at his paranoia.

Definitely sleep deprivation.

What would he imagine next? Little hairy beasties
tap-dancing on his sofa, or other fey creatures sneaking up on him in the shower?

Clicking the release of his blaster back into safety,
he lowered his weapon and reached to close the door.

Light flashed against the silver barrel of a blaster
pointed straight at his chest from the concealment of
the opposite wall.

CHAPTER 2

"Don't move," a smooth, lilting feminine voice ordered.

Syn arched one brow. It wasn't every day someone got the drop on him, especially a woman who had a voice that lent itself to seduction.

"Or what?" He wished he could catch a glimpse of whomever had outsmarted him. She had to be something, because this *never* happened to him.

She clicked off the safety release of her blaster.

Syn wasn't prone to panic, and having people level a weapon at him was pretty commonplace, but he didn't usually face unseen attackers.

Especially not in his home.

"Are you an assassin or tracer?" he asked.

"Free-tracer."

Free-tracers, unlike assassins, had a conscience as a rule. And since he was still breathing and not dead, it told him she was going after his living contract, which gave him a lot of latitude in dealing with her.

"Good." He snatched her blaster from her hands.

A blast of red sizzled up toward his ceiling, searing a long black streak across the white paint. He cursed at the mark. He'd fought too long and too hard to drag himself out of the streets and have a nice home for someone to come in and start destroying it.

"No one messes up my place." He grabbed a small, silken wrist and jerked the woman into his view. Shock jolted him as he stared into the face of a startled angel.

Damn, she was beautiful.

In that instant of hesitation, she drove her knee straight into his groin.

Pure agony spread through him. Gasping, he doubled over with a sharp curse.

Shahara pulled the reserve blaster from her boot and leveled it at C.I. Syn: rapist, murderer, traitor, and filch. He was huge and powerful. She'd have to watch him closely if she were to succeed. Keeping her eyes on him, she bent her knees to retrieve the other two blasters from the floor.

The man in front of her was not the usual type she was used to dealing with. Not only was he more refined, but something proud and primal emanated from every molecule of his body. Only one word could define it.

Sexy.

And she was far from immune to it.

Unlike the other class three and four felons she'd traced, this one possessed an air of sophistication. When he spoke, it wasn't in a gruff, ignorant street dialect, it was with a fluid, baritone voice that resonated deep from within him. His cadence and syntax were that of an educated man or an aristocrat, not a lowly filch.

With a deep breath, he recovered himself from her kick—something she'd never seen a man do so quickly before. He moved away from her with the lithe, powerful grace of a predator.

Granted he was still limping, but there was an unmistakable fluidity.

That was it. That was what she sensed from him. He had a raw animal magnetism. He moved like a caged panther—sleek, rippling, deadly.

Vicious.

And he pounced like lightning. Before she realized what was happening, he had her completely unarmed. She kicked him back. He spun and shoved her into the wall.

Shahara used the rebound to propel herself at him and caught him a stiff blow to his jaw. Grunting, he grabbed her. She flipped up and kicked him back.

Syn cursed at her skill. She was incredible when it came to fighting. And every time he tried to pin her, she escaped. He hissed as she caught him another blow to the gut.

Kill her!

But he had a bad suspicion about her identity and if she was who he thought . . .

Better to have her beat him into the ground than the alternative.

Out of her sleeves, two knives appeared. She moved at him, slashing. He put his arm up to block her attack. Their forearms collided, then she swiped his arm with the blade. It sliced straight through his padding to his flesh.

"Son of a . . ."

She stomped his foot. "Surrender, convict. I don't have to take you in alive."

He glared down at her as he tried to pin her again and failed. "Then you better get ready to kill me 'cause that's the only way I'm going in."

Shahara headbutted him, then scissor-kicked his chest. In a fluid roll, she scooped her blaster up from the floor and angled it at him.

He finally froze.

"Cute attack," she sneered, waving him back into the bedroom with the barrel of her weapon. This time she knew to keep a good distance between them.

His eyes blazing obsidian fire, he obeyed in a manner that told her he didn't often cooperate with orders.

No, she could tell by the arrogant, taunting smile that this man was a leader or a loner.

Never a follower.

"Not half as cute as yours." He rubbed his groin meaningfully.

She shrugged at his sarcasm. "He who waits, loses."

The fierce scowl Syn gave her told her he didn't like the old Gondarion proverb at all.

Disregarding the look, she tossed him a pair of laser cuffs. They landed at his booted feet with a soft jingle. "Put those on quick or I'll blast you straight to hell."

He picked the cuffs up in his fist as if they disgusted him. His black gaze hardened and she swore she could actually smell the danger that radiated from every pore of his body.

She tensed her finger over the trigger, expecting him to toss the cuffs in her face. It wouldn't be the first time a convict had reacted that way and she had a few more tricks to unleash if he chose that action.

A loud whistle blared in the room behind her. Startled, she snapped around to make sure someone wasn't coming in to help him. Before she could focus on what the noise was, Syn's hands closed around hers.

How had he moved that fast? He should still be on the other side of the room.

Her heart racing, she struggled for her weapon, kicking and punching at him with all the fury coursing through her body. If he got her blaster away, he'd kill her for sure.

His grip tightened around her hand, numbing her fingers until she could barely feel the roughened grip of her blaster. She tried to headbutt him, but he dodged too fast.

To her horror, the blaster dropped to the floor with a heavy thud.

Cursing, she reverted to her strict training and punched at his throat.

Syn caught her hand in his before she could make contact with his windpipe. Wrenching her arm painfully behind her back, he picked her up and tossed her over his shoulder.

Shahara cursed as she struggled. In spite of her best efforts and blows, he knelt down, retrieved the blasters from the floor, then tossed her on his bed.

The soft, lump-free mattress startled her for the briefest moment before true panic consumed her. He stood a few feet away from the bed, gazing down at her with dark eyes.

Her vision dimmed. Snarling, she dove for him with only one goal—to escape with her life and body intact.

Syn switched his blaster setting from kill to stun and shot her in the shoulder before she could reach him.

A soft gasp left her lips. Her eyes widened as she clutched at her shoulder, then she crumpled to the floor.

A twinge of guilt annoyed him. He'd been stunned enough times to know she'd have a vicious headache when she woke up.

But what other choice did he have? She seemed to be a determined little *cozu*.

Shaking his head in bitter amusement, he knelt beside her to check her pulse. Satisfied he hadn't hurt her, he took a good look at her peaceful features. Damned if she wasn't the most attractive woman he'd ever thrown onto his bed. Not that he'd ever made a habit of tossing women there, but still . . .

The flesh of her throat was warm and soft beneath his hand, something completely at odds with her tough demeanor. Trailing his finger over her creamy cheek, he stared at her lips, which were slightly parted while she breathed. He couldn't help wondering how much softer they might be, as well as other, more tender parts of her body.

Aching pains stabbed his groin.

Yeah, that's just what you need to add to your already fucked-up day. Sleep with a woman who wanted to hand him over to his enemies. A woman who had no compunctions about shooting him. Or, as he looked at his bleeding forearm, carving parts off his body.

If he had one single brain cell left in his head, he'd deplete her memory and dump her in the nearest hole. But he couldn't quite bring himself to be so cruel. Unlike *her,* he had a conscience about handing people over to those out to torture, kill, and maim them.

Sighing, he picked her up from the floor and carried her from his bedroom to the couch.

Damn, she weighed nothing. Didn't the woman ever eat? If he were still a doctor, he'd run a nutrition diagnostic on her. She couldn't be healthy at this weight.

But then, like him, she was a gutter rat and it was hard to find food in the sewers. That kind of desperate hunger never went away even when there was food around.

The whistle blared again. "Syn?"

He gave a small prayer of thanks that Caillen Dagan had seen the right moment to call him. That boy had always had good timing . . .

With a final look at the shapely form draped across his couch, he crossed the room and picked up his earpiece that kept him in contact with the pilots who worked for him.

"Yeah, Dagan, what do you need?"

"Kasen just called and she's accepted a run to Lyrix. She wants me to go with her and I don't dare let her go alone. You know how rough that place is. Anyway, I was supposed to do the Prinum shipment for you tonight and since I can't be in two places . . . Is there any way you can get someone to cover for me?"

Syn glanced back at the tracer on his couch, debating the sanity of leaving her.

"Syn?"

He frowned at Caillen's anxious voice. Caillen hated asking for help and Syn had never been one to deny a friend in need. Besides, Caillen protected nothing like he did his sisters, and he respected the man's devotion. If there was anything he understood, it was that family came first.

And Caillen was like a brother to him. "Sure, I'll do it."

"Thanks, bud, I owe you."

Clicking off the link, Syn tossed it back on the counter and shook his head. Caillen had always been a bit waxed when it came to his sisters. So waxed that in all the years Syn had known him, he'd only met one sister, Kasen, and that had been by pure accident.

Something bad had happened to one of them when they were teenagers and it'd severely scarred Caillen. Syn had no idea what it was, since he tended not to pry into people's personal lives.

He figured if Caillen wanted him to know, he'd volunteer it. Until then, it was none of his business.

A soft moan drew his attention back to his current problem. Intrigued by his catch, he returned to the couch.

He stared down at her, hoping he was wrong about her identity . . .

She didn't look like a Dagan. At least not Caillen or Kasen, but then genes were screwy things. He didn't really look anything like his sister or mother either.

Except for his eyes . . .

He flinched at the reminder. His father had punished him well for sharing that bit of his mother's DNA. The sad thing was, his father had actually loved her and while they'd been together, he hadn't been quite as psychotic. But after she ran off, he'd turned his hatred for her to the two kids the bitch had left behind.

He pushed that thought away and stared down at the tracer.

For now, she lay unmoving, her long, reddish-brown braid falling over the cushions, down to the floor. Picking it up, he marveled at the silken texture. He'd never seen hair quite that shade. Dark red strands were entwined with gold, brown, black, and ash. Like rich mahogany.

The leather Armstitch battlesuit she wore was of an outdated style, probably around ten years old, and by the fit of it, it looked like she'd bought it used. Still, the cut complimented her lithe, slender figure even if the color did nothing to accentuate her exotic features.

Damn, the woman was built taut and tight, and he could just imagine her wrapping those long, sexy limbs around his body while she . . .

Stop it, asshole.

That was easier said than done as he stared at her and his cock twitched. He traced the line of her full, rosy lips with his knuckle, taking delight in the slight, sensual tickle of her breath against his skin. He hadn't been with a woman in awhile. Too damned long, now that he thought about it. An obvious fact given the way his body craved a woman who wanted his head. And not the one he wanted to share with her.

There was no real reason for the long stretch other than he didn't like personal entanglements and women, while entertaining for a couple of hours, had a nasty habit of screwing him over any time he gave them a chance. The one thing Mara had taught him with crystal clarity—he couldn't do enough right in his adult life to shut out all the wrong he'd done as a kid.

More to the point, no woman would ever forgive him for the genetic link he shared with a monster.

So he always kept his liaisons to a single night with women he didn't know. Women he could keep at a safe, emotionless distance.

And for the last six months, he hadn't been able to find any woman even remotely appealing.

Until now.

I am psychotic . . . just like my dad.

He'd have to be to even look at a woman like her who was after his ass to arrest it.

And still she appealed to him for reasons he couldn't understand. Her angry, almond-shaped eyes were closed now, but he vividly recalled the odd, golden shade. There was something very familiar about those eyes. For his life he couldn't remember what.

Also there was something about her that reminded him of his own sister. The unique way she held her head when she defied him as if she'd faced the worst possible nightmare and still found the courage to continue life's brutal path. Something a typical person wouldn't notice. But to those who'd walked courageously through hell and been tested and scarred by its fires, it was obvious.

Too bad his sister had lost that courage.

Pain racked his soul as he struggled against the unrelenting grief that no amount of time seemed to dull. The sight of her lifeless body soaked in blood . . .

Regrets pounded through him and he closed his eyes, wishing he could go back and save Talia.

If only he'd been older, maybe he could have done something to help her.

Bullshit. There had been no help for either of them. He knew that for a fact and still he beat himself up with it over and over again. He hated that part of himself that couldn't let go of his past.

But this tracer wasn't Talia. She would never put herself in the line of fire to save him. To her, he was nothing more than a paycheck—a fugitive who needed to be returned because he didn't deserve to live among decent people.

Whatever he did, he couldn't allow himself to relax as long as she remained inside his home.

With that thought, Syn searched her body for more weapons to make sure she didn't have any other means of carving him up. He did his best to ignore the soft curves under his hands as he slid them over the rough leather of her battlesuit, and located weapon after weapon.

Damn, it was like disarming The League . . .

Or him.

Focus . . .

Though she was too thin for his normal tastes, her muscles were firm, no doubt from hours of physical training. He could easily imagine how attractive her lithe body would look draped in nothing but a sheet.

His blood rushed through his veins like lava as his cock turned rock hard. "Get a hold of yourself. You're not some horny teen chasing after the first girl who smiled at you."

True, but there was something about this woman. Something that put a slow burn in his blood.

Yeah, she wants to beat your ass, you masochistic bastard.

Sliding his hands over her firm calf, he located a knife tucked inside her pant leg. He pulled it out and studied the intricate design.

Shit . . .

"I knew it." The weapon in his hand was legendary. An entwined bird and viper engraved on the silver handle—the symbol of a Gondarion Seax. Only one person in her entire generation had passed seax training.

Shahara Dagan.

Suspicions confirmed, he sighed in aggravation. *You're so going to die . . .*

Shock and disgust poured through him. *Well, isn't this just typical? After months of celibacy you finally find a woman who sets your hormones on fire and not only is she after your head in the worst sort of way, she's the treasured sister of one of your best friends.*

"Just shoot me now and get it over with." Because that would be kind compared to what Dagan would do if he found out Syn had shot the older sister he worshiped.

He balanced the carefully honed blade between his fingers and looked back at the tracer whose very name made most fugitives surrender immediately.

And no wonder, given the way she fought.

"So you're the infamous Shahara . . ." He shook his

head in amazement that such a petite beauty could inspire so lethal a reputation. "I wonder what Caillen would say if he knew you were here?"

I'm going to cut your balls off, Syn.

Yeah, that would probably be it . . .

On the good side and *if* Syn was lucky. If Dagan was having a bad day . . .

He shuddered.

Rolling his eyes at his typical luck, Syn placed the knife on top of the other weapons and devices he'd taken off her. He picked up her blasters and locked them, along with everything else, in the wall safe in his bedroom.

What was he going to do with her?

Unbidden, an image of her writhing naked in his bed flashed before his eyes and he grinned wickedly. That was definitely what he *wanted* to do with her.

But hormones aside, he had to be practical.

The woman wanted to hand him over to the authorities. Seaxes were unfortunately notorious for their unshakable sense of justice and honor. And she was honor-bound to take him in no matter what argument he made.

He wasn't about to be executed for crimes he hadn't committed and he damn sure couldn't kill her without upsetting Caillen.

So where did that leave him?

Screwed blue and tattooed.

Maybe he should call Caillen after all . . .

Syn scoffed at the thought. If he knew his friend at all—and he did—Caillen would kill *him* for stunning her.

So what options were left?

Kill her. Hide the body.

If only he could . . . Damn, stupid conscience. Why

thily, in case he was in the
e slid off the couch.

sound, she crossed to the door a
ols. Before her fingers touched the key
up and gnashed her teeth in frustration.
vated the scanner.

ble bastard, rat punk!

n't really think he'd make it easy for you, did
but a woman could always hope for a brain
at would leave him stupid and make it easier

ly . . .
wanted to curse and strike out at the almost in-
beams that crosshatched the door, but she knew
did that, they'd singe her flesh with a burn far
than any fire. Worst of all, they'd trip an alarm.
e was at his mercy.

stinctively, she reached for her weapons. As ex-
ed, they were gone along with the lockbox she'd
d to breach the security system earlier.

Clenching her fists, she wished she could strangle
n. Without her lockbox, she had no hope of guessing
e scanner's code. Grimson had designed his security
ystems too carefully and the number sequences were
oo intricate to ever be guessed by random choice, or
emembered from her earlier success.

There was a nine in it . . .

Someplace.

Yeah, that wasn't exactly helpful.

Sighing, she looked around the room. She wasn't just going to stand here waiting for him to come back and discover she was awake. There had to be a weapon somewhere in this giant mausoleum.

had the gods ɑ
have come with

In the end, he
regained consciou
to talk sense into
brother's reason and

Gods, just let her
Otherwise he *would* h

And lie to Caillen fc

Yeah . . .

With that thought forei
the front door and switche
she'd have no choice excep
think of some way to escaj
with his life intact.

Shahara moaned, her temples th
Blinking open her eyes, she wor
terrible. Her sight focused on the ι
fore her where a beautiful Chinergo
she stared at the impressionist's inter₁
black bird in flight, she instantly reme
happened.

Where she was.

That slippery bastard had shot her!

With a gasp, she sat up, her head protes
den movement. Ignoring the pain, she force
eyesight to clear and scanned the room.

It was empty. Thank goodness.

Silence buzzed in her ears and she wondere
Syn had gone.

Why had he left her alone?

Well, she didn't care about the answer. As loι
he wasn't here, he couldn't kill her, or keep her t.

38

leaving. Steɑ
bathroom, sh
Without a
for the cont
she glance
He'd reactι
You do
You di
you? No,
injury th
on her.
If on
She
visible
if she
worse
Sh
In
pec
use

Sy
th
sˣ
t

She headed to the kitchen.

Maybe you should look for him first . . .

No. Better to get a weapon. If he happened to be in one of the other rooms, she didn't want him to know she was awake until she had some way to protect herself.

Gah, my head hurts.

It's what you deserve for letting him get the drop on you and you're lucky that's all he did.

Very true.

Carefully, quietly, she opened cabinets and drawers seeking a knife, but instead, all she found were empty shelves. No cutlery at all—not even a rusty spoon.

Frowning, she opened the equally empty refrigerator. What did the man live on? Air?

Aggravated at not finding anything, she had to force herself not to slam the cabinet shut—in case he was in the other room. She crossed her arms over her chest and glanced at the counter. Again she saw a bottle of wine resting near the sink.

Not quite her weapon of choice, but in a pinch . . .

A determined smile curved her lips. It should serve to at least knock him senseless for a moment or two. That should be long enough to pull a weapon off his body.

She picked up the bottle and glanced at the blue and gold label. "Hmm, vintage." Good year too. This bottle alone would probably make her fighter payments for six months. Such a shame to waste premium Gondarion grade on a worthless criminal.

Oh well.

Sliding her fingers around the cool, slick glass neck, she gripped the bottle and went hunting. With practiced, stalking strides, she inched toward the bedroom, then paused. The door to the bedroom slid upwards, which would give him ample time to pull a blaster on her and shoot her again.

Her head pounded even more, reminding her that the last thing she needed was another sharp blast.

There had to be something else . . .

She smiled as she noticed the partially opened door of the bathroom . . . it might also swing open into the bedroom.

It was her best shot.

Changing course, she headed for it.

She tried to calm the pounding beat of her heart that sent even more sharp pulses of pain to her head and played havoc with her eyesight. Damn him for *that* particular misery. She gripped the bottle in her icy, clammy hands and slipped inside the bathroom.

It was empty.

Taking a deep breath to steady her nerves, she crept toward the door on the opposite side which also had a knob. So far, everything looked good.

As silently as she could, she pushed the door open, relieved the hinges didn't creak.

She took a step into his room, then froze in shocked disbelief. She didn't know what she'd expected, but it definitely wasn't the sight greeting her.

On the opposite side of the room, Syn knelt on a red, embroidered prayer cloth, his head sedately bowed, his eyes reverently closed. His ebony hair, pulled back into a ponytail, hung just past his wide shoulders.

He wore a pair of black leather pants and a loose, black silk shirt, the cuffs rolled back from his wrists. She could see the tiniest bit of white bandage on the arm where she'd cut him earlier and a bit of scrollwork from a tattoo it covered. His gloved hands rested on his

knees, turned palm-upwards, and before him lay an
opened prayer book. The light glinted off two silver
hoops in his left ear.

Even while he rested she could detect his aura of re-
strained lethal power. See the outline of steely muscles
beneath the leather and silk, and for some unknown
reason she wished she could hear the masculine, musi-
cal cadence of his voice while he whispered a prayer.

What are you? Insane?

He's a felon.

She tightened her grip on the bottle. Pray? How
could anyone with his brutal reputation be so hypo-
critical?

The thought sent anger pouring through her.

Her eyes focused on the blaster strapped to his left
hip and a slow smile spread across her face. That was
the ticket to freedom.

Without making a sound to alert him to her presence
or intentions, she snuck across the room and reached
for his weapon. His hand enclosed hers before she
could snatch the blaster free.

He glared up at her with eyes that were . . .

Well . . .

As dark as sin.

And every bit as frigid and evil.

With a curse, Shahara raised the bottle to strike him.

Quicker than she could blink, he pulled the blaster
free and held it under her chin. "I don't like scars," he
gritted between his teeth in that deep baritone voice that
sent a shiver down her spine. "And I really hate people
who mess up my house. Put the bottle down, slowly,
and take a step back."

Shahara weighed her options as she felt the cold barrel of his blaster pressing against her jaw. The air

around her sizzled with his anger and ferocity. Two things belied by blank, emotionless eyes that stared into hers.

She knew he would kill her without a second thought.

She swallowed the tight lump of fear in her throat. There had to be some way she could gain the advantage.

A sudden idea leapt into her mind—distraction.

Yeah, but she hated what that would entail since she only had one thing she could use.

I would rather be shot than come on to a convict.

If you don't get that weapon out of his hand, you will be.

She forced herself not to show her anger or frustration. Like it or not, she only had one thing to rely on and if she didn't get his blaster, she was at his mercy for however long he decided to keep her.

And no one knew where she was to even look for her.

The first rule of a seax was to use whatever means you had at your disposal . . .

That cemented it. Curving her lips into a seductive smile, she slowly, suggestively slid the bottle down the front of her battlesuit and set it on the hardwood floor with a soft thud. She took a step back, giving him a warm, playful look.

He holstered his weapon and rose slowly to his feet.

Shahara tensed in uncertainty at his height. She barely reached mid-chest. And he had a way about him that dominated the room. A way about him that made him seem even more formidable.

He watched her like a deadly viper eyeing its prey—calculating, waiting. Ready to spring at a moment's notice.

But then men were fools. Even dangerous ones. They

lived their lives by their hormones and as long as she kept her wits about her, he would be easy prey to her tactics.

Her life and Tessa's depended on her acting ability.

Opening her mouth, Shahara licked her lips and scanned his body with a hungry look that would make a prostitute proud. "We could negotiate this," she whispered, her voice heavy with feigned desire as she gazed meaningfully at the bulge in his pants, then to the bed.

Syn stared at her in disbelief, his senses whirling at the real-life version of his fantasy. All too well, he remembered Caillen's stories about his notorious sister, as well as the rumors that circulated about her fierceness.

If he knew anything, it was that Shahara Dagan didn't practice bedroom politics.

She began unbraiding her hair. His arguments scattering, Syn watched her separate the thick, heavy, mahogany tresses. Every inch of his body burned for her as he imagined her long, graceful fingers caressing his flesh with the same tenderness she used to stroke her hair.

She climbed onto his bed.

Oh yeah, baby . . .

Resting on her knees, she arched her back and ran her hands through the soft, tangled hair that tumbled around her, framing her face to perfection.

Did she have *any* idea what such a pose did to a man?

His throat suddenly dry, he burned. He took a step toward her, then stopped.

It was a trick.

Granted, he'd had more than his share of women come on to him unexpectedly, but he wasn't dumb or conceited enough to believe for a single instant that he could inspire Seax Shahara Dagan to forget her duty.

Unlike most fools, he'd never fall for such an obvious trick. But far be it from him to tell *her* that.

He smiled wickedly, wondering how far she'd go with her ruse. This was one show he planned to savor.

Leaning her head back to expose the graceful column of her throat, she tossed her hair over her shoulders before trailing her hands slowly over her thighs and breasts.

She hesitated at the fasteners of her battlesuit.

Would she dare?

She did. Feeling as if he were being tortured, he followed the path of her hands as she lowered the opening of her suit to reveal the black lace of her undergarments. And the luscious swell of her breasts.

"Well?" Her husky voice drove him almost beyond his limit as he imagined sliding one hand inside that suit and cupping her.

She leaned forward, her breasts barely remaining inside the black lace barrier as she wiggled her way-too-attractive hips. "Would you like to join me?"

Yes . . .

If it were any other woman, he wouldn't hesitate at the invitation.

Hell, he could barely refuse her now.

But then he was used to disappointment.

It was time she learned what happened to little seaxes who played deadly games. Crossing the floor in three strides, he reached out for her.

Just as he almost touched her, she struck out like lightning. With a resounding curse, she fastened the front of her battlesuit and sprang from the bed.

Syn ducked her roundhouse kick and moved to a safe distance. "Don't try this crap with me," he growled,

his lust instantly dying as his will to survive took over.
"I'm a street fighter and you *will* get hurt."

"So am I and so will you." Rushing toward him, she
punched at his throat. He caught her wrist in his hand
and pulled her up against him. Her breath left her in a
startled gasp as she collided with the solid wall of muscle. Her heart thundered in her ears and fear scaled her
throat.

His steely hands closed around her arms.

"Let go of me!" She stomped on his instep, twisting
free of his hold.

Syn cursed, moving away from the wild *byrollo*.
What kind of shoes did she have on? They sliced like
knives even through his heavy boots.

Her eyes narrowed at him in hatred. Quicker than he
could react, she dove for the bottle and rose with it.

"Put it down." He kept his voice level. "If I draw my
blaster one more time, I *will* kill you."

She lifted the bottle higher. "Open the front door,"
she demanded in a strident tone that told him just how
desperate she was.

Only too well, he understood her panic and fear. He
didn't like being cornered either. "I'm not going to hurt
you. Put the bottle down and just talk to me."

Shahara curled her lip in disgust. Did he really think
she was stupid enough to release her only weapon? Especially after his threat? "Go to hell."

He smiled, flashing a single dimple in his left cheek.
She licked her dry lips, afraid of what the smile signified.

"Okay, keep the bottle. Just talk to me like two rational people and maybe we can find a solution to this
problem. Deal?"

She tightened her grip on the bottle, wanting to toss

it at his arrogant head. "I don't make deals with convicted rapists and murderers, I take them to justice."

His smile vanished. "I have *never* raped or murdered anyone. And I damn sure haven't been convicted
of it." The other charges were a different matter that he
wasn't about to bring up to her.

"That's not what the contract on your life says."

His jaw tensed. "I didn't rape or murder Kiara Zamir."

"Tell it to the Overseer."

Syn stifled his curse. Was there not one person in
the fucking universe who could believe the truth when
he spoke it? This wasn't going the way he wanted it to.
Kiara's father wouldn't listen to reason any more than
this headstrong tracer.

As for the court system . . . yeah, given his father's
reputation, he didn't stand a chance. He'd be convicted
and executed based on his name alone.

If she turned him over to the Gourish government,
he'd be gutted long before Kiara's father realized his
daughter was still alive. And if Zamir had already found
out she was alive and sleeping with Nykyrian, then
there was no telling what her father would do to him
for the part he'd played in their affair.

He'd been the one who signed the contract for Kiara's protection . . . That made him fully responsible
for her welfare.

And if the Ritadarions ever got their hands on him . . .
Well, their reaction was something best left to horror
movies.

"Fine." He held his hand away from his blaster, hoping to calm her. "Keep the damn bottle. It won't protect
you anyway."

That apparently was the wrong thing to say.

Before Syn could react, she ran at him, catching him

in the stomach. His breath left him with a loud *oof* as he lost his balance and the two of them tumbled to the floor. She tried to hit him with the bottle.

He caught her wrist. "Stop fighting me." He pried the bottle from her hand.

She didn't respond verbally. Instead, she raked her fingernails down the side of his neck, burning a path into his skin.

Anger darkened his vision and, for a moment, all he could think about was killing the woman on top of him. He was tired of her drawing blood every time she got within reach.

Rolling over, he pinned her beneath him. She struggled to throw his weight off, but it was useless. He outweighed her by more than a hundred pounds.

He caught her wrists in his hands before she could pull his blaster free, and held them beside her face. "Stop it!"

Shahara froze. Her blood pounded a fearful trail through her body. Tears of frustration welled in her eyes, but she blinked them back. She refused to be undignified further.

Only one other time in her life had someone held her in this manner and she hated it. She hated *him*.

Bravely, she stared up at his face.

Even this close, she could barely see the difference between his dark irises and the pupils of his eyes. It amazed her that her wrists didn't hurt from his firm grip, and that his weight didn't crush her.

"What are you going to do to me?" she asked, dreading the answer.

To her complete shock, he dipped his head down. And before she could think to turn her face away, his lips covered hers.

CHAPTER 3

The gentle pressure of Syn's lips stunned her. His kiss was so light, it felt like a feather dancing across her lips, sending a chill down her spine.

A crisp, clean scent of leather and man filled her head. He surrounded her with warmth and, for a moment, Shahara lost herself to the strange sensation of his hips lying against hers, his chest pressing intimately against her breasts. To the foreign, aching throb that began in the pit of her stomach and moved lower.

She sighed as a deep-buried need surged. No man had ever kissed her so tenderly. Most men grabbed at her with hands that hurt and pinched. And the last kiss she'd received had been a brutal assault on her lips that had left them bloody and bruised and sore for weeks.

That wasn't Syn's kiss. His soft, tender lips belied the cruelty she knew him capable of.

Closing her eyes, she breathed in the warm, manly scent of him as his tongue gently probed her mouth, dancing with hers before his teeth nipped tenderly at her bottom lip.

Syn closed his eyes, savoring the succulent velvet of her mouth as he inhaled the pure scent of female. Never in his life had he tasted anything so wonderful. So addictive.

She was sweet and soft. He released her hands and cupped her cheek. Then he left her lips and trailed a path with his mouth down her cheekbone.

Shahara shivered as his whiskers gently scraped her skin before he nuzzled against the sensitive flesh of her neck. Her throbbing intensified as chills spread all over her.

His warm breath tickled her ear while he whispered something poetic in a language she couldn't understand.

Unbidden, her arms wrapped around his shoulders, caressing the corded muscles that rippled beneath the smooth silk of his shirt. His rich, warm voice continued to soothe her with its strange, melodic language. Lulling her, hypnotizing her.

She'd never known a man could hold her without causing pain and her newfound knowledge amazed her.

Syn shifted and she felt the hard bulge of him against her thigh.

Panicked shock jolted her.

In that instant, Shahara remembered herself and why she'd come. He wasn't a tender man and he damned sure wasn't a kind one.

He was a vicious killer.

Hissing, she gripped his ponytail and pulled him away from her. *"Vanna sitiara!"* She caught him under the chin with her fingernails.

His oath matched her own as she raked his flesh. At this point, she didn't care if he killed her. She refused to ever lie with a man wanted for rape and murder. Men were cruel and abusive by nature and she'd die before she ever submitted to one.

Syn grabbed her hands again and held them by her

face. His breathing labored, he curled his lips into a fierce snarl.

Bravely, Shahara glared her hatred at him. "If you rape me, convict, I'll tear your heart from your chest and feed it to you!"

The anger fled his features. His eyes went strangely dull as if something from his past shredded him. It was as if she stared into the face of a statue without any emotions or life at all.

"I've never raped a woman, and I have no intention of starting now."

A drop of blood fell from his neck where she'd scratched him and landed on her cheek. He stared at it for a moment before looking back at her eyes. "I'm going to release you. If you attack me again, it'll be the last time you ever make such a mistake."

The icy dare in his voice quelled her more than his words. She had no doubt he would make her long regret any more moves against him. And like Gaelin, he would relish her torture. Laugh at her while he did it.

But there would come a time when his guard would fall. Then he would be hers and she'd make him pay dearly.

He released her hands and rose.

Shahara lay there for a moment, warily watching him.

Without taking his gaze from her, he retrieved the bottle from the floor. He gripped it so tightly, his knuckles protruded sharply against the leather of his glove.

"Go ahead, throw it at me."

A glimmer of shock passed across his features before he recovered his impassiveness. "I should. Hell, if I had any sense at all, I'd kill you and dump your body in the nearest slime hole."

Shahara lifted her chin defiantly. Far better opponents than he had tried and failed. "Then why don't you?"

"I have an appointment to keep."

The unexpected response was far from comforting. But it served to weaken her cockiness.

He slid his hand under his chin and cursed when he withdrew it and saw the blood on his glove. He gave her a look of such loathing that she thought he might kill her after all.

Instead, he turned around and headed into the bathroom.

She wiped his blood from her own cheek and listened to water splash against the basin. Rising from the floor, she stood in the bedroom uncertain about what to do next.

How was she going to get out of this mess?

Was he going to kill her? And just what would he do to her before he took her life? Various terrifying possibilities flashed through her mind, making her shiver.

Hesitantly, she walked to the bathroom door that he'd left partially open. He stood in front of the sink, wiping the blood away with a washcloth.

"What are you going to do with me?"

His hand paused under his chin and he met her gaze in the mirror.

The hatred in the dark stare chilled her all the way to her soul. "I don't know," he said at last. "I've never had anyone stupid enough to break into my house."

The insult brought her temper to boil. "I'm not stupid."

His disbelieving snort made her want to carve his heart out. "Breaking into my house wasn't exactly an award-winning act of intelligence. In case you haven't noticed, I don't have a landline or computer here, or any other way for you to contact anyone on the outside. You can't get through the scanner that runs over the doors and windows unless I disarm it. So where does that leave you?"

Shahara's stomach churned. It left her at his mercy and they both knew it. "I won't be your plaything."

His scathing glare raked her body as if she were the most disgusting thing alive. "Don't flatter yourself."

He rinsed out the washcloth and hung it on the towel rack to dry, then pulled out a tube of medicine and began applying it to the scratches. "I'll be gone until morning. You have the freedom of the place until then."

He turned around and faced her, his eyes piercing her with lethal coldness. "But I warn you now, there's only one thing in this life that I treasure and that's my home. If you so much as put a scuff mark on my floors, I *will* take it out of your hide."

In spite of the threat and the fact that she knew he would carry it out, Shahara narrowed her gaze. Show them no fear. That was the first lesson she'd learned as a young teen. "I don't take orders from convicts."

Faster than she could blink, he grabbed her by the wrist and pulled her to him with a steely grasp. His eyes snapped vivid black fire, provoking a potent fear inside her that she hadn't experienced in a long, long time.

In that instant, she knew this man was capable of anything.

His grip tightened. "Mess up anything, and I'll throw you to a rape gang so fast you won't even have time to protest before they cut out your tongue."

Shahara swallowed at the threat that reached the center of her panic in a way nothing else did. It was her very worst fear. Her heart pounding, she stared at him, unwilling to let him know how much his threat frightened her.

Despite her effort, she had the distinct feeling he knew anyway.

She pulled her wrist free of his tight grasp. Why was he willing to leave her in his home? It didn't make sense. "What am I supposed to do while you're gone?"

"Think up ways to kill me while I sleep."

The blasè tone didn't comfort her in the least. "I've already got a large number of them in mind."

He shrugged. "I should warn you that if you succeed in killing me, you'll never get out of here alive. You'll starve to death long before anyone misses me and thinks to come here to see if I'm all right."

Now that was something she hadn't thought of.

"Like I won't starve to death anyway if you keep me here without food," she said sarcastically, thinking about the empty cupboards in his kitchen.

Without a word, he snatched his gloves off the counter, walked past her and pressed the controls to open his closet. He pulled out a black leather jacket and shrugged it on his massive shoulders. "You can take my bed. I'll sleep on the couch. If it'll make you feel any better, lock the bedroom door."

That said, he left the room.

Shahara stood in shock at his words. One minute he threatened her, then in the next he offered her a relative amount of safety.

What kind of convict was he?

Before she could regain her thoughts, she heard the front door close behind him.

Syn leaned his head back against the closed door and took a deep breath to center his raging emotions and hormones. It'd been years since anyone had knocked him so off-kilter. A cynical stoic by birth, he'd always been able to control himself, control his emotions.

But something about Shahara made a mockery of his iron will.

He didn't know what was wrong with him. How could he be mad enough to kill her, then turn around and kiss her?

If he didn't know better, he'd swear she used pheromone enhancers.

"You're losing your edge." If he had one single brain cell left, he'd cuff her to the bed instead of giving her the freedom of his house to devise a way to kill him once he returned.

But then he knew the reasons for *that* particular stupidity. One, she was Caillen's beloved sister, and he didn't want to traumatize her too badly and have his friend never speak to him again over it. Two, she reminded him too much of Talia. The scared look in her eyes as she watched him, expecting him to throw her to the ground and tear her clothes from her.

He hadn't been old enough to protect his sister—a fact he'd never come to terms with.

And he would *never* harm a woman like that. Anyone, for that matter. It just wasn't in him.

But what was he going to do with her?

Sighing, he wished he knew an easy answer. He'd give her a few hours alone. Maybe then she would calm down enough that he could speak to her without her trying to claw him to shreds.

Or maybe he should tell her he was a friend of Caillen's . . .

Yeah, right. She most likely wouldn't care. And considering the type of people Caillen usually associated with, it would only give her another reason to take him in. She'd probably consider it a community service.

No, it would be best to keep his friendship with her brother a secret.

Surely by morning she'd be willing to listen to him. For now he had a shipment to focus on and his legitimate business affairs.

Shahara leaned her head back, letting the hot water slide against her body. It'd been a long time since she last had a hot shower . . .

And this was heaven.

In her flat, she was lucky to have lukewarm water even in the summertime.

She must be insane to shower when she should be plotting an escape, but as she'd searched his place, the temptation had been too much for her. Besides, Syn had told her he'd be gone for the night so she had hours left to plot a way home. For just a few minutes, she was going to indulge herself.

Feeling much better and with clearer thoughts, she left the shower, grabbed the long, fluffy towel on the bar and wiped the water from her face. She gasped as she realized the scent of musk in the towel smelled just like Syn.

She clenched her teeth in anger and tossed the offending towel to the floor. No matter how good he might smell or look, Syn was a convict with an extremely violent past. She must never forget that.

Just as she bent over to pick up her underwear from the floor, the door to the bathroom swung open.

Horrified, she straightened and stared into a pair of beautiful, wide dark eyes.

Syn froze dead in his tracks as all breath left his body like he'd been sucker-punched. He couldn't have been more stunned had he opened the door and found a huge lorina waiting there to devour him.

Then again, he had to admit he much preferred the sight of Shahara's well-rounded ass greeting him.

She stood in all her naked glory, her pale skin glistening from tiny water droplets. Her mahogany hair clung to her body, dripping tiny beads of water onto the floor. And one particularly attractive, long strand was curled around her right breast.

Ooo, damn . . .

Just as he'd suspected, her muscles were tight and well toned, and her breasts were made just the right size for a man's hand.

Of its own accord, his gaze dipped to the mahogany triangle at the juncture of her thighs and . . .

His tongue became terribly thick, and he hoped it wasn't hanging on the floor.

Or worse, that he was drooling.

Shahara couldn't move. Those dark, predatorial eyes hypnotized her like a snake's. He stood so still that he could have been a statue.

Only he wasn't.

He was a man, flesh and blood. And as she watched him, a slow appreciative smile spread across his face.

Her face flooding with fire, she found her voice. "Get out!" she screamed, snatching her battlesuit off the floor and holding it up to her. "How dare you! You bastard!" She rushed toward him, shoving him back into the front room. "Get out and stay out!"

Before Syn could fully recover himself, she slammed the door shut in his face.

And to think he'd assumed she was locked in his bedroom. Yeah . . . That'd teach him to assume anything.

Then again, that view had gone a long way in making up for the skin she'd clawed off him earlier. He smiled at the thought.

Until he remembered he still hadn't retrieved his pack from the bathroom cabinet.

Ah, shit . . .

He rolled his eyes as he debated going back into the bathroom for it.

Nah, that would be a mistake. This time, she might kill him. "Better leave it alone and not worry about it." 'Cause he had a feeling that if she saw him again right now after he'd embarrassed her, he'd be limping.

More.

Better to get out with all his body parts intact.

Not to mention what Caillen would do if he ever learned of the view he'd just received.

Yeah, he didn't retreat often, but in this . . .

There was no other option.

Shahara fumed as she heard Syn's deep laughter through the door, making her burn for retaliation.

Her hands shaking, she fastened her battlesuit. Her cheeks stung with heat. How could she have been so foolish? He was a ruthless felon and a liar. She knew that. Why had she bathed in such a man's home?

Thank goodness she'd been outside the shower when he found her. There was no telling what he might have done had she been trapped inside the shower cubicle.

Once dressed, she decided it was time to teach Syn a valuable lesson about how to treat a woman with proper respect. Throwing open the door, ready for battle, she paused.

The room was empty.

Frowning, she searched every corner with her gaze, but didn't find a single trace of him.

Cautiously, she entered the room, expecting a trick of some kind.

A sweet, warm aroma greeted her. Something smelled incredible. Since she hadn't eaten in two days, the delicious smell made her empty stomach ache. At first, she thought she was imagining it, but as she crossed the room, she saw three sacks on the counter.

Moving over to them, she opened the bag laying on its side and smiled at the boxed dinner tucked inside. Her stomach rumbled as she uncovered a steak, vegetables, and a roll. The wonderful aroma of gravy wafted up from the hot meal.

Closing her eyes, she savored the rush of excitement. It had been more years than she could count since she'd last eaten a meal like this. She looked inside the other two bags and saw juice, bread, cold meats, cheese, and a few snack foods.

What was it with this man?

She couldn't believe a cold-blooded killer would be thoughtful enough to bring her food. Why was he doing this for her?

Too hungry to think about it right then, she reached for the boxed dinner and took it to the sofa. It didn't take her long to power through the delicious meal and put the rest of the groceries away.

Man, that had been good. She hadn't been full in so long that she'd forgotten the sensation of it.

Looking around his immaculate home, she frowned. "You are the strangest creature I've ever met."

The hardwood floors beneath her feet were polished to a high sheen that she was sure took hours a week to maintain. Ornate, white and black, plushly woven carpets were set between the two black leather sofas and under the dining table and chairs. The dining suite was made of hand-carved ebony-wood—an expensive luxury very few people could afford.

He had four Chinergov paintings and, unless she was mistaken, they were the originals, not copies, as well as other expensive art pieces everywhere. But the most fascinating thing was the huge white piano set before the windows that looked out on a breathtaking view of the city below.

This was *high* end.

And next to it was an empty desk. Syn hadn't been kidding. There wasn't a computer of any kind here. How weird for such a renowned filch. They usually lived their lives hardwired into network systems.

He must have set it up somewhere outside his home. But even that seemed out of character for someone with his background.

He probably had a portable, then, that he kept on him.

She shook her head as she swept her gaze around his home again. What a great place to live. She'd only dreamed of an apartment like this and she'd never have imagined such a place as the home of someone with Syn's brutal reputation. Most of the places she'd been to track down her targets had been grubby holes filled with rodents and stenches that defied belief.

This place looked like it belonged to an aristocrat. Nothing was out of order. She could understand why he remained adamant she not destroy anything. She'd take pride of ownership, too.

But then, she didn't steal from others.

With that thought in mind, she went to search his bedroom, looking for her weapons. They had to be here somewhere.

At the end of the hour, she hadn't found anything. Nothing under the ebony-wood bed, nothing in the closet he'd filled with exclusive, handmade clothes. Nothing.

Not even a friggin' dust bunny.

Her gaze fell to the nightstand she had yet to open. Only because she knew he wouldn't store anything in plain sight. That would be stupid and he was anything but.

He must have everything locked in his wall safe. If only it didn't have a Grimson lock, she might have been able to breach the code. Or if she had her missing lockbox . . .

Yeah.

Shahara sighed in disgust and picked up Syn's holy book and prayer cloth from the floor where he'd left them. Even though she didn't respect his hypocrisy, she did respect the objects of his religion. She carefully wrapped the cloth around the book and moved to return them to their prayer box.

Only there wasn't one.

Must be in the nightstand . . .

She headed for it and opened the drawer. There, inside, was a large backpack. Hope flared inside her that maybe it held a computer.

Placing the book and cloth on top of the stand, she pulled it out and opened it. But her relief was short-lived as she found nothing more than a change of clothes, toothbrush, and the missing prayer box.

Crap . . .

Sighing, she paused as she realized the significance of what she held. It was an escape pack in case he had to evacuate in a hurry. So while he valued his home, he was ready to leave it all behind at a moment's notice.

What a sad way to live.

Which is why I'm not a criminal.

But still she ached at the thought of having to be so paranoid all the time. She couldn't imagine existing like that. Shaking her head, she pulled the small, red prayer box out to return the book and cloth to it.

When she lifted back the lid, she froze. Inside the box were the first really private items she'd found about her captor.

Placing the book in her lap, she pulled out a handful of documents and photos. With a scowl, she glanced at the top picture. A much younger Syn sat in a studio photograph with an extremely attractive woman and a little boy no older than four in his arms.

It was a typical family shot that stunned her.

Could *Syn* possibly be married?

Have a child?

There had been no record of it in his posted file, but there was no denying what she was looking at.

The woman was absolutely beautiful and looked very upper-crust and haughty. Syn . . . he looked sophisticated, too, but there was a dangerous gleam in his eye that only came from those who'd been raised on the street.

And as she looked at the picture, some strange, foreign emotion constricted her throat.

Unwilling to examine the source of it, she looked at

the next picture. It contained a dark-haired boy about the age of seven clutching a girl in her early teens. The girl had her arms wrapped protectively around the boy as if she would fight an army to defend him. Both of them were barefoot, filthy, and bruised, their clothes tattered and threadbare. And as she studied the large black eye and split lip on the boy's face, she realized it was Syn as a child.

Her heart lurched at the sight of his battered face. How awful. Clenching her teeth to keep her tender emotions at bay, she reminded herself that poverty and abuse were no excuse for criminal behavior.

She'd risen above her childhood and become better. He could have, too.

As she put the pictures back in the box, she saw that there was writing on the one with him and his sister. Masculine and bold, the words were as disturbing as the children's condition.

Your beloved children miss you, dearest. Send money or I'll send them for a visit to their mother and her family during your next high-society soiree.

What in the universe did that mean? And how had Syn gotten the photo that must have been used to blackmail his mother?

Most of all, what kind of mother could be threatened by a visit from her own children? The mere thought revolted her.

Putting the photos away, she turned her attention to the carefully stacked documents that were also inside. The first one was a child's birth certificate for Paden Belask with the father's name listed as Sheridan Belask.

An alias?

Why hadn't it been listed on his bounty page? But there hadn't been a single alias there. Only C.I. Syn. It hadn't even said what the C.I. stood for, which, while unusual, probably meant Syn had tampered with his records.

She studied the document more closely. By the birth date on the certificate, she knew Syn couldn't be using it as an alias for himself. The boy listed would only be sixteen.

Retrieving the family picture, she held it beside the child's birth certificate. The date of the fashions and the registration coincided. Paden must be the boy in the photo.

And Sheridan Belask must have been Syn's name at some point, which would definitely make the child in the picture Syn's son.

Where was the kid now?

Had Syn sent his wife and child into hiding to keep them safe from his enemies?

Were they dead?

Had Syn killed them? The thought chilled her.

Flipping through the documents, she didn't see either a marriage registration or one for divorce.

What had happened to them?

She scanned through the rest of the documents more carefully. There was an advanced degree in chemistry from the Derridian University of Science also under the name Sheridan Belask—an impressive feat since only the smartest and brightest were allowed to attend. There were also four false IDs, and debit and credit cards with different names, as well as several school report sheets with the name Paden Belask on them.

How strange.

As she started to return the documents to the box, there was one more piece of paper she'd left in the bottom. Picking it up, she unfolded it. Shock jolting her, she scanned the paper twice just to make sure she'd read it correctly.

She had.

It was a doctor's accreditation issued to Sheridan Belask to practice human, Kiati, and Andarion medicine throughout all of the Ichidian Universe.

And it held a surgeon's seal . . .

No way.

"You're a surgeon?" How was that possible? Why, if he'd had such a prestigious and high-paying career, would he have left it?

It had to be a forgery. Some scam he'd been working on. That made sense.

She examined the document carefully, trying to see if it was faked. If it was, it was the best one she'd ever seen. She held it up to the light. The orange and blue fibers intersected in a medical pattern. It was definitely real. But that didn't make any sense.

Why would a surgeon with three specialties turn to murder and theft?

Why would he have to?

Stunned, Shahara placed the papers back inside the box, knowing she wouldn't find an answer to her questions. Not that her answers mattered.

Regardless of the reasons Syn, or Sheridan Belask, or whatever his name, had turned into a criminal, it was her job to take him in to the authorities.

Tessa's life hinged on her ability to complete this mission. And no amount of pity would stop her from doing what she must.

Her nerves stretched almost to breaking, she waited until she thought she'd scream in anxious nervousness. But no footsteps came any closer to the bedroom.

Sliding out of bed, she walked silently toward the bathroom door.

Was he truly sleeping, or just waiting for another opportunity to catch her unawares?

She went through the bathroom and pushed open the door. She hesitated in the doorway, clenching the icy knob, ready to slam the door shut and lock it if he moved.

He didn't.

She studied the steady rise and fall of his chest and realized he was fast asleep. Breathing in relief, she released the knob.

Against her common sense, which urged her back to bed, she stepped into the room. The dawning sun brightened the area around the couch and she saw the outline of his perfect, relaxed features. He'd pulled his hair out of the ponytail and the dark, wavy strands spilled over his cheeks, softening the harshness from his face.

Asleep, he didn't look intimidating—he looked like a small, defenseless child. A warm tremor ran through her body as she remembered what he'd looked like holding his son.

Convict or not, he was an incredibly handsome man. Every bit as devastating as her brother.

He shifted on the couch.

Shahara stepped back, her heart slamming against her ribs. He didn't wake up, but his new position showed her his blaster that was still strapped to his hip while he slept.

It would cede all of her power over to him.

"Open the door," she repeated, feeling somewha. foolish.

"No."

She stared into his mocking eyes. He knew she was trapped. If she relinquished the blaster, then he'd never respect her, or free her.

If she didn't get home soon, Tessa would die.

She had no choice in this.

Lowering the barrel, she fired.

The jolt of the blast knocked Syn off his feet. His breath left him as he slammed against the hardwood floor. Pain ripped through his arm like fire.

He closed his eyes against the throbbing agony. Warm blood streamed over the hand clutching the gaping wound. Son of a . . .

He sucked his breath in sharply between his teeth as his entire body ached.

Shahara approached him like a hunting lorina. She stood over him with her feet braced wide apart. Her hand was as still and steady as any assassin's he'd ever seen.

She aimed for his heart. There was no pity or trembling in any part of her. "I said open the door, convict. Or die."

Syn stared up at her cold eyes, unable to believe he'd allowed her to deceive him so completely. So be it. He'd always been prepared for the possibility of death. Hell, he'd wanted to die since the day he'd lost Paden.

But he wasn't about to die in a Ritadarion prison at the hands of an interrogator. He would sooner take his secrets to the grave.

And if she died with him, Nykyrian would have one less tracer after him.

A glimmer of hope ignited inside her. This chance. She couldn't let this opportunity pass.

Without a second thought, she crossed the d between them and jerked the blaster from his h

In an instant, he sprang to his feet. "What the He focused on her, then relaxed. "Oh, it's yo wiped his hands across his face.

His indifference angered her. How dare he d her so readily as if she were of no more conseq than an annoying little pest.

She clicked back the safety release and levele blaster at his chest. "Open the door."

One corner of his mouth quirked up, showing his damnable dimple. "That"—he indicated the bl in her hand—"doesn't give you any leverage. If you me, you die, too."

Shahara gripped the hard, bone stock and raised barrel to his head. "I said open the door, convict. not playing a game here."

Syn sighed as if she bored him. "Go ahead. Sh me. You'll have to kill me because I have no intention letting you out of here when we both know you'll ju turn around and head back for me the first chance y get. Besides, I'm as good as dead anyway if the Ri ever lay their grubby hands on me. So go ahead an shoot."

Shahara stared at him in disbelief.

What should she do?

"Or give me my gun, and go back to bed." He reached his hand out to her.

She caught herself right before complying. She couldn't give him back the blaster. If she gave up the weapon, then she'd never get out of here.

"Shoot me," he said calmly.

Her eyes narrowed. She grabbed him by the shirt collar and pulled him up to her face.

She pressed the cold, steel barrel against his cheek. "This is your last chance. Open the door."

He shook his head slowly.

"Fine," Shahara snarled. "Then I'll see you in hell."

CHAPTER 4

Shahara stared at Syn's blank gaze. Her mind screamed at her to kill him, but try as she might, she kept seeing the picture of him as a child with the girl gripping him. The haunted look in his eyes while he held onto the girl, the bruise on his young face, and she just couldn't make herself pull the trigger.

Besides, she wasn't a murderer. She'd only killed a dozen men in her career, all out of self-defense. Every instance left jagged scars on her soul and she had sworn she'd never kill again unless she absolutely had to.

Today, she didn't have to.

With a fierce curse, she flung the weapon away from her and released him.

Syn lay on the floor, looking up at her with a taunting stare she found hard to tolerate.

Did nothing scare this man?

Did he *want* to die? If that was the case, then she was definitely in trouble. A man with a death wish couldn't be controlled or intimidated.

"No stomach for it?" he asked bitterly.

She curled her lip at him. "Unlike you, I don't find pleasure in killing people."

Without responding to her words, he pushed himself

off the floor and made his way into the bathroom. She told herself he deserved it, that he'd hurt more people in his career than she could count and he deserved to pay for his crimes. But it still didn't shut down her conscience or keep it from nagging her.

She'd shot a defenseless man and broken the code of a seax. What she'd done was wrong and no matter what arguments she might make, deep inside, she knew it wasn't justified.

When did I sink so low as to become one of the monsters I hunt? Caillen always said that if a person stared too long into the darkness, it would absorb them.

But she didn't want to be one of the bad guys. Determined to try and redeem her cruelty, she followed him.

As she entered the bathroom, her gaze focused on his bare back and she gasped in shock.

Syn looked up from the doctor's bag he was rummaging in and caught her horrified gaze in the mirror. "Thinking of ways to add to them?" His tone was frigid.

Slowly she shook her head, still transfixed by the awful scars crisscrossing the muscled planes of his back. She'd seen plenty of street people beaten by an enforcer's glazen whip, had even received a lash or two herself by desperate felons, but never to the extent of what marred his flesh.

How could *anyone* survive such a beating?

No matter how hard she tried, she couldn't stop staring at them. "Are they from prison?"

Syn wiped a pungent-smelling cloth over his wounded shoulder. "Some."

"And the others?"

He looked over his shoulder and captured her gaze with his own. Something strange and primal darkened his eyes before they turned dead.

"My father," he said simply.

Shahara bit her lip while Syn returned to tending his wound. She glanced away as he picked up a searer to seal the wound closed and did her best not to hear the sizzle of knitting flesh. She knew from her own experience how bad that hurt. To do it to himself . . . she was impressed.

And appalled.

Still she saw those scars. What could he have possibly done for his father to have beaten him so ferociously? "Did you deserve it?"

Syn tossed the searer down, then moved to stand right before her. She could feel his body heat, smell the masculine scent of his skin, and even though she was sure she imagined it, she could almost swear she heard his heart pound in fury.

She trailed her gaze up from the steely muscles of his chest to the bandage over his shoulder and finally up to the loathing that flickered in the black depths of his eyes. They were every bit as cold as space.

"Why else would he have beaten me?"

The question hung in the air between them and it left a deafening silence. She didn't know anything about his past except what the contracts read and what his prayer box contained, which wasn't much. There was no family of record. No known acquaintances or friends.

He worked part-time for The Sentella, which was a freelance assassin service run by Nemesis—one of the most feared and wanted outlaw assassins in the business. But the bounty hadn't even listed his job title there.

For all she knew, *he* could be Nemesis.

Or something worse.

So maybe he had deserved it. Maybe he'd been given his name because he'd been evil from the womb and his father had sought to curb his criminal impulses by beating them out of him at an early age.

And yet . . .

She saw the image of the beaten child. The boy Syn had looked frightened, not evil. "What did you do to deserve it?"

He paused while returning his medical instruments to their case. Without looking at her, he said quietly, "I tried to keep him from selling my sister's virginity."

A lump of emotions gathered into her throat and choked her. The loyalty of his action reminded her much of her own brother. Caillen would die to protect her.

Syn tossed his torn shirt into the garbage, then moved past her, into the bedroom.

She continued to stare at the scars on his back. Could a boy who took such a beating for the sake of another person become the menace of Syn's reputation?

Some psychologists would say no. It was people who'd lost their ability to sympathize with others, to care for others, who turned into rapists and murderers.

Still, it wasn't beyond the realm of speculation that he *could* be capable of committing those heinous crimes. Many serial killers and rapists had close friends and spouses who had never suspected they possessed such deep psychosis.

A man didn't have so lethal a reputation without cause . . .

Until she knew more, she had no choice except to believe in what his bounty sheet said: *C.I. Syn, Ruthless and Calculating. Kills without remorse. Proceed at own risk.*

She'd risked a great deal to come after him and time was running out for Tessa. She'd botched this mission and needed something to get the money for her sister before it was too late. "So how long are you going to keep me here?"

Syn tucked his clean shirt into his pants. "Until you recant your contract on me and swear that you'll never again stalk me."

"Is that it?"

"That's it."

Crossing her arms over her chest, she frowned at him. "You'd trust me that easily?"

"Hell no," he said with a sneer. "The only thing I trust in life is to get fucked over by everyone around me. But if I ever hear of you coming after me again, I'll deliver your brother to you in a box."

Shahara went cold in dread. All too well she could see her brother's lifeless form—it was a vision that had haunted her most of her life. "You wouldn't dare!"

"Wouldn't I?" He moved to tower over her. He put one arm up on each side of her, pinning her back against the wall. She trembled at his nearness, at the raw male power that emanated from every pore of his body.

"I'm a cold-blooded murderer. Remember?" He raked her with an evil grin. "Believe me, baby, I *am* ruthless and I love nothing more than the taste of blood. Yours. His. Anyone's. I'm not particular."

Outraged, she lunged for him.

No one threatened her family! No one!

Syn caught her hands and pushed her back against the wall, his chest pressing against hers. She stared up at him, wishing she could break his hold and tear him apart. Even so, she refused to be intimated or threatened by something like him. "So help me, convict, if you ever touch a member of my family, I'll come for you. There's no hole in hell you can find that would be deep enough to hide you from my wrath."

He scoffed, then released her. "Take a number."

She rubbed her numb wrists and glared at him. No matter the personal cost, she would protect her family. Oaths and morals be damned.

"When are you going to free me?"

He shrugged. "Now's as good as any time."

Her anger drained from her. She blinked, not really sure it'd be that easy to leave.

C.I. Syn, Ruthless and Calculating. Was this a trick of his to get her out of his apartment so that he could kill her and dump her body more easily?

The thought was sobering.

"I can go right now?" she asked suspiciously.

"Yep. I'll take you home, and as soon as I see you recant the contract, you're free."

Oh yeah, right . . . like she'd make *that* mistake. "Take you to my home so that you can see where I live? How stupid do you think I am?"

He gave her a deadpan stare. "You have a rundown, piece-of-shit condo at 3642 Chiton Road, in Gareth Square on Boudran. Your ship, which is older than I am, is licensed through Guidry and Associates and has two liens against it. You pay nine hundred credits a month to keep them from seizing it for back taxes and you're still paying off your father's debts, including his funeral cost."

He paused to give her a mocking glare. "You want I should go on? Remember, I'm one of the best filches to ever live. There's not a damned thing I can't find out online about you or anyone else no matter how off the grid you think you are. And I learned all that about you without even trying hard. I can also give you your social and that for all three of your siblings as well as most of the passwords and codes you use to log in to everything in your life and theirs."

A chill went down her spine. What had she gotten herself into? With that kind of information, he could ruin and kill her.

She only had one hope even if it did grate on her nerves. "I'm supposed to believe that you'll take me home and leave me there without killing me?"

Again that taunting, evil smile. "I would swear on it, but I have a feeling you wouldn't take me at my word. Believe what you will, but really you have no choice. So answer quick before I reconsider."

She ground her teeth at his offer, hating the fact that he was right. She couldn't stand being manipulated, especially by a convict. But what choice did she have other than to believe him?

Don't be stupid, girl. The only thing you can trust is that people will screw you over if given the chance. It's every man for himself.

Everyone lies.

Even her own father . . .

"What about my weapons?" she asked at last.

"Wait for me in the front room, and I'll get them. You can have them back once we get to your place."

Shahara wasn't thrilled about the prospect of having him in her home.

If only she had another way to get free . . . But, unfortunately, he had her trapped fully, and even when she'd shot him he hadn't budged.

Time was running out for Tessa. She had to get out of here. She'd already wasted an entire day. Only two were left. Would that be enough time to find another bounty that would cover the cost?

Well, if you hand him in, he won't be able to hurt Caillen.

Or would he?

He'd escaped prison before. What would keep him from doing it again? Vengeance was a strong motivator. She of all people knew that. And every molecule in her body warned her that Syn was capable of extracting a painful revenge.

First, she needed her weapons. Second, her freedom.

Without a word, she turned around and left him.

Syn sighed at her stormy exit. He didn't really care whether or not she hated him, only that she give up her quest to see him incarcerated. He'd spent enough time in prison, he had no desire to spend another second of his life like that.

He winced as old memories stung deep. *So what do we do with him? No one will take him into foster care. Not after his father's crimes. They're all scared of him.*

Put him in prison with the rest of the criminals. He might as well get used to it as it's mostly likely where he'll spend the rest of his life anyway.

The kicker was, they hadn't even put him in a juvenile facility. At age ten, and for no other crime than the fact he'd been born his father's son, he'd been thrown in maximum security with adults.

All because his father was a bastard and people were so afraid of him that Syn was every bit as guilty because he shared a genetic link to a psychotic bastard.

Yeah, he was tired of being judged for something he couldn't help.

Shahara was as guilty as the rest and right now, he couldn't think of anything sweeter than getting her the hell out of his home so that he could get some well-deserved sleep.

He opened the safe, his arm throbbing in protest. She was a lethal lorina and the sooner he expelled her from his life, the better off he'd be.

Shahara spun about as the door opened. A smile of relief curved her lips as she recognized her gear in Syn's arms.

Could it be possible that he really intended to let her go? She couldn't believe it.

Don't get excited yet. It could still be a trick.

Stiffening her spine, she promised herself to stay alert and, if he did try something, she'd be ready for it.

"Here." He tossed her a worn, leather jacket.

She caught it against her body and frowned. "What's this?"

He shrugged. "It's cold outside. You'll need it."

Shahara frowned at the dichotomy of the man. How could he be so cruel one moment, then thoughtful the next?

Not caring about that answer, she was going home and that was all that mattered.

Soon Tessa would be safe, too.

Syn stifled his disgust at Shahara's condo. Though clean, it was as rundown as anything he'd ever seen. The locks on the door were about a hundred years old and he was sure they'd collapse under the stress of even a medium breeze. A faded, old sofa had been set against one overly patched gray wall, and a tattered blue blanket covered the numerous tears in its upholstery. It looked like she'd recycled it from a landfill.

Nothing but a sheet strung up on a line separated the bedroom from the rest of the place. He hated that anyone had to live this way, but then, he remembered a time when he would have sold his soul to have this much to call home.

Ignoring him, Shahara moved to the chipped kitchen counter along the wall opposite of the sofa and turned on her laptop. Before she could type in her code, her link buzzed.

At first, she ignored it.

"Shay, this is Kasen. Please pick up if you're home."

Syn frowned at Kasen's anxious voice, wondering what trouble she was in now.

Shahara glanced up at him sheepishly before opening the channel. "Hey, Kase, what do you need?"

Syn acted like he was fascinated by the spots on the ceiling, which said she had a long-term leak there, and not interested in her call in the least.

"Have you heard from Caillen? We had a fight last night after my run and he took off again. I don't know where he is. I'm worried."

"Hang on, I'll check my messages." Shahara switched the mute on, then hit the button on her voice mail.

Syn saw her watching him from the corner of his eye. He looked at her and she quickly turned her back to him. He sighed at her coldness. It was too bad they were enemies. Half of her family actually liked him.

As he listened to her calls, pain hit him square in the chest. The first three messages were bill collectors threatening her with legal suit. The fourth message was the most disturbing.

"Fria Dagan, we cannot accept your ship as collateral for your sister's bill. You already have not one, but two liens against it. If we don't have the money by the end of the day, we will have no choice but to turn her out of the hospital. I suggest you contact us immediately to make arrangements for payment or to pick her up."

Syn clenched his teeth in anger. He'd fought that kind of crap with hospital administration on more than one account and lost. For an establishment sworn to help the needy, it never ceased to amaze him how often they refused to help the people who needed care the most.

How could anyone put a price on human life? The very idea sickened him. It was one thing to hunt and kill the corrupt who preyed on others, another to go after decent people whose only crime was being poor.

He looked at Shahara and saw the defeated slump in her shoulders. Now he understood what had motivated her to come after him. He couldn't blame her in the least.

"Hey, Trisa."

Caillen's voice. There was a tenderness in it as he spoke that Syn had never heard him use before. That told him all he needed to know about their relationship, 'cause in all the times he'd been around Caillen and Kasen, he'd never known Caillen to use it with her.

Shahara was particularly precious to her brother.

"Look, I'm making a last-minute run for the Blairus Company to get some quick cash and I'll be gone for a bit. If Kasen calls, don't tell her where I am. They paid me extra to run through the Solaras System and it's too dangerous for her to follow me—you know what an idiot she can be and I don't want to deal with it.

"I borrowed some money from a friend and paid off Tessa's debt with those loaners—you should have told me what happened. I hate learning shit like this from her boyfriend of all people. You know, I am a grown-up. Really. I can even pull my boots on by myself and everything nowadays. But don't worry. I promise I'll think up some way to pay the hospital and transfer you the money as soon as I can. I also left a few credits in Mom's trinket box for you. Don't pay no bills with it. Buy some food. You're too damned skinny. I'll see you when I get back. Love you much."

Shahara glanced over her shoulder. Syn quickly looked away. She turned off her machine and opened the channel. "Kase, he's off on sabbatical to pout."

"That's what I figured. As long as I know he's all right, I guess I'm not too upset. I'll see you later."

Shahara turned off the link and moved back to the laptop. "Did you get an earful?" she asked testily.

Syn sighed. No wonder Caillen had needed almost six thousand credits. "Look, if you need a loan—"

She curled her lip. "Not from the likes of you. If you want a prostitute you can—"

He held his hand up in disgust. "It was an offer made in good faith." *Gods, she was impossible.* "I wouldn't expect any payment other than cash when you have it."

Her eyes snapped golden flames at him. Her breast heaved with the fury of her temper. Damn, she was beautiful when pissed . . .

Syn took a step back, afraid of the thoughts in his head. He must be crazy. She wanted no part of him, and most especially not *that* part of him, and he was damned glad of it.

"Just recant the contract and I'm out of here."

"Fine." She pulled up the bounty lists. With the swipe of her stylus, she deleted her name.

Syn's temper cooled a bit as he saw that one of his threats had been removed. He handed her the Seax dagger. "Now I want you to swear on this that you'll never stalk me again."

Furious hatred burned in her eyes. She gripped the dagger. "I swear. Blood oath. I will never hunt you again."

Inwardly Syn cringed as she brought her hand away and he saw the blood where she'd cut herself. The doctor in him wanted to tend her wound, but he knew she wouldn't take anything from him willingly and he wasn't one to push himself where he wasn't wanted.

He handed her the rest of her gear and walked out.

Somehow it was the longest walk of his life as he closed her water-damaged door and stepped out into the low-rent district of her city.

Gah, that she had to live here, like this.

"What is wrong with me?" He had enough problems of his own; why did he care about her and her bills?

It was his loyalty to Caillen, he decided. Tessa was his sister, too.

Shahara stared at her screen, her heart hammering. There was nothing that could pay even close to what she still needed to keep Tessa in the hospital.

I have four hours . . .

An image of her dying mother played through her mind as she saw her lying on the hospital bed. Her mother had fought so valiantly, but in the end, it hadn't been enough.

I don't want to leave you, Shay. I'm so sorry that I won't be here for you. Please take care of your brother and sisters for me. I know it's a hard thing I ask, but I have faith in you to keep them safe.

"I can't do it anymore, Mom," she whispered, her voice breaking. She was so tired of all this responsibility. She just wanted one day where she didn't go to bed at night with a panic attack and one morning where she didn't wake up with a knot in her stomach as she feared what trouble her siblings would be in before sunset.

An image of Tessa dying tore through her.

Syn's bounty pays enough . . .

I gave my word.

Her gaze fell to the picture she had in a frame by her computer. It was them as kids. Caillen was only five and they were holding on to each other, smiling bright.

She reached out and touched Tessa's beautiful face.

The promise to her mother was much more important than an oath made to a convict.

I hate myself for this . . .

Picking up her link, she did the one thing she knew was wrong and hoped that, in time, she'd be able to forgive herself.

Hours later, Syn smiled as he turned off his laptop. He felt better than he had in a long time. Of course Shahara would want his head once she found out what he'd done, but it didn't matter.

What he did felt right.

Now, he could finally get some sleep.

Yawning, he started toward his bedroom.

A loud knock thundered on his door. Only a handful of people knew where he lived, and out of them only Caillen knocked like that. He must have returned early and found out what he'd done. No doubt he was pissed.

Without checking the corridor vid, Syn turned off his scanner and opened the door.

It wasn't Caillen.

Son of a. . . . It never failed. *Every time your defenses drop, you get screwed.*

"Well, well, what have we here?" Uriah Merjack, the Ritadarion Chief Minister of Justice, sneered.

Syn cursed. He started to pull his blaster out, but the

That he did, 'cause Syn wasn't about to give him what he wanted. If he did, the Minister would kill him.

Uriah Merjack stared menacingly at Syn, wishing to all that was holy he knew some way to break him.

As soon as they'd brought Syn into the sterile interrogation room on Ritadaria, he'd been completely stripped while they searched his entire body for weapons and contraband. Every single cavity. One could never be too careful when dealing with a man as crafty as this one had proven to be.

Satisfied that Syn had no way to fight back, Uriah had then ordered him secured to an interrogation table.

That had been nine hours ago. In that time Uriah had tried every device of torture known to them: mind probes, electrodes, orifice probes, serums.

Finally they'd decided to dispense with the table, and use a more primitive means of inducement. Securing his hands above his head with a chain and his feet with manacles, Syn was held against the wall while they tried to beat and torture the information out of him.

The light gray wall, as well as all of them, was splattered with his blood.

Still he wouldn't break. Damn him! He wouldn't even honor their efforts with a scream or pleading.

There was only one other person Uriah had ever come across with that kind of fortitude. "Just like a damned Wade," he breathed under his breath.

The warden, Traysen, turned toward him. "What was that, sir?"

Uriah shook his head at the prison warden, who had overheard his mumbling. "Nothing." He faced the interrogator who was showing signs of the same frustra-

sight of forty Ritadarion enforcers in full body ar
with weapons pointed at his heart, head, and chest k
him from suicide. Red targeting dots danced over
body, letting him know exactly where they'd be sho
ing if he tried to escape, and it wasn't pretty.

This had to be a nightmare. There was no way the
could have found him here. None.

The lease wasn't even in his name. It was in Nykyrian's.

Syn swallowed, praying he'd wake up.

He didn't.

And when one of the enforcers came forward and
slammed him into a wall he knew it was real enough.
Every bit as real as the throbbing pain along his cheekbone and shoulder.

Wrenching his arms behind him, the guard cuffed
his wrists together.

Merjack grabbed him by his hair and pulled him
around to face him. His fat jowls shook from his laughter as the ugly bastard beamed in satisfaction. Too bad
age hadn't been kinder to him.

Then again, youth hadn't been all that kind to him
either.

"I've waited a long time to find you, rat. Now you're
going to wish to God you had cooperated with me the
first time."

Too stunned to think, Syn could do nothing but
stare at the intense hatred in the Minister's eyes. He
knew the truth about Merjack's past and he was more
than sure Merjack would make good his threat.

The demonic laughter continued to fill his ears.
Merjack turned and faced one of his soldiers. "Get him
out of here. We have a long interrogation ahead of us."

tion. Neither of them was used to dealing with someone *this* damned stubborn. Most people broke within half an hour. The longest anyone had lasted to date was three.

Except for Idirian Wade . . .

Uriah looked at the interrogator. "What other means are left to us?"

The interrogator, a beefy man in his mid-forties who had the best reputation for inducing pain in the known worlds, shrugged. "Sir, I've tried everything. If you give me a little time to do research, I might find some ancient forms that could prove beneficial. But at this point . . . I've never seen anything like it."

Uriah clenched his teeth in aggravation. Of course not—because let's face it, the rat held the key to his survival while the other criminals had only been nuisances. If they didn't get this bastard to break, Uriah *and* his son would be rotting in a cell next to him.

So why should this go easy?

Crossing the floor, he grabbed Syn's hair and wrenched his head back. Blood poured from a cut above one eye and out of his nose and mouth. "Tell me where the chip is, rat."

"Still on the old block?"

Furious at yet another smart-ass retort, he kidney-punched him.

Tensing with the blow, Syn sucked his breath in between his bloodied teeth and grimaced. "Who taught you to hit? Your grandmother?" He narrowed that demented dark glare on him. "The only person you're going to scare with that is a three-year-old girl."

Just as he drew back to hit him again, Uriah's son stepped forward from where he'd been leaning against the wall.

Tall and slender with short brown hair, Jonas pushed Uriah back a step, then moved to brush bloody strands of hair off Syn's face. "I know this has to be killing you. Literally and figuratively. Why not save all of us a great deal of trouble and just tell us where you stashed it?"

Syn smiled coldly, displaying a mouth full of bloody teeth. Did they really think he was dumb enough to answer that? If he gave them that chip, he was dead.

As long as he was alive, he stood a chance of escaping.

But gods, he was tired and he hurt so bad . . . Even blinking burned. No part of him had been left unviolated or undamaged.

No, not true. They hadn't assaulted him where it really mattered.

Only his ex-wife and son could hit him there.

All Merjack and crew did was hit him on the surface, and that he could take. It felt like a typical weekend night when his dad had been on a bender and feeling particularly vicious. If they thought they could break him with these puny attempts, they had a lot to learn.

Only his father had ever reduced him to tears.

And his son.

No, this was nothing . . . just like him.

Syn laughed at Jonas's pathetic offer. "Why don't you try checking up your—"

Uriah punched him again. Pain exploded as he felt his ribs shift.

"Father, please!" Jonas snapped. "We mustn't kill him. Not yet."

The interrogator cleared his throat and addressed Jonas. "Lord President, it may be too late for that, sir. His injuries are extensive."

Jonas looked at Uriah, his brows drawn together in

concern. "We must stop this and allow him to recover before we begin questioning him again."

Oh goody . . . What a great kindness on their part. He couldn't wait.

Uriah nodded in agreement. Syn's death without that chip was useless to them. Anyone could find it. Anyone could have it. And now that Syn was up against rape and murder charges on Gouran, it was more than likely he would trade the chip to the Overseer of Justice for amnesty or at least a lighter sentence.

God help them then.

They had to have that chip!

The little bastard could ruin them and be damned if he'd lose his life and position to something as low as a Wade.

He looked at the guards and the interrogator before he replaced Syn's muzzle—it wouldn't do to have him talk to anyone but them. "Take him to solitary and keep him there until I say otherwise."

The three guards unchained Syn from the wall.

Instead of falling down like a normal person, somehow he managed to stay standing as they cuffed his hands behind his back.

Syn's strength awed him.

And before they led him away, Syn cast him a cold, evil glare that was all too familiar. One that made the hair on the back of his neck rise in fear.

But then what had he expected? Syn was the son of Idirian Wade—the sickest, most lethal criminal to have ever been conceived.

And Wades didn't buckle easily.

Jonas turned to face him. His blue eyes mirrored the same fears and concerns Uriah had. "What are we going to do, Father?"

"Relax, Jonas. You are one of the most powerful leaders in the United Systems. Fretting doesn't become you."

"Neither does a public trial and execution."

"I can control him."

Jonas shook his head. "That's what you said when he was merely a child. If you couldn't break him then, what the hell makes you think you can break him twenty-three years later? We have to have that chip! I've come too far to have some gutter rat bring me down now."

Uriah ran his hand across his jaw. Wades weren't really gutter rats. They were sharks. And if one didn't watch one's leg, it would be painfully cut off.

Along with other things.

Still, he hadn't known Syn was a Wade the first time around. Now he was prepared. After all, he'd been the one to bring Syn's father to trial and execution. A feat that had earned him the honor and gratitude of all governments.

He knew what to expect from Syn now.

"As I said, I'm in control of the situation. I will think of a way to break him. Don't worry." Even as he said the words, Uriah couldn't suppress the memory of Idirian Wade's execution.

Wade had walked into the termination booth without fear or remorse. Never in his life had he seen anyone so calm.

So purely evil.

As the gas seeped into the room, Idirian had looked at him and smiled as if to say, "I'll get you someday."

Uriah had thought then as he did now that surely evil like that didn't die.

Maybe his son was his vengeance on him after all . . .

"Sir?"

He jumped at the sound of Warden Traysen's voice. He hadn't realized Traysen had remained while Syn was taken to his cell. Had it been any man other than Traysen, he'd now be dead. But Uriah had learned a long time ago that this seax's loyalty belonged solely to him.

"What is it, Traysen?"

"I think I may know of a solution."

He exchanged an interested look with his son. "Yes?"

"You remember my colleague, Seax Dagan?"

"The girl who gave him to us?"

"Yes, sir. I think she may be of use to you again."

Jonas scowled. "How is that?"

"I think she could persuade him to lead her to the chip."

Uriah scoffed at the ludicrousness of that. "How? Syn would never trust her again after what she did to him."

"Maybe, maybe not. But if anyone in the universe exists who can accomplish this feat, it is she. I've never known anyone more resourceful or cunning. I believe if you give her a chance, she will prove most worthy."

Still Uriah wasn't convinced. He didn't like dealing with unknown people he couldn't control. "Why would she do this for us?"

"She has a family she helps support, one of whom has a severe gambling problem, and another with congenital medical necessities. Dagan is desperate and poor, and in grave need of money. For, let's say, a million credits, I'm sure she'd do anything. And ask no questions."

Jonas sucked his breath in. "I don't know, Father. She's a seax, sworn to their oaths. Why would she—"

"Traysen is also a seax," Uriah said with a smile.

"Their loyalty can be bought. Is that not right, Traysen?"

"Yes, sir. Everyone has a pricetag. It's just a question of how much."

Jonas crossed the room to stand directly in front of Traysen so that he could give him a menacing glare. "You better be sure of her greed."

"I'd bet my life on it."

"Good, because that's exactly what you'll pay with, Traysen, if you're wrong." Stroking his chin, Jonas looked back at his father. "Do it then and let's hope it works."

CHAPTER 5

Shahara paused in the doorway of her sister's hospital room that had cost her in ways Tessa had no idea of. Tessa lay on the bed looking so pale and weak. Her blond hair was mussed while the bruises still marred the beauty of her face. Several different types of monitors beeped and whirred. One to monitor her kidneys, which had been damaged during her beating, and Shahara wasn't sure about the others. All she knew was that they terrified her.

But even more horrifying than their presence was the fear that the doctors would order them removed for lack of payment, and condemn Tessa to the slow, agonizing death their mother had suffered.

At twenty-four, Tessa was almost the exact duplicate of their father. When not in pain, her green eyes sparkled with life and her curly blond hair was often unruly. Shahara had spent countless hours with Tessa as a child experimenting with different hair ointments and gels to try and tame it into a style. They'd finally admitted defeat and just grown it out long.

Shahara swallowed. She loved her siblings more than her life.

Still unaware of her presence, Tessa was lying on her bed while her boyfriend, Thad, sat next to her holding her hand. Only inches separated their faces and he stroked her cheek tenderly with his left hand.

A strange ache pressed against her chest as she watched them. How she longed to have someone look at her like that. To touch her cheek and make her smile even while her life was falling apart.

But those dreams were for fools. Nothing in life ever lasted.

Watching the two of them, she began to feel like an intruder.

What was she doing here?

Tessa didn't need her prudish sister around. Besides, she made Thad extremely nervous. He always acted like he was afraid she'd throw him to the ground, handcuff him, and arrest him.

Backing away, she turned to leave.

"Shay?" Tessa called. "Is that you?"

With a deep breath, she forced herself to reverse course and enter the room. "Hi." She moved to kiss Tessa's forehead. "I wanted to check on you. And," she held up the plastic bag in her hand, "I brought you some things I thought might help you get better."

Grabbing the bag, Tessa beamed.

Shahara looked away from her battered face as rage whipped through her. She couldn't stand the thought of anyone hurting her sister that way. God help those beasts when she got her hands on them.

And she *would* get her hands on them. There was no doubt about it.

Thad laughed as Tessa held up her ragged childhood doll. "You even brought Molly?"

Shahara shrugged. "I know you don't sleep well without her nearby."

Her sister smiled warmly. "Thank you. You're the best sister ever."

"Don't let Kasen hear that or she'll punch you."

Tessa laughed.

A nurse walked in. "It's time for her vitals. Will you please wait outside?"

Shahara led the way.

As Thad opened the door for her, his hand brushed against her shoulder. She immediately shied away.

"I'm sorry," he mumbled in a sheepish apology.

Embarrassed herself by the action, Shahara put two arms' length between them. "It's all right."

They stood on opposite sides of the hallway for several awkward minutes before Thad spoke again. "So where did you get the money?"

She watched as a group of doctors and nurses conferred down the hallway and tried to imagine Syn with his lethal air in such a refined group, wearing their scrubs.

It just somehow didn't work in her mind.

"Caillen paid them off."

"No, not the loaners. For the hospital. Caillen told me he didn't have the money for both."

Frowning, she turned her full attention to him. "They haven't been paid yet." She was still waiting for payment from Merjack.

"That's not what they told me. I tried to pay part of it when I arrived, but the clerk told me the balance was paid in full."

Now that didn't make sense. "They must have made a mistake."

He shrugged. "Maybe. Since I wasn't family, she wouldn't tell me anything more than that."

Could Caillen have come up with the money and just not had time to tell her?

Excusing herself from Thad, she went to check.

To her relief, the line inside the spartan business office was short and she only had to wait five minutes before a pinched-faced clerk motioned her forward.

Shahara stepped up to the waist-high counter.

The woman looked bored and irritable as if she'd been here way too long and wanted to go home. "Patient name?"

"Tessa Dagan."

She typed it in. "And how may I help you?"

"I need to know how much we owe."

"And you are?"

"Seax Shahara Dagan. I'm the one responsible for the bill."

The woman huffed as if annoyed with Shahara's presence. "I've already gone through this with a man. Can't you people understand? The account is paid. You don't owe any money."

Shahara stared at the billing clerk in disbelief. It couldn't be. "That can't be right. Please. Check again."

The woman turned her computer screen to face Shahara. "You can see for yourself. Tessa Dagan's account was paid in full three days ago by Sheridan Belask. He also left an open balance in the event we needed more for her treatments, and gave her and her family credit for the cafeteria and hospital store should you need something."

Shahara blanched. Sheridan Belask?

Syn?

The man whose location she'd turned in to the Ritadarion officials had paid for her sister's treatment?

Suddenly the light gray walls around her seemed a little too close, a little too bright. She felt as if someone had just delivered a debilitating blow to her stomach.

How could Syn have done such a thing after she'd gone after him?

Why would he have done this?

It didn't make sense. No one would do such a thing. Kindness was not in people's natures. Ever.

Especially not someone with Syn's brutal past.

No, he must have wanted something from her. Something more than just her oath. That was it. That made sense.

It was a good thing she'd made her pact with Merjack because C.I. Syn would have eventually come to her for repayment. Without a doubt.

Wouldn't he?

"Thank you." She turned and left the office.

But what if she was wrong?

You're not wrong. He raped and murdered that poor girl in cold blood—you saw what her father said. Her fellow tracers wouldn't be terrified of him without just cause.

And her own interaction with him had proven just how cold and dangerous a person he was.

No one would ever do a good deed without expecting payment for it. Gaelin had taught her that. And she'd learned her lesson well.

Her mind whirling, she didn't bother to stop in and say goodbye to Tessa. At the moment, she couldn't face anyone. Especially not her gentle sister who would never understand why she'd gone back on her word and turned Syn in. Even if it meant Tessa's life.

I didn't go back on my oath. Technically. She'd sworn not to stalk him. She hadn't sworn not to call the authorities and tell them where to find him.

You're arguing semantics.

Tessa would be the first one to beat her up over that, but then Tessa could afford the luxury of naivete. She couldn't.

In a daze, she made her way home.

Shahara pushed open her front door and saw Kasen sitting on her sofa, munching her last handful of friggles while she watched a small handheld viewer.

Kasen's strawberry-blond hair was pulled back into a tight ponytail that curled around the nape of her neck. Out of all her siblings, Kasen was the only who shared her eye color, which had come to them through their maternal grandfather. Big-boned and stocky, Kasen was cute enough on the outside, but her churlish personality was sometimes rather difficult to stomach.

"Hey, Sis," Kasen said absently as she kept watching her show.

"Hey, Kase." Though she loved her sister, she wished Kasen would leave. She really wasn't in the mood to deal with her right now.

Kasen frowned. "You look like you were chewed up by a wolf and shit down the wrong side of a mountain. What's wrong?"

I just remanded a man to custody who bailed me out and I feel like crap over it.

That was something she couldn't share with Kasen and her acerbic personality.

So she shook her head as she dropped her blaster on

her kitchen counter. Kasen was not one to confide in. She left such things to Caillen. But not even he could help her right now because if she dared tell him what she'd done, he'd have her head. He didn't like the idea of her being a tracer to begin with, but their desperate financial situation had made him accept it. If he ever learned that she'd taken a mission to travel alone to apprehend a man of Syn's reputation, he would absolutely flip.

Kasen went back to eating. "So how do you know Syn?"

Shahara went cold at the unexpected question. She looked up in shock from her laptop, wondering how Kasen knew of their encounter. "What do you mean?"

Kasen pointed with one crispy-fried friggle to the jacket Syn had loaned her. The one that was still slung over the back of her chair where she'd placed it after he'd stormed out of her condo three days ago. "I know that jacket. It's one of a kind. Syn bought it three years ago from some big-name auction house. Gave something like four thousand credits for it. It was the jacket High Commander Gillian was wearing when he signed the treaty that ended the Colonial Wars."

Shahara looked at the jacket, awed at the price. Just how much money did Syn have?

But then, how long did it take to steal a fortune?

Kasen dug around the bag, scrounging for crumbs. "I can't believe he'd let it out of his sight. He's real possessive when it comes to his stuff. Worse than Cai is with us." She gave a dreamy smile that was at odds with her usual caustic personality. "Syn's a great guy, isn't he?"

Shahara cocked a brow and stared at her sister, who'd returned to watching her program. Kasen never respected anyone, and the admiration in her voice when she talked about Syn was not something she needed to hear at the moment.

She cleaned up the juice spills Kasen had left on her counter and tried to appear nonchalant as she pumped her sister for more information. "Have you known him long?"

"I only met him about four years ago. Him and Cai go way back. They met through Caillen's friend, Darling. And according to what Darling's said, Syn practically raised him and still watches out for him." She threw the last bit into her mouth. "Syn's the friend who's always paying our fines and boosting Cai from jail after his fights. Hell, he even paid to repair my ship last week after I had that run-in with those Gondarion officials."

Shahara froze as she realized who Syn was. Caillen had never mentioned his mysterious friend and benefactor by name. He'd always told her that she wouldn't approve if she knew and so she'd never pressed the issue.

Now she wished she had.

The more she thought about it, the angrier she became. Syn had to have known who she was.

Why hadn't he mentioned the fact that he was Caillen's friend? His benefactor?

His boss?

Maybe because you were trying to kill him?

Like that mattered. And why hadn't she caught his slip and asked him about it?

Because he threatened Caillen and you were scared . . .

Forcing herself to calm down, she said as conversationally as she could, "Syn didn't tell me he knew you guys."

Kasen snorted. "No duh. As possessive as Caillen is

when it comes to you, I'm sure Syn figured Caillen would rip his tongue out just for speaking to you."

Biting her lip, she considered Syn's threat to Caillen's life. Had that been a ploy, or would Syn really hurt Caillen? "Syn indicated to me that he might want to hurt Cai."

Kasen laughed so hard she choked. After several coughs, she cleared her throat. "Syn hurt Cai? Lay off the hallucinogens, Sis. Syn would sooner cut off his own balls than hurt Cai . . . I'm sure it was a joke. Syn's got an odd sense of humor. Takes a while to get used to him."

She couldn't believe this. Kasen had to be wrong. She had to be.

"Hey, now," Kasen said as if an idea had just occurred to her. "Why were you with Syn anyway?" Her face turned serious, frigid. "You didn't do anything to him, did you?"

Trying to act as nonchalantly as possible, Shahara wrung out her dishrag. "What do you mean?"

Kasen stepped up to the counter and glared at her. "You know what I mean. You don't hang with men and definitely not people like Syn—you hunt them down." Her look intensified. "If you've done anything to him, I swear I'll tear you apart."

She gaped at her sister's threat. "You would choose him over me after all I've done for you?"

"No, I love you. But me and Cai would both be roasting our ass in prison if not for him. Syn even took the blame for me when I got caught filching files, and covered my tracks so that I wouldn't get arrested."

"You did what?"

"Don't you dare get mad at me." She pointed one bony finger in Shahara's face. "I've had it with your moralizing. Tessa needed the money and *you* didn't have it, as usual. I did what I had to, to help out. Besides, I already had my ass chewed sideways from Syn over it. I don't need to hear any more lectures."

Kasen scratched her nose. "Like Caillen, I get tired of always borrowing money from Syn to cover things. Even if Syn doesn't say anything, I still don't like it." She gave a short laugh. "'Course I won't do any more filching. I stink at it and I'm not about to get Syn into any worse trouble."

Shahara blinked. She couldn't be hearing this.

Had Syn paid off the hospital because of Caillen? Honestly, she couldn't fathom anyone being that nice. Not unless he was getting something out of it.

"Why does Syn help the two of you? What do you and Caillen do for him?"

She shrugged. "Nothing really. Syn's never asked for the money back or asked us to do anything for him— come to think of it, he never asks anyone for anything. Caillen makes a few runs for him every now and again, but Syn always pays him for it. Personally, I think Syn has more money than he knows what to do with."

Another gut-wrenching thought occurred to Shahara. "Do you sleep with him?"

Kasen snorted. "Oh please, I wish. He's gorgeous and ripped to the devil and back. I would give just about anything in the universe for a taste of *that* deadly Syn. But he's never been interested in me, and the last time I made a move on him, Caillen almost tore my arm out of its socket. Lesson learned. Syn off-limits."

Shahara bit her lip as she processed that latest bit.

What had she done?

You arrested your brother's best friend. Idiot!

She had the terrible feeling that she'd made a horrible mistake. One, by turning him in. Two, by signing a deal with the devil to help out her family.

If half of what Kasen said was true, Caillen would never forgive her for doing this to his friend. A friend who'd helped all of them over the years . . .

What was she going to do? She didn't want Caillen to hate her. Or even Kasen for that matter.

They were her family.

The *only* family she'd ever have. She couldn't hurt them any more than a mother could hurt her own children.

What a way to pay a man back for helping you. Gah, I suck as a human being.

Her thoughts spinning, she felt a sudden need to be alone. She had to think through this. To find some way out of the mess she'd created.

She tossed the towel into the sink. "I've got some errands to run. If you leave before I get back, lock my door."

"Get some more friggles while you're gone."

Shahara barely heard her over the buzz in her ears. She couldn't accept this latest mission. Someway, somehow she'd find a way to get them to release her from her million-credit contract.

So much for release. Merjack was a bastard of the first order and he'd insisted she see her contract for the chip through or lose her license.

Then where would she be?

In the gutter with the rest of the rats.

Disgusted, Shahara glanced at the outside of the toughest prison in the Ichidian Universe. Inside the twenty-two-foot high, white-speckled walls resided the most dangerous felons who'd ever lived.

Never in her life had she been more afraid. She still couldn't believe she was doing this. What had she been thinking when she'd made her agreement?

Tessa's life.

And the money, of course. But right now, staring up at the force field that surrounded the high walls, money just didn't seem all that important. Especially not when her life was about to be on the line.

Just one slip, and she was sure Merjack would toss her into a cell with Syn.

Or worse, Syn would cut her throat.

She sighed wearily. "Dang, Caillen," she whispered. "I really wish you'd pick a better class of friends."

Her throat tight, she walked down the cold, gray walkway where six armed guards eyed her warily.

Easy, girl. No fast moves.

Men of this caliber were like animals. They attacked whenever they sensed weakness.

Curling her lip at them, she approached the search station where they scanned people for weapons and credentials. She had to remain composed if she was to live through this mission.

You will be completely on your own. No one will acknowledge you as working with us. You will be a fugitive on the run the same as Syn until you return with him and the chip. Only then will you be cleared of this matter. Do not fail.

Because if she did, they would execute her too. Heck of a leverage tool they were using on her.

Closing her eyes, she wished she'd never even heard the name C.I. Syn.

"Papers?" the guard asked.

She handed them over. It'd taken four days to get the "forged" papers she needed to release Syn from prison.

And as each day passed, she'd feared more and more for her life. Especially if Caillen ever found out.

If only Tessa would learn her lesson about gambling and get-rich-quick schemes . . .

Yeah, like that would ever happen. *Thanks, Dad, for that life lesson.*

Once the guards cleared her, she headed for the Vice Warden's office and pressed the buzzer for entrance.

"Yes?" a sharp, irritated voice asked over the intercom.

"I'm here for a prisoner transfer."

A click sounded and the steel-gray door slid up. This was it. Just one more step and then there would be no turning back. Her heart hammering, she entered the green office, the color reminding her of mold.

There were no pictures on the walls, probably to keep some prisoner from breaking one and using the glass or frame as a weapon. Two brown, steel desks were set beside a larger one that must have been designated for the Officer in Charge. All were bolted to the floor.

At present, only one man occupied the office. A greasy little fellow who looked up from the first of the two smaller desks. "Papers?" He extended his frail hand.

She stepped up to his desk and handed the disc that contained the forgeries to him.

He put the disc into his reader and glanced at the orders for a moment, then looked back at her. "These are for Syn."

Keep your composure, Shahara. Don't move a facial muscle you don't have to.

"Yes, I know. He's also wanted on Gouran for the rape and murder of Princess Kiara Zamir. I'm here to escort him over for trial."

The little man pushed his glasses back up on his nose and frowned. "Minister Merjack won't like this. I think we should wait until he gets back tomorrow before we release C.I. Syn to you."

Shahara shrugged. "Fine. You can call President Zamir and tell him that you've authorized the delay. I'm sure he'll be understanding. After all, she was his only child."

The man gulped, his eyes widening in fear of the notoriously brutal president and military commander who was rumored to have once gutted a man for just ogling his daughter while they dined. "We . . . we wouldn't want *him* upset, would we?"

"I know *I* wouldn't want him upset at *me*. But you're the power in charge here. How did you spell your name again?"

He shuffled several papers on top of his desk as if debating, then finally he reached for his link. "Warden Traysen, I have a Seax Dagan here who is waiting to transfer Syn to Gouran. I need your approval, sir."

"I'll be right there."

Shahara took a deep breath in relief. So far everything was going as planned. Just a few more minutes and she'd be safely away.

But how long each second was turning out to be . . .

When Traysen showed up, she reminded herself not to acknowledge that they knew each other in any way.

He eyed her with a cool, warning stare.

Without a word of greeting, she followed him down a series of locked and guarded hallways until they entered the detention area.

Scanning the facility, she couldn't squelch her revulsion over the living conditions of the prisoners. The lower into the facility they went, the worse the conditions in each cell—which literally were holes cut out of the masonry. Holes that were barely large enough for a small child, never mind the men and women who were forced to live inside them.

Unidentified odors assailed her until she could barely breathe. Human excrement littered not only the floors of the cells, but also spilled over into the hallways.

Little to no light reached the prisoners who moaned and begged for death and mercy as they passed.

The seax in her rebelled at their inhumane conditions and she vowed to see to it that the Overseer's council was notified of this violation. No one, regardless of their crimes, should have to live like these people did.

How did Traysen work here day after day and not report it?

"Merjack ordered me to keep Syn penned in solitary." Traysen swung open an armored door, which led to an underground area. A brisk, cold wind blew up the stairs, freezing her. "I warn you, he's one tough son of a bitch."

"Merjack?"

Traysen shook his head. "Syn. I've never seen anyone like him in my life and I thought I'd seen it all in my day. I'm not quite sure if a little thing like you can handle him."

"I've handled worse," Shahara said with a confidence she didn't feel. Last time they'd tangled hadn't gone all that well for her.

She just hoped she had better luck this time.

And right now she wasn't too sure if Syn wouldn't kill her on sight. Who could blame him? She had a hard time picturing the immaculate Syn residing in such a filthy place as this.

The cells down where Traysen led were made of titanium instead of stone. Clear, steel-glass walls sealed off the front of the cells and allowed her to see into them, but no audible sound could be heard. The prisoners, male and female, were naked and chained down by stakes on the titanium floor or secured to the walls or ceiling. Shahara's stomach churned in horror. Given their condition and the frigid temperature, she didn't know what kept them from freezing to death.

When they neared Syn's cell, it was all she could do not to retch. His hands were chained together over his head, and another chain suspended from the ceiling kept him two feet above the floor. More chains were secured to his feet on a short line to prevent him from being able to kick.

Every muscle in his upper torso was stretched taut by the unnatural position. It had to be killing him.

Bruises and lacerations marred every inch of his naked body, and his long, tangled hair obscured his face from her. She bit her lip as guilt gnawed at her conscience.

This was all her fault. How could she have been so stupid?

They'd beaten him well. She could only imagine how much pain he must be in. "How long has he been like this?"

"A few hours. Release the holding hook," Traysen said into his handheld link. "And send me backup . . ." He looked at her before he added, "A lot of backup."

Instead of being lowered gently, Syn dropped to the ground like a sack of vegetables. She grimaced.

He lay on the floor, unmoving. Her heart stopped

beating. He didn't appear to be alive. Had they killed him?

Eight enforcers joined them an instant before the narrow glass door raised. Slowly, the guards moved into the cell.

"A real tough son of a bitch," Traysen repeated before moving her to the side of the door as if to protect her from something.

When they seized Syn's chains, he sprang to life, striking out at them. With his fist wrapped in the chain, he decked the first guard to touch him, then he went after the second. For several seconds, he put up a good fight. But with his hands and feet chained together, he didn't have enough mobility to finish them off.

The guards beat him down with clubs, knocking him back to the floor.

Shahara dug her fingernails into the palm of her hands, trying to keep herself from crying out for them to stop this.

If she did that, it'd mean both their lives.

Steady. Play it cool.

Still, she couldn't stand to see a defenseless man beaten and just do nothing. How did Traysen manage to look so stoic?

Finally, the enforcers released the chains on Syn's legs and pulled a pair of pants on him. With his legs free, he renewed his fight with vigor and determination. While he struggled with the guards, he was thrown back against the glass and Shahara saw the fresh lash wounds crossing his back. The raw skin and blood . . .

Bile rose in her throat.

When they turned him around to unchain his hands and recuff them behind his back, she couldn't stifle the gasp. Bruises and blood covered his face. He'd been beaten so severely, he could barely open his left eye, but when he finally saw her standing there, he rushed for her.

"Varisha, espolin krava!"

Traysen shielded her with his body. Shahara didn't know the language Syn used, but she was certain he wasn't giving her a "Hi, how you doing? Good to see you again" greeting.

The enforcers clubbed him with their staves until he stopped moving.

"Take him to my ship," she ordered, trying to act like none of it bothered her. But inside, she died a little every time they struck him, and her conscience took hold with steely, unforgiving claws.

One guard seized his feet while the other carried him by his shoulders.

"Here." Traysen handed her a small injector gun.

"What's this?"

"It'll help revive him when you get where you're going."

"Is it adrenaline?"

"No, it's seranac."

She arched a brow at that. Seranac was a potent drug that worked on the hippocampus and frontal cortex. An interrogation med, it loosened memories and blurred a person's ability to separate the past from the present. It also caused hallucinations, since the person couldn't tell one from the other and could become caught up in the past and think that it was happening in the present. And since it held a stimulant to it, it could be most dangerous for all involved.

Usually the person was held down when it was administered.

"Don't you have something a little safer?"

"Not here I don't, and it is much safer than adrenaline—can you imagine *him* on that?" He shuddered and indicated the injector with a jerk of his chin. "That's the only thing I have that can revive him. But don't worry. It's a small dose. It won't last for more than a few minutes—just enough to get him inside someplace and he'll be unconscious again."

He had a point about the adrenaline. With a nod, she slid it into her pocket and followed the guards.

The walk out of the facility seemed to take forever. Each minute, she half expected someone to rush toward them and demand both their heads.

Luckily, it never happened and, at long last, they reached the landing bay.

The guards roughly dumped Syn into the back of her fighter. The tallest of them also took a moment to add a couple more blows to Syn's unconscious body before leaving.

"That's for cutting me, you rank bastard dog," he snarled. As he turned to face her, Shahara noted the long jagged cut along his jaw that Syn must have given him.

While beaten and chained . . .

You are so dead when he wakes up.

With a trembling hand, she took her copy of the forged transfer orders and climbed aboard.

She half expected Syn to lunge for her again, but she realized he was still unconscious. Breathing a sigh of relief, she hoped he stayed that way until she could get him home and tend to some of his wounds. The last thing either one of them needed was a fight that would only hurt him more.

She shook her head in regret. How had she come to this pass?

How had she turned a man over to these beasts? Even if he was a convict, he didn't deserve this.

Her mother would be so disappointed. And if the truth were known, she was more than just a little disappointed in herself.

But worse than her guilt was the question of what he'd do when he woke up and found himself back in her home.

What kind of vengeance would he seek?

Well, she'd fought worse, she supposed, but something inside denied it. She'd never gone up against anyone who could handle a beating so well.

Her heart heavy with dread, she programmed in the coordinates and launched.

It didn't take more than a couple of hours to return to her home.

Uncuffing his hands and getting Syn out of her ship was no easy task. "Gah, could you be any larger?" As she moved to help him out, she realized he was burning with a fever.

Great, just great. She struggled to pull his huge form from her backseat.

It was useless. She was going to have to use the drug even though something told her it would be a stupid thing to do.

But if she didn't, she'd have to leave him in her ship, which would have some busybody calling the enforcers on her.

"Suck it up." She pulled the injector out and shot him in the arm. Maybe it wouldn't be so bad and he had happy childhood memories.

Not with your luck, babe.

It took several minutes before it revived him.

He blinked open his swollen eyes as much as he could. "Talia?" he whispered like a fearful child.

"Sheez, you're already hallucinating." This was the last thing she needed. A man twice her size dreaming of who knew what. Hopefully it wouldn't be a violent dream he was having—at least not until she could get him inside and put a safe distance between them.

But his semiconscious state made it easier to get him out of her ship. He leaned heavily against her. She looked around the neighboring flats, hoping no one saw them and called the local enforcers.

How in the world she would explain *this*?

With a sigh, she tugged him toward her condo.

"Where are we going?" he asked in a fearful whisper as he leaned on her. "You know he's going to find us again. He'll just get madder if we run. Maybe we should just wait for him to come back. If he's drunk, we can hide and he won't see us."

"Yeah." She moved him into her home and toward her bed. "Why don't you just lie here and wait." She pulled the sheet back and helped him lie down.

He curled up like a child.

Shahara went to the sink and grabbed a bowl of tepid water and a fresh washcloth.

By the time she returned to the bed, Syn had rolled on to his back and appeared to be asleep. It was probably for the best. He needed to rest as much as possible. They had a long journey ahead of them and not a lot of time to complete it.

As gently as she could, she bathed the caked blood from the side of his full, sensuous mouth. His steely jaw.

Long, aquiline nose.

One large bruise had formed over his left eye, swelling it shut. As she continued to sponge him, she noted another bruise on his forehead that looked like someone had slammed him head first into a wall.

Repeatedly.

"They certainly made a mess of you," she whispered, running the washcloth over the discolored area of his neck. All too well she could detect the outline of someone's fingers as they'd tried to choke him.

"Wow, I'm not the only one you bring out the worst in. What? You tick off everyone you meet?"

But all kidding aside, she couldn't understand his condition.

Why had they beaten him like this? It wasn't like the types of punishment they used for misbehavior. He'd been *thoroughly* and *brutally* interrogated. From the cuts and bruising, it looked like they'd used every known probe to cause as much damage and pain to him as possible.

Why would Merjack, Chief Minister of Justice for the Ritadarion Empire, do such a thing?

What was on that chip that was worth killing a man over? Merjack had said it was a matter of international security, but . . .

This was ridiculous.

Tenderly, Syn reached up and cupped her cheek. Shahara paused and met his gaze, amazed at the gentleness of his fingers against her skin.

Love and protectiveness blazed bright in the dark depths, taking her breath. "I'm sorry, Talia," he said so quietly she wasn't sure she'd heard him. "I did everything I could. I swear I'll make sure no one hurts you anymore. When I'm big enough, I'm going to get us out of here. I swear it. You'll be safe then. Just please don't cry."

Shahara's heart lurched as she realized he thought she was someone else. His sister from the sounds of it. "I won't cry anymore."

He seemed to take some comfort from her words. With a deep sigh, he drifted back into unconsciousness.

Grateful for the reprieve, Shahara removed his pants and started bathing the dirt and blood from his body.

His tawny chest was bare with hard, well-formed pectorals that tightened and flexed under her hands. Well-defined, bruised biceps and triceps warned of extreme strength, as did the tight muscles of his forearms, and the tendons on his long, lean hands.

His wide shoulders tapered to a washboard stomach and narrow hips. On the left side of his stomach, just beside his navel, ran an old jagged scar from a knife or dagger. She flinched at the thought of how much such a wound would hurt.

As gently as she could, she rolled him to his side and washed the blood from his back. Clenching her teeth in unexpected anger, she couldn't even begin to count how many more lashes had been added.

Her bed sheets were ruined. Not that it really mattered. That was a petty concern given his condition.

How she wished she could afford fredavine to smooth over the red, swollen cuts to help them heal and take the sting out. What had Merjack been thinking? Beaten like this, it'd be weeks before Syn would be mobile again.

If he didn't die . . .

With that thought in mind, she began washing the blood out of his hair as best she could. She'd never seen hair so dark and the softness of it surprised her. It was the only thing about him that was soft. The rest of his body was like coiled steel.

As gently as she could, she rolled him over, then wrung out her cloth.

Moving back to him, her gaze dipped down to his . . .

Her face burst into flames. She'd been doing her best not to look, but now that she had, *it* was all she could see.

She let out a low, appreciative breath. He was nicely formed all over.

Stop that! What was wrong with her? She had no interest in male anatomy and most especially not *that*.

Reaching for her sheet, she quickly covered him and moved on to safer areas of his body.

Running her cloth over the tiny hairs of his leg, she couldn't help noticing the corded muscles. Even prone, they held the promise of agility and speed. Like a marathon runner.

He was such a strong man and yet she sensed a deep vulnerability in him that she was sure would embarrass him if he knew what he'd told her, his enemy. That was the role she'd cast for herself and yet some part of her rejected it.

What do you care?

Yet she did. For reasons she couldn't even guess, she didn't want him to hate her.

I'm insane . . .

Returning the bowl and cloth to her kitchen, she opened up the envelope the warden's assistant had given her that contained his personal effects. Inside was a silver religious medallion that was used to protect children.

Wondering if it was his or his son's, she returned to the bed and fastened it around his neck.

As she pulled away, Syn grabbed her wrist. Shahara panicked at his fierce grip, amazed that he could find such strength after his beating. "What are you doing here? Come to gloat?"

She trembled at the raw hatred in his voice. "I would never gloat."

She watched the anger drain from him. "Why did you betray me?" he asked, his voice searching, pleading.

"I needed the money for my sister."

His glare darkening, his grip turned brutal. "I gave you everything you ever wanted, everything you asked for and this is how you repay me? You fucking bitch . . . What did I *ever* do to hurt you or Paden? Tell me!"

Shahara realized he wasn't talking to her. He was still caught up in the demons that tortured him.

His grip tightened on her arm until she cried out in pain. "Syn, please. You're going to hurt yourself. Please lie back and sleep."

Somehow, her plea reached him and he lay back.

"Why did you take my son from me?" he whispered weakly. "He's all I ever had. The only one who ever loved me and you made him hate me. Why would you do that to me after all I gave you? I'm not my father. I would never have hurt him. I never hurt you. I'm not my father . . ."

He kicked back the covers and tried to rise.

"Syn! You need to lie down."

He shook his head. "I have to get to Nykyrian. I have to warn him."

Nykyrian . . . he was the other person listed on the

Gourish contract for raping and murdering Kiara Zamir. "Warn him about what?"

"Kiara's using him. She's going to get him killed. Stupid idiot. She doesn't love him. She's lying. Why won't he listen to me?"

"You killed her to protect him?"

He looked at her. "Who are you?"

"Did you kill Kiara Zamir?"

He didn't answer as he tried to push past her.

Shahara held tight. "You can't get up. You need to stay here."

He looked around her condo. "Where am I?"

"Where do you think you are?"

"I want my sister." The anguish in his voice brought a lump to her chest. "Why did she have to leave me?" A tic worked in his jaw. "Because I'm not worthy." His tone was deep as if he were quoting someone. "She couldn't stand looking at me anymore."

Finally, he closed his eyes.

Shahara sighed in relief, hoping he didn't have anymore of these episodes.

Thanks for the drug, Traysen . . .

She stayed awake all night, bathing him in serin gel, trying to get his fever down. While she maintained her lonely vigil, she kept thinking over his words.

Who was this man? He had so many secrets, so many demons that they made hers appear weak in comparison. Why had his wife taken his son?

That explained why Syn wasn't in the more recent photos. He must be keeping up with his family from a distance. Which meant he still loved them.

I can't believe how badly I've screwed all this up . . .

Closing her eyes, she wished she could take away

the pain she'd caused him. It was obvious he had enough to bear without the misery she'd added to his life.

She stretched to ease the aching muscles of her back. In the end, she'd done what she had to and there was no going back. All she could do for now was see to it that he suffered no more than he had to.

As a seax, she owed him that much.

Just before dawn, his fever broke. Shahara drew a thick blanket over him, before finding her way to the sofa.

As soon as she closed her eyes, she drifted off to sleep.

Shahara awoke with a start. She glanced around her home, trying to figure out what had startled her. When her gaze fell to the empty bed, she had a moment of severe panic.

Where was Syn?

In answer, the door to her bathroom opened. In all his naked glory, Syn leaned heavily against the door-frame. Even weakened, he filled the room with an aura of raw, masculine power.

As he moved toward the bed, every muscle in his body rippled. Never in her life had she seen a man with a better body and if things were different . . .

Yeah, right. You wouldn't do anything.

His cheeks were grizzled with the beginnings of a beard and the cuts on his cheeks and lips made a mockery of the handsomeness she knew he possessed.

Her gaze swept over him and she couldn't suppress the chill that spread through her. He made an imposing figure and she had to agree with Kasen. Even beaten and bedraggled he was gorgeous.

From the expression on his face, she could tell how much pain he was in.

She went to offer her help, but he greeted her with a fierce snarl.

She took a step back, realizing he was lucid and angry.

"What am I doing here?" he growled.

She disregarded his question. "You need to get back in bed and rest."

Though his eyes were still swollen, she could see the hard glare he pinned on her. "Why? So you can heal me, then turn me back over to the Rits?"

Her throat tightened, then she fell into the lie she'd created. "I'm sorry about that. It was a mistake. But as you can see, I fixed it."

"You have my undying gratitude." The sarcasm in his voice cut her deep.

She deserved that. After all, how would she feel if she were in his place?

At least he wasn't rushing for her throat. That was an improvement.

"Can I get you anything?" She moved toward the kitchen. "Something to drink. Eat?"

He let out a sound she assumed was an aggravated snort before he pulled a blanket off her bed and limped toward her sofa. "Yeah, I need a drink of something so potent it'll inebriate me in one shot and a painkiller chaser." Draping the blanket around him, he took a seat, then rubbed his hands over the whiskers on his face.

Syn cursed as he accidentally bumped his swollen lips with his hand. Damn Merjack. He was going to kill him for this.

And with that thought, he glanced to Shahara, who eyed him nervously.

Yeah, you ought to be nervous, babe.

He should kill her too. But at the moment it took all his strength just to move. He'd forgotten how much a beating hurt.

He took a deep breath. Severe pain sliced across his chest. *You know better than to breathe like that, you idiot!* How in the hell had he *ever* forgotten that pain?

Shahara watched him warily, still not sure if she was out of danger. Once again he turned that dark, probing stare to her while he raked his fingers through his thick, black hair to comb it out. Oddly, her own fingers ached with the memory of how soft his hair had been.

"Why did you free me?" he asked at last.

"You helped my sister. Thank you, by the way."

Good, he seemed to accept her explanation. After a long minute, he looked up at her. "How'd you do it?"

Transfixed by the play of steely muscles, it took a moment for his question to register. She paused. "Do what?"

"Get me out."

She fetched her hairbrush for his hair. As she handed it to him, his fingertips brushed hers, sending a strange tickle to her stomach.

Attributing it to the fact that she'd never before conversed with a naked man in her flat, she stepped back and cleared her throat. "I forged transfer papers for you."

The look on his face made her insides shrivel. "What name did you use on the release?"

"Mine."

The curse he snarled caused her cheeks to flame. He

immediately rose, then quickly sat back down with a groan.

She put a safer distance between them.

"How long have we been here?" he asked between clenched teeth.

"How many questions are you going to ask?"

Even from her distance, she could feel the heat from his stare. "If you used your *real* name on the papers, how long do you think it'll be before the Rits come knocking on your door to question you about my whereabouts? Merjack isn't going to just blithely let me go."

"Oh my God," she breathed. She hadn't even thought about that. What an oversight. If she wasn't careful, she'd tip her hand and be caught for sure.

Syn rolled his eyes toward the ceiling. "Jeez, woman, couldn't you at least think it through?"

"Well, excuse me. I don't normally pull people *out* of jail. I'm the one who puts them there."

With a grimace, Syn pushed himself off her sofa. "We've got to get out of here before they find us."

"And go where?"

"Wherever."

Crossing the room, she was aghast at his suggestion. "I don't want to leave my home. I have things to take care of. People to take care of."

He grabbed her by the arm, his gaze branding her with heat. "Well, how do you propose to take care of them from a hole similar to the one you found me in?"

He looked her up and down with that evil grin she was learning to despise. "And believe me, *sweetie,* they're a lot harder on a woman than they were on me. The guards don't normally rape male prisoners. But they would sure get their jollies passing around a little thing like you."

Her stomach dropped at his words and for a moment, she thought she might vomit.

Syn grimaced as if pain cut through him. "We have to get out of here. Now!"

Rushing toward her nightstand, she pulled out her weapons and module for her fighter. "Let's go."

"Just one problem." He dropped the blanket and stood in her room completely naked. "I need something to wear."

Once again heat suffused her cheeks. How in the universe could she have forgotten his nudity in such a short time?

Stepping around him, she rummaged through her closet and pulled out some of Caillen's clothes that he left here for those nights when he stayed over. She handed them to Syn then stepped into her living room and pulled the sheet closed to give him privacy while she waited by the sofa.

"Damn it, Caillen," Syn growled several minutes later. "You must wear the same size boot as your sisters."

He gave a fierce groan and she couldn't help laughing. Poor Caillen.

"If my injuries don't kill me, these tight boots will." Just as he opened her makeshift curtain, a knock on her door startled her.

She went cold. "Oh God, they're here . . ."

Syn grabbed her blaster.

Suddenly, a familiar voice called out through the door. "Shay? You home?"

Relief coursed through her at her sister's voice. Opening the door, she pulled Kasen in. "What is it?"

"I just heard over Caillen's scanner that the Ritadarion government is sending agents over here to find you. And I was . . ." Her voice trailed off as she looked past Shahara and saw Syn by the sofa.

"Oh," Kasen mouthed.

"We've got to go." Syn handed the blaster to Shahara. "Have they gone by my place yet?"

Kasen shrugged. "It sounded like they had, but I'm not sure."

He growled deep in his throat. "I think I know a place where they won't find us."

Kasen scowled. "Where are we going?"

Syn gave her a sincere, charming smile. "You, my nosy friend, are going home to wait on Caillen while I take Shahara to a safe zone."

Kasen let out little puffs of breaths in aggravation. "Where are you two going?"

"If I told you, it wouldn't be safe."

"Yeah, but—"

Syn lost patience with her. "Not enough time to explain. Go home, Kasen. Now."

Shahara lifted a brow at the fierce voice he used and for the first time in her life, her sister actually obeyed.

Syn jerked her out the door of her condo and around the side of her building.

She tried to break free. "You could loosen your hold on my arm. It's not like I'm likely to run off anywhere."

"Sorry." He released her.

An instant later, the pain returned as he again seized her arm.

"What the—"

"Shh." He pulled her down beside a group of hedges. "Lean against the wall," he whispered.

Without question, she obeyed.

Just as she was about to ask him what was wrong, she saw the Ritadarion enforcers.

Her heart pounded. They'd found them. And worse, they blocked the entrance to the landing bay she shared with two of her neighbors.

Her throat dry, she wanted to curse.

We're so caught.

CHAPTER 6

As soon as the enforcers passed their hiding place, Syn pulled her up and in the opposite direction of the bay.

Shahara was aghast. "What are you doing? We need my fighter."

He looked back over his shoulder to where the men had vanished, then shook his head. "Not today, we don't."

"Then how are we going to get out of here?"

The smile he gave her sent a chill down her spine. "We'll get out of here *my* way."

"But what about Kasen? She's still in my house." She started back to help her sister, but the grip on her arm was steel.

"Go back and they will make you wish you were treated as well as I was. Kasen can handle herself. Trust me, I've seen her get out of much worse situations than this. And I promise I'd never let anyone harm her. Caillen would beat my ass if I did. She'll be okay. We, on the other hand, are going to be dog meat if they see us."

Okay, Syn was definitely nuts, she decided as he pulled her down the street, away from the landing bay. Otherwise how could he remain so calm while the transport? You think they're not going to check them in a few minutes and figure out where we went? The only thing that saves us is the address I entered just now won't show up on their end if they check—a fake one will. Because, yeah, I *am* that good. And we're lucky they don't have sats trained on this area or we would be seriously screwed right now. But you don't know about tracking satellites or deja vu loops and ghost codes because you don't ever have to use them. Now, if you don't mind, I'm going to sit over here with my throbbing feet and bleed in silence until we get to our destination."

Damn him, he was right. She'd always acted in the open—like using her real name on his transfer orders. She'd never been one for subterfuge. Sneaking maybe, but never any long-term incognito operations. She didn't know the first thing about hiding, or places to go for shelter.

What was she going to do?

How was she ever going to get through this mission intact? If the imbecile enforcers didn't kill her by mistake, Syn more than likely would. Especially if he ever found out the truth and whose side she was really on.

Oh God, I'm a wanted criminal . . .

She wouldn't be able to go home until after all this was over and she had that chip in the right hands. She couldn't even be around her family without endangering them.

It wasn't that she hadn't known it going in, but the reality of it was a whole other matter.

If she was caught, she would go to jail.

With the criminals I put there.

For a full minute, she couldn't breathe as that sank in. Damn her stupid sense of justice. She should never have allowed Traysen to talk her into doing this. There was no amount of money worth her freedom or her life.

What would happen to her family without her?

How was she going to survive?

She looked over at her churlish companion. Syn knew. He'd been running since he was a kid.

But would he continue to help *her*?

Not if he suspects you in any way . . .

Maybe he wasn't quite the beast his bounty sheet claimed. Maybe he liked Caillen enough to keep her safe in the name of their friendship. Grasping that small hope, she turned to face him. "Since we're in this mess together, care to tell me why you're so important to the Rits?"

He opened his eyes and cocked a questioning brow.

When he didn't answer, she tried again. "Come on, Syn. I'm not green. I know governments don't expend this kind of energy to go after a run-of-the-mill filch or even a murderer. Nor do they routinely beat their prisoners to a pulp. You were seriously interrogated by someone who knew exactly how to wring the most pain out of you while keeping you alive and able to speak. There's a lot more to this than what's on the surface and they want you for something significant. What is it?"

He let out a heavy sigh. "Yeah, there's a lot more to this."

She waited.

When he refused to say more, she gently poked him in the ribs.

He hissed and smacked at her hand, but not hard enough to hurt her. Then he winced as if his own actions had caused him pain. He glared at her before he spoke again. "Do you really care to know?"

"Yes."

With another deep sigh, he ran his hand over his whiskers and she watched the play of lean tendons under the bruised skin. "When I was fourteen, I was doing a filch for a certain political candidate on Ritadaria. The information he wanted was pretty routine, just dirt about his opponent and their party. I was going along my merry way, recording and scanning secure chips in their offices, when I accidentally came across Merjack's personal diary."

"Chief Minister of Justice?"

"No, his son, who later became president." He paused. "What I discovered was that the Minister and his son were responsible for President Fretaugh's death."

She gaped at his disclosure. "They killed him?"

"In a manner of speaking. Back in the day, the Minister was only a vice warden in our fun little prison. He released one of the assassins for the hit and, once the assassin killed the president, Merjack's son killed him to keep the man from talking."

She scowled at his far-fetched story. "That seems like a lot of effort to go to. Why not kill the president themselves?"

"They needed an airtight alibi. What better one than being directly beside the man when he's executed and the whole thing is being covered by every major news organization in existence? All the assassin had to do was shout out a political statement against the president as he killed him and everyone assumed our friends had nothing to do with it. And no investigation was held since everyone plainly saw it was a psycho zealot who took the president out. Likewise, no one thought twice about the hero who ended up killing the zealot while trying to apprehend him. Ironic really, by killing the man they'd hired to murder the president and covering their tracks, Jonas Merjack was able to secure the presidency for himself. Living proof that there really is no justice in the world."

Shahara digested that slowly. Now this was an interesting snippet and it went a long way in explaining why Merjack wanted Syn so badly.

Then again, Syn could be lying. Filches had a nasty habit of doing that sort of thing when it suited their purposes. "And you have the chip to prove all of this?"

"Had it."

She looked at him in disbelief. "What do you mean you *had* it? How could you let something like that out of your sight?"

He gave her a droll stare. "It was a long time ago and I was a scared kid. Merjack had a separate security feed on the diary which I didn't discover until it was too late. They were bearing down on me and I stashed the chip barely a heartbeat before they caught me."

"Why would they go to such extremes to hide their actions only to put it down as hard evidence for someone to find?"

Syn shrugged. "Why do people do anything they do? I gave up a long time ago trying to figure out the stupidity or arrogance of the average person. Maybe he was so proud of it that he had to let it out and since he didn't dare tell a real person, he told his recorder. I don't know. All I know is it's his voice and his confession."

She wasn't so sure. This was just a little too much to believe. "How old did you say you were? Fourteen?"

He nodded.

"Do you honestly expect me to believe that a serious political candidate would entrust something as important as gathering campaign secrets to a mere child?"

His features turned to stone. "I don't give a damn what you believe."

She scoffed at him. "You really are a piece of work. I almost believed you."

"You should. It's the truth."

Yeah, right. "I doubt you'd know the truth if it came up and slapped you down."

He glared at her. "And what makes you so sure that I'm lying?"

"Because I was orphaned at sixteen and I know people don't hire children to do much of anything. The best job I had at that age was scrubbing floors."

He snorted. "They do when it's something highly illegal and they know you were trained by the absolute best."

"And just who trained you? Idirian Wade?" she asked sarcastically, using the name of the most notorious criminal who'd ever lived.

His look was as cold as steel. "Yes."

Shocked, she stared at him. Now *that* was one fact omitted by both his sheet and her contact.

Could it be true?

Surely he was lying.

But if he wasn't, that made him even more dangerous. Because anyone spending time with Wade had been spending time with the devil himself.

Syn looked so serious that he was either a consummate liar or he was telling the truth.

Which one was it? Honestly, his story was way too much to be believed.

"Why would Wade train *you*? Especially as a kid? He wasn't exactly known for having partners or letting them live once someone made the mistake of thinking he wouldn't skin them. Literally."

His look was completely cold. "Why do you think?"

She shrugged. "I can't imagine how a criminal like him would have any interest in a snot-nosed kid."

He rolled his eyes. "C'mon, Seax. You're not this dense or that stupid. Your father was one of the greatest smugglers ever born and what was the first lesson he taught your brother?"

"How to . . ." Her words broke off as she finally understood. "You're telling me Wade was your father?"

He gave her a sarcastic salute. "Give the woman a hero cookie."

Shahara couldn't breathe as those words sank in. Dear God, she was sitting next to a man descended from the most psychotic killer ever known? Someone who was notorious for killing hundreds, if not thousands of people—men, women, and children. And he didn't just kill his victims, partners, and friends, he tortured and mutilated them.

He'd even cannibalized some of the bodies.

Wade was a man so evil, that even decades after his death, decades after his ashes had been scattered in space and every possible trace of anything that might contain even a micro hair or skin cell from him had been seized and destroyed, governments were still terrified someone would use his DNA to bring him back.

And she sat next to the son he'd trained . . .

For a moment, she thought she'd be ill.

Syn tensed as he saw the look in her eyes that he despised most. It was the one that said he contaminated her air with the filth of his past. That if the car wasn't in motion, she'd be running out through the street to get away from him. Not for anything he'd ever done.

But because he'd been unlucky enough to be fathered by a psychotic animal.

Just once couldn't someone surprise him and separate the truth from their fears? Only Nykyrian had ever really accepted the fact that his genetic link to a madman hadn't corrupted him, too.

What did you expect?

Nothing, really. It was the same reaction Kiara Zamir had given him. But what killed him most was the knowledge that if he really were his father, he'd have butchered them over those looks and then kept their eyes as trophies.

Provided he didn't eat them.

Disgusted, he looked away.

Shahara sat perfectly still as she came to terms with the fact that she was sitting next to the devil's spawn. No wonder he was so good at what he did. His father had eluded custody for decades. Those who'd come close to finding Wade had been gutted, skinned, and pinned to walls as a warning to anyone else who had dreams of bringing him in.

In fact, he would have never been caught at all had someone not . . .

She licked her lips as a shot of hope went through her that said Syn might not be quite as corrupt as his father. "You're the one who turned your father in, aren't you?"

Syn cringed at a question only one other person had ever asked him. No one but Nykyrian had ever figured that out.

He started to lie to her, but why bother? It wasn't like her opinion of him would change. "Yeah."

"Why?"

"Seemed like a good idea at the time." If only he'd known then what hell was going to rain down on him, he might have reconsidered. But at the time, he'd wanted to get away from his father's brutality so badly . . .

He'd had these stupid dreams of the authorities giving him to a family where he could go to school like a normal kid and have a life like everyone else.

Even at ten years old, he should have known better. He'd seen enough of the darker side of human nature by that point . . . but the kid in him had been dumb enough to believe in happy endings and rainbows.

"So how much money did they pay you to betray him?"

He loved the way she phrased that. Like he'd betrayed the father who'd never done anything for him except make him suffer. Yeah, his dad had given him a certain set of criminal skills that had served him well over the years, but that benefit was far outweighed by the rest of the damage the bastard had done to him physically and mentally.

"I was a kid, Shahara. They didn't give me shit for it. It was my civic duty." He almost choked as he repeated the words the Overseer had said to him right before they put him in cuffs and hauled him to jail.

"Then why did you do it?"

To retaliate for his sister's death. He hadn't been big or seasoned enough to kill the bastard himself. So he'd allowed the authorities to do it for him.

But that was something he'd never admit to. In the end, he got what he deserved, too.

No good deed goes unpunished.

I'm coming back for you, you little bastard. And when I do, you'll suffer like no one ever has. So help me, gods. I should have let your mother drown you when you were an infant. See what mercy gets you? A bastard seed who betrays you to the grave. May the gods make you suffer every day you live and may each one be more painful than the one before it.

Those had been the last words his father had ever spoken to him. To this day, they warmed the cockles of his blackened heart.

And it proved the one point Syn had lived his life by ever since.

Everyone betrayed.

He'd sold out his father and his son had turned his back on him. And just like he'd done to his own worthless father, his son called the authorities any time he tried to visit.

Poetic justice really.

"Syn?" she asked insistently. "Why did you turn your father in?"

"I told you. It seemed like a good idea at the time."

Shahara shook her head, unwilling to accept that. He was hiding something more, but it was obvious he didn't trust her with it. And why should he? She hadn't been exactly trustworthy where he was concerned.

So she changed the subject to something less volatile and to the only thing that could save her life. "Fine. Let's assume you're telling the truth about all this. Why didn't the Merjacks kill you? If you're the only person alive who knows what they did, why would they take the chance on you telling someone else your story?"

"Because they couldn't find the chip. That's the only reason they haven't killed me . . . yet. After all, who's going to believe *me?* A lying, sack-of-shit convict whose father's memory can still make seasoned assassins piss in their pants?"

Confused, she tried to make sense of it. "I don't understand. If you're dead, why would it matter where it is?"

"Anyone could find it and expose them," he said as if he were talking to a small child. "I'm actually surprised no one has found it yet. It would have been real easy to locate. We're just lucky they haven't."

"Then why haven't you gone back for it and exposed them for the murderers they are?"

"Because until you showed your pretty little neck in my home, they've mostly left me alone. I mean, sure they tried seriously to find me for a couple of years after I escaped prison, but I changed my name and they eventually went away. I was practicing the live-and-let-live social policy of survival."

"But if they killed someone, how could you not—"

"Look," he snarled, cutting her off. "Better *him* than me. Believe me, I'm sure Fretaugh had skeletons aplenty in his closet none of us know about and I don't have your wonderful little sense of justice. That's one luxury I've never been able to afford. The only law I answer to is the law of survival. And that law says for me to keep my ass as far from Ritadaria as I can."

She clenched her teeth in frustration. She'd never understood people like him. People who could turn a blind eye to corruption, to crime.

If what he said was true, how could he just let criminals get away with . . .

Oh, he *was* a criminal. No wonder he lacked her morals. If he'd had them, he would never have done all the things he'd done. And that was something she'd have to come to terms with for the next few days until they located the chip.

"So where are we going?"

He opened one eye and pierced her with a glare from it. "You're not about to let me rest, are you?"

"Well, I would like to know where it is I'm heading. Seeing as how I *am* a part of all this . . . now."

"Fine," he said in a voice as equally aggravated as hers. "First we need to get a ship to tel-ass out of here. Then we need to find someplace to stay for a night until I can protect myself, and unfortunately you, from the bastards after us."

"And then?"

"Then we go to Ritadaria and find that damned chip."

She frowned in disbelief. "I thought you were practicing the live-and-let-live law of social survival stuff."

"Yeah, well, screw it. I was never all that bright anyway."

Damning himself for stupidity, Syn closed his eye and took as deep a breath as he dared. He ached from one throbbing molecule to the next and all he could think about was the betrayal that had caused each fierce blow.

She'd done this to him.

He'd been living a quiet life with only a few inconveniences as certain morons came after him. But no one had ever found his address before. He'd been very careful about it.

Until now.

Now he was once again a hunted animal with nowhere to call safe and no one to turn to. No one except the person who'd put him in danger.

Trust no one at your back unless you want them to bury a knife in it.

And he'd actually pulled her to safety with him. What the hell had he been thinking?

That Caillen would be upset if he let her get hurt. Of course, not nearly as upset as Syn would be if he died over it . . .

He must surely have brain damage.

Where had he picked up a conscience? And when? He'd always lived his life alone, without encumbrances.

No good deed goes unpunished—that was the one mantra he believed in above all others.

Now he was going to pay the price for his sudden tender heart because, no matter how much he might want to strangle Shahara, he knew he couldn't let her go to prison for helping him.

Even if she did deserve to find out firsthand what it was like to live in hell. And no doubt when all of this was said and done, he'd be back in prison and she'd be free. It was just the way things went.

"Hello?" she said, poking him once more in the side.

He stifled the urge to strike out. "What?"

"Why are we going to Ritadaria?"

Crossing his arms to protect his damaged ribs from her finger, he sank lower in his seat. "Maybe I'm tired of running. Maybe I'm still a fool for a pretty face. Ah, hell, maybe I'm just tired of living and I really don't care if they do catch me anymore."

Shahara sat back. What could one say to that? She certainly had no response.

Suddenly, the shuttle stopped. As the door swung open, she saw the small, city spaceport just a short distance away.

Stepping out onto the busy street, she glanced around at the various spacecrafts docked in neat isolation channels that lined both sides of the port. All of the ships were small to medium in size with only a handful used for anything other than shuttles to larger crafts docked in a hangar that orbited the planet—large-bulk craft that weighed too much to ever be landed on a planet's surface.

She frowned. "Why are we here?"

He sighed as he stopped by her side and looked at her as if she were dense. "I told you, we need a ship."

"We have no money to buy passage."

"Must you always get caught up in the details?"

She grabbed his arm and pulled him to a stop. "Look, I've already broken more laws in the last two days than I've ever broken in my entire life. *I'm* not a criminal. I can't do what you do."

He sneered at her. "How nice for you. I'm so glad your precious morality was never compromised. Some of us weren't so lucky." He pulled his arm free of her grasp and gave her a look that froze her all the way to her toes. "Now if you'll excuse me, I have a ship to commandeer. Make sure you stay right by my side so that none of the cameras pick you up and transmit our location to our friends."

He took a step away from her, then paused and turned around with an amused smile. "Or stay here and give the Rits my best, won't you?"

Shahara growled low in her throat. She was going to kill this man. No doubt about it.

But first, she had to get away from the people who were tracking them and complete this godforsaken mission.

Trailing along after him, she crossed the bay. She couldn't believe the open way he walked about, as if he were on honest business.

How could anyone be so sure of himself? Especially since he was about to steal a ship?

No wonder he never got caught.

He paused several times, looking at various ship markings, before he finally decided on one. He gave her a smug, taunting grin. "This one will do nicely, don't you think?"

She clenched her teeth to prevent herself from speaking the lecture that blistered her tongue. He wouldn't listen anyway. Why bother?

Besides, she admitted, it *was* a beautiful ship. Painted red and gold, it was the largest of the rounded Fropane class. A freighter of renowned maneuverability and speed. Her brother had always dreamed of owning one. But they were for rich shippers. Not destitute pilots like Caillen who couldn't even afford a place to live.

One of the bay's attendants approached them. "May I help you, *Frion*?"

Syn inclined his head toward the ship. "Where's her manifest and log?"

"They're recording them now."

"Has she been fueled?"

"Yes, sir. They did that first."

"Good. Open her up."

Without question, the man complied. Shahara frowned. It was that simple to steal ship?

Who knew?

Now that she thought about it, no one had ever questioned her when she'd docked her fighter here. Of course, no one in their right mind would ever want to take that rust heap.

Maybe it was just that Syn's voice held such authority to it, his presence so much power, that no one dared to question his commands.

Still . . .

Like a graceful dancer, the hatch lowered. Automatically, the ramp extended itself for them. Thick, dark green carpet lined the walkway and Shahara fought the urge to take off her worn boots before she damaged the pristine fabric.

Syn took her elbow and led her up the ramp.

"Is there anything else you need, *Frion*?" the attendant asked.

Pausing, Syn looked back at him. "Yeah, tell Eamon there's a shipment due in later tonight. He can take that flight or a passenger shuttle. Whatever he prefers. Just have him bill it to the account."

"Yes, sir."

Her jaw dropped. "You know the ship's owner?"

He laughed coldly as he walked past her. "*I am* the ship's owner. Eamon is just the captain assigned to her."

Following him up the ramp, she had a strong urge to kick him. He'd been playing with her all this time? "What do you mean you own this ship?"

He pushed the controls to retract the ramp. "I own one hundred and six of them to be precise. Contrary to your information, I happen to be a shipper, not a thief."

"You mean your flat and everything you own is—"

"Paid for by honest coin." He started past her but she stopped him.

"I don't understand."

"No, you don't. And that's your problem. Now, if you'll excuse me, I have a flight to plan. We have to get clearance before the Rits get smart enough to lock down this port. I can't afford to shoot my way out of a port we use all the time for my real business."

Dumbfounded, she stood in the narrow corridor while her mind whirled with this new information. Was he a doctor, a shipper, a thief, or a filch?

Just who was this man?

Unsure of what to think, she went to the bridge. Syn sat in the navigator's chair where he was pulling up course information and coordinates.

Shahara headed for the captain's chair. No sooner

had she seated herself than she noticed the cut above his eye had reopened.

Absently, he brushed the blood aside while he scanned the electronic files.

"Here," she said, pulling out her small handkerchief from the tiny pocket above her breast. "I can get it."

She moved to his side.

As she brushed the thin, worn linen over his brow, she could feel his warm breath fall against her throat where it tickled, raising chills the length of her arm, tightening her breasts. He looked up at her with an unfathomable stare. One that hypnotized her.

Even with the bruises marring his face, she couldn't lose sight of his handsomeness. And as she watched him, his gaze darkened with some thought she couldn't name.

The handkerchief fell from her hand and she touched his roughened whiskers. They made him appear so rugged and raw, a far cry from the clean-shaven man she'd met just days before. Now he really looked like a dangerous criminal. Like a man who could steal her most private thoughts.

Her very soul.

She should be afraid of him and yet no part of her recoiled as she normally did when a man stood so close. He wasn't groping or pulling. He just sat there, looking up at her as if waiting for something.

Suddenly she felt his hand at her waist. He trailed it up along her spine until he touched her cheek. Before she could react, he gently pulled her closer.

"So pretty," he whispered an instant before he claimed her lips.

Shahara trembled at the foreign sensation. His lips weren't demanding, they were asking. Gentle and kind, they teased her senses . . . whetted a hunger that she'd never known existed. Surrendering herself to her whirling emotions, she leaned into him and allowed him to pull her onto his lap.

Again he whispered his language to her and her body arched for the kisses he began to rain down the column of her throat. Throbbing heat assailed her. She wanted more.

Syn knew he should stop, but for his life he couldn't pull away. It had been way too long since he'd last held a woman. And this one stoked his passions to the highest level imaginable. She was so brazen and yet so timid.

And her body tasted like honey and spice.

He moaned as she ran her hands through his hair, stroking his scalp. Running his hands over her spine, he felt her move against him an instant before her knee brushed against his bruised ribs.

Pain exploded, blotting out all the pleasure. He gasped in agony.

She tensed a moment before she jumped away. "I'm so sorry! Are you okay?"

"Other than the fact that I feel like my rib just punctured a lung, sure, I'm all right." He leaned forward, trying to shift the pain.

If he ever got his hands on Merjack . . .

And speaking of, it was probably a good thing she'd accidentally done that. They needed to get out of here. Quickly.

Hormones be damned.

Pushing himself up, he took a shallow breath to steady himself. "If you want to punch in coordinates, I'll do the preliminaries and fire the engines."

She nodded and took his vacated chair. Syn paused

for a minute as he noted her reddened cheeks and swollen lips. His whiskers had burned a path all the way down her throat and, for some unknown reason, he liked that sight. Somehow it marked her as his.

Don't even go there.

What was wrong with him? He knew better than to put any claim on a woman. He could never depend on one. Women lied and they betrayed.

The only one he could trust was himself.

She's already looked at you like you were shit.

Yeah, but she also let him kiss her. Usually when a woman learned the truth about his past, she ran.

Don't. You're nothing to her and that's all you'll ever be.

With that thought in mind, he took the captain's chair and prepared their launch.

Just as he was about to press the launch code, Shahara reached out and touched his arm. "Look." She inclined her head toward the side window.

Looking over, Syn saw the Rits coming in to question the flight staff. "Stay calm. They won't mark this ship. And we've already been cleared for the launch."

"Are you sure they can't make us?"

"The ship is registered under the name of Darling Cruel. They wouldn't dare push that button."

Shahara took a deep breath. He was right. The Cruels were renowned for their political power and wealth. No one messed with them unless they had a death wish.

Still, her heart didn't stop pounding until he put the throttle down and launched them.

"If you own this ship, why is it registered to Darling?"

He gave her a droll stare. "I couldn't very well run

the business under my own name now, could I? Every half-wit moron in the galaxy would be after me."

"Aren't you afraid the Cruels will find out and get angry?"

His look was snotty and offensive. "Ryn and Darling are friends of mine and have been for a long time. It was actually Darling's idea that I register my business assets under his name."

"Why would he take such a risk?"

"What risk? Who in the universe would take his family on? For all they know, it is his business."

She had to give him that. No one in their right mind would dare question one of the Cruels. "So how do you know him?"

He sighed irritably. "I knocked on his door one day and said 'Hi, I'm here to rob you. Hope you don't mind. Oh, and by the way, will you be my friend?' "

"You don't have to be so sarcastic."

He gave her a lethal glare. "I'm getting tired of answering your questions. I swear you must have been trained as an interrogator."

"Well, excuse me for being curious. I don't have the benefit of knowing all about your family or friends. Caillen never mentioned you."

"If you were trying to cut me with that remark, you missed. I made Caillen swear a long time ago that he'd never tell anyone he knew me. If anyone ever found out he was a friend of mine, his life wouldn't be worth any more than that plastic ring on your hand."

Shahara clenched her right hand into a fist. In spite of the hard shell she kept on her emotions, tears welled up in her eyes. Gritting her teeth, she blinked them away, angered that he'd been able to stab her there. She knew her mother's wedding ring had no monetary value, but her mother had cherished it and to her it was priceless.

How dare he insult it so.

Syn saw the sadness that darkened her eyes and he was instantly contrite. "I didn't mean that. I'm sorry."

In an effort to distract her from the pain his thoughtless words had caused, he quickly asked, "So tell me, how did you find my apartment? It's not registered under my name either."

With a shake of her head, her eyes cleared. "I researched purchase orders." She cleared her throat, then spoke louder, "I knew you flew a black Pritan fighter that was only a year or two old."

He sucked his breath in as he cursed himself for *that* oversight. "I purchased it under my name."

She nodded. "I cross-referenced the fighter's serial numbers with a list of landing bays until I found the one where it was registered. Once I knew the location, it was merely a matter of asking people in the area if they knew anyone who answered to your description."

Oh, I am an idiot . . .

But he had to give her credit. No one else had thought of that.

"Clever."

"Some days more so than others." She glanced back at the coordinates. "I take it your fighter is also registered to Darling?"

"To another friend . . . as is everything I own."

She cocked her head. "Aren't you afraid one of them will betray you? Take it all away?"

Syn shrugged. "I'm sure one will eventually, but that's the least of what keeps me up at night. Trust me, there are a lot worse things in life than losing a few credits."

"Such as?"

"Strangling the older sister of one of your best friends because she can't shut her mouth."

Suddenly a warning light went off.

Shahara jerked toward her panel, afraid they were being attacked.

"You need to okay the course I just entered. Hit the approval sequence. The code is listed to your right."

As she reached to comply, her gaze fell to their heading. All of a sudden she felt ill.

Very, very ill.

"We're going to Rook?"

"Yeah, something about that bother you?"

She was aghast at his nonchalance. "Yes, it does. That is the most dangerous place in the universe. Are you out of your ever-lovin' mind? We go there and we'll be dead in three minutes."

CHAPTER 7

Syn gave her a dry stare. "Quit being such a baby. I thought you'd been to the 'worst parts of the galaxy in search of your targets'?" That last bit was said in a tone that mocked hers and it really pissed her off and made her want to throw something at him.

Reigning the impulse in, Shahara eyed him coolly. "I have, and I'm not being a baby. Only a complete waco goes to Rook." Waco was an assassin's term that meant walking corpse—something they used in reference to their targets, which was exactly what she and Syn would be the moment they placed one foot on Rookish soil.

The people who called Rook home were the worst of the worst. There was no security, no enforcers, nothing but blood on the streets. Literally. Life on that planet had no value whatsoever—not that it had all that much in the rest of the universe, but . . . She'd heard of people there being butchered for their shoelaces.

And Syn looked completely unconcerned about it all.

Then again, he was related to the worst scum imaginable. To him the rest were just posers.

He swiped at the cut on his forehead, and grimaced at the blood on his fingertips before he wiped it on his pants leg. "Yeah, well, this corpse needs a resting place. So Rook it is. Maybe we should call ahead and have them get our tombs ready. What do you think?"

Shahara grimaced at him. He was categorically insane—that was probably what the C.I. stood for. It had to be. "You have some severe mental problem I need to be aware of, don't you?"

He flashed a half-dimpled smile that sent shivers the length of her body. When he continued, it was in a strange accent that sounded more than just a little too creepy. "Just because I eat babies for breakfast and pick my teeth with their bones doesn't mean I'm nuts."

She rolled her eyes. Given who his father had been, he probably shouldn't be making jokes like that. No doubt that had been his father's favorite delicacy. "Any other weird habits I should be aware of?"

"Just my need to dance naked in the streets under the light of a full moon."

"I'll make sure we wrap this up before the next full moon, then." In spite of her words, a wonderful image of his naked body flashed in front of her open eyes. No matter how much it pained her to admit it, the man was gorgeous, and even beaten within an inch of his life, his body was hot. "Naked in the street, huh? Now there's a sight I'd love to see."

A wicked grin curved his lips. "Well, I'm certainly up for a private viewing any time you want."

"I wouldn't be so cocky," she said with a wicked grin of her own. "If my memory serves, the part of you that might be up to it will probably be the first part of you the inhabitants of Rook cut off."

Shaking his head, he turned back around in his seat. "Hit the approval sequence."

"All right, it's your funeral." But all kidding aside,

there was a lump the size of a large asteroid that burned a hole in her stomach. She didn't like the idea of stepping foot on a planet ruled by convicts, pimps and slavers. It was just too dangerous. Even for a seax.

She wasn't afraid, merely cautious. And the one thing she'd learned early in her career: Arrogance kills. Never assume there wasn't better out there and that it wasn't coming for you.

Because the moment you were convinced of either one, it was over. End game.

Syn watched her from the corner of his eye. By the look on her face, he could almost hear her thoughts. Not that he blamed her. He hated the idea of crawling back to Rook himself. It'd been decades since he'd escaped the dismal alleys and street gangs so violent his father would be proud of them. The hell that had once been his life. Years since he'd given much thought about his father's old running buddies and the neighborhood that had birthed them both. He'd sworn long ago to put it all behind him.

Now he was crawling back like a wounded pup. And he hated that most of all. Nothing sucked more than having to face the worst part of his past.

Too bad he couldn't go to Nykyrian. He knew his friend wouldn't hesitate to help, but Nykyrian had problems of his own and the last thing Syn wanted was to bring another one to his door. Yeah, it was a great time to be wanted since most of his friends were in hiding themselves. As for Caillen. . . .

Yeah. . . .

No. He could handle this himself. As he'd always handled things.

Only this time he wasn't on the run alone. He had to watch out for Shahara as well. Her presence should have annoyed him, yet for some reason it didn't. Instead, it was almost comforting to know that if he didn't make it, she'd be there to help.

Or would she?

Come on, Syn. Where's your brain? What the hell makes you think she'd help you again? The only reason she came back for you was guilt over her sister and you were lucky she had even that much sympathy for you. Don't count on that happening twice. You, my friend, are nothing to her. Nothing but a convict.

And Shahara hated convicts.

Sighing, he realized how true his thoughts were. He was just living an illusion like he'd done with Mara.

And just like Mara, Shahara would leave him behind without a moment's hesitation, pausing only long enough to call the authorities on her way out the door.

He knew that as well as he knew that the Rits would kill him. So why did his mind betray him with thoughts of her? Her smell, her softness, even the little crease she got in her brow when she looked at him as if he were crazy—all were etched deeply in his conscious thoughts.

She was a beauty and he would give what little soul he had left for one night with her.

But that was a bullshit dream and he was tired of reaching for the stars, only to get body-slammed by fate.

Resigned to the brutal reality of his life, he checked their settings.

Shahara felt Syn's stare. Why was he watching her?

A quick glimpse told her it wasn't anger.

So then what was it?

Some part of her she couldn't name delighted at his attention. His eyes radiated heat to her and her body responded to him of its own accord.

Even now she could remember the feel of his skin, of his hands running over her body. Not since her teens had she dared think of a man other than her brother as anything but an enemy.

Now for the first time, she saw one as something more. Unbidden dreams resurfaced from the darkest corner of her mind. Dreams that tormented her with notions of a lover, of stripping his clothes from him and running her hands over his incredibly hard body until he begged her to stop.

But that wasn't her. She'd iced her hormones a long time ago and it bothered her way too much that he was thawing them out with such ease.

"If you don't mind . . ." Syn pushed himself up from his chair. "I'm going to lie down for awhile. I've set the autopilot. Let me know if we come up on anything unexpected."

"Sure." She watched him leave and, once she was sure he'd had enough time to reach sleeping quarters, she turned on the ship's monitors.

Her conscience reared its ugly head over her obvious spying. She didn't care. She wanted to observe him without the weight of those dark eyes probing her as well.

And what better time than when he was sleeping . . .

She found him in the captain's lounge. The room was large for a craft this size, and plush, with a double-sized cot mounted against the far wall. Syn headed straight for it and sat down. Grimacing in pain, he pulled off Caillen's boots and tossed them aside before stretching out. With a deep sigh, he draped his arm over his eyes.

Caillen's shirt was stretched taut over the broadness of his shoulders and with his arm lifted, the whole of his hard, washboard stomach was exposed. She stared at the bared flesh, wondering what it would feel like to rub her hand over the indentations.

Nip it with her teeth . . .

Syn was a commanding figure even while lying prone. Something innate in him warned of his deadly abilities. And though he wore the air of danger around him like a comfortable old shoe, he was also well-mannered and charming.

When he wasn't being a smartass, anyway.

How she wished she knew his thoughts.

Or at least more about his past, which had to be horrifying.

His name, she thought all of a sudden, realizing that she still didn't know what the C.I. stood for. She had so many questions and so few answers.

Most of all, she wondered what it would be like to call Syn friend. Her brother and sister seemed to find it easy enough. Why couldn't she?

Because she'd been betrayed by everyone she'd ever trusted. Her father had been so obsessed with his inventions and schemes that he never paid any attention to her while he pursued them. He would promise her and her siblings time and then conveniently forget.

Or get frustrated when things didn't work out and then he'd vanish for day or two to "get his head straight" while the rest of them were left to pick up the pieces.

Her mother had tried to comfort their hurt feelings, but she'd been sick for so many years that Shahara could barely recall the time before her mother became ill. And her mother had depended on her for everything. To beg for more time to pay bills, to help dress and care for her mother and siblings, to hide money from their father . . .

There'd always been something to worry about.

Then there'd been Gaelin. He'd seemed like some mythic hero swooping down to help her just when she needed it most. Her father had barely been dead a year and she was just starting her training as a tracer. She'd met him outside the market and he'd followed along after her like a lovesick puppy.

"Come on, baby. Give me a little smile. That's all I ask. Here, let me carry that box for you. Don't worry, I don't bite. I'm one of the good guys."

He'd seemed so harmless that in no time she'd dropped her shields.

God, she'd been so stupid. Why had she not seen through him from the beginning?

But she knew. She'd been so strong for so long that it was nice to be able to lean on someone else for a change. And he'd seemed so interested and nice . . .

Young and innocent, she'd wanted to believe that there was goodness in the world. That happy endings were possible and that people were decent.

Yeah, right.

All he'd been interested in was her body and what little money she had. And after he'd felt he'd waited long enough, he'd taken what he wanted and left her bleeding.

That day, she'd died, too. Not physically, but inside. Every hope or dream she'd ever held about her future vanished. From that day forward, she knew there would be no children—Gaelin had seen to it that would never happen.

No love, no husband.

Nothing but a long life spent serving her siblings and trying not to let it turn her bitter. Making sure that they were able to have the dreams she didn't dare have anymore. Making sure that no one ever took from them what had been brutally taken from her.

Her throat tightened and she wished she could cry. But what was the use? Tears were cheap and she wasn't one to wallow.

Still, she wished she'd never met Gaelin. Wished she could have met Syn under another set of circumstances.

Wouldn't it have been great to meet Sheridan Belask, medical student? Ignorant of his past, she could have probably liked him a whole lot.

Gah, Syn's right, you are a crybaby. Enough. What was done was done. She couldn't go back, and right now they had much bigger problems ahead.

Switching off the monitor, she promised herself that she would think no more of what could have been and no more about him.

She couldn't afford to.

Hours later, Syn came awake to the sound of the intercom buzzer. "Yeah," he said, his voice ragged from the new pain that had seeped into his bones while he rested.

Don't move. Don't breathe.

Someone, shoot me and put me out of the misery . . .

Why did it have to hurt so much to move? He rolled his eyes as the medical reasons shot through his head. *Shut up, brain. I know why I hurt. I just don't want to.*

"We're coming up on Rook. I thought you might want to come up here and talk to the controller."

"Not really," he breathed. But she was right. She'd get them shot out of the sky. His luck, she'd even admit who they were and the fact that they were coming in to hide.

Grinding his teeth in expectation of more pain, Syn carefully pushed himself off the bed, pulled on Caillen's hated boots, and went to join her.

"How'd you sleep?" she asked as soon as he entered the bridge.

"Like a baby vorna that's been caught in a steel trap." He took the pilot's chair and tried not to breathe anymore.

She shook her head at him. "They started asking for our letters and registration a second ago."

"Did you give them any?"

"No."

"Good girl." He flipped open the channel. "Cut it, moron, if I had this thing registered, I wouldn't be here. I lifted her on Gondara. Let us pass before I hunt you down and beat you for wasting my fucking time."

The channel buzzed for several seconds until a gruff voice came back. "Who's her captain?"

"Chryton Doone."

"Dock in Bay Nine, Hangar Delta Four."

Shahara lifted her brows in surprise of both his new name and the ease with which they were granted landing approval.

Was Chryton what the *C* stood for?

No. Chryton couldn't be it. The name just didn't suit him.

She sat back in her chair. "That was easy."

"Don't go optimistic on me." He brushed his hair out of his eyes. "I promise they'll have a welcoming party for us. So keep quiet and pray no one recognizes *you*."

Yeah, that could be bad. Bringing a tracer on board a planet of criminals was suicide indeed. And if any of them marked her, she was sure not even Syn's reputation would see her through. And while she could fight with the best of them, they seriously outnumbered her here.

Maybe this wasn't such a good idea after all.

In a few minutes, Syn had them docked and locked.

Just as he predicted, a group of three armed men and two armed women came out to greet them. They waited just outside the doorway, weapons held at ready.

Syn sat at the console for several seconds, flicking his finger back and forth over the lateral controls as if he, too, were debating the sanity of being here.

At last, he rose to his feet, shrugged on his jacket, and headed for the boarding ramp.

When he reached the end of the corridor, he paused. A small mirror had been placed just to the left of the hatch and he took a moment to look at himself.

"Ah, jeez," he sneered, fidgeting with his hair to help conceal the bruise on his forehead. "I look like I climbed out of a hole in hell."

"Well then, you ought to fit in here."

The look he gave her would have iced fire. He pulled a pair of shades out of his jacket pocket and put them on to cover his black eye. "Hand me your blaster."

"Why? You planning to shoot me?"

"Not quite yet." Then he added, "If I go out there unarmed, they'll know something's not right."

Shahara debated a minute longer before finally handing it over to him.

He tucked it into his left pocket. "Do you still have the small one in your boot?"

"Yeah."

"Take it out and keep it in your hand, in your pocket."

She didn't like the sound of that, but she obeyed.

"Now give me your other hand."

She frowned before dutifully giving it over as well. He grabbed a small stylus from a notch in the wall and quickly wrote down a name and address on her palm. His touch tickled her hand and did incredibly strange things to her belly while she watched. What was he doing?

"In case something happens to me, that's the address for a man named Digger. It should be two blocks down the street on the right. It's a large apartment building. You can't miss it." He took the silver necklace off and placed it around her neck. His warmth still clinging to it, it sent a chill over her back. Her breasts tingled. "Show him this and he'll help you."

"What about you?"

"If I go down, don't worry about me. I don't have a brother and two sisters who need or love me. You just make sure you get away."

She didn't like the sound of that at all. "You don't think you can make it two blocks?"

He didn't answer. Instead he changed the subject. "Stay here while I go talk to the guards."

Frowning with concern, she watched him extend the ramp, then walk down to meet their landing party. Only a slight limp gave away his injuries. Well, that and the bruises that still marred his neck. Bruises that made her feel guilty for the part she'd played in handing him over to Merjack.

With a masculine, in-control-at-all-times nonchalance that astounded her, Syn approached the guards and exchanged a few words with them.

As the guards walked away, he motioned for her to join him.

She took a deep breath in relief. "What did you say to them?"

That wicked grin returned, flashing his dimple. "I'm not about to repeat it to you."

She narrowed her eyes. "Careful, convict, I might finish what the Rits started."

He just laughed and threw his right arm over her shoulders. Her alarm bells ringing, she stiffened at his touch.

"Relax," he whispered, his breath tickling her neck. "I need a crutch and I can't very well be seen on the street here with one. If one of the natives detects any weakness, we're both roadkill. So just look mean and don't make eye contact with anyone."

She smiled seductively. "Gee, hon, you take me to the most wonderful places."

"Don't make me laugh. It hurts too much. Now quit talking and start for the door."

As they started walking, she couldn't help noticing the muscles flexing beneath her hands, against her side. Hard and strong, they made their presence known in a way that disturbed her breathing. Her hunger for his body begging for appeasement, she did her best to think of something disgusting—like Caillen's dirty underwear.

It didn't help.

And it only served to remind her that Syn didn't wear any . . .

Once outside, she almost stopped as dread consumed her. Only Syn's constant pull on her kept her in motion.

Filth lined the street and an odor that smelled way too much like human waste, garbage, and alcohol assaulted every olfactory gland she possessed. Bile rose in her throat, effectively distracting her from the tantalizing form next to her.

"Relax." He tightened his arm around her shoulders. "Breathe through your mouth."

"My God, what *is* that stench?"

"Hell."

As he continued to lead her down the street, a funny feeling settled deep inside her stomach. She was putting a lot of trust into a man she barely knew. He could take her to some remote location and dump her.

For all she knew, he might even be taking her to a slaver so that he could get enough money to hide. *Good grief, Shahara, what are you doing?* This wasn't her. Shahara Dagan trusted no one.

Ever.

The last time she'd made that mistake, she'd been robbed and raped. And if Syn ever learned the truth about why she was here with him, she was sure that was mild compared to what he would do to her.

"Where are we going?"

He gave her a puzzled look. "To an old friend."

"What kind of old friend?"

With a weary sigh, he shook his head. "I'm not going to dump you here with no money and no way home if that's what you're thinking. I'm not half the bastard your bounty sheets say I am. I wouldn't leave a rabid dog at the mercy of the vermin who inhabit this place. So relax. The less you know, the safer you'll be."

She still couldn't stifle her nagging doubts. "Why are you helping *me?*"

"Ah hell, I don't know. Stupidity, I guess." He glanced at her and must have seen the worry in her face. "You're Caillen's revered big sister. Remember?" His voice was suddenly void of aggravation. "I'm not about to face him after I let something happen to you. It would kill him and I think too much of him for that."

His explanation brought an unexpected wave of disappointment to her.

She tensed. *What were you expecting? Gee, Sha-hara, I'm helping you because I care about you?*

Wake up. You know better than that. People only help when they have to.

With a sigh of her own, she readjusted her grip on his lean hips and directed her gaze away from him.

The buildings that surrounded them were the strangest hodgepodge of glass, steel, brick, and wood. It looked as if the architects had used spare parts and designs they'd thrown out. And every person they passed eyed them with an interest that made sweat bead on her forehead.

Footsteps approached from ahead. Remembering Syn's warning, she focused her gaze on the sidewalk before them.

"Hey, how much for the woman?"

Syn pulled her to a stop.

Shahara couldn't resist a quick glance to see the tall, bald man who stood in front of them to the right. Beefy and intense, he put the scare in scary. He had a shorter, gray-haired companion about a foot behind him.

She looked up at Syn and watched the almost imperceptible way his eyes narrowed underneath his shades. "Your life would be about right." He raked him with a sneer. "You still interested?"

The stranger looked to his friend. An arrogant, amused smile passed between them before the man turned back to face Syn. "C'mon, *friend*. It's two on one. You sure don't look like you're up to those odds."

With a casualness that astounded her, Syn removed his shades and put them in his pocket. The only inkling she had to his deadly mood was the subtle shift of his jacket with his left hand to expose her blaster for his grip. He rested his hand casually against his tight buttocks. "You can't be talking to me. I don't have *prokas* for friends. And I assure you I could gut you both before your stench had time to catch up to your fall."

Rage contorted the man's features. He took a step forward.

Syn didn't move. He didn't even tense. He just stood there, taunting them with his eyes and deadly silence.

Waiting.

Like a vicious, lethal viper who knew it could take down its enemy with a single bite.

The man behind him paled. "Wait a sec, Chronus. That's Syn. I saw his face on Blade's scan."

A flicker of fear dispelled the rage an instant before doubt wavered in his gray eyes. "I thought he was dead."

Syn gave him a menacing grin. "Not as dead as you'll be if you don't walk on . . . friend."

His buddy grabbed him by the shoulder. "C'mon. Don't mess with him. Remember what he did to Durrin and Blade. The Partini still can't walk right."

Syn gave an evil laugh. "I sure would like to get an eye's view of your kneecap, too. What say we play doctor for a bit?" He checked his chronometer. "I got time . . ."

With that, the two men took off at a dead run.

Shahara was impressed by their quick flight. Most of all, she was impressed that Syn had inspired that kind of panic in them without having to draw a weapon. "Just what did you do to a Partini?"

He draped his arm over her again. "It's a long story. And there's nothing in the universe more boring than an old war tale."

She was amazed by that. Any other man, her brother included, wouldn't have hesitated to bore her with a tale of his masculine bravado. But Syn didn't seem to need to prove himself. She smiled at his confidence. It was such a nice change from the people she'd known.

As they walked on, she looked up at him and watched how well he managed to keep the pain from showing on his face.

How did he do that?

If not for the bruises and slight limp, she'd never be able to tell that he was hurt, and she wondered what internal scars he must hide with the same predatorial grace.

Syn was like hardened steel. And it must have taken the very fires of hell to forge a man this strong. Which left only one question. What was his weakness? Surely he had one.

Without any more confrontations, they approached the apartment building. Twin bright yellow towers stretched up toward the liquid blue sky.

From a distance the place had looked habitable but, with every step that drew them closer, it became less and less attractive. Broken bottles and litter lined the sidewalk. Several bodies lay stretched out in front of the doors.

Tempted to check them for a pulse, Shahara reminded herself that many thieves used that type of ploy. Once someone bent over, they pounced.

Just like Syn in prison.

Syn took her by the hand and led her toward glass doors that were covered with red graffiti. He pushed the control to open them.

As the doors pulsed open, she thought about an old story she'd once read that described the entrance to hell. This place certainly looked the part. If not for Syn, she'd probably be running in the opposite direction.

For some reason, she took a great deal of comfort in his presence. Much more comfort than she ought to.

He led her across a dirty, dank, empty lobby where even more graffiti was painted, some of it highly vulgar and obscene. It even had pictures of lewd acts and body parts.

As they approached the lift, a huge reptilian thing appeared and cut them off. It had the body of an upright lizard and the face that was half human, half snake. Its shiny blue and green scales gleamed in the dim light.

A scream lodged in her throat as she forgot Syn's words and looked into the yellow eyes that were broken only by the black slit of its pupils.

He leveled a blaster at them. "Put your hands up, humans. Now."

CHAPTER 8

Syn let go of her as he faced the reptilian creature. "Stand down or I'm going to shove that weapon some-place real uncomfortable for you and I know enough about your anatomy to know exactly where that is."

It didn't look convinced. "What do you want here?" it asked in a lethal raspy whisper.

"I'm here to see Digger."

"And you are?"

"Syn, as in *the* original."

It gave a rumbling sound she assumed was a laugh. "You don't look like Syn to me. And even if you were, what would you want with that old piece of dried-up mud?"

Syn's gaze turned deadly. "Why don't you ask him?"

The lizard being took out a comlink and pressed a number sequence. After several seconds a gruff voice answered.

"I hate to disturb you, *Frion*. But I have a human here who says he's Syn, as in *the* original."

"Syn, huh?" It was obvious the man was older by his shaking voice. "Then ask him what his birth name is."

The lizard looked at Syn.

Shahara also turned a questioning brow. Now she would find out what C.I. stood for.

"Sheridan Wade," he said with an odd note in his voice.

Sheridan Wade? Just how many names did he have? But that one made sense given who his father had been.

"That's my boy!" the voice said excitedly. "Send him up."

The lizard turned back to them. "My pardon, *Frion* Syn," it said before pushing the control for the lift. He stepped back to clear the door. "Digger is in flat 554."

Syn said nothing, but Shahara could sense a strong, indecipherable emotion from him.

They stepped inside and the doors closed behind them. The lift cruised up the air channel with a smoothness belied by its ramshackle appearance.

Syn released her hand and went to stand in a rear corner.

"Just what *is* your name anyway?"

"Does it really matter? I'm a man without family, name, or country. I'll answer to just about anything as long as it's not degrading or insulting."

"That's not what I asked. I want to know what the C.I. stands for."

He looked up with a smart-aleck grin. "Created In."

"Created In Syn," she repeated. "Cute name. Your mother must have really hated you."

His smile died. "With a passion," he said with such sincerity that it gave her pause.

Before she could say anything more, the lift stopped and he left her without so much as a backward glance.

Promising herself that she'd force him to tell her, she went after him.

The rundown hallway was deserted except for the

lines of graffiti that were scribbled everywhere. At least the apartment was close by.

This was not encouraging.

As Syn reached up to knock, the door swung open.

Tall and extremely lean, the man was probably around sixty-five. Though wrinkles obscured his features, which were also covered my a full beard, something about his demeanor told her that he'd probably been quite handsome in his youth. He had a thick head of white hair and eyes so blue they practically glowed.

And when he looked at Syn, it was like a father greeting his long-missing son. "Well, I'll be crimped and shanked, it really is you. I thought someone else was screwing with me." He pulled Syn into a tight hug.

Syn cursed. "Careful, old man." He quickly extracted himself. "Don't break my ribs . . . any worse."

"Break your ribs?" He looked Syn up and down. "Good Lord, boy. What happened to you?"

"I went drinking and fell off the stool . . . what do you think happened?"

Digger snorted. "Still the same sarcastic asshole you ever were. But you're here, so that tells me just how bad it is. God knows you wouldn't come here by choice and I damn sure don't blame you for that. You running from the pinches?" Pinches was an old slang term used for the enforcers.

"I'm a Wade. What do you think?"

He nodded. "You know you're always welcome here." He opened the door wider and finally took notice of Shahara. "And who might you be, beautiful?"

"Someone who's allergic to archaic playboys and who's young enough to be your granddaughter," Syn answered. "Call her Shahara, but watch out. She's responsible for about half of my injuries."

A charming smile curved Digger's lips. "Well, I'll keep my hands to myself, but make no promises about where my eyes might wander. Now come on in, you two, before someone shoots you in the hallway just for being there."

At least the inside of the small apartment was a lot cleaner than anything they'd found on the outside. Pieces of electrical equipment were strewn about, but the underlying areas were basically clean.

Digger rushed to the threadbare sofa to clean off paper and wires.

Syn leaned against the wall with one arm wrapped around his ribs. His breathing was labored and he was starting to sweat profusely again. "Dig, you have any Prinapin?"

"Wouldn't be caught dead without it at my age. 'Cause dead I'd be if I needed it and didn't have it."

Shahara lifted her brow at the mention of the illegal drug. A potent healer, it was banned due to the number of physical defects and mutations it could leave behind. Not to mention about half the people who took it didn't wake up again. "Are you really crazy enough to take that?"

Syn shrugged. "We can't afford for me to be on my back any longer than necessary."

Still, she admired and was repulsed by his courage. "All right, but if you grow another head, don't say I didn't warn you."

Digger laughed so hard, he started coughing.

"Ha, ha," Syn said with a lopsided grin. "C'mon, Dig. Give me a bed and the drugs before I fall down."

"To the back, boy, and you," he said to Shahara with a charming smile, "just make yourself at home. I'll be right back."

Running her hands down the front of her battlesuit, Shahara took a seat on the old green sofa. A spring squeaked in protest.

As she sat there waiting for Digger to return, she glanced around the room, trying to get a feel for who this man was and how he fit into Syn's life.

From the things in his apartment, she'd peg him as some sort of electrician or technician, but if he lived here on Rook, he must be doing something else, something very illegal, with his electronics.

And as she sat there, she spied an old-style photo on the desk by the window. Getting up, she went to it and saw Digger holding Syn. His sister Talia stood beside them, her young head hung low. Even though she couldn't be any older than nine or ten, she already looked defeated by life. Syn looked as defiant as always. The same angry fire burned in his eyes that he still had.

Clean-shaven in the photo, Digger was every bit as handsome as she'd suspected. And the love on his face as he looked at Syn was heartbreaking. It reminded her of the way her father would look at them until the day he'd died of simple pneumonia.

She swallowed against the pain of that memory. Though her father hadn't always been the best morally, he'd loved them all and they'd never doubted that one fact.

It brought tears to her eyes. She didn't mean to be so hard on her father. She still loved him. But he'd made all their lives difficult while he chased after shifting rainbows. Yet underneath that, she knew how lucky she'd been. While they hadn't always been fed or even had a roof over their heads, they always had love.

And each other.

Unlike Syn. How awful it must have been for him.

Looking around the room, her eyes became heavy.

How long had it been since she'd slept?

She couldn't remember. But then sleep had never been her friend. She'd fought against it all her life. First, because she was afraid her mother would die while she slept, then because she was afraid that someone would hurt her siblings.

She should be probably afraid of Digger. She didn't know him at all, yet something inside her told her that Syn wouldn't let harm befall her. He trusted Digger.

Yawning, she put the photo back and returned to the sofa.

I'll just close my eyes for a sec . . .

And before that thought finished, she was fast asleep.

Syn tossed two pills into his mouth and swallowed while he leaned wearily against the wall.

Digger curled his lip in disgust as he finished covering the double-sized bed with fresh sheets. "I don't know how you can swallow that shit without water. I'd be choking all over the place."

"Necessity is the mother of invention."

Digger snorted. "I wish you'd come up with a fresh saying, but at least it's not as annoying as that old no-good-deed-goes-unpunished crap." Digger smirked as he pulled a blanket out of the storage drawer beneath his bed. Covering the bed with it, he turned to Syn. "I know it ain't as fancy as that place you've got now, but it's clean."

"You don't have to apologize to me." Compared to some of the slime holes where he and Digger had slept in the past, this was a mansion. "My only requirement is that it's dry and nothing crawls around and bites my ass."

Digger motioned for him to lie down. "Well, you don't have to worry about any of that."

Slowly, Syn removed his clothes, then obliged. He let out a long sigh as he finally lay down. It hurt like hell, but it was infinitely better than standing.

"It's good to see you again." Digger fussed with his pillows like a spinsterish aunt.

Syn didn't say anything. He wasn't sure what to say. He owed Digger a debt that could never be repaid, but he'd never wanted to see the old man again.

Digger belonged to the past. A past he would sell his soul to forget.

But it didn't change the fact that he did love the old bastard even when he didn't want to. "I'm sorry I haven't been around these last few years."

Digger snorted. "Don't you dare get soft on me, boy. I wouldn't want you to come around my old sorry self either. I never wanted you to live like this. You know that."

Syn nodded.

"Now what can I get for you while you heal?"

"The two of us need gear."

"Full infiltration?"

"The best. I know you can hack my accounts and pay for it. Take whatever you need. Just make sure to hide your IPs. Make them think we're on Gondara . . . that should piss off the old bitch."

"All right. Anything else?"

"Yeah, give Shahara some food. She's too damned skinny. And for the sake of the gods, buy me some boots that fit." Syn draped an arm over his eyes to shield them from the glare of the overhead lights. "I wear the same size *he* did."

Digger started to leave, then paused. "I heard them

Rits were after you again. There's been some talk around here about certain people who are making bets on bringing you in dead."

"Yeah, I know. I'll leave as soon as I can. Don't worry, I'd never bring trouble to your door."

Digger stiffened as if that offended him. "You know better than that. I owe you, Sheridan."

"Don't call me that." It made his skin crawl to hear it.

Only Nykyrian got away with using that name anymore. Ironically though, even he seemed to know not to use it. Syn had never told him it bothered him. Somehow Nykyrian just knew it did and only used it when he wanted to make a point, get his attention, or annoy him.

But then, as an assassin Nyk was good at intrinsically knowing what pissed people off.

"Sorry, old habits die hard."

Syn looked over at Digger and grimaced. "Yeah, and so do gutter rats."

Digger's gaze turned hard, reproachful. "I done told you all your life, boy, you ain't no gutter rat."

Syn withheld the contradiction. There was no denying the truth. Shit was shit, no matter how much sanitizer and perfume you put on it.

Digger sighed. "You stay here as long as you need to. I won't let anyone in."

Syn offered him a smile. "Thanks."

Shahara came awake ready to fight. She snapped upright, her lip curled, her hand going to her blaster. Looking around, it took her several minutes before she recognized her surroundings.

"You're all right, sweet." Digger rose slowly from the stuffed arm chair a few feet away. "No one here will hurt you."

She took a deep breath to steady her nerves. "I'm sorry. I didn't mean to wake up like that. It's just habit when I'm not in my own place." She pushed back the blue blanket that covered her. A smile curled her lips at the kindness of him covering her while she slept. "Thank you."

He inclined his head to her. "No problem. I do the same thing when I wake up." He disappeared for a moment before returning with a warm plate of vegetables and a huge steak. "Why don't you try some of this? I ain't the best cook around, but it ain't killed no one yet. Well . . . just that one rat what came in and took some. But that was more from the blaster shot I gave him for being a thief than from him eating the food . . . I think."

She laughed. "I assure you it can't be any worse than mine. I can't cook for anything. Even my brother cooks better. Sad really."

He laughed.

While she took a few bites, Digger brought her a bottle of water. "That there's the best in the whole Ichidian Universe. It comes from a spring on Laquata."

She lifted a brow. Laquata spring water was a rare luxury indeed. She'd never even thought to have a sip of it, never mind a whole bottle. Rumors said that it held magical healing properties. Not that she believed that. It was most likely a myth made up by the owners to help sell it to gullible fools.

Still, it tasted good.

He scratched his chest and resumed his seat. "I know what you're thinking. However, I'm not quite out of my prime yet. I still can do my business and not get caught. Though I must say I came mighty close to getting caught with that shipment of water. But it was definitely worth it."

Shahara swallowed fast—she was drinking contraband? Why was she even surprised?

Not like your brother doesn't do it. Or your father for that matter either. Half your wardrobe as a kid fell off the back of someone's transport.

Shut up and drink it.

Setting it aside, she wiped at her chin, then changed the subject. "How long have you known Syn?"

His eyes turned gentle. "I've known him since the day they brought him into this world. I was even the first one not in a medical uniform who held him."

Now that was interesting. "Really? Before his mother or father?"

He nodded. "His mama had a hard delivery with him. She was too weak, and his father . . . He couldn't make it." There was a note in his voice that made her suspicious but she didn't pursue it. "I was the one who took her to the hospital and stayed with her while she struggled." He sighed. "I'd give anything to have had a son like Sheridan. But he's as close to one as I ever got. Not that I'm complaining, mind you. He was even named after me."

"Sheridan?"

"Sheridan *Digger* Wade. I'm his uncle."

Ah, that explained their closeness. "Maternal?"

His eyes went blank as he looked away. "No."

Shahara choked on her food as that settled in. Good gods, he was . . .

Idirian's brother.

She wanted to run.

Digger sprang to her aid and pounded her on the back until the food dislodged from her throat. Taking a few gulps of air, she blinked back the tears in her eyes.

She gaped at the old man as he took a seat next to her on the sofa. "How can you be related to that psycho?" she asked, eyeing the old man warily.

His look turned harsh. "Indie wasn't always like that," Digger said defensively. "He was a good kid. He just fell in with the wrong kind of people."

Oh yeah, right. What a load of crap. That was the one excuse that made her want to hurt someone. "Are you telling me other people led him into that kind of sadistic slaughter?"

He returned to his chair, his shoulders slumped in defeat. "No, child. I'm not a fool. Indie became everything you ever heard and worse—I know the real stories that didn't make the news—the ones they deemed too gruesome for public consumption."

Now that terrified her, given how grisly the released stories had been. How much worse could they get?

"At first, I stayed around thinking I could change him back into the innocent kid he'd been or at least browbeat him into some form of decency. But once he had the taste of blood in him, he decided he liked it, and the power people's fear gave him. There was nothing I could do. It's hard when you're kicked down your whole life and people mock you for being beneath them. Then when you find a way to pay them back . . ."

He shook his head. "Indie got high off it and he felt it was justified for the way we'd been raised and treated." His gaze seared her. "I'm not about to excuse it. I was never blind to my little brother's shortcomings. But to the end, I did love him and I wish I could have saved him from himself."

On one level she could admire that. Yet on the other . . .

She shivered.

Still, she didn't understand why Digger had stayed with such a man. "Once you saw that you couldn't change him, why didn't you walk away?"

Digger sighed. "It wasn't that easy, and there for a time, Indie got better. Not because of me, but for Sheridan's mother. She was a decent lady from a good family and, believe it or not, he loved her like nothing I ever saw. She was under his skin and he'd have done anything for her. But it wasn't that easy to leave his past, which hadn't been all *that* bad up until then."

"So what happened?"

"Her parents," he spat the word. "Stupid interfering bastards. They refused to even call him by his name 'cause he was so far beneath them. They told her that so long as she was with him, she couldn't come home. Even when she took Talia there to see them, just a few weeks after Talia had been born, her parents had her thrown out and told her they didn't want to see no bastard lowborn baby—said it was no grandchild of theirs."

He winced. "I was there with them when it happened. She'd been so convinced that as soon as they saw the baby, everything would change and that they'd forgive her for falling in love with a pleb. But her father was colder than Indie had ever been. And she was so tore up over it. After that, Indie went insane 'cause he couldn't make it better for her. He wanted her to have the life she'd had with her parents and to not regret marrying him. Since he couldn't find a legal job that paid anything, he went back to what he knew. Filching."

He let out a tired sigh. "And something happened to her after that meeting that day. She became real demanding about everything. Like she felt that she'd given up her entire life and dignity for Indie. Suddenly nothing he did could please her and she rubbed his

nose in everything she didn't have. She kept reminding him that she was a high-bred lady and he was
shit."

Shahara scowled. "Why?"

"I don't know. She became an entirely different person and nothing Indie did was good enough. She started
to take it out on Talia and then Indie would take out his
anger on her for hurting his daughter. Then when she
got pregnant with Sheridan, it only got worse . . . I half
expected her to abort him."

"Why didn't she?"

His eyes turned dark. "Indie told her he'd kill her if
she killed his son."

Shahara was horrified by that. How could parents
act that way? It was bad enough what they did to each
other, but to do it to their children? "I don't understand.
Given the way he treated Syn, why did he care?"

"Indie still loved her at that point. I don't know why,
but he did and he worshiped Talia because she looked
like her mother. Then when Sheridan was born, he was
so proud and happy to have a son. Until the day he
caught that bitch trying to drown Sheridan when the boy
was only three weeks old."

Her stomach hit the floor as disbelief consumed her.
"What?"

He nodded. "I don't know what made her snap, but
she'd been holding the baby down under the water while
she was bathing him. But for Talia running to her father
to tell him Sheridan was dead, we'd have never known.
Indie beat her down so bad that I don't know how she
lived. Not that I blamed him for that one. It's the only
thing that was justified." He swallowed audibly as he
glanced out the window. "She left not long after that and
when she took off, it killed Indie. Whatever kindness he

had inside him went with her. And he hated Sheridan from that point on."

That didn't make sense. "I don't understand. Why hate him? He was just a baby."

Digger rubbed a tired hand over his chin. "Indie blamed him for losing her. He had this screwed-up idea that if Sheridan hadn't been born, she'd have stayed, and so he wanted to make Sheridan pay for running her off. He even turned on Talia . . . again because she looked so much like her mother. And I felt even sorrier for her than I did Sheridan. She knew what it was like to have a father who loved her. Sheridan didn't. She used to cry herself sick wanting to know what had made her father hate her."

Shahara wanted to cry for all of them. "Who was his mother?"

The hatred in his eyes singed her. "I'll never say that bitch's name. May that old whore rot and die for all eternity for what she did. She could have saved Indie and pulled him back from his life had she not been so selfish. But she wanted her fancy baubles and houses. We weren't good enough and that was what turned my brother psychotic. He got it in his mind that we were trash and that the only way to get respect was to take it and to kill anyone who wouldn't give it to him."

His gaze turned hard. "Syn don't know none of this and I want to keep it that way. He thinks his mother left because she couldn't take living with his father. No offense, I'd rather he keep thinking that, too."

Because it was easier than to know his own mother tried to kill him. "Don't worry. I would never tell him."

He inclined his head to her.

Shahara pushed her food around on her plate. "So what about Syn? What made him a criminal?"

"That boy ain't no criminal!" he snarled so defensively that she pulled back from him. "Sheridan never done nothing but survive and there shouldn't be no crime in that."

His unwarranted hostility surprised her. There was no denying what Syn was, reasons be damned. The man broke the law. A lot.

His gaze probed hers with an intensity that chilled her. "Tell me what you'd have done if you were only ten years old and found yourself without a family and no home. Them Rits took every last credit of Indie's. Not a cent was left for Sheridan. He had nothing at all. I was thrown in jail when they arrested Indie and I thought that, as bad as it was for me, that at least he'd have a good home with decent people. But I overestimated those so-called decent people. None of them would take him in. Not even the government wanted him in an orphanage."

She winced at that harsh reality. "Because of who his father was?"

He nodded.

The sins of the father are forever visited on the son. Conventional wisdom would say that whatever genetic defect had caused Idirian Wade's behavior would manifest in his child. It was a rampant fear that she was more than familiar with.

"So what did they do with him?"

Sighing, Digger raked his hand through his hair. "Put him in prison. They said he might as well get used to it since he'd most likely end up there anyway."

She set her fork down in stunned shock. "At *ten*?"

He nodded darkly. "And not kiddie jail. They sent him to maximum security."

"At ten?" she repeated.

"At ten." His tone was ice cold and brutal. "There's your League justice for you. Put an innocent kid in with the garbage and see if he survives. But that was all right. His father had taught him well on how to hide, fight, and take as much pain as anyone wanted to give to him. As you've seen. He don't go down easy."

Still . . . he'd been a baby. How was that even possible? How had he survived? "Someone had to get him out. Did they release him?"

He laughed. "You have to remember, Sheridan was big for his age and precocious as hell. That resourceful little bastard escaped within a year and went out on the streets by himself. He managed to stow away on a ship that came here and he made a home for himself in the gutter."

Shahara tried to imagine it. She knew how hard it'd been to survive without her parents and she'd been almost twice his age when her father died.

And though her condo wasn't much, at least it was one of the few things her father had paid for before his death.

"Where was his mother then?"

The look he gave her killed the words on her tongue. "He went to that bitch when he was twelve and she threw him out into the street like he was trash. Said she was back where she belonged and she didn't want nothing to do with the past. Said she never wanted to lay eyes on him again and that if she did, she'd put him in jail for the rest of his life. Then she called the pinchers to come pick him up."

Shahara swallowed in horror. How could a mother react that way? Why? It was so cold and needless.

If she could only have a child, she'd make sure no one ever hurt it.

"And his sister?"

Tears welled up in the old man's eyes. "She was an angel. So gentle and timid. Never once raised her voice or said an unkind word about anyone. Sheridan loved that girl like you wouldn't believe. He would have slit his own wrist if she'd just asked him to."

"Surely she helped him?"

He shook his head. "She killed herself the day before Indie was arrested."

She gaped at that unexpected bomb.

Talia had killed herself?

Please don't leave me, Talia. I won't let him hurt you anymore. I promise. Syn's pleading tone tore through her. She knew how much he'd loved his sister. He must have gone crazy with her death.

And suddenly she knew why he'd turned his father in . . . No doubt he blamed him for it and had wanted revenge. It made perfect sense and yet . . .

How had Syn survived?

He'd been just a baby when everyone in his family had deserted him. She couldn't even begin to imagine the fear and pain he must have felt. No matter how bad her life was, she'd always had her family. A family who, even with their problems, protected her to the bitter end.

"What did Syn do after his mother . . ." She couldn't even bring herself to say what the bitch had done.

Digger shrugged. "I don't know how he survived. Worst of all, I don't know what was done to him either in jail or after. He never would talk about it. But I thought about him the whole while I was in prison. I was sure he'd get killed in no time . . . or something much worse. He was such a smart little thing and so good-looking. I just knew *if* he managed to survive he'd fall prey to some slaver or pervert. And I still don't know if he did."

He gave a sad laugh. "But I guess living with Indie had taught him how to suffer in silence. How to go a long while between meals. How to move like a ghost around people so they wouldn't see or hear him." He looked down the hallway to where Syn was sleeping. "How to take a beating that would kill most people and not surrender to the pain."

And that explained it, too. No wonder Syn didn't react.

He was used to it.

Digger took a sip of water. "One of the few times Sheridan talked about being on the street, he told me that he used to crawl up under Dumpsters to sleep and keep the scum away from him at night. Can you imagine? The filth, the smell . . . the rats?" he shuddered. "Sheridan either ate out of the garbage or stole what he needed to eat and, when he was old enough, he took up Indie's primary occupation."

"Murder?"

Digger snorted in indignation. "Sheridan would never kill anyone what didn't try and kill him first. I told you, he ain't his father." He gave her a nasty glare. "Filching was what started Indie off on his criminal career. He was the best at it. He could hack into any security system, and he designed them so well that no one could even begin to breach his codes . . . except for Sheridan, and that used to make him insane. He never could keep Sher out of whatever file he wanted."

There was pride in his eyes when he spoke about that—like he'd had something to do with it. "When Sheridan was old enough, Indie taught him how to work the systems."

Then his look turned dark again. "If he messed up, on a good day, Indie would break some of his fingers for it. On a bad day, he'd break Talia's."

He shook his head, his features tormented. "And you know the saddest and sickest part of it all? She was buried right after his father and me was arrested. Sheridan, in custody at that point, was the only one at her funeral, and I remember them newspeople broadcasting how cold he was over it. They had a picture of him at her grave, dry-eyed, and they painted him as a monster, which is another reason why they sent him to jail and no one would take him in. 'Ten years old and already his father's son,' that's that they said. A second-generation Wade psycho in the making."

He spat in fury. "Sheridan didn't cry because Indie would burn or scald him anytime he cried until he learnt not to. That boy was never allowed to shed a tear without making it worse on himself. So when Sheridan didn't cry, the media crucified him for it. Son of the devil, as heartless as his father. May they all burn in hell."

Anger burned deep in his eyes. "Some of the victims' families were there when they returned him to jail just so they could spit on the ten-year-old boy who'd lost everything in his life, including his freedom, for nothing more than the fact that he was born and that he didn't die when his own mother tried to drown him. The media painted it like he deserved that, too. Can you imagine going to bury your sister wearing armor and handcuffs and manacles? Alone? Having people throw things and spit at you?"

Shahara flinched, her stomach churning at the thought. No, she couldn't. She'd barely made it through her parents' burials, and at least she and her siblings had known their parents were sick and had had time to prepare themselves—even though that was a myth. No one was ever ready to let go of a loved one. Not if they actually loved them.

Poor Syn . . .

I deserve to be flogged for what I've done to him. Never in her life had she felt more wrong.

She could tell herself that she didn't know about his past. But that was only an excuse. She'd hurt a good man who watched out for her brother and sister . . .

She looked down at her palm where he'd written Digger's number and at the necklace she wore—Syn's necklace. Given to her to keep her safe even after she'd handed him over to his enemies.

Clenching her fist where his writing was, she wanted to cry. But like Syn, that had been kicked out of her long ago by her own brutal memories.

Digger ground his teeth before he continued. "When he was executed, Indie had a list as long as my arm of business clients he serviced, and they paid well for information about their competitors and other people they wanted to watch . . . or hurt. Sheridan used that list to make contacts and get jobs. He was *that* good."

So Syn hadn't been lying about that. Just how many times had he told the truth to uncaring ears? And why did she have to be yet another set of them?

"Until he got caught."

"Until he got caught," Digger breathed. "That's when I came back into his life. As luck would have it, I was on yard detail and saw him while they were leading him down to interrogation."

He fell quiet for several minutes as if reliving the horror of it. When he spoke again, she had to strain to hear him. "I tell you I haven't ever seen anyone so beaten. Even what was done to him now can't compare to what he looked like then. And he was only a kid. Those Rits were on him like nothing I ever saw. They kept him locked down under the tightest security and were always questioning him . . . torturing him. I can still hear his young screams for them to stop hurting him. Those sounds would cut through the yard and even hard-core prisoners would all stop as a cold shiver ran down our spines.

"But I knew those screams. For me it was like listening to him with his father all over again. Hell, I figured it had to be easier on him to be tortured by a stranger than by someone who was supposed to love and protect him. But I knew if I didn't do something, they were going to kill him. The fact that he knew not to tell them anything—to stay strong—still amazes me."

"You're how he escaped that time?"

"That I am. I'd been working on an escape for years when they brought him in. It didn't take but a couple more bribes to get him out, too."

Shahara sat back and thought about what Digger was telling her. If what he said was true, then Syn's story about Merjack was also true.

That wasn't good. Not for her anyway.

Glancing back at Digger, she asked, "And the two of you came here?"

He shook his head. "No, I came alone. Sheridan was afraid to stay with me. He kept saying that the Rits would come to kill him and anyone around him would be dead, too. He said he had to go back and find something he'd left behind before he could be safe again. That was the last time I saw him until today. But we keep up. He's always made sure that I was taken care of and had what I needed. And he calls whenever he gets to a secured line."

"No emails?"

He shook his head. "A very few here and there. He's always paranoid a filch like him can trace it to me and hurt me to get to him or trace it back to him. So mostly it's through links we talk."

"Then you don't know what happened after that? What he went back to find?"

"I try to keep my ears open about what he's up to, but he keeps a low profile, so I don't hear too much."

That was too bad, because she still needed answers, especially if she was to help him. "Then you don't know why he raped and killed Kiara Zamir?"

He slammed his hand down on the arm of the sofa so hard it made her jump. "Now that's stupid. I said it that day I first heard about that contract. Sheridan wouldn't hurt no defenseless woman. He had too much love and respect for his sister for that. He'd never shame her memory."

His old gaze burned into her with his indignant sincerity. "I done told you and you need to listen and understand. I've *never* seen him go after someone who didn't go after him first. He's not his father and he never has been. He ain't got that cold streak. Like Indie, it woulda come out by now and the first one he'd have killed would have been that bitch who turned on him."

"His wife?"

"*Ex*-wife. She was cold to the marrow of her bones, like Indie. I never heard of anything so malicious. Like his mother, she told The League and Rits where to find him because she wanted the reward for turning him in. She even set a trap for him, using their son as bait, and he barely escaped that time, too."

Shahara started at what he described. "No, she didn't."

"Yes, she did. She told him that he could come to Paden's birthday party and when he showed, she took the present, then led him, not to his son, but to a room full of enforcers."

"How did he get away?"

"Same way he always does. He fought his way out and has the scars from six blaster burns to show for it. All he wanted to do was see his kid . . . Stupid bitch."

He cursed even more foully. "What kind of woman does that after he'd already left her a fortune that would have made even a king giddy? Every cent he'd ever made after scraping himself off the streets he gave to her without hesitation. He didn't contest nothing she wanted and she took everything he had. *Everything.* All he asked for was to see his son once a year on the boy's birthday, and she wouldn't even allow him that much. She turned that boy against him and he won't even speak to Sheridan now because Sheridan's trash. Even though Sheridan still sends the boy money and has put that kid through the best schools in the galaxy— anything he wants, Sheridan makes sure he has it, and he can't even see him. If the bitch don't call the pinches on Sheridan, his own son does. And he still loves that kid more than anything. Would give him a kidney if he asked. And you know the hardest kicker of that?"

"What?"

"That boy ain't even his and he knows it."

Shahara sat stunned. Had she heard that right? "Excuse me?"

Digger nodded. "That whore fucked around on him the whole time they were married. Sheridan was a doctor . . . a surgeon no less, until the bitch took that from him, too. He worked at one of those high-end, well-respected hospitals where Paden was born. When

patronizing tone he'd used. She'd only been a scared child . . . afraid that he'd leave her and go to her sisters, who were sleeping at her condo, and do to them what he was doing to her. He'd relished every hour he'd tortured her.

Until then, she'd fancied herself in love with him. And when she'd asked him why he'd done it . . .

I take what I want, baby. That's what a man does. You done gave me all your money. You want me nice. Get some more and come see me. He'd tossed her torn clothes at her. *Now get out. You call the enforcers on me, and I promise you I'll see you and those other little whore sisters of yours in the ground.*

At seventeen, she'd been forced to walk home with no money, in torn clothes. Bleeding and hurt. No one had even stopped to ask her if she needed help. They'd only stared at her or hurried away as if afraid her condition might rub off on them. Meanwhile, because she didn't have money and couldn't be treated for it, she'd lost her ability to have children that day.

And she'd lost a whole lot more . . .

That was why she'd killed him. The other reasons only made it easier for her to swallow that dark side of her personality that she wanted to pretend didn't exist.

So she knew exactly where Syn was coming from. What she didn't know was how he could forgive either of them.

How he could forgive her.

"How old was Paden when . . ."

"Seven when Sheridan left. He graduated from school last year. Wouldn't see Sheridan even though he tried, but he's taking all the money Sheridan sends him for his prestigious university classes." He curled his lip. "Kid ain't never held a job a day in his life while he lives off Sheridan's trust fund. Worthless little bastard . . ."

He sighed. "But there's nothing I can do and, as Sheridan says, it ain't none of my business what he does with his kid." He rose to his feet and stood before her, arms akimbo. "By the way, do you know how many times I watched him get beat protecting little Talia? He weren't no bigger than my knee and he'd stand against his father, who was even taller than Sher is now. Sheridan would hold up his little fists and stand like a man while Indie bounced him off furniture and walls until he lost consciousness." His eyes turned dull, sad. "I never understood how a father could hurt his children so."

Grimacing at the image, she thought about the photograph she'd found of Syn and Talia in his prayer box. Even though he'd protected his sister didn't mean he wasn't capable of hurting someone else. Caillen protected the three of them and she couldn't even begin to count how many women he'd treated like dirt.

All the people he'd lied to and the laws he'd broken . . .

"How can you be so sure he wouldn't have killed Kiara Zamir?"

"I told you, I know that boy. I've seen him walk through the fires of hell and I know every scar it cut into him. He ain't never been mean. Pissed off a lot, but never mean. He ain't my brother."

Shahara sat back, her mind whirling with all the new information she'd learned about Syn.

And she'd thought it would be so simple when she first took the contract. C.I. Syn: Cold-blooded criminal. Pure and simple.

But that wasn't the man she'd found. And the more she learned, the further from that he became.

Digger let out a long breath as he took her barely touched plate from her and walked it to the kitchen. "Well, I've said probably more than I ought to, and I'm sure it'd anger him to know what I've done." He looked at the clock on the wall. "It's getting late so I guess I ought to lay these old bones down for a little sleep." He moved to a corner and started making a pallet on the floor near his desk.

"What are you doing?"

"Making my bed."

Guilt consumed her. She couldn't let a man of his age sleep on the floor. He looked so frail, she doubted he'd last the night.

"Why don't you take the sofa?"

"And let a lady sleep on the floor? I wouldn't hear of it. Just 'cause I'm old don't make me weak or less of a man."

Shahara bit her lip. Where else could he sleep?

"Why don't you sleep with Syn?"

He snorted. "He'd have a fit if he woke up to my old body lying next to him. Not that I'd blame him, mind you. If I had a choice, I wouldn't want to sleep with me neither."

That just left one option.

It was scary and unnerving, but it was the only one she could think of.

"Then why don't I sleep with Syn? You can take the sofa."

He hesitated. "You sure about that?"

No.

She nodded.

He smiled warmly as relief shone in his eyes. "All right. I must admit I like that better. Just follow me and I'll show you back." He took her down a narrow hallway, past the tiny kitchen, to the small bedroom at the end of the hall.

Shahara glanced around the minuscule room which barely accommodated the bed. She'd thought she could sleep on the floor in here, but one look and she knew she'd have to sleep *under* the bed for that. Except it had a drawer there and, as small as she was, she didn't think she could sleep in *that*.

"Good night." Digger turned and left her alone.

Shahara sighed. What should she do?

Syn slept completely silent and still. If not for the gentle rise and fall of his chest she might have worried.

Moonlight from three moons lit the room with a soft glow, spilling over Syn and giving her an ample view of his face.

And other attributes.

Mesmerized, she watched the play of moonlight in the dips of his washboard stomach, and across his hands . . . He had a brightly colored tattoo that ran from the crook of his elbow to his wrist. It was of a sword covered in blood and with words written in an alphabet she didn't know.

Did she dare crawl into bed with him? A strange wave of excitement poured through her at the thought. What would be the harm? She'd shared beds with Caillen all her young life.

Caillen is your brother.

Good point.

With that thought, she attempted to stretch out on the floor. She bumped her knee into the bed frame. Cursing from the pain, she moved her legs only to smack her head against the small chest of drawers.

Oh, this was so not working. "Ouch," she snarled,

cupping the pain at the back of her skull. The room was just too small.

Aggravated, she rose. "Okay, Syn. You stay on your side of the bed and I promise *I* won't beat you."

That said, she pulled back the covers and lay down beside him, keeping her body rigid and as far away from his as she could.

Why couldn't the bed be larger?

But after several minutes of his not moving, she began to relax. And before she knew it, she fell asleep, too.

Syn came awake slowly, the remnant of pain hanging on the fringes of his sleep. He felt infinitely better. The deep throbbing ache in his head had subsided to a dull, manageable ache, and he could actually take a deep breath without wincing.

Definitely an improvement.

As he started to move, he became aware of a soft form pressed up against his naked body. One that smelled of lilac and spring.

But that didn't make sense.

Opening his eyes, he stared into the startled face of Shahara. Her large gold eyes were wide and her face flushed from embarrassment.

Damn, that was the best sight he'd ever seen. And this moment alone had made his beating worth it. He hadn't come awake in bed with a woman since Mara had thrown him out. "Hi, beautiful."

She didn't say a word.

He didn't know how she'd gotten into his bed but he enjoyed the soft curves that fit snugly against him, even if they were covered in an armored battlesuit. The tiny hand that rested on his bare chest . . .

And especially the long leg that rested between his knees. She felt good in his arms. Too good.

Shahara stared into those dark, searching eyes. For the first time, she didn't see what his bounty had listed about him. She didn't see a filch or a traitor or a convict. She didn't even see a man.

What she saw was a human being who'd been betrayed and hurt by everyone around him.

And I'm no better than they are.

Because in the end, she was going to betray him, too.

For what? The name of justice? Or was that the same *noble* sort of excuse she'd used for Gaelin?

But right now, lying here with him, she didn't see anything except someone she wanted to know. To understand how he could carry on with a kindness toward others that she'd lost.

How could he do it?

How could he even trust another person? Even Digger? Never mind put all of his assets in someone else's name after his wife had already stolen everything from him.

Unable to fathom it, she placed her hand on his whiskered cheek.

Syn was afraid to move for fear of scaring her. Something was different about her now. She looked at him, not with fear or anger or pity.

But with . . .

Understanding.

And before he could move, she closed the distance between them and kissed him. Growling at the taste of her, he carefully pulled her into his arms and held her close as every hormone in his body fired.

Shahara lost herself to the feeling of his body against

hers. Of his bare skin under her hands. She'd always wanted to be like a normal woman.

Unafraid of trusting a man in her life.

He's a convict. How can you trust a convict?

He shifted and she felt his arousal against her stomach. In that instant, involuntary horror flooded her as she remembered Gaelin holding her down by her neck and tearing at her clothes.

Panic tore through her. "Let me go!" she snapped. "Don't touch me!"

Syn understood that anxious tone and knew it wasn't directed at him. Instantly he let her go and moved as far away from her as he could so that no part of him was touching her.

That had been the irrational cry of someone whose past had just risen up and tackled them to the ground.

"You okay?"

Shahara scowled at his question, but even more baffling was the concern on his face and the tender note in his voice. She'd expected him to be angry or offended.

But he wasn't.

"Yeah, sorry."

"Hey, don't apologize. We all have shit to deal with. I have the same reaction sometimes, too."

She scoffed. "I find that hard to believe."

"It's true. You ever want to see me really wig out? Hand me a candy bar."

She rolled her eyes. That was ridiculous. "A candy bar?"

"Yeah. A bad thing happened to me over a candy bar once when I was a kid. Never got over it. I break out in a sweat just at the sight of one."

She gave a short, sarcastic laugh. "You're messing with me, aren't you?"

He held his hand up and gave a Ritadarion gesture of honor. "I swear it. To this day I won't even look at chocolate. Breaks me out in hives."

A slow half smile curved her lips. "I think you're just trying to make me feel better."

"Is it working?"

It really was. "Thanks."

He scratched at the dark whiskers on his face. "So how did you get in here last night? Don't get me wrong. It was a great surprise, but I would have thought you'd rather sleep with our lizard friend from yesterday than bed down with me for even a nap."

"I don't know . . . lizard man or you . . . Nah, you're right, the lizard would have won it."

He laughed. "Seriously, what prompted you to come in?"

"Well, for one thing you were pretty harmless and you *were* drugged. But mostly I couldn't let Digger sleep on the floor while I took the couch, even though he insisted."

Syn didn't know why, but that touched him. It seemed out of character for her tougher-than-nails facade. And it had been a decent thing to do for an old man. In his world, decent acts were rare enough that they always shocked him whenever they happened.

But now it was morning and they had a lot to do. He couldn't afford any more down time. Sooner or later, the Rits would remember he'd had an uncle and come here to check.

Shahara frowned as he moved away from her. The sheet fell away and she realized he was completely naked. Her face flamed at something she hadn't realized when she'd crawled into bed with him. That would have definitely made her reconsider her actions . . .

Sheez!

Oblivious to her mortification, he retrieved his clothes from the other side of the bed. Most of the bruises from yesterday were gone, making the sight of his bared flesh all the more yummy.

Delectable.

Her cheeks blistered. Turning to face the window, she heard his low laugh.

"Sorry, I wasn't planning on company."

"Don't you ever wear bed clothes?"

"No."

She heard him moving around behind her. "You really should develop some modesty."

He laughed again. "Why bother? I never have enough people around me to worry about it, and in jail you don't have any privacy anyway, so you learn to not think about other people's sensibilities, or your own."

Her heart clenched at a fact he joked about. She knew from her own brief experience how brutally kept they were. And he didn't even talk about the routine cavity searches and other horrors prisoners were subjected to.

Her own brief experience with having no control over what was done to her body had been bad enough. She couldn't imagine how many times he'd been violated and at an age when someone should have still been rocking him to sleep.

It offended and disgusted her on his behalf.

He cleared his throat. "It's safe now. I'm dressed."

Not sure if she could trust him when he seemed to delight in embarrassing her, she turned around slowly and sighed in relief. He really was dressed.

As she looked him over, she realized the bruises had all but healed on his face and neck as well. Only a faint

telltale sign of light yellow across his left cheek betrayed the fact that he'd been severely bruised just the
day before.

"Wow," she said, drawing closer. "Prinapin does
work." And before she thought about her actions, she
reached up and fingered his stubbled cheek, his arched
brow, and the little wrinkle between his brows.

His eyes darkened. Mesmerized, she watched the
emotions flicker behind his dark gaze. Mercy, he was
gorgeous and . . .

Suddenly a voice growled behind them. "Hands up,
scum. You're under arrest!"

CHAPTER 9

Syn snapped around, ready to attack.

Then he gaped in utter disbelief. No . . .

It couldn't be . . .

"Vik?"

The little metallic bird postured on the window-sill, eyeing him coldly. Vik's paint was iridescent and glossed—something the mecha had never liked, since he said it made him look like a girlie bird. "I'm surprised you remember my name." Vik paused before he added an acerbic, "Asshole."

Syn laughed as he rolled away from Shahara. "You prickly little shit, get over here."

Vik swooped in to land between the two of them on the bed. He burst apart, shifting from bird form to that of a more traditional mechbot. With his hand, he smacked Syn in the arm. "I thought you were coming back for me."

"I tried. I really did, but by the time I could, I figured you'd be gone."

Vik hissed then looked at Shahara. "He lie to you like that?"

Shahara's mouth worked as she tried to place this creature in Syn's life. "Who exactly are you?"

He literally bristled. His skin flicked up like spikes before it settled down again. "Oh, that's great. Your girlfriend doesn't even know me." He smacked Syn again. "Traitor."

Syn grabbed him by the arm and pulled him up to dangle by it. "Hit me again, and I'm putting you in a compactor."

"You might as well. You two-timing bastard."

Shahara frowned. "What are you two to each other?"

Syn set him back down on the bed. "Vik is one of the first things I created when I was a kid."

"I was your partner."

He smiled. "Vik was my partner. When my father used to send me on jobs, Vik was my eyes and ears to make sure I got in and got out."

"Yeah, and how does he repay me? He abandons me the first chance he gets."

"That's not true. You were supposed to watch out for Digger."

Vik ignored him. "Does he call? No. Does he email or even text me? No. He just ran off and left me here to rust and die." He turned back to Syn. "You really suck as a friend."

"I do suck as a friend. I'm sorry."

"Mmm-hmm. You think you can sweet-talk me? Who you been two-timing me with anyway? Some low-tech battery-operated device? I hope it shocked you every time you touched it."

Syn laughed. "There's no one else, Vik. You're the only mecha I could ever stand."

Vik shook his head. "Lies, lies, lies. They just roll off your tongue like slobber off a dog's snout."

Shahara wrinkled her nose at the graphic image.

"Hey, if it makes you feel better, I went to prison because I didn't have you at my back."

"I would say you deserved that, but even I'm not that cold."

Shahara was fascinated by the AI. It was extremely sophisticated and very well programmed. "How old were you when you created . . ." She stopped herself from saying "this" as she didn't want to offend the mecha. "Him?"

"Seven, and I did some modifications over the years."

Wow. She was impressed. This showed a level of skill that was unrivaled and to have been so young . . .

Syn had never been a typical kid.

"Is there anything you can't do?"

He gave her a droll stare. "Find a woman who won't stab me in the back and betray me. Oh wait, you stabbed me in the arm, didn't you?"

She deserved that, and what stung most was the fact that it was true. But she didn't respond, especially since he hadn't said it in a snotty tone. Just matter-of-factly.

Vik moved to sit down by her arm. "You want to leave him for a real man?"

Shahara laughed. "You're not my type, Vik."

He tsked. "Yeah, it's hard for you fleshy types to admit that we're better in bed. 'Sa'ight. I understand." He sniffed. "Not like I don't have a crush on a lamp."

Syn smiled. "You know I have missed you."

Vik gave him a shaming stare—something incredible given the intricacies of programming that went into facial expressions. "But not enough to come back."

"I'm truly sorry, Vik. I didn't know it would hurt your feelings. I thought you liked it here with Digger."

"He all right. But he not you. He so cautious, it boring.

You ever try to run with an old man? I miss what we had." He paused before he added. "Can I come with you now?"

Syn hesitated. On the one hand, he'd like that a lot. On the other . . . "What about Digger?"

"He not doing much these days. Please, Sheridan. I don't want to stay here. I'm going to rust and die from inaction."

That was the last thing Syn wanted to happen to him. "All right, but don't call me Sheridan. I don't use that name anymore."

"Asshole? That works for me."

Syn rolled his eyes. "Syn. Call me Syn."

Vik snorted. "Syn? What kind of stupid name is that?"

"Better than Vik."

"Not really, but okay. If that be the terms, I abide by them." He returned to his bird form and flew to sit on the sill. "By the way, I knew you were back when I heard some bonebags talking about the price on your head. They gathering men to come get you. You might want to prepare."

Syn cursed. "We need to get up and get out of here." And with that came a streak of worry over Digger. Wondering where he was, Syn headed to the front room.

The room was empty except for a pile of dark material and a note placed on the sofa. He picked it up and glanced to see Shahara as she came forward to stand in the doorway. "Digger went to buy some food."

Folding the note, Syn's gaze fell to the clothes. He tossed the smaller set to Shahara before he saw the black boots. "Hallelujah," he breathed in relief. "I can finally put my feet into something that fits."

"I've never seen a man so obsessed with shoes. Is

there something else about you that you need to tell me? Any other weird fetishes like wearing my underwear?"

He snorted as he remembered all the times in his childhood when he'd sliced his feet open because he'd been forced to go barefoot. "Hey, where I grew up, shoes that fit were a rare luxury and it's one I've since grown way too accustomed to." He noted the two backpacks at the foot of the sofa. Good. It looked like Digger had found the equipment they needed. He'd check it out more fully later. Right now he was dying to get cleaned up. And to get the ragged, scratchy hair off his face.

"I'm going to shower. Digger said in his note to make yourself at home."

Shahara moved aside to let him pass. She watched him walk into the bathroom and didn't move until she heard the water come on. All too easy, she could imagine him and that naked, ripped body glistening from the water.

Leaning back against the wall, she closed her eyes and took a deep breath to steady herself as a wave of fierce desire went through her.

What she wouldn't give to be like Kasen. Her sister would be peeling off her own clothes right at this moment while she headed straight for Syn and that shower.

And she was sure it was a wondrous sight to watch the water drip off his chiseled features, catch in his dimple. See his wet, black hair curling around his neck and broad shoulders. Watch the water catch in the fine hairs on his legs, and other more intimate places.

To follow those droplets with her tongue while she suckled hard muscles that . . .

She let out an appreciative breath.

He would be magnificent. If only she were different.

Still, she couldn't quench the fire in her blood. What

would it be like to make love to a man like him? To feel his strong arms hold her tight while he kissed her softly until she begged for mercy?

Shahara bit her lip in indecision. Was all of his kindness just a deception?

Was Syn like Gaelin, deceiving her with a false facade, waiting until he'd weakened her defenses before he struck?

Something told her Syn wasn't like that and yet she couldn't bring herself to trust him. She couldn't afford to be wrong again.

Sighing, she pushed herself away and went to find something to eat.

A very short time later Syn joined her in the kitchen.

"What smells so good?" he asked, walking to the counter.

Shahara wanted to answer, but the sight of him cleaned up was the only thing she could focus on.

His black pants hugged his hips and other parts in a way that was pretty much obscene and left very little to the imagination. Not that she had to imagine. She knew only too well what resided beneath that tight fabric.

Blood droned in her ears as her body became white-hot.

He'd draped his shirt over his muscular shoulder. He reminded her of some mythic god emerging from the mists. Perfect in every way. Never, ever in her life had she seen a man so gorgeous.

When she didn't answer, Syn turned around and stared at her. "Do you mind if I have some?"

Shahara forced herself to swallow. "Go ahead." She diverted her gaze down to her own plate and hoped he didn't notice the color on her cheeks.

As he turned his back to her, she couldn't resist another look at his tantalizing form. Without a doubt, he had the nicest, firmest ass she'd ever seen. And for the first time in her adult life, she wouldn't mind a healthy serving of *that* rump roast.

Once he had his plate full, he joined her at the table. He took a bite, then made a terrible face.

Before she could blink, he dodged from the table to the compactor and spat his food out. Upset at his reaction to her cooking, she put her hand on her hip and gave him a chiding glare. "It's not *that* bad."

Grabbing a glass of water, he took two long, deep drinks. "No wonder you're so skinny. I'd die of starvation too if I had to eat that."

"Thanks a lot."

He turned contrite. "I'm sorry. But you could have warned me it was deadly."

Rolling her eyes, Shahara took a bite of her eggs. In all honesty she did have to agree with him. The eggs were runny and salty, the bacon burned, and the rolls wouldn't be too bad. Provided you used them as a doorstop.

"What can I say, Tessa and Caillen are the cooks in the family, not me."

Syn grabbed a piece of bread from the glass container on the counter and shoved it in his mouth as if he were trying to kill the taste.

She'd probably be more offended if she hadn't grown up with Caillen being every bit as a cruel to her whenever she cooked.

"So what's our agenda?" she asked, changing the topic.

He took another drink. "First thing, I need you to help me tape my ribs."

"The Prinapin didn't work?"

"Prinapin is good for minor injuries, pain, and

cosmetic fixatives. But it won't do anything for more serious injuries, such as cracked ribs. And the last thing we need is for me to puncture a lung."

She set her fork and plate aside. "Then what are we going to do?"

"I'm going to commit suicide."

She looked at him in shock.

"Not literally. I need to go back to my place for a few things. If I know the Rits, someone will be there watching for me. So I need to leave you here and go it alone."

"Now wait a min—"

"Don't argue. I was trained from birth to break into buildings without being seen. You, on the other hand—"

"Did a remarkable job breaking into your flat without your detecting me."

"Yes, but you *did* get caught."

She couldn't argue with him there.

"It won't take me long, then I'll come back for you."

Would he?

She didn't know for sure. And she wasn't sure how much she trusted him on that issue. "Well, I think it's time for my shower," she said, reaching for the clothes she'd placed in the chair beside her. "That is, if you left any hot water."

"Nag, nag, nag."

Shahara rolled her eyes.

"Wait," he said, stopping her before she left the room. "My ribs."

Some wicked, buried part of her jumped in delight at being able to touch him so intimately.

Shahara crossed the room and took the white, ribbed sterile wrap from his hand. "How do I do this?"

her. At t moment, it was all he could do not to curse her. Sur unwrapped cracked ribs would have been a lot less nful than the unsatisfied heat that stabbed his groin.

She anced down briefly at his tight pants where he was su his arousal was standing at full salute, and her face t ned bright red.

W out a word, she spun on her heels and took off for t bathroom.

"Don't take too long," he murmured, trying to shift himself into a more comfortable spot. "I'm definitely going to need a cold shower to stamp out this fire."

Picking up his glass of water, Syn considered dumping it inside his pants to help cool his lust. Instead, he took a deep drink and went to the front to look through the backpacks and to inspect his boots.

As he searched their gear, he smiled at Digger's thoroughness. There was nothing he'd left out. When it came to thievery, the old man was the best in the business and knew what any good filch would need to confront any ordeal.

Grateful for that fact, Syn set the packs aside, then pulled on his boots and shirt.

The door opened. Digger paused with an armload of groceries. "Nice to see you up and about."

"It's nice to be seen up and about." Syn grabbed the bags from him and took them to the kitchen.

"I was hoping I'd get back before you got up. Your girlfriend said she didn't know how to cook, so I was thinking I'd get you something solid for your ribs."

Syn laughed. "I'm afraid you're too late. She already poisoned me."

"Well, when a woman looks that good, she don't need to cook, now does she?"

He opened the roll and held a piece just
vel. "Wind it tightly about my rib cage. But
sure it's not so tight that you cut off my circu

Shahara did as ordered. She lightly wrapp
dage around his upper torso, her fingers brush
the hard, firm muscles. As her hands glided o
she watched as they twitched and jerked in
He really did have an amazing body . . .

Her breathing ragged, she did her best not t
about the desire throbbing like fire in her most
places. Or the chill bumps that spread over his fle:
hardened his nipples as her fingers brushed his sk

But the worst, most torturous part of it all wa:
step into his arms she had to take every time she d
the roll around his back. A step that brought her brea
straight up against his hard stomach.

Syn licked his suddenly dry lips as he watched he
work. It took every piece of control he possessed not to
pull her into his arms and sample her lips. He put his
hands on the edge of the counter and held on so tight
that his knuckles cut against his flesh, and the counter
bit into his palms.

This was an even worse torture than anything the
Rits had ever used on him. Hell, a few hours of this and
he'd be begging for mercy.

She looked up at him and he saw the desire burning
deep in the golden depths of her eyes. His control shattering, he dipped his head to hers.

Instead of fleeing, she leaned forward and then, just
as he thought he'd have his taste of heaven, she pulled
back.

"All done," she said, her voice strained.

His body on fire, he couldn't bring himself to thank

Agreeing with him, Syn set the bags down on the kitchen counter. "Did you hear any talk while you were out?"

"Naw." Digger pulled the groceries out of the bags and put them away. "I put in a few inquiries, but the word so far is silent."

Syn rubbed his neck. "Yeah, well, there were two guys on the street yesterday who made me, and Vik said he'd heard some things. I figure it's just a matter of time before they gather up enough courage or alcohol to come after me."

"Damn pity when a man can't even have a minute's peace." Digger looked up at him with an indescribable stare. "But then I guess you're used to that."

Yes, he was. Syn helped him put the food away.

Silence fell between them until Digger cleared his throat. As Syn turned around, he noted the sudden awkwardness. "What is it?"

Digger pulled out a chopping block and knife. He unwrapped a package of cheese. "I know it's you who's been stuffing my account."

"What account?"

Digger thumped the knife down on the cheese, slicing a thin piece. "Now don't you treat me like a fool, boy. Ain't no one else who'd bother. I know it's been you all these years. And I know why you sent Vik to me. I want to know why."

Syn leaned back against the counter. He started to lie, but why? The truth was, he loved his uncle. He always had. "I owe you."

Digger scoffed. "You don't owe me nothing."

"That's not true. You got me out of prison."

"Yeah, but I helped put you there. If I'd been a man, I'd have taken you and Talia away from your da when your mom left. I should never have allowed the two of you to stay with him."

"You didn't know what he was capable of where we were concerned."

"I should have."

Syn sighed. "Yeah, well, if ifs and buts were candy and nuts, then we'd never go hungry."

Applause sounded. Syn looked to the doorway to see Shahara standing there. She wore the same black armored outfit as he, but he had to admit it looked much better on her.

"I'll have to remember that."

Digger looked up. "Sheridan here tells me that you tried to poison him."

She cast an accusing glare at Syn.

Before he could respond, Vik flew into the window and whistled so harshly, it made all three of them flinch.

"Vik!" Syn snapped. "Stop it."

"Stop, my ass. A group of vigilantes just crossed the street. They're coming for you and your girlfriend so you better run or get splattered."

Shahara cast a frantic look at Syn whose face was impassive. "What do we do?"

Syn went for the packs and slung one over his shoulder before tossing the other at her.

Digger locked the front door. "I can hold them off for a few minutes."

Shahara's heart pounded. Digger wouldn't last long against young men. They were doomed.

Syn grabbed her hand and started pulling her to the bedroom. "What are you doing?"

"Do you trust me?"

She snorted. "Not even a little."

"You better learn," he said before releasing her and throwing open the bedroom window.

As he started climbing out, panic took hold of her over what he would want her to do next. "Oh, no way I'm climbing out there."

"C'mon, Shahara." He held himself precariously in the window that was five stories up. "We have no choice."

She shook her head. "No!" she said emphatically.

His dark gaze narrowed as Vik flew through the window. He swooped down, then returned to hover over Syn's shoulder.

Vik ruffled before he shouted, "They're almost here."

"Shahara!" Syn's gaze turned deadly. "Move your ass. Now. We have to get out of here."

But it wasn't that easy. She couldn't do what he asked. She couldn't. "I'm terrified of heights."

He ducked his head back in. "You're what?"

She swallowed as old memories surged. The pain and broken arm, most of all the raw fear . . . Had she not landed on a pile of garbage that had cushioned her fall, she'd have been killed. As it was, she'd been seriously injured. "I fell out a second-story window when I was a kid and ever since I get sick from heights, Syn. Really, really sick."

Just the thought of it . . .

She wanted to run.

He let out a slow breath. "Great, leave it to me to find the one tracer in the universe afraid of a little height." He clenched his teeth, then looked back at her. "Give me your hand."

"Why?"

A loud thud sounded against the front door. "Open up, old man. Or we're blasting through!"

"It's me or the Rits, Shahara. Who do you choose?"

That was a choice?

But in the end, she knew he was right. She had to suck this up and be a woman. "I choose option three," she said, giving him her hand.

Syn pulled her into his arms. "Hold tight and don't look down."

Shahara did as he said and swallowed her panic. Strong arms wrapped around her in a protective cloak an instant before they shot upward at a dizzying speed.

She looked up at his steely features. "What the . . . ?"

"It's a spring-loaded cord." He pushed her up over the lip of the roof.

Trembling, Shahara crawled to safety and did her best not to think about how far above the ground they were. "What did this accomplish?"

"Not much." Syn pulled himself up over the ledge and pressed the button to rewind his cord into its wrist compartment. He surveyed the surrounding rooftops, then pulled a baton from the pocket on the outside of her backpack. "Grab the one out of mine."

Frowning, she did as ordered while Vik circled back to them with another report that more were coming.

Syn pressed a button in the center of the twelve-inch metal cylinder and the baton expanded to six and a half feet. Before she could ask what it was for, he pole-vaulted over the lip of their building to the top of another.

Her head went light at the mere thought.

Surely he wouldn't . . .

"C'mon," he said, looking back at her.

Oh, hell no . . .

"You're crazy!"

"Certifiably insane." He flashed a charming grin. "Now move before we get caught."

I'm gonna die . . .

She heard the blasters firing in Digger's apartment and knew she had no choice except to follow.

Holding her breath, she duplicated Syn's pole vault even while she feared her limbs or the pole would collapse. It seemed to take forever before she reached his side.

He gave her a chiding stare. "Now that wasn't so bad, was it?"

She glared at him.

With an irritating laugh, he left her side and skipped over two more roofs like a graceful dancer.

Shahara watched with envy. "You make this look so easy," she breathed. "If I fall I swear I'm going to kill you."

Once she caught up to him again, he retracted the poles. "Remember where this is. It's the best friend a thief ever had."

"I'm not a thief."

"Oh yes, you are, baby. You stole me from the Rits. And I assure you Merjack considers it a worse crime than grand larceny."

"I really *hate* you. And stop calling me baby!"

He pulled her up against his steely chest. His eyes twinkled with merriment and he dipped his face so close to hers that his breath tickled her lips.

"As long as I evoke *some* strong emotion from you," he said, rubbing his nose against hers, "I'm happy. Anything beats apathy."

He released her and looked around as if considering his options. She had to admit, he made a sexy sight as he stood tall and proud while surveying the rooftops that surrounded them. There was a feral grace to his stance that the woman in her couldn't help but appreciate.

Shouts erupted as Vik swooped down. "They're on the other roof."

Her panic swelled. There wasn't a door or any other means of leaving the roof they were on. "Where do we go from here?"

He leaned over the side and looked down. "How much do you weigh?"

"A hundred and three, why?"

He didn't answer as he pressed the keys on his wrist computer.

"How are we getting off this roof?"

That damnable grin she was learning to despise returned to his handsome face. "You don't really want me to answer that question."

A cold chill crept up her spine. "Why?"

He spread his arms wide. "Come to papa, darling. We're going to take another ride."

She shook her head. "If you think I'm scaling down the side of this building . . ."

"We don't have time to scale it."

"Then what are we going to do?"

He spread his arms wider and winked at her. A horrible lump grew in her belly. She must have died and been sent to hell.

Shots fired around them.

Vik dipped below the building. "Better hurry, bonebags."

"C'mon, Shahara."

Cursing, she moved to stand in front of him. He took out a strap.

"What are you doing?" she asked as he wrapped it around her buttocks and secured her to him in a most distracting way.

"Hold tight."

She was beginning to despise that phrase. Dutifully, she wrapped her arms around his neck.

"Wrap your legs around my waist."

She glared at him. "I don't think so."

"It's not sexual. Just do it."

She obeyed, then wished she hadn't. They were locked in such an intimate embrace that it brought fire to her cheeks. Between her legs, touching the very part of her that begged for him, she could feel the tight muscles that lined his stomach. Her breasts were pressed firmly to his chest where they took up a dreadful throb of their own.

What was she doing? She never touched a man like this.

And before she could finish that thought, he put his arms around her waist and stepped over the edge of the building. "Oh my God," she screamed as they plummeted toward the alley far below.

"Stop that shrieking before you pierce my eardrums." His arms tightened around her. "Just hold on to me and pray."

Shahara buried her head against his shoulder and locked her limbs tightly around him.

Suddenly, she heard him curse over the rushing wind. "What is it?"

"We're going to die."

"What!"

"Hold on."

"Hold on," she repeated in stunned disbelief. "What do you mean *hold on*?" If she held him any tighter, she'd snap him in two.

Then she felt it. They were finally slowing down.

With one last jerk, they stopped falling. Or maybe they were dead . . .

Syn's arms tightened around her and when he spoke, there was a note of humor in his voice. "You can open your eyes now. We're safe. But you can stay in my arms as long as you like."

Shahara looked up at him, wanting to kill him. But her body wouldn't cooperate. Weak with relief, all she could do was hold him close. "I hate you, convict."

He laughed, causing his stomach muscles to touch her in the most intimate of places.

Shahara just glared at him. "How can you find this funny? You almost killed us."

"Me? You're the one who lied about your weight."

"I don't think so. When was the last time you stepped on a scale?"

He cocked a brow. "Good point."

She extracted herself from his arms, then punched him in the shoulder. "You could have told me you had antigrav boots. I thought we were dead."

"I didn't want to tell you what I was doing in case you decided not to jump."

"That was mean."

"You'll get over it."

"Only after I kill you."

"There they are!"

They looked up in unison to see two men running toward them. Syn grabbed her by the arm and headed in the opposite direction as Vik flew toward their pursuers to slow them down. As they ran, Shahara decided she didn't like being on this end of the chase. At all.

She much preferred being the hunter.

Syn led her down a dark alleyway. They jumped over garbage bins and homeless derelicts, and all the while, she could hear her pursuers coming ever closer while Vik insulted them and they shot at him. Her heartbeat drummed in her ears. Syn looked so calm as he ran, checking over his shoulder every now and again, that she felt like strangling him.

Suddenly, a fence cut them off. She started climbing it only to find razor wire lining the top. "What are we going to do?"

"Jump down."

She did and he caught her against him.

Terrified, Shahara looked past him to see two men coming straight at them.

Syn pulled a hand-sized canister out of his pack, then tossed it at their pursuers. Smoke exploded.

"Hold your breath," he said, taking out his baton. He extended it to half its length and used it to pry up the bottom of the fence. "Go."

She crawled through the space, then looked back at him. With one graceful move he rolled under the fence, retracted the baton, and put it back inside his pack.

She heard their pursuers scrambling through the smoke and taking more shots at Vik. "How long will that hold them?"

"Not long."

Grabbing her hand, he headed for a temple across the street.

She ran to keep up with him. "What are you doing?"

"Trust me." He opened the door to the temple and slid inside.

Her trust wearing thin, she followed.

Inside the dark foyer, racks of unlit white candles lined the pale pink walls. Syn grabbed two and handed her one. "Just do what I do."

He opened the intricately carved wooden door to the

chapel and walked slowly down the aisle. Her legs trembling, she kept wondering if the men had seen where they'd gone.

And if they had, would they follow?

The last thing she wanted was a confrontation inside a holy place.

Realizing they were in a Kiloran temple, she looked at the intricately carved statuary of various saints that stood on pedestals every few feet. It was actually quite beautiful and serene.

With his heels clicking lightly against the hardwood floor, Syn led her past their watchful eyes to the velvet-encased altar, where an eternal oil lamp was set. He knelt before it and tapped his forehead twice before touching his heart. Then he kissed the candle and lit it from the lamp.

"Now you," he whispered.

She duplicated his gesture. He cupped his hand around the flame and walked to a prayer bench just to the right of the altar, near a small door. Kneeling down on the bench, he placed the candle in a small holder.

She followed suit. All around the elaborate, gilded temple, she could hear people whispering their prayers.

All except Syn.

With his head sedately bowed, he said nothing as he appeared to pray. Until she noted that his eyes were open and he was discreetly searching the temple for something.

The chapel door creaked open. Shahara turned her head to see one of the men entering.

"Syn . . . they've found us."

He looked to the door, then blew out his candle and took her hand. Shahara barely had time to blow out her own before he pulled her through the side door.

Her heart lodged painfully in her throat and choked her. He wasn't actually going to lead them through the temple's private grounds, was he?

Wasn't that illegal or something? Or at the very least a grave sin?

The cold, dark hallway went on forever without a door. Syn pulled her down it until they came to a small alcove. He wrapped his arms around her, pulling her back into the shadows with him. Wanting to protest, she held her breath as she heard the door open and heavy footsteps approach.

Then she heard the gruff sound of a man coughing. Her heart stopped. This time, they were definitely caught. There was nowhere else they could go.

CHAPTER 10

Syn held her close against his chest. So close, she heard the pounding of his heart. Felt the rigidness of his body. And even though she should be terrified of what was about to happen, she found his presence soothing.

Another door opened just ahead of them and she heard several female voices whispering in a language that sounded an awful lot like the one Syn used.

The man came to a stop.

"What are you doing here?" one of the women demanded in an angry, intimidating tone.

At first Shahara thought they were talking to them, until she heard the unknown man respond. "I saw a murderer take refuge here. I'm looking for him."

"Not on our private grounds you're not. Get out."

Two priestesses walked past their hiding spot without seeing them. As a third one paused beside them, Syn reached out and touched her arm.

The priestess glanced at them, then gaped. Closing her mouth, she took a step past their alcove so that she could shield them with her own body. She cleared her throat. "See to it that this man is thrown out on the street. Make sure he never disrespects our temple again."

Once the doors closed behind the man and the two

priestesses, the remaining priestess turned back to them and smiled tenderly at Syn. "My goodness, child, trouble is definitely your handmaiden."

Syn released Shahara and straightened up like a guilty child confronting an irate parent. He hung his head and she cocked a curious eyebrow. She'd seen Syn angry, hurt, and contrite. But shame was a new emotion and she wondered what about the priestess made him feel it now.

"I'm sorry, Mother Anne. I shouldn't have come here while I was being pursued. It was wrong to bring them here. But I didn't know where else to go."

The priestess touched his cheek. "Never be sorry for needing help, child. We all do at some point."

Still, shame burned in his dark eyes and it made Shahara want to comfort him.

She shifted her gaze to the priestess and her golden robe. It shimmered in the dim light like a vibrant candle flame and it looked as soft as a cloud. Her bearing as regal as a queen, the priestess's gray hair was braided and then wound around the crown of her head.

Though the priestess was probably thirty or more years older than Shahara, she held the look of a vibrant teen. Only a few wrinkles creased her kind face, and those marked the woman's years of laughter and smiles.

No wonder Syn trusted her. It would be hard not to trust someone with such kind eyes.

Mother Anne's sharp gaze fastened on her. "And whom have you brought with you?"

"Shahara," she answered.

Mother Anne smiled a smile that lit up every corner of her face. "You are as beautiful as any angel. Never let anyone tell you differently."

Turning back to Syn, she gave him a reproachful

stare. "I wish you'd come under better circumstances. For years I've wanted to show you what we do with all the money you donate."

Syn looked embarrassed. "I have no need to check on you, Mother. I knew you'd do good with it."

Ushering them out of the alcove, she tucked her hands into her shimmering sleeves and led them the rest of the way down the hall back toward the temple. Syn opened the thick wooden doors that led to a wondrous courtyard.

Shahara stared at the quiet garden. Flowers bloomed everywhere with a bright colorful bounty that stunned her. Birds sang sweetly while chimes swayed in the wind, making a lilting sound that whispered serenity. Even Vik sat silently, sparkling on a branch, as he eyed them with a cocked head.

A fountain, with bubbling waves, marked the center of the yard and, just a few feet away, she saw a huge maze made of hedges that took up much of the left side of the garden.

Mother Anne led them toward it. "You know, Sheridan, we have just opened another home with your last donation, on Kildara this time. And we now have over three hundred homeless children living here in the Talia Wade Memorial Home."

Shahara started at her words. Just how much money had he given to them that they could provide for so many?

Syn said nothing.

Mother Anne smiled at him. "Every night we have them offer a prayer for you, child."

Syn shook his head and some strange emotion hovered in his eyes. "Not for me, Mother. My soul was lost a long time ago. Just have them pray for Talia."

Mother Anne pursed her lips and Shahara could tell

she longed to argue, but knew better. So they walked past the fountain and to the maze made of bright green shrubs.

"Anne?" an angry voice snapped.

Syn moved quickly and pulled Shahara behind a tall shrub. He placed a finger to his lips to warn her to silence.

"Yes, High Mother," Mother Anne answered.

"Please send Omera to the infirmary. There is a patient there in need of her special talents."

"Yes, High Mother. I will see to it right away." Mother Anne stepped to their hiding place.

Syn shook his head. "I can't believe she's still alive."

Mother Anne pursed her lips together. "Yes, and extreme old age hasn't mellowed her in the least. If she catches you in our sanctuary this time, she will demand your blood."

"I'm sure of that." He looked at Shahara. "We need to get to the catacombs."

Shahara gaped as a wave of apprehension went through her. She could just imagine a crypt of stacked bones and decaying bodies. "Catacombs? As in where dead people are buried, catacombs?"

He rolled his eyes. "Don't tell me a fierce tracer, a sworn seax no less, is scared of a little tomb. Good Go . . ." He looked to Mother Anne and blushed. "Gracious," he corrected himself. "Is there anything you're *not* afraid of?"

"You for one," she snapped. "And I'm not afraid of the tomb. I . . . just don't want to go there."

The look on his face told her his thoughts: *Me or the Rits.* Well, at the moment, she was definitely leaning toward the Rits.

Mother Anne smiled reassuringly. "You'll be all right, child. Sheridan knows his way around them better than anyone."

That was supposed to be comforting?

And she noticed that Syn didn't correct the Mother from using his real name.

Very interesting . . .

Mother Anne stepped around Shahara and placed a gentle kiss on Syn's forehead. "Walk with the gods, child. Remember they will always be with you."

Syn nodded. "Thank you, Mother Anne. For everything."

He motioned for Vik to follow them. Then, taking her by the hand, he led Shahara through the maze.

With every step they took through the winding, green bushes, apprehension swelled more and more in her chest.

"Syn . . . I really don't like being around the dead. I've buried too many members of my family. I really don't think I can do this."

Syn paused just outside the marble entrance as he heard the note in her voice. He turned to her with a curse scalding his throat but, as he faced her, it died. Stark terror flickered in the golden depths brighter than the eternal flames that burned on either side of the catacomb's door.

"Aren't you afraid?" she asked, her voicing sounding much like a little girl's.

He shook his head. "The dead won't hurt you, Shahara. Only the living can do that."

"But Syn . . ."

He let go of her hand and brushed a stray strand of hair off her cheek. "Listen to me, I swear there's nothing in there to be afraid of. I used to live in the catacombs and they're the safest place to be found on this planet."

His words shocked her so much that she forgot her fear. "You did what?"

"He lived here as a kid," Vik said as he joined them and flew into the entrance. Opening his mouth, he shined a light for them to see into darkness.

Syn held his hand out to her. "It'll be all right. I promise."

Gathering her courage, she took his hand and allowed him to lead her into a waking nightmare.

Once inside, she decided he was right. It wasn't so bad. As far as the light carried, all she could see were bronze plaques placed on the black-veined marble walls. It simply looked like an endless government corridor, not a cryptic tomb.

Thank goodness. She just hated the thought of what happened to people when they died. Most of all, she hated the thought of it being her family.

Silence buzzed in her ears, broken only by an occasional mournful cry of the wind and the sounds of their boots clicking against the ceramic floor and the metallic whisper of Vik's wings.

To her eternal relief, no bodies or bones could be seen. And other than the coldness, it bore no resemblance to a burial shrine at all.

Syn squeezed her hand comfortingly. "I told you there was nothing to fear."

Not willing to admit aloud that he was right, she asked, "Where are we going?"

"There's a secret entrance that lets out near a spaceport. It was built four hundred years ago during the Religious Wars, when the temple was used as a military outpost, to allow the priestesses to escape if they were attacked by enemies. I figure we'll wait there until dark, then head out and find a way off this place."

They passed several intersecting hallways. Resisting the urge to look down them lest she see something to dislodge her courage, Shahara focused her stare on the floor directly in front of them.

Syn navigated the corridors like a pro.

"Just how many priestess are buried here?" she asked, noting the endless rows of plaques.

"A little over thirty-two thousand."

Her eyes widened. "You counted?"

"I spent a lot of time here as a kid."

Vik made a sound of agreement. "He used to pretend they were his guardians who watched out for him."

He cast an evil grimace at the mechbot. "Thanks, Vik. Want to emasculate me a little more?"

"Okay. You have many other more embarrassing moments."

"Yeah, and for your own personal safety, you might not want to go there."

Shahara shook her head at their snipes. "You two argue like an old married couple."

Syn didn't respond as they finally reached the end of the hallway. He knelt down and brushed dust out of a barely noticeable crack in the marble. "It looks like it'll still open."

Shifting his position, he sat down. "Are you going to stand there or what?"

She sat down opposite of him and wrapped her arms around her chest. As she leaned back against the wall, cold seeped into every part of her body. There was a bit of a breeze that whispered through the hallway, cutting to her bones. "It's kind of chilly in here, isn't it?"

He gave her an odd half smile before spreading his

arms and legs wide. "Well, you know what they say about conserving body heat."

She debated the sanity of sitting in the circle of his arms. If he were anyone else, she'd gut him for the mere proposition, but after all they'd been through, she found her body moving toward him of its own volition.

She tensed for a moment.

"I won't hurt you," he said, his voice soothing. "Just pretend I'm Caillen."

Yeah, right. Caillen had never felt this good. And the rush of heat through her body . . . it would be disgusting if it were Caillen who made her feel like this.

Shahara relaxed against his chest and allowed the scent and warmth of his body to engulf her. He rested his arms on his bent knees and she found herself longing for him to put them around her, to hold her tight.

His breath fell down her cheek, rustling her hair and bringing a tingle to her arms.

Syn watched the way her breasts tightened beneath the thin fabric of her black shirt. His mouth watered, aching for just a tiny taste of the warm soft flesh he'd glimpsed when he'd stumbled onto her naked. It was all he could do to keep his hand away from the taut peak.

Never in his life could he remember wanting a woman this badly. If only she would cooperate, he would really enjoy the next few hours of their wait.

In that instant he knew he was going to have her. That he *must* have her.

But not here on the cold floor like some animal satisfying a basic itch. She deserved better than that.

First, he had to find some way to make her trust him. To make her willingly submit to his touch. She was terrified of men; his kiss had proven that.

But at the moment, she wasn't terrified of him.

She frowned as she looked at his arm where his sleeve had slid back, showing a glimpse of his tattoo. She pulled the cuff further up, her fingers lightly brushing against his skin. "The words are in Ritadarion, aren't they?"

"Yeah."

"What does it say?"

Syn hesitated as he remembered the origin of his tat. What it signified. Since he'd left prison, only Nykyrian, Digger, and Mara had ever seen the entire thing—aside from Merjack and his guards, but they'd ignored it.

Then again, those bastards were probably illiterate.

Mara had never asked what it said. All she'd done was nag him to have it removed because it disgusted her.

Decent men don't mark themselves, Sheridan. What possessed you to do something so crass? Really, you should have it removed before one of the hospital administrators sees it. Imagine what they'd say?

But he'd managed to keep it hidden from all the "decent" people at the hospital where he'd worked. Hell, maybe he should have had it removed, but it reminded him of his past and it kept him grounded.

Nykyrian had never commented on the words at all, even though he could read them. Maybe because he understood the underlying meaning without their talking about it. His friend was eerily astute that way.

"Syn?"

He took a deep breath before he answered her. "It says . . ." He clenched his teeth, then finished, " 'Nobody's Bitch.' "

She arched a single brow at him. "Okay . . . Care to elaborate?"

He gave her a flat, dry stare. "I was in prison, Shahara. I think you can imagine why it's there."

Shahara heard the note underlying his bland words. Leaning against his leg, she locked gazes with him and saw the hurt that was deep inside his eyes. "What happened?"

He looked away.

She caught his chin and forced him to look at her. "I won't think bad of you, Syn. I know what it's like to be hurt so deep inside that you think it'll never heal. To struggle every day with memories you wish you could purge out of your mind and can't."

"You already think I'm scum."

"No," she said honestly. "I don't." Maybe she had at the beginning, but she was quickly learning that there was a lot more to him than what she'd heard.

Syn let out a tired sigh as he remembered his past and the humiliation that still tore at him whenever he let his guard down. He'd fought so hard and it hadn't been enough . . .

"I was attacked the first night I was in prison. Like you, I couldn't fight them off at the time. But the next day, one by one, I hunted them down and killed all three with a shiv I'd stolen from another inmate. Orius, another prisoner doing a life sentence, was so amused by it that he *gifted* me with the tattoo as a warning to anyone else who wanted to mess with me. He told me to always wear it with pride."

Shahara's heart wrenched at what he described. "How old were you?"

He looked at her blankly and she realized it must have been the first time he'd been sent to prison. She winced at his bitter words.

"I'm so sorry, Syn. No one should have to suffer that and especially not a child."

"Yeah, well, it wasn't the first time I'd been raped. It was merely the last."

Her stomach hit the ground at his dry tone. "What?"

A tic worked in his jaw. "You know who my father was, Shahara. What he was. Did you really think he'd only sold my sister?"

For a moment she couldn't breathe as those words slammed into her. Honestly, it had never crossed her mind that his father would have been *that* cold.

Poor Syn.

She placed her hand to his cheek. "Did Digger know?"

He shook his head. "We didn't tell him. There was nothing he could do. Had he tried to stop him, my father would have killed him for it."

Tears stung her eyes as she realized the true horror of his past. One that made a mockery of hers. Placing her hand over his arm where the tattoo was, she leaned her head against his chest and hugged him close. "I'm so sorry."

Syn was stunned by her hug. Most of all, he was shocked by the sincerity of her tone. His body erupted with heat. "I've never told a single soul about any of that. Only Talia ever knew." And he had no idea why he'd shared it with her.

Maybe because she'd been through it herself. She knew, like him, that they'd done nothing to cause it. Some people were just cruel shits who preyed on others for no other reason than the fact that they could inflict pain.

In the end, he was grateful that, unlike his father, he'd never understood how people could be that way, nor had he ever found joy in hurting someone else.

Closing his eyes, he held her against his chest and let

the sweet scent of her hair soothe him. "What about you? What did you do to your attacker?"

"Killed him." She looked up at him. "Guess that means I'm nobody's bitch either."

He gave her a half smile. "Guess so."

Shahara listened to the strong beat of his heart under her ear. This was the first time since Gaelin that she'd allowed a man to hold her.

And it felt really good.

But there was still a part of her scared of what he might do. A part of her that waited for him to change into a monster.

"How did you do it?" she asked, trying to distract herself from that thought.

He frowned. "Do what?"

"Learn to trust and be intimate with someone after that happened to you?"

"Who says I did?"

She frowned. "You were married. I just assumed you trusted her."

"And I told her nothing of my past. I knew she couldn't handle it and I was right. She was married to a character I created and not the person I was or am. She thought I was the orphaned son of a respected business-man who was living on a trust fund and that I'd had a bland, boring childhood." He sighed. "It was the child-hood I'd wanted to have. Totally fabricated so that other people wouldn't know the truth of me."

"But, you were with her. I can't stand to be touched. The thought of sex still terrifies me even though I know it's not supposed to be violent or painful. I just can't bring myself to go there with another person."

His features softened. "I think it was different be-cause I wasn't attacked by a woman . . . at least not until you. I never really associated the two and honestly, I can't stand to be touched by a man either. Not even casually to shake hands. It makes my skin crawl. And like you said, it doesn't hurt when you're with someone you want to be with. It's actually extremely pleasant."

Syn stared into her trusting face and wanted to show her what he meant, but she wasn't ready for that. Honestly, it'd taken him years before he'd learned to enjoy sex himself. For the longest time, he'd viewed it as a tool. An act to be bartered for something else.

Then Mara had come along and for the first time he'd been able to fully enjoy himself. He'd found pleasure by sharing himself with her and making sure she never left his bed without multiple orgasms.

Until he'd learned about her adultery. That had shattered him worse than anything.

But he didn't want to think about that. It was a long time ago . . . and yet it still pricked him soul deep whenever he thought about it. Why hadn't he been good enough for her? Where had he been lacking that she needed to find another man to satisfy her?

Wanting to distract himself from that, he leaned his head back against the wall. "Why don't you tell me a story to kill time?"

She scowled. "What?"

"Caillen said that you used to make up stories to tell to him at bedtime. He said you were best at it."

Shahara gave a light laugh, remembering how many stories Caillen used to demand from her.

Please, Shay, make it a funny one!

She missed those days of her little brother making shadow puppets on the wall to illustrate her tales.

"It's been a long time since I even thought about any. I don't think I can do it anymore."

"Why did you stop?"

She shrugged. "After my father died, there were no more stories to tell. They just seemed too trivial to bother with while I had bigger concerns like feeding three hungry siblings."

He reached up with one hand. She tensed, half expecting him to touch her. Instead he paused momentarily, then scratched his chin. He returned it to rest on his knee. "I told you I wouldn't hurt you."

"I know. It's just hard."

Suddenly, his hand was on her cheek, brushing a stray curl away. "Are you scared of me?"

"Yes," she answered honestly.

His blaster appeared in her hands. She grimaced at him. "What's this for?"

"If I hurt you, you can kill me."

She scoffed. "This is stupid." She tried to return it to him.

He pushed it back into her hands. His gaze locked with hers and it held her transfixed. For once there was no mockery in his eyes, nor did they appear quite so glacial. "Fear is never stupid."

"That's not what you said earlier."

He laughed and she marveled at the rich sound echoing around her. "Well, I had to goad you in here for your own sake. Besides, it worked."

Shahara set his blaster by her foot and relaxed, allowing him to continue to brush her hair back from her face. Chills spread over her and she thought about his strength. Since all this began, he'd been unbelievably courageous.

Just what did it take to scare him? "What are you afraid of?"

"Nothing."

"Nothing?" She was skeptical over that. "Surely something has to scare you."

Syn licked his dry lips as his gaze trailed over her breasts and down to the legs she'd crossed in front of her. The way she sat, her thighs were open, inviting his hand to touch the most intimate part of her body.

He felt himself harden to the point of pain. What he wouldn't give to trail his fingers over her breasts, her tight stomach and plunge them straight into . . .

Damn it, boy, get your head in the game. If he didn't stop this, he'd burst his seams.

Clearing his throat, he compromised by trailing his fingers over her soft, parted lips. "The only thing left that I haven't faced is death and, after all I've been through, it would probably be a relief. So no, there's honestly nothing left that scares me."

Shahara thought about that while her body turned liquid in his arms.

What would it feel like to fear nothing? Her multitudinous fears ate at her constantly.

"Tell *me* a story, Syn. Tell me how a ten-year-old child survives alone in a world like ours."

His body turned rigid and his hand stopped moving. "That's an old story that's best forgotten."

Suddenly she knew what made him afraid. "You lied to me. You are afraid. You're afraid of letting anyone close to you, aren't you?"

"That's ridiculous. I have plenty of people who are close to me."

"Name me one person you confide in. One person who knows all about you."

Silence answered her.

"Well?"

"Nykyrian."

She shook her head. "No. You just told me something he doesn't know about you. How many other things have you kept from him?"

Syn dropped his gaze to the ground as he realized the truth. "You're right. As a rule, I don't let people get too close to me."

"And why is that?"

"Because when they look at me, they don't see me. They only see my father's son."

Shahara had to strain to hear those words. Even in the dim light she could see the torment in his eyes. "I don't hold you accountable for your father's crimes. And I want to know *you*. I want to know why you, who have more reason than anyone I have ever met, have never turned into the animal your father was."

He offered her a quirky grin. "I could have sworn you accused me of that."

"Well, I say a lot of things I don't mean and you're trying to change the subject."

"All right, fine," he said, his eyes turning dull. "You want to hear a story, then a story you shall have."

Swallowing hard, he turned his gaze up to the ceiling. "There was once a little boy who was born on a cold rainy day to parents who'd learned to hate each other. He was told that his mother had been a good girl who'd fallen in love with a bad boy who ruined her. But the truth was, she was every bit as heartless."

His deadpan voice tore through her and she noted the way he omitted referring to them as his parents. It was as if he recited a book he'd once read, or talked about a stranger.

"One day, the mother tried to kill the baby and the father beat her so bad, she took off."

Shahara froze as she remembered what Digger had said to her. "How do you know that?"

"My father rammed it down my throat every time he got angry at me. 'You worthless bastard. I should have let your mother drown you, instead of saving you.'"

His voice was still hollow, but she knew he had to feel the bite of that. "You hate your mother, don't you?"

He looked down at her and sighed. "I don't know her well enough to hate her. The only memory I have of her is when she threw me out the door and threatened to call the enforcers on me if I ever darkened her threshold again."

She wanted to weep over his mother's cruelty. "So what happened after your father was executed?"

He took a deep breath. "You know the answer. I was sent to prison."

"I still don't see how they could have done that to you. Couldn't they tell that you were different?"

He shook his head. "The child wasn't all that different from its father in those days. All he knew was violence. How to take pain and how to give it. The boy was angry and bitter, and he lashed out at anyone dumb enough to get in his way. Believe me. That little bastard took down three grown pedophiles without even flinching. He cut their throats and stabbed them until they were dead at his feet. He was so violent and cold in their execution that none of the other prisoners would even look at him after that."

No easy feat and it said a lot for what he'd done.

But it didn't change the fact that Syn wasn't cold-blooded or cruel. She knew better.

As Digger had said, he'd only attacked them after they'd brutalized him.

"The boy didn't listen to anyone. Not even the guards, and since the beatings didn't curb the boy's mouthy comebacks, they started locking him up in solitary. One day they made the mistake of choosing a cell with an electronic lock. The boy had been trained well and in no time, he had it deactivated and was out of there."

"It must have been so hard on your own."

He shrugged. "It could have been worse."

"Worse?" she asked in disbelief. "You slept under Dumpsters."

"Digger told you that, eh?"

She nodded.

"Well, I could have still been in prison being raped and beaten, so trust me. The Dumpsters weren't so bad."

How could he be so accepting? How could he not hate his mother for turning him out?

To this day, a part of her despised her father for his neglect and shortsightedness and he'd never put her through anything like Syn had suffered.

"So how did you end up here?"

"I stowed aboard the first ship I could find with an open hatch." He gave a bitter laugh. "I guess I should have checked its log first to see where it was headed. Not that it mattered. This is where I'd lived with my father so I wasn't used to anything better."

Shahara leaned against his knee so that she could better see his face. "When did you meet Mother Anne?"

"Who's telling this story?"

"Sorry. You are."

"All right," he said, leaning his head back against the wall again. "Once the child arrived, he realized

eir private chambers and kept me bathed
as the first time in my life I had some-
stay, where no one tried to hurt me."

d at the thought.

d his hand over to her neck where he
backs of his fingers against her flesh, doing
e things to her body. Again the needful throb

Iothers taught me how to pray and how to
hey showed me that some people spend their
ng to help others and that helping people wasn't
weak. That not everyone was a user."

t's why you're pious now?"

h. It's the least I can do. I owe them every-

they raised you in their chambers?"

ot entirely." He moved his hand down the line of
aw, sending waves of pleasure through her. His
rs trailed over her lips, her closed eyelids and then
n the side of her neck. She drew a ragged sigh of
asure.

When Syn continued, his voice was a full octave
eper. "The High Mother found me and had a connip-
on. Men aren't allowed to take holy vows and she con-
dered my presence a desecration to the temple."

"What did you do?"

"I moved back into the catacombs."

She cringed at that. "No, you didn't."

"I had no choice. But this time, I at least had blankets and a pillow. The Mothers would bring me a hot
meal at night and they helped enroll me in the local
school."

She became distracted by his touch as he trailed his

that surviv
the boy had
needed."

"You stole?

"Everything
didn't care who
And one day, the
wallet of a man wh

"He caught you?

"No, just as he wa
dodged into a vacant t
out in the spaceport. Th
and debris until he foun
trance of the catacombs."

"The man didn't find yo

"No," he said, switchin
around down here for hours
was a tomb, and two, the ma
me. After sleeping here a few
that no one ever came here. It wa

"So you made this your home?

"What can I say?" He flashed h
was the cleanest, safest home I'd ev

She shuddered at the thought. "Yo
me how you met Mother Anne."

He reached out and fingered her c
fingers a stark contrast to the icy air.
eyes, savoring his touch, his smell.

"One day one of the priestesses died and
her down here. I stayed hidden until they le
I'd fallen asleep, Mother Anne and Moth
came back to conduct Final Rites."

She opened her eyes. "They found you?"

He nodded. "Their kindness changed my life

took me into th
and fed. It w
where safe to
She wince
He move
brushed the
wicked littl
started.
"The N
forgive. T
lives tryi
stupid o
"Tha
"Yea
thing."
"So
"N
her j
finge
dow
plea
de
ti
s

fingertips back across her lips and under her hair. "Did you use your real name?"

"Hardly. I quit using Wade the day my father was executed."

She still didn't know where C.I. Syn came from. "Was it the Mothers who named you Syn?"

He laughed, his lips dangerously close to her own. "No. For an obvious reason, they refused to ever use it."

"Where did it come from then?"

"Given my parentage and youthful occupation, it seemed to be the only appropriate name."

She shook her head at him. "You're worth so much more than that."

He moved to kiss her.

As much as she wanted his kiss, she didn't want to distract him. Not while he was actually telling her about his past.

Pulling back, she asked, "So what does C.I. really stand for?"

Disappointment flickered in his eyes and he sat back with a sigh. "Certifiably Insane."

She rolled her eyes at him. "Why won't you tell me?"

"It's too embarrassing."

Crossing her arms over her chest, she sat back and looked at him from under her lashes. "It can't be any worse than Gildagard."

He frowned. "Gildagard? What the hell's that?"

She snorted at his disdain. "It's my real name, you goob. After my maternal grandmother," she said with a smile. "My father hated the name so much, he started calling me Shahara when I was still a toddler."

His rich laughter warmed her. "Gildagard Dagan. You have to admit it's pretty gruesome."

Yes, it was, but she wouldn't admit it to him. "Now that I've confided my greatest embarrassment . . ."

He shook his head. "I'd sooner turn myself over to the Rits."

"How bad can it be?"

"*Real* bad."

With that, she knew she'd never get a straight answer out of him. So she changed the subject. "Okay, if the Mothers were taking care of you, then how did you get back into filching?"

"How many questions are you going to ask?"

She shrugged. "How many hours did you say we—"

"Good Lord, woman. Didn't anyone ever tell you that men have a specified word count set aside each day and if I don't stop talking, my tongue will explode?"

She snorted. "Did you get that from Caillen or he from you?"

He smiled a smile that sent a rush of excitement through her. "I told you it was universal."

She gave him the little pout she used on Caillen to swing him around to her way of thinking. "Please finish telling me your story."

He kissed the tip of her nose, then pulled back to a safe distance. "School was expensive and the Mothers were misappropriating funds on my behalf. I began to fear that they'd get caught and punished. So I decided to use the one *gift* my father had given me."

"Filching for major companies?"

He nodded.

"Shame on you."

"I know. But if you knew the High Mother, you'd understand why I started. Had she ever caught them, she'd have tossed them into prison without a second thought. And from personal experience, I can assure you, they wouldn't have survived five minutes."

"But you did."

"What can I say? I'm a tough bastard."

Yes, he was.

And maybe it was his story or maybe their close proximity, Shahara wasn't sure what had made her suddenly so bold. But before she could stop herself, she reached out and touched the stubble on his cheek that still held a faint discoloration from his beating.

He nipped playfully at her fingers.

Embarrassed, she dropped her hand and thought to distract herself. "So how did you meet Nykyrian Quiakides?"

He picked her hand up and toyed with her fingers. The circular motion of his thumb against her skin sent electrical waves up her arm and straight to the center of her body. "He was wounded from a mission gone awry and I went to pick his pocket. He started to kill me and then when he realized I was just a starving gutter rat, he tossed his wallet at me and told me I looked like I needed it more than he did."

She scowled at what he described. Nykyrian was a trained League assassin—someone not known for any kind of compassion. All assassins killed without remorse or hesitation. "You're messing with me again, aren't you?"

"No. I swear. I knew he was dying from his wounds and I started to leave him to it, but I couldn't. Not after he'd been kind to me—the Mothers had taught me not to turn my back on people, especially those who helped me. Before I could think better of it, I helped him back to where I was staying and tended his wounds."

"An assassin?"

He nodded. "Because I saved his life, he paid for me to go to school."

"Out of the goodness of his heart?"

"Yes and no. I also worked for him."

"And what did you do?"

"Helped him gather information on targets. Provided a few toys for him to use while tracking and fighting. All legal." He lifted her hand to his mouth and began to suckle the pad of her forefinger. His tongue slid sinfully over her flesh, doing terrible things to her will. "And he paid a damn good salary."

"Which kept you off the street."

He inclined his head.

"So tell me about Sheridan Belask. How does he fit into all of this?"

His entire body turned rigid. His eyes returned to their normal frigid state and he pulled her hand away. "What?"

A wave of embarrassment consumed her. "I saw your surgeon's certificate."

His breathing intensified with the anger that flickered in his eyes. "Why were you searching my things?" And before she could speak, he answered for her. "That was a stupid question. You were looking for a weapon."

Shahara nodded. "So how did you become Sheridan Belask?"

Something strange passed between them then, a shared flickering heat that she couldn't define. Shahara realized then that she was probably the only person he'd ever told about this part of his life.

It made her feel so . . .

She didn't know what the word was. All she knew was that in spite of how they'd come together and what might happen in the coming days, she was glad she was here with him at this moment.

He lifted her hand again and brushed a kiss along her fingers before nipping her fingertips with his teeth. "I was always interested in chemistry and biology, so I started taking courses in that. One day one of my professors suggested I think about a career in medicine."

"And you became a doctor."

"Well, it wasn't quite that easy." He took a deep breath and swapped her hand for her braid.

She watched as he brushed it against the palm of his hand, then twisted his fingers in it. "I knew I didn't want to be a filch the rest of my life. For one thing, my activities had a way of getting back to the Rits and I had to stay on the move. And besides that, filches have very short life expectancies. So after a while I started thinking about what the professor had said."

He touched her braid to the tip of her nose. "It started looking like a great opportunity. All my life, all I'd ever craved was respectability."

"And doctors are always respected."

"Exactly." He raised her hair to his face and ran the tip of her hair across his chin. If she didn't know better, she'd think he was savoring it.

"How did you get into school? Don't they require birth certificates or records?"

"Nykyrian forged everything I needed. He used his League contacts to give me a whole new identity."

"Ah. So what happened that you left it all behind?"

He dropped her hair. "I was found out."

"By?"

"It's not important."

And though she longed for an answer, the note in his

voice told her that he was through confiding in her. He'd exceeded his word count.

She started to point out that his tongue had yet to explode, but she thought better of it.

Besides, he would just come up with another smart-ass retort.

Even though it was probably more than he'd ever told anyone, it still left her feeling on the outside of him. She wondered what it would take to breach his defenses, to make him trust again.

But then, trusting her would probably be the worst thing he could ever do.

"Now that I've dumped my sordid past on you, I want you to answer a question."

She lifted her brows. "Okay."

"How did the daughter of a fifth-rate smuggler end up as a trained seax? I thought seaxes followed a strict bloodline."

"They do. My uncle on my mother's side was a seax and he marked me for training when I was just a toddler."

"Why not Caillen?"

She stopped just short of confiding a secret not even Caillen knew about his birth. Even though Syn had told her so much about himself, she couldn't bring herself to tell him that Caillen was a foundling they'd adopted. Her brother had no memory of it and to their family it had never mattered that he wasn't theirs by blood.

Except for the matter of seax training.

So she told him that alternate truth. "He didn't think Caillen had a warrior's spirit."

He laughed. "No, I guess he doesn't. He is a bit of a fly-by-the-crotch kind of pilot."

She joined his laughter. "He is indeed. I swear I

should have gelded him when he hit puberty. Gah, he's been unbearable since the moment he discovered girls were good for something other than throwing rocks at."

"Darling's pet name for him is manwhore."

"So is ours."

He started to reach out for her again, but something made him pull his hand back. "So what made you decide to be a tracer?"

Shahara thought back to her childhood and sighed. "I think I did it in part to spite my father. He always hated tracers. Said they were too full of themselves for his tastes. And too, out of all the occupations open for me at the time of his death, it not only allowed me to uphold my oath as a seax, but also paid the best. And it gave me a loose schedule that allowed me to be home when Tessa and Kasen needed me."

He nodded. "I used to envy the way the four of you pulled together to survive. But the last few years of Tessa's gambling debts have made me realize how lucky I was that I never had anyone else to look out for."

It bothered her that he knew so much about her family already. It put her at a terrible disadvantage. "I must admit that there were a couple of times when I seriously thought about running away from them. I was too young to have so much responsibility dumped on me, but I knew if I surrendered us to the government we'd be separated and I couldn't stand the thought of them being abused the way I'd been. Not to mention, I couldn't survive without them and while Caillen would have managed all right without us, I don't think Kasen or Tessa would have survived on their own."

"No, they can't even survive *now* on their own."

That was very true. "I think the hardest thing for me was watching Caillen drop out of school to help out.

He was so smart and made such good grades I know he could have gone on to university and done something great with his life. Instead he's now a low-rate smuggler like our father."

"He's not low rate. He's one of the best pilots I have."

She smiled. "Thanks."

He inclined his head to her. "Personally, I think you should have made Kasen get off her lazy ass and work."

"That's harsh," she snapped with a frown. "You know she really likes you."

"Yeah, well, considering I'm one of the extremely few people she can stand for more than three seconds, that's not saying much."

Her frown deepened. "She's had a hard time with it all, especially with her asthma and diabetes. There's so much she can't do and she has to be so careful not to overexert herself. Who can blame her for being a little difficult?"

"Difficult?" he choked. "She took Caillen's last paycheck and blew it on a new dress and shoes."

Shahara gaped. "Tell me she didn't."

"Yes, she did. I thought Caillen was going to kill her and I almost helped."

Shahara rubbed her eyes as a dull pain started in her temples. Kasen would never grow up. And neither would Tessa. "I suppose it's my fault. Tessa was only ten and Kasen eight when our father died. I was so afraid they'd be pushed to grow up too soon like I did that I overcompensated and allowed them to never take any responsibility at all." She let out a tired breath.

He took her chin in his hand and forced her to look at him. "You should never apologize for loving someone too much."

"No, but I fear I may have ruined their lives."

"You shouldn't take responsibility for their short-comings. Those are their problems, not yours."

Shahara offered him a timid smile, thinking about what he said. Maybe he was right. Maybe it was time she stopped covering for them all the time and allowed them to fall once in awhile.

For several seconds, they sat quietly.

Until Vik raised up and took flight. He buzzed past them. "There are footsteps approaching and they're headed straight for us."

CHAPTER 11

"Footsteps?" Shahara repeated, grabbing his weapon from the ground and rising to her feet. "I thought you said no one ever came down here."

Syn stood by her side as he took the weapon from her hand. "They don't. Not without a good reason."

"Like they're chasing after two imbeciles who were dumb enough to stay put while they searched?" she whispered angrily.

"Sounds like a good reason to me." His nonchalance was seriously pissing her off. "So I misjudged our safety. It's not the first time I've made that mistake."

"Now you tell me?"

"Shh," he said, holding up his hand.

Out of the silence, a voice called out, "Syn, where are you? I have someone here who wants to speak with you."

"Run, Sheridan!" Mother Anne screamed.

A myriad of emotions danced across his face, replacing his usual stoicism—concern, stunned disbelief, and finally he settled on rage. Shahara took a step back. Never in her life had she seen anyone so terrifying. This was the man her sheets had warned her about.

Deadly. Evil. Cold.

"Vik—" His tone was lethal. "Total dark. Now."

Vik cut his light off.

"I can't see," she whispered.

"I can."

She realized he'd left her. Holding her arms out in front of her, she felt her way along the walls, wishing her eyes would adjust to the darkness. It was like it engulfed her. Oppressed her.

The total sensory dep was disturbing as she strained to feel or experience something.

She couldn't even hear Syn's footsteps.

Suddenly she heard the man who'd spoken moving closer. His feet, along with the Mother's, echoed off the marble walls so it sounded like an army was trampling through.

A light came closer.

Shahara dodged into an intersecting hallway and watched in awe as the number of the group grew . . .

And grew.

This wasn't just a single pursuer. There were twelve of them. And Mother Anne wasn't alone. Another priestess had been taken as well.

"Where the hell is he?" one of the men growled.

"Shh," the one who'd spoken originally barked. "I don't want him to know our numbers. Let him think I'm alone."

"You're not alone," Syn said out of the darkness. "But you will be."

Instantly, one man went down, his neck twisting.

"Where is he?" the first man cried.

Four more fell.

"He's everywhere!" another shouted.

Seeing her chance to join the fray, Shahara ran at the two holding the priestesses. She caught one in the windpipe a second before she kicked the other's knee out.

"Run," she told the priestesses. They quickly disappeared into the darkness while she swung around to deal with the next man near her.

"You bitch!" He aimed his weapon at her.

She knocked his arm aside and pulled out her dagger. Slicing his arm, she headbutted him, then kicked him down and turned to take on the next.

The four remaining men advanced on her.

Syn paused as he watched Shahara take down the rest of their attackers with an ease that was impressive and a little frightening.

Damn, she was good.

A slow smile curved his lips as she emerged over the bodies. Her torso twisted slightly, it was a stance of power and skill.

And it was sexy as hell.

She met his gaze and returned his grin. *"That's* what I'm good at."

Yes, she was.

Her gaze narrowed on something behind him. Before he could move, she flew past him to kick at one of the bastards who'd been trying to lunge at his back.

She knocked him to the ground and stomped him in the tenderest part of his anatomy. Falling back, he whined like a baby.

Syn sucked his breath in sharply between his teeth as he involuntarily jerked and cupped himself. "You've got to quit doing that."

She rolled her eyes. "Why are you bitching? It wasn't you this time."

"Let's just say your last kick at my jewels is still fresh in my memory." He walked over to the guy and *tsk*ed at him. "I know that hurts. She kicks like a mule, huh?" He shook his head.

"What are you going to do to me?" the man asked, his voice trembling.

Shahara frowned while Syn dug around his pack until he found an injector. He held it up in front of his face as if inspecting the dosage. When he looked back at the cringing man, his expression was glacial, deadly. "I'm going to kill you." He shot him full of the contents.

Shahara's heart stopped. Was he truly that cold-blooded?

He moved to inject another man on the ground.

Grabbing his arm, she pulled the injector away from the unconscious man's throat. "What are you doing?"

He looked up with a startled gaze. "C'mon, don't play the innocent with me. You shot me while I was unarmed."

"I didn't kill you."

He shoved a vial into her hands. "And I'm not killing them. Relax, it's just a sedative to make sure they don't come after us for awhile."

Still skeptical, she glanced at the container in her hand. A slow smile curled her lips as she read the label. He was being honest. "Then why did you lie to him?"

"Why not? He's lucky I didn't kill him. Anyone else would have."

More footsteps approached. Shahara held her breath, waiting to see if it was more attackers. She tossed Syn his blaster, which he caught with one hand before he stepped back into the shadows.

Bracing herself, she waited for them to approach.

Instead of rugged men out to kill them, the two priestesses returned. Mother Anne stayed back while the other one rushed to Syn and drew him into a tight hug.

"I know it was foolish to come back, but we had to make sure that you weren't hurt."

Syn tightened his arm around her and the expression of appreciation on his face brought a lump to Shahara's throat. He let go of her and stepped back. "It's good to see you again, Mother Omera."

Mother Anne cast a worried grimace over the men on the ground. "Are they dead?"

He scratched his cheek. "Resting. They'll be up and about in six or seven hours." He looked at Shahara. "Which doesn't give us that much of a head start. So if you'll excuse us?"

"Sheridan?" Mother Omera put her hand on his arm to keep him from withdrawing. "You have done us proud."

Syn paused at words that meant a lot to him, but they were wholly untrue and undeserved. "No, but I intend to." With that, he led Shahara back to the end of the catacombs and pulled the release for the secret entrance so that they could leave this place.

Shahara frowned up at him. "Are you all right? I'm getting a weird vibe from you."

"I feel about normal." He stooped to crawl through the opening.

Shahara sighed. Well, that was certainly ambiguous enough. As she followed him through the entrance, she stopped. This time she knew the odor that filled her nose with a rotten, sour smell. "We're in a sewer?"

"Did I forget to mention to you that we'd have to go through the sewers to reach the landing bay?"

She narrowed her gaze at him, wanting to beat him to the ground. "You forget to mention a lot of things."

He laughed.

Vik came to rest on her shoulder. "Don't feel bad, Lady Bones. He forgets to tell me things, too. Like the fact that he wasn't going to come back and get me."

Syn turned away from them. "I'm obviously outnumbered, so before you two combine forces and kill me, I'm walking this way." He paused to look back at her. "You want Vik to light the way again?"

She paused as she heard creatures scurrying in the darkness. "Depends. How many furry, little critters will I see run away when he turns it on?"

"Let's just say, if the thought of them makes you squeamish, you might want to wait."

Her stomach dropped. She'd just been kidding but now that she thought about it . . .

A hundred horror stories of vile things in sewers flashed through her mind. Were they rodents or something far more sinister? "Do they attack?"

"Not as long as we keep moving."

Shahara cringed. "Can *you* see?"

"Unfortunately, yes. I see better down here than I do in daylight." He took her hand and led her forward through the filth and stench.

"How?"

"It's a Ritadarion birth defect that hits about one in every three hundred babies born. Some scientists speculate it's because we lost our primary sun two hundred years ago and the one left behind is so dim that children are mutating in order to adapt to our darker environment."

"That's . . ." she searched for the most appropriate word. "Creepy."

"Thanks."

"No problem."

His grip tightened on her hand. "What?" She hated the fact that she couldn't see what had made him tense.

"I thought I heard something." He came to a stop.

Shahara strained to hear, but nothing came to her, other than the painful reminder that vermin were running entirely too close to her stationary self. "Maybe it was one of the little beasties at our feet."

"Maybe." He tugged her hand again. "C'mon."

She didn't say anything more as she followed after him, while Vik made whirring noises on her shoulder. She couldn't believe she was alone in the dark with a man and not terrified. But the longer she stayed with Syn the more used to him she became.

It was strange to her. Strange and somehow wonderful.

Too bad it couldn't last. For them, there was no future. All she would have of him was this time.

Spent in a sewer . . .

Instead of being happy about the prospect of putting this mission behind her, a horrible pain stabbed her chest as she realized how soon they'd part as eternal enemies.

Unwilling to examine it, she promised herself to let him get no closer to her. She couldn't afford to. Her future and that of her siblings depended on it.

At last he stopped. "There's a ladder just above my head. I'm going to pick you up. Crawl to the top and you'll find a small grate. It has a spring latch and, once you're close to it, you'll see how to release it."

He took her by the waist. The strength of his hands burned her as he effortlessly lifted her up. Shahara seized the ladder and did as he told her while he climbed up behind her.

When she reached the top, she gave a sigh of relief. Thank heaven they were finally out of that smelly hole. But all things considered, the surface air really wasn't all that much better.

She turned to help Syn up. It was then that she noticed the man standing in the fading light of the afternoon sun.

And the blaster he had angled at her chest.

"Say one word of warning and you're dead," he whispered.

Shahara froze as she quickly assessed the threat. There were sixteen of them, fully armed and ready to kick ass, and Syn would be temporarily blinded by the brighter light when he came out of the darkness . . .

Someone seized her from behind.

All her senses alert, Shahara could no longer think. Her training took hold. Stomping an instep, she whirled on her attacker with a fierce growl.

Syn squinted in her direction, but for his life he couldn't open his eyes wide enough to see anything. The glare from the fading sun had him completely blinded. His gut told him that they were in trouble, but damn his eyes, he couldn't do anything. All he could do was hear Shahara fighting and blasters shooting.

"Vik?"

"To the right."

Syn struck out and felt his attacker go down. Vik landed on his shoulder so that he could talk him through the fight.

By the time his eyes adjusted, the fight was over. Vik fluttered his wings as Syn surveyed the damage. And honestly, he was stunned.

He'd taken out two. Shahara had handled the others on her own.

Her features stern, she stood over one unconscious man with her hands clenched at her sides. The rest lay on the street, piled up around her. By their clothes, he marked them for Ritadarion trackers.

In awe, he looked at Shahara. "Remind me not to *ever* piss you off."

She had a glazed expression an instant before her legs buckled. Syn barely caught her before she hit the street.

"Shahara?" he gasped in startled alarm, holding her against him. "Shahara . . . answer me." It was only then that he saw the blood seeping from her scalp.

What was he going to do? He couldn't take her back to the temple or Digger's. Those places were no longer safe.

Scanning the area around them, he knew they had to get off the street before more Rits or desperate natives decided to try their hand at apprehending him.

Picking her up, he cradled her against his chest. She felt so tiny in his arms that it momentarily stunned him. She was so vibrant while awake that he'd forgotten just how small she really was.

And she wouldn't last long without medical attention. That thought foremost in his mind, he ran with her toward the spaceport.

Over and over his mind kept flashing on Talia and the way she'd looked when he'd found her in his bedroom. The pale blue tint of her skin. Her eyes half open. Her body drenched in the blood that had drained out from her slashed wrists . . .

It wouldn't happen again. Not on his shift.

Entering the port, he quickly assessed the ships around him. Most were small freighters and shuttles. But two were fighter class—just what he needed.

He ran at them full speed.

"Hey!" one of the attendants called, rushing toward him. "You can't take that ship."

Shifting Shahara's weight in his arms, Syn spun on the woman with his blaster raised. "Unless you want to die, I suggest you stand down."

She put her hands up in the air and moved away from him.

Syn kept his eyes on her while he continued to move toward the ship, more slowly this time.

At the base of the fighter, he stared up at the ladder and cursed. Now how the hell was he going to hold on to Shahara while climbing aboard a fighter? True, he was nimble, but that defied even his abilities.

Then he saw his answer. "Move the docking crane over to the fighter."

"I can't do that."

He clicked back the release of his blaster. "You have five seconds."

She ran toward the crane as Vik flew into the cockpit.

Once she had it in place, Syn warned her away. He climbed the stairs two at a time, all the while watching the worker, half expecting her to gain enough courage to try something. It wasn't until the three of them were aboard and the cockpit solidly latched that he began to calm.

A little.

As soon as the cockpit shield had begun its descent, the worker had vanished. Syn was certain she was running for help so he wasted no time firing the engines. A bit of worry swept through him at not running a preliminary check, but he didn't have time.

He threw the throttle and launched the craft's thrusters straight up. His stomach dipped as the g-forces played havoc with his body.

Within a few minutes, they achieved escape velocity. He swung the ship out toward space, and in no time they broke through the planet's atmosphere.

Once they were safely tucked into the bosom of space and he was certain no one was tracking them, Syn turned his attention to the small form draped in his lap. The control lights glinted softly against her pale cheeks and he noted her blood had soaked his pant leg.

Gingerly, he shifted her head until he could examine the wound. It didn't look quite as bad as he'd first thought. He should have remembered that head wounds bled a lot, even when they were slight.

But hers was deep and could use a couple of stitches.

He shrugged his backpack off and pulled out the first-aid kit. In just a few minutes, he had her wound cleaned and wrapped.

"Will she live?" Vik asked.

"I think so."

"Will she be pissed over it?"

"Probably. I'm sure it's going to hurt when she wakes." He looked over at Vik who was now in his mechabot form, perched on the control panel. "Why didn't you warn me?"

"She was kicking butt on her own. Thought it was safer you not fight blind. But then you stuck your head up and I had to help you."

"You still could have warned me."

"And you could have taken me with you instead of abandoning me all these years."

Those words made him ache. "I am really sorry,

Vik. If I'd known how much it would hurt you, I swear I wouldn't have done it."

"Okay, I'll drop the subject. But if you ever do that to me again, I'll stab you in the penis, which I'm sure will hurt."

"Yeah, it would."

"Good. Now I'm powering down for a bit to conserve my power."

Shaking his head at his strange invention, Syn shifted Shahara's weight and pulled her up to sit in his lap more comfortably. Leaning her head into his shoulder, he held her like he used to hold Paden when he'd crawl into his lap for a nap. The thought brought tears to his eyes and he quickly pushed his memories away. It didn't do any good to look to the past.

Paden wanted nothing to do with him outside of maintaining his bank accounts.

He was Syn again and Syn had never had a son. Syn was a street survivor.

As he looked into Shahara's peaceful features, a long-forgotten part of him begged for something he knew he couldn't have. Mara had brought that harsh reality home. Decent women didn't want to spend their lives with filth like him.

They wanted husbands they could be proud of. Not functional alcoholics with a hair trigger on their temper. But at least the alcohol was a step up from the drugs that had once ruled him.

That was what cut him the deepest. Mara had never seen the darkest side of his past. The animal that had crawled through the streets and sewers looking for his next mission and fix that would get him through one more day. He'd been a pathetic waste of humanity at one time.

If not for Nykyrian, he'd still be a worthless junkie, wallowing in a hovel.

Or he'd be dead.

Would it really matter? Could hell really be worse than the life he currently lived?

But at least he didn't have to deal with the shakes and cravings.

Bully for me.

Yeah, his life basically sucked. And it was so lonely. He'd long grown tired of the comfortless nights. But what could he do?

He sighed at the thought. What he wouldn't give to hold Shahara like this forever. Only, he knew better than that. People never stayed. It wasn't worth the pain to get to know them because, sooner or later, one way or another, they were gone and he was left alone to pick up the pieces.

Right now, he didn't have another fresh start in him. He'd used up his lives and his names.

He had nowhere else to go.

Shahara heard the faint sound of a heartbeat pounding against her ear. At first, she thought she was a child again and her father was taking her to her room after she'd fallen asleep waiting for him to come home. But her father had never smelled this good. Felt this delightful.

No, that was Syn. Syn, wicked, warm, and sweet. Beguiling. A champion who held her with gentle arms that never frightened her.

"Are you awake?" Concern marked his voice.

"Sort of." As he shifted her, she felt a stabbing pain between her eyes. "Gah, what did you do to me?"

Then she remembered.

Straightening up, she bumped her legs into sharp

metal as her head exploded with even more agony. "Where are we? What happened?"

Syn pursed his lips. "Which question would you prefer I answer first?"

"You pick."

"Where . . . I commandeered a fighter."

"You mean you stole it?"

"Semantics, semantics."

She glared at him. If she thought it'd do any good, she'd box his ears for the theft. "How did we get here?"

"You finished off the Rits, passed out from your head trauma, and I carried you on board."

She ran her hands along the bandage and felt the knot forming where one of her attackers had brought the butt of his blaster down on her head. She hoped he woke up with an equal amount of pain.

I should have kicked him so hard he'd need a testicle retrieval.

But that didn't change the fact that Syn had committed another felony while in her presence. Growling low in her throat, she narrowed her eyes at him. "You know I would never have climbed aboard a stolen ship."

He smiled, flashing that damnable dimple. "You didn't say that when I stole my own."

"I was going to until you told me it was yours."

This time he laughed. "Well then, I guess it's a good thing you were unconscious."

He was hopeless.

"Would it make you feel any better to know that it was more than likely stolen by whoever flew it—"

"No, it wouldn't." She shook her head. "I thought there was honor among thieves."

"Only in your dreams."

Or my nightmare. "So where are we headed?"

He showed her their heading. "I need to get a couple of things. Our first stop is at my office and then I need to go by my apartment."

"What are you? Insane? Do you know how many trackers will be there watching for you?"

"Yes, I do. Which is why I told you to stay with Digger. But ye stubborn curse wouldn't listen, so here we are. Me with brain damage and you with a head injury."

She looked at him skeptically. "What is there that is so important we have to risk our lives to get it?"

"The map that tells me where to find the chip."

Shahara drew her brows together into a deep frown even though it sent even more pain through her head. "If the map is in your flat, why are we going by your office?"

He sighed as if aggravated with explaining himself. "Before I stick my ass into the fryer, I want to do some hacking and see what the Rits are up to. I'd like to get a few satellite details of where they're located in and around my building. I need to be in my office to do that."

"Oh." Then another thought struck her. "What if they're at your office?"

He shook his head. "Not a chance. My office is a space station under heavy security."

"And registered under someone else's name, no doubt."

"Exactly. They'd never find it."

"That's what you said about the catacombs."

And for a minute they both sat still with dread hammering in their chests.

CHAPTER 12

Once they reached his company's headquarters, Shahara was amazed by its size. The space station spun around slowly in the center of the galaxy where the giant intergalactic freighters could access all the major routes.

The station had probably a dozen spikes that reached out into space to allow the freighters to dock and hook into air locks where passengers and supplies could be loaded and unloaded.

Smaller landing bays were built further in so that smaller ships could be set down on thruster pads and not interfere with their larger counterparts. It was truly top of the line and cutting edge.

"Precision Shipping." Shahara read the logo off the side of the station. "Nice name."

"Thanks. Our motto is 'Be happy with our service or we'll kill you.'"

She smirked at him and his sarcasm as Vik powered up and yawned.

As they neared one of the smaller bays, she admired the clean lines of the bay and the size of the crew in this one terminal alone. "This location must cost a pretty sola."

"And worth every credit."

She gave a low whistle. "How in the universe did you ever afford something like this?"

Syn brought the fighter in for a smooth landing. "After my ex-bitch took everything I had, I borrowed money from Nykyrian to buy a used freighter. I started small, watched my bottom line and, after years of extremely hard work and sound investments, I've accumulated what you see."

She narrowed her eyes at him suspiciously. "And how much of it did you get from accessing the secured data of your competitors?"

He met her gaze evenly. "I only hit them when they come at me first."

She looked at him doubtfully.

"Honest," he said, holding up his hand in a Ritadarion symbol of honor. "I'll gladly admit every crime of which I'm guilty. But I'm not about to admit to something I didn't do." His gaze burned into hers. "I've lost a lot of business to their filches. Every time I think I have a system hack-proof, up comes some little snot with my codes. When I find them, I make them pay for it."

He set the fighter's locks and pulled the gear for the cockpit to open. "And I usually send a little bonus bug their way just for shits and giggles while I repair the damage they did to me."

She couldn't help but smile. He just looked too adorable. "If you say so, then I'll believe you."

Syn climbed out of the fighter while Vik transformed back into a bird. He paused to look back up at her. "You coming or am I too corrupt for you?"

Instead of following his lead, she jumped over the side.

Syn grimaced. "You'll ruin your joints doing that."

"Don't be an old man." But her head did not appreciate it in the least. In fact, it was all she could do not to whimper from the new pain splitting her skull.

I should have killed them . . .

You shouldn't have jumped down like that, you idiot.

He gave her a knowing grin. "Bet that head of yours hates your guts right about now."

"Shut up." Then she added testily. "Asshole."

He grinned as he led the way out of the bay and into the station's corridors. "I live for your endearments."

Rolling her eyes, she followed him through the hallway, touching the bandage he'd wrapped around her head. He'd done a great job with her injury considering what little he'd had to work with. He must have been impressive as a surgeon.

Shahara looked around at their surroundings. The entire station was clean and white with an antiseptic odor that stung her nose. Twelve freighters of varying sizes and styles were docked along with two small fighters.

Loaders and several mechbots were stowing cargo on one of the ships while fuelers drove a tank over to the freighter.

Everything ran so smoothly that it amazed her. Every time Caillen or Kasen flew, they ran around in circles trying to scrounge up papers, fuel distributors, and cargo. Syn had been gone over a week and still everyone went about their job without hesitation.

"I'm impressed," she said, catching up to him. "A filch, a doctor, a Sentella member, and a shipper. You're a man of many talents."

"Yeah, well, it's easy to get a lot accomplished when you don't have any distractions."

"Such as?"

"Nosy tracers who ask way too many questions."

As they headed out of the bay, a uniformed worker came forward. *"Frion* Syn," she said, opening up a computer ledger. "What do you want me to do to your fighter?"

Syn looked at it over his shoulder. "Have someone refuel her and set her down in the main port of Rook."

"Yes, sir." She left them alone.

Shahara was aghast at his orders. "You're returning it?"

Syn tensed at the doubt in her voice.

Face it, rat. You were born a thief and you will die a thief. No one will ever see you as anything more. He should have come to terms with that years ago. Still, it didn't stop the ache he felt over her incredulous question. For some unknown reason, he expected better from her. "I have no reason to keep it. It doesn't belong to me."

Shahara wondered at the hurt on his voice.

"C'mon, my office is down here."

Wondering if she'd actually hurt him, she walked down the carpeted hallway. Along her right side were windows that looked out into space. It was a breathtaking view even with the bright fluorescent lights that dimmed it.

As they walked, they passed several workers, but none of them spoke a word to Syn. They merely nodded their heads in acknowledgment while going about their business.

At last Syn stopped and pressed the controls to open a door. Pulsing open, it displayed an office about four times the size of her condo.

Shahara held her breath as the lights came on and she stared at paradise. "Whoa," she breathed.

Syn led the way inside. "C'mon, it won't hurt you."

Shahara moved into the room, her jaw agape as she scanned the contents and fought an urge to take off her boots before she desecrated the perfect white carpet.

To her direct right was a small kitchen unit with a black marble table and one black, stuffed dining chair. To her left were three large, glass desks with several different types of terminals and other electronics she couldn't even begin to identify. A huge electronic star chart hung on the wall behind the largest desk. And, of course, expensive art pieces were littered about.

Along with another expensive piano.

In front of her was a huge stuffed chair that faced a solid steel-glass wall. Stars and gases twinkled and swirled in the depths of space with varying colors that looked like a living garden. She felt as though she were out in space and not in a station at all.

Syn took the backpack from her shoulder. "Are you hungry?"

Her stomach rumbled an answer.

"I guess you are." He dropped their packs by his desk before heading toward the kitchen.

"This place is enormous." She walked over to the kitchen counter.

"It beats what I grew up in, that's for sure." He paused in front of a food processor, then pulled her around to see what he was doing. "Here's a list of the various menus. Choose what you want by simply pushing it." He touched the screen and the item he'd chosen immediately flashed, then changed screens. "When you pull up a dish, it displays the ingredients and you can add or delete whatever you want."

She was awed by the device. "Wow, this is high-tech."

"Yeah, well, I can't cook any better than you can and this was a lot cheaper than hiring a cook to hang around."

Shahara gave him a wicked grin. "I've never had synthetic food before—how is it?"

He gave her a droll stare. "Given what you fed me this morning, why are you even questioning it?"

He did have a point.

Then he continued, "Most of the time you can't tell a difference, but stay away from the fish. It comes out rubbery."

"Gotcha."

Syn showed her where he kept the silver and linen, then left her to play.

"You want anything?" she asked as he walked to his desk.

"No thanks, I'm not hungry."

Nodding, she returned to playing with the menu. This was the coolest thing she'd ever seen. It had food from all kinds of planets and cultures.

What I wouldn't give to have this in my house. Of course it probably cost more than her entire building, but still . . .

Syn began filtering through his voicemail.

Shahara listened to them and was instantly bored. They were all from clients wanting to hire him or discuss shipments with him, sales people trying to schedule appointments, pilots wanting jobs, or his employees with various problems.

Taking her food out of the small countertop cubicle where it appeared, she moved to the table. As she pulled back the solitary chair, she made a startlingly realization.

Everything in this office was designed for only one person.

Everything.

She glanced around to make sure she wasn't jumping to conclusions, and sure enough, there was only one arm chair, one dining chair and the one desk chair he was currently sitting in.

He was utterly alone.

Her heart wrenched for him. It wasn't that she'd never made that connection before, but it was only now that the full implication of it hit her that she really understood what that meant.

And it was a brutal realization.

No one in any message ever asked him how he was doing or bothered with friendly chitchat. No more so than any of the people they had passed in the hallway. He'd been gone for over a week, tortured, beaten, and almost killed, and there was no one asking him where he'd been. No one worried that something might have happened to him.

I should warn you, you'll starve to death long before anyone misses me and thinks to come here to see if I'm all right. His words echoed in her head. He hadn't been joking that night in his apartment.

That was what he'd meant by not having distractions. No one ever bothered to talk to him. Spend time with him.

He was alone.

While he and Caillen were friends, they didn't really spend that much time together.

And to think, she'd spent years bemoaning the fact

that she couldn't have five minutes of peace without one of her siblings either calling her or stopping by.

If she'd ever left without telling one of them exactly where she was and when she'd be back, they would take turns jumping all over her.

Syn had never known that.

No one ever missed him. Except for Vik, who was lying next the computer where Syn worked. How sad that the one thing to miss him most was a robot he'd created in his childhood.

Because he had no other friend . . .

Shahara swallowed the sudden lump in her throat. How lonely it must be. How tragic that a man so giving had no one but strangers to give to.

"What do you do for holidays?" she asked before she could stop herself.

He stopped the playback and looked up from the notes he was taking. "What?"

Feeling somewhat embarrassed, she cleared her throat before she spoke again. "I was just wondering what someone with your kind of money did on special occasions."

His expression bland, he answered drily, "I drink." He returned to his work.

Biting her lip, Shahara looked back at her food and realized she wasn't hungry after all.

God, how she wanted to walk over to him and hug him. To let him know that he didn't have to be alone like this. It would be so easy and yet it was far too difficult for her. She would never be able to give him that comfort.

After all, it wasn't her place. They were strangers trapped in a desperate situation. She was nothing to him.

But as she watched him, she realized she didn't want to be nothing where he was concerned. She wanted to be like her brother and call him friend.

She'd seen enough to know that he was the best friend anyone could ever have.

At last the calls stopped. Syn turned his back to her and began hammering away at an old-fashioned keyboard.

Shahara pushed her food around her plate while she looked around the room again. Her gaze paused on the piano. He must really like to play, given that he owned two of them. But that, too, seemed incongruous to her.

When had he learned it? Who had taught him?

"What's your mother's birthday?"

She looked back at Syn. "What?"

"Your mother's birthday. What is it?"

Her defenses went into hyperdrive. "Why do you want to know that?"

He let out a sound of utter aggravation. "After all her questions, she won't answer one simple one for me." He shook his head. "I'm leaving a message coded for Caillen. I thought I'd lock it with something only he would know."

Shahara raked him with a skeptical look. "Are you telling me that the great computer filch can't find out a simple birthday?"

He snorted. "Yeah, I could access her medical records, but it'd be a lot faster if you simply gave it to me."

"8510.25.3."

"Thank you."

Shahara carried her plate to the sink, then, taking her drink, she went over to the desk. "What are you doing anyway?"

"Nothing."

As she scanned what he'd been working on, she gasped. "Is that your will?"

He darkened the page. "It's nothing."

Setting her glass down on his desk, Shahara was stunned by his actions. "Why would you leave everything to Caillen?"

Syn started to move away.

She reached out and grabbed his arm. "Why?"

"I don't have anyone else to leave it to," he said, shrugging her grip away.

"What about Nykyrian?"

"He doesn't need any more money and neither does Darling."

"What about your son?"

"He has a large enough trust fund already. Believe me."

His features impassive, he moved to stand before the windows and stare out into the darkness. Shahara wondered how often he did that and something inside told her that he must do it a lot.

She ached for him. Ached for a way to ease the pain that must haunt him.

What would it be like to be all alone? To have no one to talk over problems with? No one to share birthdays with?

He'd lived that way most of his life. Yes, he had friends but they all lived independent lives.

Wanting to comfort him, she went to stand beside him. "Tell me about Kiara Zamir's murder. How were you involved?"

His jaw turned to steel.

"I'm not accusing you of it," she said quickly. "I just want to know how you got blamed for it."

His jaw eased a little. "It's simple really. We were

hired to protect her. Because of his past with The League, Nykyrian has a lot of enemies out to kill him. One of them took the contract out on Kiara and Kip as just bonus pay."

"Kip?"

"My nickname for Nykyrian. Anyway, we were keeping her at her flat when one of the assassins and his team showed up for them. We had to move her before her father could approve the new location. Needless to say, he overreacted to us moving her without his knowledge."

"Where did you take her?"

"Nykyrian's place. It's where they both are right now, shacked up in suicidal bliss. Crippin' idiots."

She didn't understand the problem, if that was all there was to it. "Why doesn't Nykyrian return her?"

The look he gave her was chilling. "He would rather die than give her up. They are *in love*." Could there be any more loathing added to his tone?

"And you're caught in the middle of it?"

He nodded. "I signed the contract and took responsibility for the princess. In her father's mind, I'm as guilty of kidnaping her as Nykyrian is."

"What about the rape charges?"

"That one baffles me, but I guess in his mind we are low enough that if we have her, we must be animals enough to rape her. 'Cause let's face it, we're unconscionable scum."

She hated the fact that he was right. To the upper crust, they were garbage, barely one step up from rodents. "Surely you can explain it to him."

He snorted. "Have you ever tried to reason with an aristo? Mercy and understanding aren't exactly things they concern themselves with. Killing us plebs is."

That was certainly true enough.

"Doesn't it anger you?"

"Every minute of my life, but there's nothing I can do about it. It is what it is. Just like I can't help being hunted down and tortured because I know a secret about another aristo." His look cut through her.

She glanced away, ashamed of how wrong she'd been to do to him what she had.

"I'm going to call Caillen," he said quietly. "You want to speak to him?"

Before she could answer he added, "On second thought, let me call first and then you call him. He'd have a fit if he knew we were together, and I'm really too tired to deal with his crap right now."

Shahara nodded at his wisdom and watched him while he made the call. She sighed as the line buzzed. As usual, Caillen wasn't home.

"Hey, Cai," Syn said as he left a message. "I wanted you to know that I've already taken care of this week's pay and I'm leaving you a hefty bonus. If you need more, just pull it from petty cash and we'll settle it up later. I don't want you doing another run through Solaras. Damn, boy, get a brain. Stay safe and I'll catch up to you soon." He cut the transmission. "You want to call?"

She shook her head. "I'll wait." If she called too close after Syn, he might get suspicious. Especially if Kasen had told him the two of them were last seen together.

That could get really bloody.

Syn let out a long breath. "I'm sure you're tired, so follow me to the bedroom." He went over to the door beside the kitchen and pressed the controls.

Once more, her mouth dropped. A jumbo-sized, ebony-wood bed was set next to another window with a breathtaking view. The cream-colored silk comforter and pillows looked as soft as a cloud.

The bed's ornately carved headboard matched the geometric design of the ebony-wood dresser and nightstand. There were also more paintings on the walls, originals she was sure.

He stepped into the room and opened another door to the left. "The bathroom's in here. You'll find plenty of fresh linens and soap. I don't really have anything for you to sleep in, but if you want to clean your clothes, you can borrow one of my shirts from the closet."

Putting her head inside the bathroom, she saw the personal-sized clothes washer and dryer set into the wall.

"Do you need anything else?"

Just you, she thought, but she knew she could never say that aloud. "I think I have it."

"All right, I'll be outside reviewing data on the Rits and their activities if you need me."

And then he was gone.

Shahara took a seat on the bed and wondered how many nights Syn had lain here, alone, and watched the quiet peacefulness of space. Did it soothe him? Or did it just make him feel all the more lonely?

"Oh, what does it matter?" she whispered. "He has his life and you have yours." And the two of them could never be together. She couldn't even stand for a man to touch her.

So why did she keep imagining fantasies of them together?

It just wasn't meant to be.

"At least you have a family," she said with a sigh. But right now, that wasn't much comfort at all.

Syn heard Shahara moving around in his bedroom and it made him hard enough he could hammer a steel spike with his erection. She'd left the shower several minutes ago and he was sure she was digging around his closet. An image of her wet, naked body flashed before his eyes and he cursed.

"Focus, rat," he snarled, looking back at his sat read-outs. "You've got a lot of info to cover and not that much time."

Still, his mind tortured him with thoughts of her beneath him until he feared he'd lose what sanity he had left.

What was wrong with him? He'd tried this before and look what had happened. He'd had his heart torn apart.

His past would never let him be and it would forever separate him from any other person.

Caillen doesn't see you that way. Maybe she won't either.

He paused at the thought. It was true. Neither Kasen nor Caillen ever threw his past back at him. They treated him like a friend.

And if they could, maybe, just maybe, Shahara could too.

"Stop it," he growled at himself. "Don't do this. You're being stupid." Because at the end of the day, they didn't know as much about him as Shahara did. They only knew a very sanitized version of his past.

Hell, for that matter, she only knew a sanitized version.

Even so, he couldn't quite stifle the tiny voice in his head that begged him to take one more chance.

Hours later, Shahara came awake to the most beautiful sound she'd ever heard. Floating through the heavens, she could hear a soft melody that whispered around her, cajoling her, soothing her.

Then she realized it wasn't a dream. Opening her eyes, she tilted her head to catch all the strains of the haunting melody. Played with such passion and skill, it brought a lump to her throat.

Curious, she rose from the bed and went to investigate. The outer room was dark except for two electric candles that flickered next to the piano. Syn sat on the bench, his hands flying over the keys as he played with his eyes closed. The shadows played against his dark skin, making him look even more dangerous than normal.

He'd taken off his tight black shirt and wore a loose-fitting cream one very similar to the one she'd chosen to sleep in. With the candlelight around him, he cut a dazzling picture.

She stared in amazement. Wherever had he learned how to play like that?

Suddenly, he opened his eyes and jumped. The music instantly stopped. "Ah, jeez," he gasped. "You scared the hell out of me. I thought you were asleep."

"I was."

He closed the cover over the keys. "I'm sorry. I thought I had the volume turned down to where it wouldn't disturb you."

"It didn't disturb me," she assured him. "I just wanted to hear more. It was incredible."

He offered her a shy smile. "Not really, but thanks."

Without thinking, Shahara moved to sit next to him. "I always wanted to play one of these. My uncle had one in his house, and whenever we'd go to visit when we were kids, I'd fiddle with it." Back then she'd have given anything to be able to play like he did.

"Why didn't you take lessons?"

She looked at him drily.

"Sorry, stupid question."

"How did *you* learn to play?"

Shrugging, he reached for a glass of wine and took a sip. "Too much time on my hands. I taught myself."

She shook her head. "It seems like a strange thing for . . ."

"A street rat, filch, trash—"

She cut him off with a growl. "No. I was going to say a man like you to want to do. What made you want to play?"

He paused as if thinking about something in his past before he answered. "There was a woman who lived across the street from us when I was a kid. She gave lessons each afternoon and I'd sit out on the stoop and just listen to them play. It was the most beautiful thing I'd ever heard. Like a piece of heaven. My father hated music, so to me it made it all the sweeter. After I'd started working for Kip, I was walking past a store one day and saw the one I have at my apartment in the window." He closed his eyes and clenched his teeth as if he were savoring the memory. "It was the most beautiful thing I'd ever seen. So I bought it without a second thought and then sat there until I'd learned to play it."

"So Mara didn't get everything then?"

Pain flickered deep in his eyes and she hated that she'd inadvertently caused it. "No, I walked out on it and left it with her. But Kip . . . he bought it off her and returned it to me. He said he knew how much it meant to me and he wasn't about to let the whore sell it to someone else." The ragged emotion in his voice brought an ache to her throat.

"You love him?"

"Like a brother. He's the only person I can fully trust at my back."

And that was why he was willing to die rather than take Kiara home to her father and clear his name. It made sense to her now. He wouldn't hurt his friend for anything.

Better he should die . . .

The candlelight flickered against the burgundy liquid of his wine and flashed in his entrancing eyes. He cleared his throat and Shahara became aware of where she sat.

What had made her stray so close to him?

Still, it didn't seem wrong or frightening to her. Somehow it felt only natural to be beside him.

"Do you mind?" she asked, touching the cover.

"No, go ahead."

She flipped it back and stared at the black keys.

"Here," he said, turning the volume up. "Pound to your heart's content."

Syn watched as she played with the keys and set a disjointed melody. Maybe it was the wine—and he'd drunk a lot of it—or the scent of lilac that drifted from her hair, or maybe his earlier thoughts, but something sent wave after wave of heat to his groin. And every minute she sat next to him wearing nothing but one of his shirts, the more uncomfortable it became to just sit and not touch.

He shifted slightly, his pants suddenly way too tight.

She frowned as she struck an ugly chord.

He took another drink of wine and set the glass to the side. "Here," he said, marking the spot on the keyboard. "This is C." He showed her how to arch her fingers and alternate them down a simple scale.

She duplicated his movements and finally produced something that was harmonious. "I did it!"

When she looked up at him, her gaze sparkling, his breath caught in his throat.

Candlelight flickered in the golden depths of her eyes, catching the raw spark of vitality that glowed from deep within her soul. The thin shirt she wore was drawn taut over her hardened nipples and her unbound breasts shook with her excitement. Gods, she was beautiful.

Her smile slowly faded. Her breathing sped up and she licked her lips.

Syn tensed, his control slipping as he watched her tongue moisten the very thing he wanted desperately to taste.

Was it an invitation? The last time he'd kissed her, she'd been so afraid that he hesitated to try again.

But as he watched her, a fierce hunger gripped him and he knew he'd die if he walked away unsatisfied.

Shahara opened her mouth slightly. She wanted to beg for a kiss, but the words were lodged in her throat. And just when she was sure he'd never comply, he dipped his head down and took possession of her lips.

This time there was no panic. Instead, he teased her lips lightly with his own while his right hand came up to cup the back of her head. Shahara moaned at the sensation. How she wanted this man.

For the first time since Gaelin, she wanted to know what pleasure could be had between a man and a woman.

Even though the thought almost overwhelmed her with fear, she knew that Syn was the only one she could trust. He would never hurt her. And she knew she would never feel this way again about any other man.

He alone made her feel safe.

Protected.

I'll never have this chance again.

Pulling back, she stared deep into those dark eyes that hid an unfathomable pain. "Teach me, Syn," she whispered against his lips. "Show me that it doesn't have to hurt."

His eyes mirrored shock. "What?"

"I want you to make love to me."

previous lovers had known many men before
But Shahara was still technically a virgin.

e'd been taken, but never loved.

s mouth went dry at the thought. Who was he to
ith her like this?

Syn?" Shahara asked hesitantly as she watched
. Sadness darkened his eyes and he looked as if he,
man who feared nothing, was scared of her. She
ached out and took his hand, then pulled him to sit
ext to her. "Are you all right?"

"I need a drink."

She laughed at his ragged whisper. "I need you."

He looked up at her words an instant before he re-
claimed her lips with a hungry kiss that told her how
much he needed her as well.

Shahara trembled at his touch and the knowledge
that this man who needed no one at all wanted her. Her
body was alight with a thousand flickering sensations.
She touched his loose hair, his face, and marveled at
the raw masculine strength of him.

Of everything he'd been through . . .

And still he was whole and here. A survivor like her.

Not a rat, but a wolf who fought to protect his den
and those he cared for.

Tonight, she wanted to care for him.

Hating the barrier of his shirt, she pulled the tail of
it out of his pants and ran her hands up under it and
over the corded muscles of his chest, careful not to hurt
his wrapped ribs. Chills spread over his flesh and she
felt his nipples harden beneath her questing palms.

He trailed kisses down the column of her throat and
in that instant she thought she'd pass out from the sheer
pleasure of it. He laid her back against the soft mattress. Her senses whirling, she delighted in his touch.

CHAPTER

Syn stared in total stupor at her request. I
it? One look into her eyes and he saw the s.

No . . . I'm dreaming. Or high.

Brain damaged.

Something's happening 'cause I definitel
hear what I think I did.

There was no way Shahara Dagan would ask a
of shit like him to make love to her. That would
happen in a drunken hallucinatory fog.

You are *drunk.*

Yeah, but not *that* drunk.

"I trust you to take away my fear." She fingered a
piece of hair by his ear. "Show me, Syn. Show me what
it's like to be unafraid."

That was enough to actually sober him. His body
sang in response. And before he could argue or have
his conscience rear its ugly head, he stood and swept
her up in his arms. He claimed her lips once more.

Taking her to the bedroom in record time, he placed
her gently on the bed. As he looked down at her, he was
awed by her beauty.

He'd never been with a woman like her before. All

Until he shifted and she felt his bulge against her thigh as he trapped her against the bed.

Syn felt her stiffen beneath him. Pulling back, he saw panic flickering in her eyes. It was his weight, he realized. She must feel trapped beneath him like she'd no doubt been by her attacker.

Moving to her side, he tried to imagine how hard it must have been for a woman with her strength and self-esteem to find herself weak and ineffectual against someone so much larger. He knew from his own experience how awful it was. To this day, he hated to feel pinned, and if anyone held him down by his throat . . .

It was on in the worst sort of way.

"I'm sorry," he whispered, wishing he could tear the bastard's heart out for hurting her so.

She looked embarrassed until he returned to kiss her. When he pulled away again, he saw her desire burning deep in her golden eyes.

That look mystified him. Why did she want to be with something as foul as he was? Of all the men in the universe, why would a woman like her want to sleep with a no-account filch who had no real future and the bloodiest of pasts?

It defied his comprehension.

Suddenly, her fingers began stroking his chest and all logical thoughts vanished. All he could focus on was the heated desire that swept through every fiber of his being.

Rolling to his side, he pulled her on top of him, buried his hands in her hair, and kissed her lips.

Shahara smiled at her new position, delighting in the feel of his narrow hips between her legs. It was wicked and sweet. Just like him.

The thought made her smile. Sweet . . . a word that

really didn't fit with the predator she knew he could be and yet there was no other word to describe what he was toward her. And it made her treasure him all the more.

She pulled his shirt over his head and feasted on the sight of him beneath her. His eyes liquid, he stared up at her with such a tender expression that it took her breath.

A smile curled his lips, showing her his dimple as he reached up and fished his medallion out of her shirt. His warm hand rested between her breasts while he studied it. "Do you want it back?"

He shook his head. "It looks much better hanging between your breasts."

Syn let go, then cupped her buttocks. Pulling himself up, he nibbled at her neck. Shahara squealed in delight. Never before had she felt anything so wonderful.

"Ah, wait," he growled, lying back against the mattress with a fierce grimace. "I forgot to take off my boots."

Poking her lips out, she slid to the side of him. He sat up and quickly snatched his boots off, then threw them to the floor.

Shahara moved behind him. Leaning against his muscular back, she wrapped her arms around his waist and inhaled the scent of his skin. Gah, he felt incredible. All she wanted to do was hold on to him.

Syn moaned at the intimate contact of her breasts against his spine, her hands splayed across his pectorals. Gods, to be held like this forever . . .

"You can do that all night."

For the rest of my life . . .

Shahara brushed his hair back from his neck and

placed a tender kiss right at his hairline as she fingered the bandage she'd wrapped around his ribs earlier. Then his jaw. And his dimple. "I just might do that," she whispered, nipping one earlobe between her teeth.

He sucked his breath in sharply.

She delighted in her power over him. Drunk with it, she found the courage to move her hands over the smooth planes of his bare skin, over the bandage and down to the patch of hair that ran from his belly button and disappeared into his pants. Unlacing the stays, she dipped her hand lower, into the thicker patch of curls until she found what she'd been seeking.

As soon as she touched him, Syn threw his head back so hard it collided with her brow.

"Ow!" she snapped, jumping away.

Rubbing the back of his own head, he turned to face her. "I'm so sorry, I wasn't expecting you to do that. I mean, I'm glad you did it . . . was hoping you would . . . but I wasn't expecting it."

His nervousness made her smile. So, he *could* lose his composure. Who knew?

But it wasn't when he was under attack or being confronted. It was a tender hand that knocked him off-kilter. She filed that knowledge away for later examination.

"It's all right." She smiled even though she was still seeing a few stars. "I think I'll live."

With an evil grin, Syn pulled her close and began kissing her forehead where he'd accidentally hit her.

She moaned in pleasure. "I'm definitely feeling better."

He unbuttoned her shirt and trailed a path of kisses to her breasts. She bit her lip as his tongue flicked across the taut peak of her nipple. "I think I just bypassed the whole better thing and have gone straight into the great category."

He nipped at her playfully. "Want to try for ecstasy?"

She arched one brow. "You mean it gets better?"

"Just wait." He stepped away from her and removed his pants.

Shahara's mouth went dry as desire and panic mixed inside her. He was magnificent. And terrifying. Her heart pounded as she looked at the evidence of his attraction to her.

I'm about to have sex . . .

Me.

She swallowed and fought the urge to run for the door. This was it. She couldn't back out now, and deep inside she admitted that leaving was the last thing she really wanted to do.

No, she'd be strong. She wanted this.

She wanted him.

Syn returned to the bed. Hesitantly, he moved his hands to the opening of her shirt. "May I?"

Warmed by his question, she nodded.

He pulled it off and left her bare before him. A chill stole up her spine as the cool air brushed against her naked skin. She felt terribly vulnerable and shy.

And then Syn was there, pulling her into his arms. Once again he rolled over, placing her on top of him.

"You are so beautiful," he whispered, running his hands over her.

Heat stole up her cheeks as she leaned forward to claim his lips. She skimmed her hands through his hair, delighting in the silken strands that slid through her fingers as her own hair cascaded forward to drape around them in a dark curtain.

He ran his hands over her back and down her buttocks. Fire coursed through her veins and a painful throb started that erased her memories of Gaelin's brutality.

Even though a part of her was scared, she knew this was the one man who wouldn't hurt her.

And she ached for him in a way unimaginable.

Syn closed his eyes as he savored the taste of her body. He'd never made love to a woman who knew anything about him. At least nothing more than the lies he'd told her.

But Shahara had stared into the abyss of his soul and seen the monster that lurked there. And she hadn't run. Why?

What made her able to see the man when no one else ever had? In this one moment, he would give her anything.

Even his life.

I'm lost.

Lost in a way he'd never been before. Not even with Mara. Shahara made him want to be something more than a drunken thief and a paid killer.

She made him want to be a hero . . .

Pulling back, he stared at her dilated eyes and saw the ragged pleasure on her face. And as he gazed at her, he realized the truth.

I'm not lost. I'm found.

She'd pulled him out of the darkness of his past and brought him into a light he'd never known existed. Here in this one moment, he understood intimacy in a way he'd never known it before.

Shahara knew him. She knew the horrors of his past. The degradations and humiliations he'd suffered, and still she was with him by choice. Closing his eyes, he savored the sensation of her fingers laying against his cheek. He covered her hand with his own and marveled at how such a gentle touch could bring him to his knees.

Blows he could take. But it was the gentle hand of a woman that could truly destroy him.

How was that possible?

I'm a fool.

But only for her.

Shahara hesitated as she saw the troubled look on his face. "Is something wrong?"

He shook his head. "Not at all."

"Then why do you look so stern?"

Syn gasped as her soft hip brushed against his cock and his body exploded with pleasure. For a moment, he thought he might actually come from it, but he bit his lip hard enough to make sure the pain kept his release at bay.

When he could finally speak again, his voice was raw. "It's not directed at you, love. I'm just trying not to embarrass myself."

"How?"

He laughed as he realized that for a woman who knew her way around the universe and could handle the deadliest of criminals, Shahara was terribly naive. "Have you ever heard the expression, ladies first?"

"Yes."

"Well, it's truer in bed than it is anywhere else."

"I don't understand."

He kissed her brow that was wrinkled by confusion. "Trust me, sweetness, you're about to."

Shahara was completely baffled until he brushed his hand against the part of her that was on fire. She shivered as his fingers stroked her. For a moment, she was paralyzed by how good it felt. Never had she experienced anything like it.

His gaze held hers as he rolled her over and placed himself between her legs. A wave of embarrassment hit her, but before she could even move, he scooted down in the bed until he was able to dip his head and take her into his mouth.

Throwing her head back, she cried out at the sheer ecstasy of what his tongue was doing to her. "Syn?" she breathed.

He answered her by gently scraping his whiskers against her cleft.

A fierce tremor shook her as he licked and teased until her body exploded into the most incredible pleasure she'd ever known.

Syn growled as he felt and tasted her orgasm. He looked up and took pride in the fact that he'd given her something no one else had. His breathing ragged, he slid himself up so that he could lay by her side and stroke her breast.

Shahara was dumbfounded by her body as Syn pulled her on top of him and kissed her lips.

He nibbled and teased. "Did you like that?"

She nipped his chin. "Not even a little. It was completely horrifying."

He laughed at her sarcasm, then his eyes turned dark while he slid his hand down her back, to her hip. "Are you ready for what comes next?"

Him inside her.

Biting her lip, she was overwhelmed by his kindness. *Because he knows exactly what was taken from you.* His innocence had been stolen from him, too.

"I'm ready."

His gaze held hers as he lifted his hips and slowly

impaled her. Shahara gasped at the strange thickness of his body filling hers. It didn't hurt, but it wasn't exactly comfortable.

"You okay?" he asked, his entire body tense.

She nodded.

He cupped her face in his hands. "All right, love. It's entirely up to you now. You set our pace and I'll abide by it."

"I don't understand."

He lifted his hips up, driving himself even deeper inside her. She gasped as a wave of intense pleasure pierced her body. Slowly, he showed her the rhythm.

Syn watched as she took over and found the pace she was most comfortable with. He watched her with hooded eyes, amazed by her spirit and passion.

This was the kind of woman a man dreamed of keeping in his life. The kind of woman who would fight for him and defend him to the end.

If only he could have been someone different. Someone she deserved.

Shahara delighted in his touch as he slid his hand down to stroke her cleft while she moved against him. Leaning her head back, she savored the raw feel of his body inside hers and the sweet satisfaction that pounded with each thrust and stroke.

Suddenly, she forget all the fear that had haunted her most of her life. Syn freed the part of her that had been locked away and she wanted to laugh with the triumph of it. It bubbled up through her with wave after wave of happiness until she was sure she couldn't keep her laughter inside.

But that would probably not be a good thing to do while he was making love to her. He just might misinterpret the source of her humor.

So instead, she leaned forward and kissed him.

He stopped moving and, before she could withdraw from her kiss, he leaned her back against the mattress.

He left her lips and hovered above her. At his hesitation, she looked up into his eyes and saw that he was waiting to make sure she was all right. She smiled, and again he entered her and took over their play.

Syn's heart sang as she dug her nails deep into the flesh of his back. Never in his life had he felt like this. She wasn't some acquaintance he barely knew, this was a woman he cared for, a woman he'd protected. A woman who had fought for him. And the union of their bodies gave him more pleasure than he'd ever thought possible.

For the first time in his life, he felt as if he mattered to someone. That maybe, just maybe people didn't have to use each other.

Maybe Shahara was right. Maybe life was better than his cynical view.

Shahara saw his eyes change and, if she didn't know better, she'd almost swear she saw love shining back at her. But that was ridiculous. He didn't love her. He was only doing what she'd asked him to.

Teaching her that this one act wasn't something to be feared.

Syn growled in her ear, then buried his head in her neck. Smiling, she wrapped her legs and arms around him as he sped up the pace. A thousand flickering flames danced in her body, each one burning hotter than the last as she arched her back to draw him in deeper to help ease the new ache that had started throbbing deep inside her.

She clenched her teeth, needing release, and when it finally came she screamed out in relief. She tightened

"It's not what you think."

Actually it was, but—

Caillen caught him with a right hook to his left cheek. Caught off guard, Syn stumbled back, his face stinging from the blow.

When Caillen pulled back for another punch, Syn caught his arm and wrenched it behind his back. "Damn it, listen to me."

"I'm going to kill you, you worthless piece of shit!" Caillen shouted. "You hear me, filch? I'm going to rip your heart out and shove it down your throat!"

Shahara sat up in bed, holding the sheet to cover her body. Her senses dazed, she scowled at Syn. "What are you doing? Let Caillen go."

Without thinking, Syn obeyed. Caillen swung around and knocked him to the floor, then sat down on his chest. Syn blocked his punches, but couldn't dislodge his weight.

"Stop it!" Shahara came off the bed and caught Caillen by his ear. She pulled him to his feet.

He cursed but, to Syn's complete shock, didn't hit her for the hold. "Let go, I'm not a child."

"Then stop acting like one." She continued holding him by the ear until she'd dragged him a safe distance away. "What do you think you're doing?"

His face dark, Caillen ground out between clenched teeth, "I'm going to kill him for raping you."

Shahara started at his assumption. Looking at Syn, who was now on his feet, she saw the hurt on his face. "He didn't rape me, you goon. Gah, are you totally stupid?" She let go of his ear.

Caillen turned to face her in stunned disbelief. "You mean *you* slept with *him?* By choice?"

"Not that it's any of your business, but yes, I did."

Even more rage darkened his brow and Shahara wondered at its source.

"How could you do such a thing, Trisa? How could you crawl into bed with a common filch?" He looked her up and down as if she were unclean. "How could you ever willingly spread your legs for a convict? My God, I thought you were better than that."

His lip curled in disgust, Caillen gave one last disparaging glare at Syn, then quit the room.

Shahara started to go after her brother, but one look at Syn, and all thoughts of comforting Caillen vanished. He looked like a lost child—bewildered and wounded. Suddenly, she realized what Caillen's words must have sounded like to him.

"Syn." She moved to touch his arm. "He didn't mean it."

Syn just stared at her, his sight dulling. Caillen had meant it, all right. After all these years, he finally knew why Caillen had kept him away from his sisters. It wasn't just that he was protective of them.

Caillen thought he was trash and he didn't want to sully his precious sisters with Syn's presence.

How could you crawl into bed with a common filch?

All this time he'd deluded himself with the belief that Caillen was actually his friend, that his past didn't matter to him. Now he knew the real truth. Caillen, like everyone else in his life, had used him.

Gods, he was such a fool.

"Syn?"

He looked at her and the concern on her face. Curling his lip, he decided he was through with it. He didn't need her pity and he sure as hell didn't need her. To hell with all of them.

"Don't touch me," he snarled as she raised her hand

toward his face. "Go be with your brother." *He has your devotion, I don't.* He'd never had anyone's love like that, except for Talia's, and she'd abandoned him to their father.

With that thought, he started pulling on the rest of his clothes. Fine, he didn't need anyone. He was used to it.

He would clear his name so that she could go back to her life and then he'd vanish. Clearing her name would make them even for her rescue. Then he would owe neither her nor Caillen a damn thing.

She followed him as he searched for his boots. "Syn, would you please talk to me?"

He sat on the edge of the bed and jerked his boots on. "What do you want me to say?"

"Caillen was just upset—you know how he gets when he's mad. He spews out all kind of stupidity. He'll calm down and be sorry for it later. You'll see."

He curled his lip at her. "Don't patronize me. I'm not an idiot. He meant every word."

Shahara wanted to argue, but realized Syn might be right. She didn't really know how much of it Caillen had meant. But if those were his true feelings after all Syn had done for him, she was embarrassed to claim Caillen as family.

How could her brother have hurt Syn like that?

Or worse, use him? If he'd only been using Syn all this time for his money, she vowed to make Caillen pay dearly for it. She'd taught him better than that. Expected better than that from him.

"What are you doing?" she asked as Syn strapped his blaster to his lean hips.

"I'm getting ready to leave."

"Where are you going?" For a moment, she feared he was headed after Caillen to finish their fight.

He turned on her with a snarl. "After the damn map, remember?" Pulling his hair back off his face, he secured it with a black band. "You stay here and I'll be back later."

Something inside told her that if he left her, he'd never come back. Shahara had learned a long time ago to listen to that inner voice. She ran into the bathroom and hurriedly pulled her clothes out of the dryer.

Once dressed, she met Syn in his office by his desk.

"What are *you* doing?" He looked her up and down.

"I'm going with you."

"Like hell."

"Like hell, nothing." She stood toe to toe with him. "I'm going with you and you can't stop me."

Syn wanted to choke her even more than he wanted to beat the shit out of her brother. "It's too dangerous for two. Stay here where it's safe."

Shahara arched an angry eyebrow. "I don't think so. I started this with you and, by God, I'm going to finish it. And the last thing I need is some overly macho guy telling me that I can't take the heat. If I can pull you out of prison, kick the ass of everyone who's come at us so far, then I think I'm qualified to pilfer a map from your apartment."

Syn clenched his teeth. He didn't want her along. He was used to working alone and that's the way he liked it.

He ignored the part of him which laughed a bitter denial.

Shahara grabbed her pack off the floor and slung it over her shoulder. "Okay, convict, what's the plan?"

His teeth still clenched, Syn had half a notion to knock her over the head and leave her behind. But as stubborn as she was, she'd just come after him once she woke up.

With his luck, she'd lead about a dozen or more Rits to him.

At least if she were with him, he could keep his eye on her and make sure she didn't do something stupid that would get them both caught. "All right, you can come. But if you so much as sneeze without my permission, I swear I'll cut your throat and run for cover."

Instead of angering her, his words made her smile.

She's as crazy as the rest of her family.

But then what did that make him?

A first-rank idiot who deserves whatever the Rits do to you.

Syn growled low in his throat, wishing to the gods that he'd never been born. Without another word, he picked up his own pack and led her to the landing bay and into the belly of a small shuttle.

She dumped her pack in the copilot's chair. "Why are we using a shuttle?" She took a seat in the navigator's space.

He sighed, wondering why he'd ever involved himself with her. She was far too naive for the danger in his life. "If the Rits come after us, a freighter wouldn't stand a prayer of escaping and a fighter would be too suspicious. I'm sure the authorities have a Search and Hold on every fighter that docks anywhere near Broma. Therefore we're relegated to a shuttle." That said, he took the helm and launched them.

Once they were safely away and he had their coordinates programmed in their directionals, Syn grabbed her pack out of the chair beside him and dropped it into her lap.

She looked up with a puzzled frown.

Opening it, he began pulling out various items. "This—" he held up a black, cloth hood, "is part of your suit. You hook it up like this." He pulled it on and showed her how to fasten the small metal hooks around the hem of the hood to the collar of his shirt. "The hood will protect you from any infrared or bio detectors they might use while scanning."

"Are you serious?"

"Deadly," he said quietly. "If I pull my hood out for any reason, whether you understand it or not, you do the same immediately and keep it on."

Syn swallowed as her fingertips brushed against his hand. She took the hood from his grasp. For several seconds, he could do nothing except stare at her, wishing for things he knew he could never have.

I am a total idiot.

Clearing his throat, he forced himself to finish his instructions. He watched as she fastened the hood and then he checked it to make sure she'd done it correctly.

"Good." Next he pulled out several explosives.

Shahara inclined her head to him. "Cloaking smoke, numbing gas, and a light bomb." She touched each type of canister as she named it.

"Very good." He repacked her gear and made sure her baton was back in its pocket. "Now take off your blaster and put it inside your pack."

"Excuse me?" she asked in disbelief.

"Do it."

Shahara bristled at his stern command. She'd never been one to take orders without a fight. "Why?"

He took a deep breath as if he needed patience. "If light hits your *silver* blaster, it'll reflect off the barrel. Why the hell do you think mine's black? Also, the way you carry your blaster, it dangles loosely and could thump against something and alert our enemies to where we are. Something that would be very bad."

Shahara narrowed her gaze at his sarcasm. "Is there anything else I do wrong, while you're at it?"

Some of his anger dissipated. "It's not wrong for what *you* do, but in my line of work, it'll get you killed."

Sighing at the harsh reality of his world, she put her hood within easy reach and prayed that this time everything went smoother for them.

Syn continued his warnings. "You also have to remember that if the authorities have the right equipment, the fuel inside your blaster will be picked up on their scanners."

Now there was something she'd never heard of before. Dang, technology changed faster than she could keep up with it. "How is that possible?"

"Most blaster charges are coated with *trissem* to allow individual makers and suppliers to identify their merchandise. About a year ago, the authorities came out with a scanner that can pick up the *trissem* and expose a concealed weapon."

"But how will putting it in the pack—"

"The pack is lined with *deluva*. To date, there's no scanner that can infiltrate it. So long as we have them, we're relatively safe."

What did he do? Stay up every night researching all this? She unstrapped her blaster and did as he'd ordered. "You're good at this."

"Yeah, well, on the street a filch's life expectancy is only twenty-two and I'm doing my best to double that."

She flinched at his words. "You can't be serious? Even League assassins have longer life expectancies."

He turned to face her, his features completely stoic. "Assassins have a home quarter with allies. A filch has no one to trust. You're just as likely to get it from a client as you are from an enforcer. Or a competitor. Believe me, I carry multiple scars from all three."

Shahara drew her leg up into her chair and thought about his words. She'd never before considered how much danger such a life would hold. It was terrifying. At least as a tracer, she only had to worry about her targets getting her. While she did compete with others for missions, tracers didn't kill each other over them.

"Yet you trusted Digger, Nykyrian, Darling and the Mothers."

"I also trusted Caillen."

A lump burned her throat. Did Syn hate her for her brother's words?

"I'm really sorry, Syn."

He didn't say anything as he turned back to the controls.

For several minutes, Shahara sat in her chair, watching him run data through the computer. The light of the console flickered across the handsome planes of his face. Desperately, she wanted to take him in her arms and hold him tight, but he held himself so rigidly that she was afraid to even try.

A light began to blink. Syn sat back and looked at it, then thumped it with his fingertip.

It stopped.

"What was that?" she asked, suddenly anxious.

"A malfunctioning light."

"Oh."

They both fell silent while Shahara wondered about his thoughts. Would he ever forgive Caillen for what he'd said?

Could she?

Her brother's words had been harsh and if she were lucky enough to have a friend like Syn, she'd never betray him.

At that thought, her stomach flipped and she considered the irony of life. What Caillen had said to him was not nearly as bad as what she was *doing* to him.

What am I going to do?

Syn watched her from the corner of his eye while he continued to test various scenarios with the computer strategist. She sat in her chair with one leg drawn up beside her as she absently twisted a finger in her mahogany hair.

He sighed. This was not the way he'd wanted his morning to turn out. He'd wanted to spend hours holding her, exploring her body, and instead he was headed straight into suicide with a hangover and a fury that was so raw in his throat he could taste the acid.

Damn you, Caillen.

But then, what did it really matter? He'd known better than to ever hope for anything. How many times would he try for something and watch as all his hard work crumbled around him?

Well, this time, he'd learned his lesson. Shahara was only experiencing halo syndrome. It was common enough. Hell, he'd taught a number of classes to interns about it back when he'd been a doctor. He'd saved her life and taken care of her so she naturally looked at him as a guardian angel and had deluded herself with infatuation. But once all this was over, she'd gradually come to her senses and see him for what he really was.

A no-account thief.

And she was a tracer, a seax, no less.

There had never been two more incompatible people born. To even hope for one more moment in her arms was complete madness.

No, he had to keep his distance. For her sake as much as his own.

He closed his eyes and tried to banish the ache that seized him over the thought of letting her go. *She doesn't belong to you. You were meant to be alone. Why do you fight it?*

Because all he really wanted in life was for one person to say "I love you" and have them mean it. Just one human being to stay with him no matter what.

How he damned such thoughts. They'd tortured him all the nights of his life.

No more. He was done with it all.

To hell with love and to hell with people. He didn't need either one.

As soon as he could, he'd dump her and that would be that. And if his heart and soul didn't like it, then they could both go to hell and roast. He'd had plenty of disappointments over the years and, at this point in his life, he was used to its bitter taste.

He was definitely done with her.

CHAPTER 13

Shahara came awake as someone touched her gently on her arm. Instinctively, she drew her blaster and aimed at his head.

Syn caught the barrel and disarmed her before she could shoot him . . . again. "Are you all right?"

She started to fight back until she realized who it was. She calmed instantly, grateful she hadn't inadvertently hurt him. "Sorry about that."

He shook it off without offense. "It's okay. I do the same thing myself." He returned the blaster to her.

Sliding it back into her holster, she yawned. "Where are we?"

"Broma. I landed almost twenty minutes ago." He picked her pack up off the floor in front of her feet and handed it to her.

"Why didn't you wake me sooner?"

"You looked like you needed the sleep, but we've only got about three hours of darkness left. So we need to get out of here soon."

Shahara rubbed her eyes and yawned again. "Okay, Captain. After you."

He arched a brow. "What? No convict insult?"

She stood up and placed her hand against his cheek.

Even though his tone was steady and even, she had the distinct impression that he only brought it up because her use of the word offended him. "I see you, Syn. I know what you are."

Syn didn't respond as his body erupted at the sensation of her gentle touch.

Don't be an idiot. Mara touched you with a loving hand once upon a time, too.

And it had been a lie. First time he did something Shahara didn't like, she'd turn on him just like Kiara had done after they'd risked their lives to save hers. In one second of confession, he'd been reduced down to the filth of his past.

Just like Mara and Paden.

Just like Caillen.

The truth of his past had never set him free. It only enslaved him more.

And he was tired of it.

Stepping back from her, he pulled on a pair of black gloves, then handed her a matching set.

Shahara wanted to curse as she saw the veil come down over his face. He'd retreated back into himself and she had no idea why. Disappointed, she accepted the gloves, noting the little bubbles of hard-formed plastic that lined the palm and fingers. Tracing some with her finger, she looked up with a puzzled frown.

"We're going to rappel down the side of my building. Those should keep you from slipping."

Her body went cold. "Rappel?"

"Just don't look down."

Her stomach shrank at the thought. "You are one seriously sadistic bastard, aren't you?"

"It comes with being a Wade." His tone was so low she wasn't sure she heard it.

Never in her life had she wanted to reach out to someone more than she did him right now.

You are not your past, Syn.

But her words wouldn't reach him and she knew it. He was the kind of man who only believed in actions. Not lip service.

And she was going to have to betray him.

Pushing the thought aside, she followed him out of the shuttle.

In just a few minutes, they were headed down a dark, quiet street. The moon had taken refuge behind a group of clouds, and the outside landscape showed up only in spots where streetlights made tiny puddles of butter-colored light to help guide them. Vik soared up to scout the area in front and behind them, looking for anyone who might threaten them.

Wind whistled through the alleyways between the buildings with an eerie cry. Goosebumps sprang up all over her and she wished she'd thought to bring a jacket. Clenching her teeth to keep them from chattering, she stayed one step behind Syn.

"What time is it here?" she asked, her voice seeming overloud after the quiet.

"About three in the morning."

"It's rather creepy out, isn't it?"

Syn paused for a minute and looked around the deserted city streets before he shrugged. "Not really. I always preferred this time of night. It's peaceful. Even the worst predators are usually asleep or home by this hour." He gave her a strange look. "Except for filches. We do our best work after dark."

He headed into an alley. She watched as he climbed to the top of a Dumpster, then he held his hand out to her. Accepting it, she allowed him to pull her up to stand beside him so that they could balance on the edge of its lip, above the garbage.

An instant later, he pulled a grappling hook out of the small black plastic pack he must have strapped to his arm while she'd slept. He shot the hook upward toward the building's roof, where the prongs exploded and it vanished over the edge. After it landed, Syn tugged on the rope, testing the line. Her mouth went dry at the sight of his steely, catlike muscles beneath the tight bodysuit.

And before she could blink, an image of his naked body flashed before her eyes, sending a most inappropriate wave of desire crashing through her.

Syn wrapped the cord around his torso and looked at her. "C'mon," he said, pulling out the thick strap he'd used to tie them together the last time they'd scaled a building. "I'll help you up. But you're on your own once we reach the destination."

"No problem." She noted the seriousness of his tone. He wasn't the same man who'd teased her before. He hadn't been the same since his confrontation with Caillen, and she wondered how long it would be before he returned to the Syn she'd grown to care for.

Saddened by the thought, she stepped into his arms. His embrace was cold, mechanical.

Syn's breath caught as the heat of her body warmed his. Standing here, it was hard to let his rationale reign, especially since all the blood in his head was rushing south.

I should have never slept with her. All that had done was whet his appetite for more and make him crave things he couldn't have.

Dreams were lies manifested by worthless desires. And the last time he'd made the mistake of giving himself over to a woman, she'd stabbed him straight through his heart. Twisted the knife and left him bleeding.

If only those wounds were fatal.

Get the map, the disc, and get her out of your life. Then he could go back to . . .

Hell.

But at least he knew the rules there, and people's misconceptions of him didn't hurt.

"Hold tight."

She complied and they raced toward the top.

Once on the roof, he freed her. "We'll have to vault three buildings over before we hit the right roof."

"Do you think the Rits will be expecting us?"

He retracted the grappling hook back into its case. "I don't know. I couldn't get a decent sat link to check. But the good news is they can't get one on us either." He tapped the link in his ear. "Vik? Report."

"I don't see anything, boss. It looks clear, but I'm not betting on those odds."

"Keep looking and let me know when you make them." Syn took out his baton and faced Shahara. "If we're lucky, which I seldom seem to be, they'll have given up and be gone by now. But if my typical luck holds, they'll have at least two people staking out my building. I doubt they'll be this far back, though, and I seriously doubt they're looking up for our approach, which is why we're here." He paused, then added, "I guess we'll find out soon enough."

Shahara rolled her eyes. "Great." She just loved his optimism. It was one of her favorite things about him.

Pulling out her baton and extending it, she watched him run, then vault over the edge. He soared across the wide space like a graceful bird taking flight—like all this was second nature to him. The saddest part of all was the fact that it *was* second nature to him.

Her element was fighting. His was being one with the darkness around them . . .

"Go ahead," she groused at herself. "Make it look easy. But if I fall, I swear I'll haunt you forever."

Which would only be fair since he was already haunting her.

With her heart lodged painfully in her throat, she took off at a run and vaulted over to the next building. Her heart didn't beat again until she landed safely on the other side.

He shook his head at her panicked expression. "What did you say you did for a living? Play video games?"

Shahara took a deep breath and thought about where she'd like to plant her extended baton on his body. "I prefer to face my enemies on the street. In the open." Stealth was also her friend at times, but she was only stealthy until she reached her target.

Then it was full-on.

"And I prefer to live." With that, he vaulted to the next rooftop.

Not soon enough to soothe her frayed nerves, they landed on his roof.

Syn walked over to the opposite edge of the building and leaned over its ledge. With an indifference to danger she greatly envied, he stared down at the street for several minutes before looking back to where she was keeping a respectful distance. He motioned her forward.

Her heart still lodged in her throat, she obeyed even though she hated the thought of looking down.

"I see two tracers," he said once she joined him. "What about you?"

She stared down at the dark street and her stomach hit the ground. For a minute, she was ill, but she swallowed her panic and forced herself to look around. It wasn't until a piece of paper blew across the street that she finally saw one man walking.

"Right there," he said, pointing to the man pacing between two lamps that she'd noted. "And over there."

She looked at the other man sitting on a nearby bench, looking like a homeless urchin. How had she missed seeing him before?

As she stared at them, she realized their clothes were far too new and clean for them to be homeless and she couldn't imagine any other reason for them to be about. "Why did they choose such obvious vantage points?"

"They're decoys."

She turned toward him with a raised brow. "Where are the others?"

He shrugged. "No telling. They might be looking at us right now."

Then how could he be so calm about it? "And to think I turned down the chance to get a good night's sleep at your office."

"Yeah, well, I told you to stay put."

"Next time I'll listen."

He pulled his hood on, then secured two lines down the side of the building. "Vik?" He tapped his earpiece that kept them in contact with each other. "You see anything?"

"Nope."

He glanced to her expectantly.

She pulled her own hood on and tucked her braid into it. A bead of sweat ran between her breasts as she thought about what would come next.

She would be hanging about three hundred feet above the ground. One misstep and she'd die.

Painfully.

As if completely unperturbed, Syn swung over the edge and began his rapid, fearless descent. She swallowed hard and watched the expert way he danced down the side of the building, his boots clicking ever so slightly against the two-inch metal piece that separated the mirrored blocks.

Well, she couldn't let him get the better of her. Licking her dry lips, she carefully climbed over.

As she began her much slower descent, the chilly wind whipped against her body.

How could Syn do this for a living? How could anyone?

Just one tiny slip and . . .

Well, whoever had the unpleasant task of cleaning up the mess would probably be able to use a sponge on her remains.

With that thought foremost in her mind, she looked up at the roof and tried to think about someplace safe. To her complete dismay, the only safe place that came to her was an image of Syn holding her.

Good Lord, what was with her? She'd never had such delusions before. Never even had a single hormone rear its ugly head.

Until him.

Something about Syn had chiseled away her indifference and invaded her thoughts and heart in a most terrifying way.

Out of nowhere, two hands grabbed her legs.

"You're almost there," Syn said, guiding her to land on the balcony beside him.

Letting go of that rope was the easiest thing she'd

ever done. She rubbed her hands down her sides, trying to use the material of the gloves to absorb some of the clamminess.

Syn pulled several little discs from his pack and placed them at each corner of the windows.

"What are you doing?" she asked.

"They're light filters. They'll keep anyone on the outside from seeing a light while we're inside."

"Wow. I've never heard of anything like that."

"That's because I invented it and I'm not real eager to share it with other people."

"Did you really?"

He paused and turned toward her. Even though she couldn't see his face, she was certain he was giving her a look to rival the winds for coldness. When he spoke, she was even more positive. "I can do a lot of things that don't involve stealing."

Crossing her arms over her chest, she narrowed her eyes. "Did I say you couldn't? You, my friend, are seriously defensive when it comes to your past."

"You should try me on my future sometime."

Before she could ask what he meant, he slid open the door and stepped inside. Once she entered, he pulled it closed.

All of a sudden he froze, as if something had stunned him.

Was it the Rits?

Her heart pounding, Shahara squinted into the darkness, but couldn't see anything. "Where's a light?"

It flared on.

Her breath caught as a sick feeling washed over her. *Oh no . . .*

His immaculate home looked like a city's waste facility. His paintings had been torn from the walls and slashed. The sofas looked like they had met a huge bird of prey and lost their battle to survive.

Papers, chips, and discs littered the entire floor. Even the food she'd left behind had been pulled from his cooling unit and dumped on the floor where it'd rotted and filled the place with a very *lovely* little odor.

How could anyone do such a thing?

If there's one thing I value, it's my home. She winced at the memory of Syn's words. Looking at him, she saw that he hadn't moved. He just stared at the mess.

His expression pained, he swallowed. "My cleaning lady is going to be really pissed."

Deciding laughter would be the worst possible response, Shahara added, "I'll take the odds that say she's going to quit the minute she sees this."

It was then that his icy facade slipped under a mask of ultimate fury. "Damn them," he ground out between his teeth as he jerked the hood off his head. He pulled his hair free of the ponytail and raked his hands through it. "I hope you all rot in hell, slimy bastards."

Shahara wasn't sure how to react. He reminded her of a spring that was too tightly wound, and at any minute she expected him to explode. Every single muscle in his body was tense. Even his eyelids, and she'd never known that those could get tense.

He released a hissing breath and started kicking at papers with the toe of his boot.

Suddenly, he froze again.

"No . . . gods, no," he breathed as if some horrible thought had just occurred to him.

He took off to the bedroom like lightning.

Cautiously, she followed after him, afraid of what she'd find.

He stood before the open wall safe and pulled chips

and papers out. "Where is it?" he growled as if the safe
had contained his very soul.

"What are you looking for?"

He ignored her. Instead, he fell to his knees and
started frantically searching the floor of the bedroom.

Her heart clenched. She'd never seen him like this
before. After all they'd been through, she thought nothing could rattle him. But he was completely torn up by
whatever was missing.

"Did they get the map?"

When he looked up, her breath caught in her throat.
Primal, evil hatred blazed in the stormy blackness of
his eyes. He looked like a wild lorina about to attack.

Shahara swallowed. How had she ever forgotten just
how dangerous this man was?

"You want the fucking map?" he snarled. "You can
have it."

He charged at her so fast she half expected him to
hit her. Instead, he stepped around her and lifted his
enormous ebony-wood dresser with one brutal shove.
Glass shattered as the mirror hit the floor and broke
into a million pieces.

After flipping the dresser on its side, he kicked one
of the intricately carved legs off of it. He handed it to
her.

Shahara looked down to see a folded piece of paper
and a disc concealed inside a hollowed-out space.

He returned to searching the floor.

Okay . . . the map wasn't what had him upset.

She pulled it out and put it in her pack, then knelt
down beside him. "What are we looking for?"

Again he turned on her with a snarl. "Get out!" he
shouted. "Just get the hell out of my sight!"

His fury stunned her. Not that she blamed him. What

they'd done here was uncalled for. And he must blame her for this.

After all, she was the one who gave them his address.

How could I have been so stupid?

She had destroyed his life. Caused him to be beaten, chased.

And now this.

The one and only thing he valued.

Clearing her throat, she gathered as much dignity as she could and went back to the main room. She pulled the hood off her head and sighed as she surveyed the utter destruction around her.

What had she done?

It had all seemed so simple at first. Hand over a convict and save the four of them. How much simpler could it be?

Only it wasn't simple. She'd destroyed an innocent man.

No, not entirely innocent, but he didn't deserve this. No one deserved to have their home ripped to pieces.

Over and over she saw his beaten body, heard the thump of him hitting the prison floor. The sight of his young, battered face in the photograph.

He'd been amply punished for anything he'd ever done. He surely didn't deserve any more.

At the moment, she hated herself for her part in it all.

He saved my life, took my fear away, and I repaid him by kicking him in the teeth.

Shaking her head to clear her blurry vision, she gazed down at the mess surrounding her and saw a fragment of one of the photos he'd kept inside his prayer box. She knelt down and picked it up. It was his sister. Though the lower half that contained him had been torn off,

Talia's face still remained untouched. Maybe she could find more.

With that thought, she began to hunt frantically through the debris. Granted, it wouldn't rectify what he'd lost. But at least it would give him something to hold on to.

Just as she found several more pieces, a loud shattering sound came from the bedroom.

What the . . . ?

Terrified that a sniper had shot through the window, she entered the room and saw Syn standing just inside a large gaping hole in the windows, where he'd thrown his office chair through them. The wind rushed in, billowing the white curtains toward him. Papers whirled and danced while he just stared out into the darkness with his hair whipping around his handsome face. He looked primal. Fierce.

Lethal.

A statue of a man ready to take on the universe and destroy it.

Thinking about the trackers below, she rushed to the window. She looked out to see five people running toward the building. "They're coming for us," she warned him.

"Let them." His tone was as sinister as his stance.

She stared at him in disbelief. "What?"

Ebony strands of hair whipped around his face, some catching in his whiskers.

When he looked at her, his eyes were brittle obsidian. Bereft. "I don't care what they do. I'm tired of running. Fuck them. Let's fight."

She was aghast. "Well, you picked a fine time for that attitude, buddy. You know, you could have at least consulted me before you turned suicidal. Especially since my life is currently tied to yours. Thanks a lot, asshole." Her heart racing, she glared at him. "Stay here and die, then. I'm at least going to try to live through this."

Syn watched her leave. He tried to tell himself that it was good riddance. Let her find her own way.

But even in his feral and furious state, he knew she wouldn't get far on her own. And for some insane, stupid reason, it mattered to him whether she lived or died.

Let her go.

He couldn't. Too weak to fight his conscience anymore, he chased after her.

Shahara heard her pursuer pulling himself up on the rope next to her. Expecting the worst, she looked down, ready to fight. Instead of a tracker, she saw Syn climbing up behind her.

As he drew even with her, he grabbed her by the waist and swung her over to another balcony.

"What are you doing?"

"Saving our asses." With that, he shot the grappling hook toward the roof. She wrapped her arms and legs around him an instant before they shot upward.

She stared at his stern features. "Thank you for not disappointing me."

His answer was a grunt as he helped her over the lip of the building. Once he was safely beside her, he scanned the rooftop. A strange, throbbing beat echoed around them, shaking the roof under their feet.

Shahara frowned at the noise.

Whatever could it be?

Before she could ask, Syn grabbed her arm savagely and pulled her down to squat behind the building's atmospheric control unit. He shielded her body with his own and, in spite of the danger, she trembled with the familiarity of his body pressing against hers.

Suddenly, a bright light exploded across the rooftop. Her breath caught in her throat and in an instant, she knew the source of the noise.

They had a rover after them.

CHAPTER 14

Harsh bright searchlights crisscrossed the rooftop, turning the darkness almost as light as if it were the middle of the day. It would be only a few minutes before the craft located them.

Her heart sliding into her stomach, she looked up at Syn. "What now?"

"I'm thinking."

"Could you think a little quicker?"

He cast her a dark glare. "You're not helping."

Not helping? She wanted to choke him. "You're lucky you're still breathing and not limping."

Vik swooped down and literally crawled into Syn's pack like it was a mother's cocoon.

Shahara scowled at him. "What are you doing?"

He poked his beak out. "I don't wanna die, man. They're not playing. Have you seen how many of them are out there?" He shivered. "One just took a shot at me, so unlike you morons, I'm hiding. Hiding is nice."

She huffed at him. "You can't die, Vik. You're a mechbot."

He vanished completely into the pack. "They can pull me apart and reprogram me. Trust me, that's death.

"How would I know? I've never been here before."
He latched the door closed behind her by reaching over
her shoulder.

"Then how did you know this was here?"

"I saw the opening and decided this was a better
place to be than on top of the roof, in plain sight." He
pulled out sealant and pushed it into the crevices to keep
the Rits from coming in on top of them.

"So which way do we go?"

He pulled Vik out. The mechbot dangled in his hand
like an angry pet. "Go scout, buddy."

"Screw you, Syn. Really." Turning into a large rat,
Vik scurried off, but not before calling back over his
shoulder. "Bet you're wishing you'd made me bigger . . .
and with weapons."

Ignoring him, Syn, on all fours, headed to the right
at a much slower pace.

She hissed as her back scraped against the tight
walls and bit into her flesh. "You know, I'm getting
really tired of following after you like a lost puppy."

Pausing, he laughed evilly. "Feel free to stop any time
you want to."

She heard clicking sounds across the roof that she
was sure were hundreds of feet. Well, okay, maybe not
hundreds, but it was certainly more people than she
wanted to confront on her own.

Quickening her crawling, she muttered, "I think I'll
wait until after our *friends* go home to cut you loose."

"Here." He placed her hands on each side of his
hips. "Hold on to me and don't worry about where we're
going."

Grateful for his eyesight that didn't need any noticeable light, she did as ordered.

Beneath her hands, Shahara felt the hardness of his body as he led her through the endless, winding duct until she was hopelessly lost. Still, his presence comforted her and gave her hope that they would survive.

It amazed her that she'd given him her trust. Something she'd sworn long ago that she'd never do with anyone outside her family. But then, she'd found herself doing a lot of things with him that she'd sworn she'd never do.

And thank the gods that he had yet to betray her.

At last, he opened a small vent and led them into a rundown, empty office. Cobwebs and debris littered the floor, while off in the darkness, she heard animals scurrying. A foul odor assaulted her nostrils. Pressing her hand to her nose so that she could breathe, she looked at Syn. "What is this place?"

"I think it's the condemned building a few blocks away from my apartment."

That would certainly explain the decaying mess and the lovely dank, moldy odors.

Syn went to look out the windows. The blinds crackled from their brittle state as he spread them open ever so slightly. "I think we lost the ones chasing us from the roof. At least I don't hear them any more."

"Neither do I."

He tapped his ear, and she waited while he listened to whatever Vik reported.

"Pull on your hood." He put his own on his head.

Good idea, she thought as she complied. The Rits would scan the building soon and it would be easy to trace two large targets.

Lights danced around the fogged glass of the office's door.

"They're coming." Syn pulled her away from the glass to keep their pursuers from seeing their shadows.

Once again her heart picked up its heavy staccato rhythm as they pressed themselves flat against the wall. Syn held her plastered there, his arm draped protectively across her breasts. The door creaked open. Her breath caught in her throat as a personal-sized searchlight traveled across the room.

When the man entered, Syn grabbed the arm holding the light, then decked him. The blow had no effect on the tracker. Cursing, Syn shook his hand as if he'd broken it.

The tracker smiled evilly as he grabbed Syn by the throat and slammed him against the wall.

Without thinking, Shahara stepped around Syn and drove her knee into tracker's groin as hard as she could. He let out a loud wail before doubling over. She brought her hands down on either side of his head, against his ears, for a nice percussion blow.

He fell to the floor where she groin-kicked him again, just for good measure.

Syn stood over the tracker. "Bet the next time a guy hits you in front of his girl you'll fall down, won't you?" He bent over and began searching him for something.

The tracker said nothing. He just lay on the ground moaning while holding himself.

Syn straightened and she saw the communicator he'd found. He set his blaster to stun and shot the tracker. He shook his head at her. "Damn, woman, you really *do* need to stop with those groin kicks. You make my cock hurt just looking at him."

"It was more effective than your punch."

"I can't argue with that." He started down the hallway.

As he walked, she noticed the slight limp. "Are you hurt?"

"No," he said in a low voice. "It's sympathy pain for that tracker you downed."

She rolled her eyes. "Yeah, well, I didn't kick *you*."

"Like I said before, your kicks have a way of staying with a man for a long time."

"Quit being a baby and get us out of here."

He grunted. "What do you need me for? I ought to turn you loose and let you kick them down."

Voices crackled over the communicator in a language she couldn't make out. "What are they saying?"

He held his hand up to silence her and listened.

Once the voices stopped, he turned to face her. "They're cordoning off the block. They have two rovers on each side of the building and a group of local enforcers." He rubbed his neck. "I don't mind taking out a tracker or two, but I'd sure hate to kill a local."

"Too bad they don't have the same compunctions about us."

He cocked his head. "I thought you weren't bloodthirsty."

"Let's just say I'm getting sick of people coming after me all the time when . . ."

He stopped and faced her. "When what?"

She clamped her lips together. For the first time, she began to actually feel what he must have felt for years. Abandoned. Alone. Hunted for something he couldn't change, for something he'd done out of necessity.

It was a nasty feeling, and one that had been rammed down his throat. Who was she to complain to him over these last few days?

How had he managed all this time to remain free?

It gave her a whole new respect for him and his abilities.

"How are we going to get past them?" she asked in order to change the subject.

"We're going to get to the first floor and find a quiet place to hide."

"Why?"

"Just trust me."

And with those three little words, she found herself trailing along behind him again.

When he finally found them a place he called "safe," she began to wonder if the night would ever end. He stopped beside a row of old employee lockers.

She raked a doubtful stare over them. "You're not thinking what I think you are . . ."

"We'll fit."

She wasn't so convinced. Reaching out, she touched his hard stomach, then wished she hadn't as a wave of misplaced and definitely mistimed desire hit her. "I don't know, chubby. You're not exactly small."

The sound of feet kept him from responding as he opened one door with only a whisper of noise and wedged himself inside. When she headed for a different unit, he caught her arm and pulled her in on top of him.

She grimaced as he bumped her breast with his elbow and sent a sharp flash of pain through her. "I really wish you'd find us better places to hide."

He said nothing.

Shahara let out an aggravated breath. How the two of them had wedged themselves into the thin metal locker to begin with, she couldn't imagine. It would have probably been okay for one person, but for two, it was a little too tight. Every inch of her body was thrown against his and, as they waited, she began to feel part of him grow.

So he wasn't quite as mad at her as he pretended. She smiled at the thought and realized that for once she didn't mind a tight place.

Syn held his breath, trying his damnedest to ignore the soft mounds of her breasts pressed intimately against his stomach. Her neck was just beneath his lips and that flesh was much more enticing than he wanted it to be. Not to mention her arms, on either side of him, made him long to have her actually hug him.

I am so fucked up . . .

A painful ache set fire to the entire lower half of his anatomy. And for a moment, he didn't care if he got caught so long as he had a taste of her first.

What the hell is wrong with me?

Personal safety and survival had always been his first instinct. But tonight, his instinct was to protect the very woman who threatened him most.

And as those soft, golden eyes looked up at him, he was lost. Her parted lips beckoned him and it was almost impossible to keep from kissing her.

Why couldn't she see him for the man he was and not the past he'd been through? But he was old enough to know better. People betrayed, and sooner or later everyone screwed him over for themselves.

She would be no different.

Yet right now, looking at her trusting face, it was hard to resist doing something he knew would be suicide.

Shahara heard his breathing change and her own instantly followed. She moved her hands to his hips, which were pressed intimately against hers. His entire body jerked. With a wicked smile, she couldn't resist lowering her hand and cupping him. It was bold and she couldn't believe she'd done it, but the look of heat on his face made it all worthwhile.

Licking her suddenly dry lips, she had a terrible urge to reach up and take his hood off and kiss him until he begged for mercy.

Just when she thought she'd give in to her impulse, she heard approaching footsteps.

His entire body went rigid as he pulled her hand away from him.

Shahara held her breath.

"See anything?" It was a woman with a deep contralto.

"No," an older man replied. "Just the same old broken-down stuff. Nothing on the scanner, either."

"I don't know why they're bothering with the first floor. No one but an idiot would try and hide down here. I bet they're up on top trying to find some way to get past the rovers."

"I bet we find them up on the tenth floor."

"Half a week's pay?"

"You're on."

Shahara saw him touch his ear. Vik must have been talking to him, but Syn didn't respond.

Once the pair left, he eased open the door. "Stay here," he whispered before closing her in.

Was he leaving her for them to find?

Don't be stupid. The two of you have come too far for him to leave you now.

Still, she couldn't quite stifle the voice that kept telling her he was taking his chances and leaving her there to face the Rits alone.

Maybe it was just her guilty conscience nagging her.

Suddenly the door flew open. Shahara struck out with one fist.

"Relax," Syn hissed as he ducked her blow. "It's just me." He shoved a uniform into her hands. "Change as fast as you can."

She held the red enforcer's uniform against her chest and scowled at him. "What did you do?"

"Just hurry."

With no thought to modesty, she obeyed. While she pulled her new clothes on, she couldn't resist a quick look to see Syn's bare skin. The full curve of his naked hip and bare derriere.

Syn *never* wore underwear.

Hmmm . . . She'd have to tuck that tidbit away for later . . .

He looked up and caught her gaze with his eyes. "Would you quit wasting time? Get dressed."

Syn snapped his uniform together while he tried to blot out the image of Shahara in her bra and tiny, tiny panties he desperately wanted to pull off with his teeth. His body ached with the memory of her squeezed up against him.

Or better yet, naked in his bed.

What was wrong with him? They were about to be gutted and all he could think about was sex.

He was definitely losing his mind.

But then, if not for her, he'd be in custody right now.

Part of him wished that he were. He really didn't feel like going through this anymore. Every survival impulse he'd ever had had died in his flat.

Who do I bother fighting?

He'd kept so few things from his past. So few were worth keeping. Goddamn those bastards for finding his escape pack. It was pathetic, really, that everything he valued in his life fit in such a small space, but it had.

And now it was all gone.

Every piece. There was nothing left of the tattered remains of his past. Not one tiny memento. There was nothing to ever say that he'd even existed.

So why bother?

One look at Shahara and he knew why. She had people who depended on her. She still wanted to live. He'd dragged her here and he would see her to safety.

One way or another.

"You ready?"

Shahara nodded. She smiled as she realized his uniform didn't quite fit. "What if someone sees you?" She pulled at the extra fabric hanging over his stomach.

"They won't be paying attention to us. They're looking for someone out of uniform."

Not sure if she bought his argument, she folded up her clothes. "What are we doing with our gear?"

"Tuck your clothes into the pack and hold it down to your side and to the back."

She frowned. "Won't they see it?"

"Not if we're lucky."

"You have a lot of faith in luck, don't you?"

"Not at all. She's a vicious bitch who seldom knocks on my door." His voice was frigid. "I have a lot of faith in people's inability to see what's right before their noses. Now come on."

As she followed him out of the room, she thought about his words. He was right. All these years, people had searched for him and he'd been living in the middle of a major city, running a major company. It said a lot about being able to hide in plain sight.

He was simply amazing.

Syn kept a tight grip on his pack as he led her through the hallways that were crawling with armed enforcers and trackers who scoured the area for them.

Vik was already outside the building. "It's scary out here, boss. They're hot for your ass in the worst sort of way."

He would have responded, but didn't dare in case they were using a scanner to ID his voice. They'd been relatively safe inside the metal lockers that shielded them, but now that they were out in the open, it was a new set of rules.

"Hey! I think we found them."

A group of enforcers ran past them, to whatever someone had thought they found. Two trackers dressed in brown ran past with a third one coming up with a slow, deadly swagger.

There was something about the last one that stood out, and it wasn't because he was dressed all in black with spiked vambraces and custom blasters. He, like Syn, was alert to things the others missed. This wasn't some run-of-the-mill tracker or low-IQ enforcer.

He was a predator.

Syn tipped his head down as the tracker went past. But his attention was so focused on the one he needed to be wary of that he missed the next one who slammed into him.

Shit . . .

The tracker stopped and eyed him intently. Recognition registered.

Syn dropped his pack and punched him hard.

"They're here," the tracker snarled into his link as he returned the blow.

Syn cursed as they became the focal point of every person there. "Run," he shouted to Shahara.

To his shock, she didn't. She pulled out her blaster and shot the tracker.

Targeting lasers danced all around them as the trackers and enforcers swung on them. Syn ducked the fire, slung his pack over his shoulder, and pushed her forward as he pulled out a smoke bomb and threw it.

Shahara repeated the gesture, tossing hers in the opposite direction. Shots flared all over, some narrowly missing them.

Acting on pure instinct, she grabbed Syn's arm and pulled him toward an alcove.

Syn followed her, then realized they were completely trapped. Cursing, he looked at her and saw the fear deep in her eyes.

"We're not going to make it, are we?"

"Yeah, we will. It'll take more than these bastards to bring me low."

But before he could make good on that, a shadow fell over him.

It was the predator he'd seen, and he had his sights trained right between Syn's eyes.

CHAPTER 15

Shahara couldn't breathe as she waited for the final shot that would end their lives.

It didn't come.

The tracker scowled at them—something that was truly eerie given the black eyeliner that emphasized his merciless steel-gray eyes. "Wade?"

Syn returned the expression. "Scalera?"

A slow smile spread across the tracker's handsome face. The dot vanished off Syn's forehead. Scalera shook his head. "Leave it to you to be neck deep in this shit."

"Fuck you."

Shahara had no idea what was going on, but as more soldiers headed for them, Scalera shielded them with cover fire.

"Go, Wade."

Syn didn't hesitate as he took her arm and obeyed, all the while shooting at anything that moved.

"This is suicide." Shahara aimed at her own targets.

But as they ran, she realized that Scalera was Trisani—and a powerful one at that as he threw their attackers to the ground with nothing more than a hand gesture and used his telekinesis to cover them. He caused some of the trackers to fire on each other, while he slammed others into the walls, transports, and other objects.

Man, to have those powers for five seconds . . .

As they started for their shuttle, Scalera teleported to cut off their escape and stop them. His ankle-length black leather coat rippled around his body with fluid grace. "Your ride's compromised." He jerked his chin to their left. "Head to Bay Eight. We can commandeer another one."

Syn looked as doubtful as she felt, but he did as Scalera suggested. When a guard moved to confront them, Scalera held his hand out and threw him to the ground.

They kept moving until Syn stopped next to a green ship. "Vik? You better get here now." He pushed the controls to extend the ramp while she and Scalera covered his back with drawn weapons.

Vik flew in over their heads. "They're getting reinforcements. You bonebags better tel-ass or lose them."

Syn ran in first with her and Scalera coming in behind him. Scalera retracted the ramp while Syn went to the bridge to start the launch sequence.

Still not sure if they should trust Scalera, she went to help Syn.

She took the navigator's seat while he fired the engines and ran a preliminary check.

"Nero," he said into the intercom, "I need a cover blast at four o'clock and you better use your powers to open the bay's door or this is going to be a fatally short ride."

Shahara watched as the bay doors stretched open slowly. It was obvious they were locked down and fighting Scalera's efforts. Syn didn't wait for them to open. He put the throttle down and gunned the engines.

The ship lurched forward at a velocity that plastered her against her seat. Unlike her, the ship had no idea they were about to impact with that wall and burst into flames.

Syn's gaze narrowed with a deranged glint. "Do or die, baby. Do or die."

Her heart hit the floor as she realized they really were going to slam into the closed doors. Nothing was moving.

This was it . . .

Bracing herself, she prayed.

Syn didn't slow even a bit. He went forward without hesitation.

She bit back a scream.

Just as they reached the doors, they snapped open with only the lower section scraping against the bottom of the ship. The sound of steel on steel was painful but at least it wasn't fatal as they popped through and soared into the atmosphere.

She leaned her head back and took a deep breath in relief. "I seriously hate you, convict."

Vik snorted. "I just oiled myself, boss."

Syn gave them both a droll glare. "Stop your bitching. We made it." Then under his breath, he added, "Granted it was by our short hairs, but I haven't killed us yet."

Scalera joined them, his face white as he collapsed into the gunner's chair.

Syn glanced over at him. "You all right?"

He nodded weakly as he breathed in ragged gasps.

The one bad thing about Trisani was that the use of their psychic powers also drained them physically. If they overused it, it could cause them to lapse into a coma, have brain damage, or die.

His dark blond hair was streaked with black in a becoming tousled mess that fell around an angelicly perfect face. Every feature appeared to have been chiseled by a master artist and yet there was nothing pretty about him. He held a raw masculine grace that was ruthless and angry.

Stubble marked his face, adding an even more rugged air to him. It was obvious he lived the same way Syn did.

By his wits, strength, and brutality.

Nero draped one long arm over the chair and rested his hand next to Syn's shoulder. "I have to be a raging idiot to cover your ass, Sher. Damn, why did it have to be you?"

"Just lucky, I guess."

Nero made a mocking sound. "When did you change your name, anyway?"

"A while back." Syn set their course and introduced them without looking at them. "Shahara Dagan, meet Nero Scalera. Nero, Shahara."

One finely arched brow shot up. "As in Seax Dagan?"

Syn banked and shot them into hyperdrive. "One and the same."

He sucked his breath in sharply. "I'm impressed. Didn't know seaxes hung out with people like us."

Syn snorted. "Everyone slums eventually."

Unamused by Syn's words, Shahara had to give Nero credit—he was recovering well from the power expenditure that had left him ragged a few minutes ago. "How do you two know each other?"

Nero inclined his head to Syn. "Little bastard saved my life."

"When?"

Syn answered as he programmed the autopilot. "He was in prison with me."

That was interesting. "The first or second time?"

Nero gave him an arch stare. "You went back?"

"Not by choice."

He let out a low whistle. "Damn, Wade. You were always an unlucky bastard."

Syn shot her a sullen glance. "Tell me about it."

"So what happened?"

"Got busted hacking, what else? I was a stupid kid trying to eat." Syn swung his chair around to face him. "What about you? How did you end up working for the enemy?"

"Like you said—gotta eat and I grew tired of clients trying to rip me off, or worse, kill me."

Syn gave him a mocking salute. "Tell me about it. My current situation was caused by a fucking client trying to screw me over when all I did was save his daughter's life."

Nero wiped his gloved hand over his chin as he cracked a charming grin. "People suck."

Syn's gaze went to her, but he didn't say anything. He pushed himself up from the chair and went to check on Nero. He pulled out a light and shined it into Nero's eyes to test the dilation. "You burn anything out?"

He shook his head and moved out of Syn's grasp. "Not even a nosebleed. I'm good."

"Cool. Can you take the helm while I go clean up?"

Nero scowled. "What? You piss your pants or something?"

"Definitely something. I just need a little time alone to regroup."

Something passed between them that Shahara couldn't read.

Nero stood up. "Sure. I got it. Take your time."

Syn didn't even look back at her as he left her alone with Nero, who moved to take the captain's seat.

She watched as Vik shifted into his mechbot form and plugged into the computer. He didn't say anything as he settled down into what looked like a nap.

"You and Syn seem really tight," she said to Nero as he checked their readings.

"We were."

"What happened?"

He turned in the chair to face her. "Nothing, really. We were both being hunted, so we split up to have a better chance at survival. He went his way. I went mine."

She had a feeling there was more to it than that, but Nero didn't seem to want to elaborate. "How old were you when you were in prison with him?"

"Nineteen."

She arched her brows at his age. That would make him almost ten years older than Syn, yet she would have guessed he was no older than his mid-twenties. "You don't look that old."

He shrugged. "Trisani don't age like other races. One of our better gifts."

Definitely. She wouldn't mind having that gene herself. "And what did you do to go to prison?"

Something dark passed over his face. The electronics around him popped and hissed as if he had a power

spike that rattled them. "I'm a full-blooded male Trisani who survived infancy. Any idea what people do
to us?"

Trisani males were even more powerful than the
females. The only problem was that their powers had a
bad tendency to kill them before they were old enough
to master them. If that wasn't bad enough, because of
their abilities, their entire race had been hunted to the
brink of extinction. Other cultures and beings either
feared them for what they could do or wanted to har-
ness and use their powers for themselves.

Even though the Trisani were a peaceful race, their
entire history had been one of bloodshed and brutality.

"You were enslaved?"

A tic started in his jaw. "I was sold to the warden
when I was five—after my parents and sister had been
slaughtered. He kept me in prison so that he could use
my powers for his own advantage. I didn't belong there
any more than Syn did."

And it was then she remembered something he'd al-
luded to with Syn. "So how long have you been hiding
your powers from others?"

"Long enough to remain free and not have to run
every other day. I only use them when I have to."

Yet he'd used them tonight . . . Not for his own survival.

For theirs.

And the most miraculous part about that was the
fact that he didn't strike her as particularly altruistic.
"Why did you expose yourself to save us?"

He cast his gaze in the direction Syn had taken when
he left them. "Sheridan could have escaped prison on
his own, but he refused to leave me to what they were
doing to me." He winced as if the pain was more than

he could bear. "You have no idea what that kid did to free me. But I know, and it's a debt I'll never be able to repay."

There was a strange catch in his voice. "What?"

A tic started again in his jaw as shame darkened his eyes. "He sold the only thing he could."

She frowned. "His skills?"

"Yeah."

Gasping, she realized what he meant. Syn hadn't sold his computer skills . . .

He'd sold himself to get them free. Horror filled her. "Why would he have done that?"

"Hell if I know. It damn near cost him his life to get me out. And to be honest, if it'd been anyone other than him, I'd still be in that prison rather than escape."

"How do you mean?"

"I'm Trisani. The only thing worse than a warden keeping me drugged and using me against my will is a criminal. I knew Sheridan would actually free me once we were loose. True to his word, he set me free and never tried to come back to use me. There's not much I wouldn't do for him."

She felt the same way. "He's a good man."

"Yeah, and that's a rare thing in this world." Nero indicated the door with a jerk of his chin. "By the way, he's seriously torn up right now. I don't know what you are to him, but if you have any feelings where he's concerned, you might want to check on him."

"He said he wanted to be alone."

Nero gave a light, mocking laugh. "A lot of people say that when they don't mean it. He's emotionally hurting worse than I've ever seen him, and believe me, I've seen him hurt. There's something inside him tearing his guts out and while I can sense the pain, I can't pinpoint the cause."

Concerned about him, Shahara got up to search for Syn. It took a few minutes to locate him in the crew's rest area.

She froze as she saw him wearing nothing but a damp towel twisted at his lean waist. His hair was wet as if he'd taken a quick shower. But it was the wound on his shoulder that concerned her most.

"You got shot?"

He didn't bother looking at her while he tended it. "A couple of burns. I'll live."

How could he be so blasè? And how had she missed seeing that he was hurt while they escaped?

Her heart heavy, she closed the distance between them. He started to move away, but she took his arm and kept him by her side.

"What happened at your apartment?"

He gave her a droll stare. "What? You blind? It was torn apart."

Shahara had to stifle a smart comeback to that. But the one thing she knew about him was that he used sarcasm as a defense and a cover for his real feelings. "No, not that. You were searching for something. What was it?"

Syn was completely unprepared for the wave of emotion that ripped through him over her simple question. It tore a hole straight through his heart and left it ragged and bleeding.

Something he would never share with someone else. "Nothing." He stepped around her.

But she was relentless in her pursuit. "Don't lie to me. I know better. They took something extremely valuable to you." She pulled a small handful of tattered bits from her pocket and handed it to him. "I found this in the debris."

Grief choked him as he saw Talia's bruised face staring at him. That one expression took him straight back to his childhood. Back to the horror and pain that had battered him every day of his life.

His hand shook as he reached for this last tie to the sister who had meant the world to him. "I tried to save her, you know."

Shahara heard the pain in his voice and it cut through her soul. "What happened to her wasn't your fault."

Syn didn't believe that for a second. "If I had gotten home sooner . . . I was supposed to come straight back . . ." He paused as he fought down his tears. "But I didn't. I stopped in a park and . . . I was so stupid and selfish. I just wanted to have a few minutes where no one was yelling at me or hitting me. A few minutes to sit in the sun and feel like I was normal. Gah, I'm such a fucking idiot. Had I just gone home . . ."

Shahara pulled him into her arms and held him close. How could he call *that* selfish? A child shouldn't have to feel so much pain.

And neither should this man. He who gave so much to others. He put the world first. Too bad no one had ever done that for him.

If only she could take away his pain.

Syn let the softness of her skin soothe him even as his bitter memories surged.

"You were just a kid."

He shook his head in denial as her thumb stroked his cheek, sending waves of pleasure through him in spite of the pain that ravaged him. "I was never a child any more than you were. She was my responsibility and while I sat on a bench, watching a group of kids play ball, she was slicing open her wrists." He felt his tears well as he remembered that day so clearly.

Why did you leave me, Talia . . .

In a life marked by betrayals, hers stung the deepest.

Closing his eyes, he inhaled the scent of Shahara's skin. But not even that could soothe him. "I stole a flower from the park and took it home to her, hoping it would make her smile. When I opened the door to give it to her, she was on the bed, covered in blood."

Everything had gone black and white in his vision as he saw her lying awkwardly on the bed, except for the bright red blood that haunted him to this day. It stood out starkly against the other colors.

Dropping the daisy to the floor, he'd screamed out, "No!" A cry of agony that had come straight from the deepest, darkest part of his young being as he ran to the bed to try and wake her.

But he'd known it was useless.

She'd left him alone in a world that hated him as much as it had hated her.

He'd slipped on her blood that had soaked the floor and had crawled on his hands and knees while he sobbed, begging her to live. Begging her to open her eyes and tell him he wasn't so bad. Sobbing and desperate, he'd taken her cold hand and held it to his face. "Why would you leave me, Talia? Why?" But in his heart he'd known the answer.

It was the same reason Mara had left him.

He wasn't good enough.

Now Shahara held him close as he tightened his grip on her. "It's all right, Syn. I have you."

He didn't believe that. No one had him or wanted him. They never had. He pulled back from her and handed her the photo remains. "Thanks for finding this, but it's not what I was looking for."

"Then tell me. Maybe I saw it. Talk to me, Syn. Please."

Syn wanted to tell her to go to hell. But she reached out and cupped his cheek in her hand. It was such a tender touch. No one had ever comforted him like this.

Not even Mara.

And he was helpless before it. Before he could stop himself, he answered. "It was a note."

She frowned at him. "A note?"

Syn closed his eyes as more agony ripped him apart. Even now he could see Paden's bright, happy face as his son had run to greet him when he came home from work the night before the reporter had ruined his perfect lie of a life. He'd scooped the boy up and laughed as he hugged him close, grateful to have such a pure, untainted love to call his own.

Paden had bounced in his arms. *"Daddy! Daddy! Look what I made!"* He'd stuck a piece of paper in his face so close that at first all Syn could see was a bright blue color.

Laughing, he'd kissed his son's cheek and pulled the drawing back until it came into focus. It was the two of them standing in the hospital with a rainbow over their heads. And in the rainbow, Paden had scrawled the words: *I lov you, Dedy.*

Nothing had ever meant more to him than those precious words that had been written from his son's heart. That one moment of pure joy, knowing that after all he'd been through, he had one person alive who really loved him. One person who saw him as he wanted to be.

He could still feel those tiny arms around his neck as Paden kissed his cheek and laid his head on his shoulder.

A perfect, untainted moment . . .

Gods, to have that back for a single second . . .

But it was gone, along with the love and respect Paden had had for him.

"Get away from me, you lying bastard. I don't want anything from you. Thank the gods you're not my real father. You disgust me. I never want to see you again." Those were the last words Paden had said to him.

But not even those harsh words could erase that one precious memory . . . or that drawing that he'd kept all these years in a watertight container sewn into his backpack.

His last memento of the life he'd wanted so desperately to live. A life he'd fought so hard for and one he missed every single second of the solitary hell he was now living.

Somehow they'd found it, and it was as gone as his son's love.

I should have never kept it.

"Syn?"

He stared into a pair of golden eyes that even now looked at him suspiciously. Couldn't one person ever see *him*? "It was just a stupid note, Shahara. Nothing more."

Shahara didn't believe him. There was too much pain in his eyes. She brushed his hair back from his forehead and even without him telling her, she knew what it had to be. Only one thing could have shredded him like this.

"It was from Paden, wasn't it?"

He pulled away from her.

"Talk to me, Syn."

"I'm not a woman, Shahara. Yes, it was from Paden. Now can we leave it alone?" He moved to pick up his clothes.

Her entire being ached at the knowledge of his tender soul that had been pulverized by everyone around him. And what had he treasured most?

A note written by a child he'd loved. One he continued to love and care for even while the child spurned him.

It was so unfair.

How could anyone ever leave him? What kind of fool had Mara been that she could shove away a man capable of such love and devotion even when she didn't deserve it?

And in that instant, she realized the most frightening thing of all.

She loved him. This man, this stranger, had infiltrated not only her heart, but her very soul. The more she learned of him, the more she cared. The more she wanted to soothe him . . .

Life had dealt him the worst possible hand and still he'd survived without losing his decency. She didn't know how he'd managed to keep what so many others, including herself, had lost.

But then, he was one of a kind and that was what she loved most.

Not since childhood had she ever allowed herself to think of the future, to hope for someone to call her own. She'd given up all hope of ever loving someone outside her siblings. Of caring so much about them that she'd lay down her life to keep them safe.

Now she did.

She wanted Syn. She wanted to spend every single

moment with him and him alone. There was no way to change his past, but she could make sure that he'd have no more lonely holidays. That his future included someone he could talk to, someone he could trust.

And that person would be her.

He deserves better than you. It was so true, but those better than her didn't see the beauty that was his battered heart. They didn't appreciate what a rarity he was.

Most of all, they couldn't protect him from a world that was hostile and cold. But she could make sure no one hurt him anymore.

Ever.

You have an oath to uphold. He's a wanted criminal. Even without Merjack's and Zamir's warrants, he was still under indictment from thirty-five other systems.

Being with him would cost her everything.

No, that wasn't true. Not everything, because being with*out* him would cost her her heart.

Doing something she'd never done before, she threw her common sense aside and kissed him. To hell with her oath of office. None of that mattered to her anymore.

Only he did. And she would see to it that no one ever hurt him again.

Syn's mind whirled at the unexpected contact. Her lips were as light as a feather as they tugged against his. Instinctively, he held her against him, pulling her closer until her breasts were pressed flat against him.

She tasted so good, felt even better. All he wanted was to spend the rest of his life holding her like this. But that could never be. Fate had conspired against him from the moment of his conception and, the way things were going, it wasn't about to give him a break for anything.

Still, he had this one moment. This instant to call his own. How could he turn away?

He pulled back from her lips and stared into her passion-darkened eyes. Her hungry look took his breath away. There was no accusation there. No restraint.

It was open and inviting.

How could she want him after she'd learned so much about him? It was amazing. Never in his life had he made love to a woman who knew much of anything about him. And none of them had ever known his past, his *true* identity.

But Shahara did. She knew the horrors and the scars that had been left behind. It made him feel vulnerable and afraid.

She ran her hands over his bare skin. Chills spread down his back and arms as she gently rubbed the muscles of his chest.

With a wicked smile, she leaned forward and suckled the hollow of his throat.

Growling with pleasure, he tensed as his body erupted in flames. Gone were all thoughts of anything except the pure joy of her hot lips on his throat—of her hands soothing him.

Shahara felt a moment of shyness as he removed her top, but it vanished the moment he kissed her. His hands gave her pleasure everywhere they touched, her arms, her breasts, and the throbbing ache between her legs.

She pulled at his towel, needing to feel him inside her again. It fell in a puddle at their feet.

With her own insatiable hunger, she tugged at his lips with her teeth, wanting to devour him.

"I need you, Syn," she whispered softly. She wanted to tell him that she loved him, but he wouldn't accept that from her. He was too jaded to believe in something as easy and paltry as words. It was something she'd have to show to a man like him.

He sank to the floor with her before he removed the rest of her clothes. Shahara bit her lip, amazed that she still had no fear of him. Amazed that she welcomed his touch when she'd never been so easy with anyone else.

Syn soothed her. He silenced her doubts and her insecurities. With him, she was finally whole. She was the woman she'd always wanted to be. One who could be touched without fear. Most of all, she could rely on him. When everything was falling apart, when enemies had her cornered, he stood by her side to protect and help her.

Her eyes misting, she touched his newest wound on his shoulder. A wound he'd taken for her . . .

He was all she'd ever wanted, wrapped up in a package that should offend her to the core of her being.

But that was Syn. Ever full of surprises. Ever full of strength and integrity.

Most of all, loyalty.

Reaching up, she pulled his lips back to hers.

Syn trembled at the wave of emotions her simple kiss evoked. Gods, how he wanted to believe in her, but how could he? He'd been wounded so many times by those he trusted.

Would she be any different?

I don't have another fresh start in me. He'd had to start over one time too many. He was tired now. Soul-weary.

But as he looked into those eyes that seared him, his heart wouldn't listen. It wanted to believe in her and it wasn't listening to reason.

"Hold me," he breathed in her ear. She wrapped her arms around him and he closed his eyes to savor the feeling.

One perfect moment.

Lying naked on the floor with her breath tickling his neck, with her arms holding him against her body. This was heaven.

If only it could last.

She cupped his cheek in her hand and smiled at him. "I won't hurt you, Syn. I'm not like the others. I will stand by you. Forever."

Sure you will. But he bit back his sarcasm. It was a defense mechanism and he didn't want to hurt her. In this one instant, she meant what she said.

Whether or not she meant it in the future remained to be seen. For now, he would take it and be grateful that she at least felt it today.

Kissing her lips, he separated her thighs with his knees and slid slowly inside her warmth.

Shahara threw her head back and groaned as the sweetest pleasure assailed her. Never in her life had she experienced anything so wonderful. The weight of his body bearing down on hers, the feel of him moving against her. His body filling hers.

She wanted to scream out her love, but fear of his reaction kept the words inside her. It was too soon to tell him something he would only reject.

No, she would keep her secret for the time being, but soon she would tell him.

Syn buried his face against her neck and inhaled the sweet feminine scent of her body. With her arms and legs wrapped around him, he knew what true peace was. Gone were his demons and doubts, and in their place were emotions he couldn't even begin to define.

She moaned with each thrust of his body, fanning the flames inside him even higher.

Suddenly, her grip tightened and she screamed out in pleasure. Syn gave a deep throaty laugh at her reaction as he joined her in paradise.

His body satisfied, Syn didn't want to move. He wanted to stay within her for the rest of eternity.

If only he could.

"Syn? You're crushing me."

Pouting, he looked down at her. "I don't want to move."

A smile spread across her face. "And I kind of like you where you are. But you weigh about a ton and a half and this floor is really hard."

He snorted. "Excuse me, I take great exception to that. I only weigh a ton." He rolled to his side and pulled her on top of him where he could see the sparkle of her eyes as she watched him.

Shahara marveled at his handsomeness. And once again she wondered how his wife could have possibly left a man like him. What had the woman been thinking?

With that came another terrifying thought. How much had his wife meant to him?

Had he loved her as much as her father had loved her mother? Even after her mother's death, her father had never looked at another woman. He'd once told her that the gods had only made one real woman and he'd been the only man lucky enough to find her.

"Did you love your wife?" she blurted out before she could stop herself.

"No."

She frowned at his lack of hesitation and the certainty in his voice. "Then why did you marry her?"

"I was in love with the *idea* of her."

"I don't understand."

Sighing, he lifted up a handful of her hair and twisted it between his fingers. "I'd just completed my residency when she entered the emergency room with a friend of hers who'd been injured at work."

"What kind of work?"

"Does it matter?"

"I'd like to know."

He brushed her hair against his lips before he answered. "She worked in an art gallery and her friend had been injured moving some paintings around. She'd cut herself so badly she needed surgery."

"Is that why you're so interested in art? Because of your wife?"

"Not because of her. She merely exposed me to it and taught me about it. Since I'd never been around anything beautiful in my life, I liked spending time in galleries. After she left, it was the only thing I kept. Again, not because of her, but because I wouldn't let her take that from me, too. Everything I'd ever enjoyed had been spoiled by some selfish asshole. The bitch robbed me of enough. I refused to let her sully the one thing I found comfort in."

Shahara respected that. It took a strong person to keep others from ruining things that gave them pleasure.

And it made her wonder about the day they'd met. Syn must have met a lot of women as a doctor. "What made you ask her out?"

His eyes turned strangely dreamy. "She looked so pure and frail. Completely feminine and soft. I'd never known anyone like that before. All the women I'd been around were tough and sarcastic. The kind who'd slap a man before she kissed him."

Just like me.

Shahara's insides shrank at his words.

"But not her," he continued. "She was so sheltered and unjaded. I knew in an instant that she'd never had a moment of fear or hunger. No demons haunted her. She had a past that I envied. And I thought that maybe, if I spent some time with her, maybe I could pretend I'd had a different past, too."

"And she loved you." Shahara's voice caught on the last words.

"No. She wanted the prestige of being married to a doctor. For some reason I never understood, she was embarrassed by her parents and their *lowly* pleb status. Her father was a salesman and her mother a computer tech." He laughed bitterly. "Ironic, huh? I would have killed to have parents like hers and she wanted nothing more than to forget they existed because she wanted better."

Though his voice was flat, she couldn't shake the feeling that he still cared for his ex-wife. His eyes had belied his indifference while he described her.

"How long were you married?"

"Six *long* years."

Nonplussed, she lifted herself up on one elbow to look down at him. "If they were so miserable, why did you stay?"

"Because she was respectable. Our life together was respectable and that was all *I'd* ever wanted. So what if she was the most pretentious woman alive? At least she was a lady. In public, she was the most gracious, enchanting woman you could imagine. She knew every tiny piece of etiquette. Hell, she even knew which piece of cutlery went with what dish."

Unlike me. Shahara's heart broke with the knowledge. Whether he admitted it or not, Syn still craved that life. She could see it in his eyes. Hear it in his voice.

She would never be that type of woman. They both knew that.

He could never be happy with her.

She wanted to die. How could she have been so foolish not to see it before?

He frowned at her. "What's wrong?"

"Nothing." She cleared her throat and changed the subject. "Do you ever wish you could go back?"

"No. Not to her. I wish I could be a legitimate doctor again. And I would sell my soul to have my son's love back. But the rest . . . What the hell, I guess. I've sold myself for a lot less over the years."

Shahara raised up to look down at him. "Mara was a fool, Syn. If she couldn't see all the wonderful things you are, she definitely doesn't deserve you and I'm glad you're rid of her."

Syn's breath caught at the conviction he heard in her voice. For a minute, he could almost believe her.

And when she lowered her lips to his, he could almost believe in miracles again.

Don't be stupid.

Dreams were for fools, and honest, decent women like her didn't involve themselves with trash like him. Not for long, anyway.

Unwilling to lie to himself anymore, he pulled back and sighed. "We need to get cleaned up. It won't be long before we reach Ritadaria."

"You think we're going to find that chip?"

"No. I personally think we're going to die."

CHAPTER 16

Syn hissed as Shahara nipped his chin with her teeth. Hard. "That. Hurt."

"Be grateful I showed restraint after that last comment, buddy." But there was fear in her eyes as she looked at him. "Just out of curiosity, where did you leave the chip when you hid it all those years ago?"

He rubbed his hand over his chin in an effort to dispel some of the pain she'd given him. "In an office down the hallway from Merjack's."

She gaped at him. "You what?"

He shrugged. "I told you, I was a scared kid. I only had a few seconds to stash it before they took me. I figured it was the safest place."

Shahara was flabbergasted by the news. What an act of supreme stupidity. "You don't honestly think the chip's still there?"

"Don't know. It's been a couple of decades since I dumped it. Let's hope for a miracle."

A miracle? A flippin', farkin' miracle?

Was he insane?

"You're on drugs, aren't you? Go ahead and admit it."

He snorted. "I haven't done drugs since I was in my teens and Nykyrian threatened my life if I ever used again. Bad thing about having an assassin as a friend. When he makes a threat against your life, you know it's not one. He means it."

She didn't find his dry humor amusing in the least. Not when their lives were hinging on a miracle. "And where in the office did you dump it?"

"I secured it to a piece of statuary."

Oh, it just got better and better. Her stomach hit the floor as she stared at him in contemptuous disbelief. They were so wasting their time. The odds of that person still being there . . .

Of the statue still being there . . .

She might as well shoot herself now and save the Rits the cost of the blaster charge. "Do you at least know whose office?"

"No. That's why I made the map."

She ground her teeth. "I'm going to kill you. Why are we even bothering? Do you know what the odds are that it's still there?"

"I don't play the odds, love. Never have."

She rolled her eyes and wanted to beat him until he bled . . . more. "And if the statue's gone?"

"We're screwed."

She let out a long, irritated breath. "That's what I like about you, convict. You always keep things interesting." Meeting his gaze again, she frowned. "How did you get the map, anyway?"

"I drew it once I escaped jail."

"Then I was right—you did intend to one day clear your name."

A strange look crossed his face an instant before he rolled over and got up.

"Why did you wait, Syn?"

He growled as if aggravated by her interrogation. "Things came up. I didn't have the time nor the inclination."

Her frown deepened. That didn't make any sense. The Syn she'd grown to know wouldn't have been so lackadaisical about his freedom. "Like what?"

Syn sighed as he remembered all the reasons he'd made for not exposing Merjack. In the end, it came down to one thing—who would ever believe the son of Idirian Wade accusing the man who was credited with bringing down his father? Sheridan Wade was filthy trash, and if his stints in prison had ever taught him anything, it was that people like him got screwed while people like Merjack screwed everyone else and got away with it.

Had he even tried to clear his name, he would have probably been executed for it. The way the media skewed things, they'd have called it a vendetta accusation and crucified him over it. The only reason he was trying to set the record straight now was that Shahara's sterling reputation as a seax might negate the stigma.

Maybe.

But he didn't want to share that with her. She would dismiss it and call him paranoid—because in her world, honesty prevailed. In his world, it got people killed.

"Forget it."

Shahara wanted to curse. His tone told her that it'd be wise to heed him. This time, anyway.

Still, the mystery tantalized her.

How she wanted to understand his reasoning. What would have caused him to continue running when all he had to do was turn the chip over to the authorities?

That had to be simpler than living with all the people who'd been sent to track him down over the years.

Maybe she didn't know him so well after all.

Once they were showered and dressed, they joined Vik and Nero on the bridge. Nero didn't say a word, but Shahara had a feeling he knew exactly what they'd done.

"We're coming up on Ritadaria," he told Syn. "Bet you never thought you'd be back here."

"Not alive, anyway. What about you?"

"As a tracer and tracker, I bill them, but it doesn't mean I like it here any more than you do. I try to avoid coming to the planet as much as I can."

Shahara frowned. "Aren't you afraid they'll arrest you?"

Nero snorted. "I wasn't a convict, Dagan. I was an illegally purchased slave. My *owner*"—he sneered the term—"has no legal claim on me. And I'm no longer a kid learning my powers. I'm a full-grown man with an ax I want to bury in the forehead of anyone dumb enough to come at me. I defy the bastards to try something now."

A chill went down her spine as she realized he was every bit the predator Syn was. And she never wanted to be on the bad side of either man.

Syn took the copilot chair to help guide them in. "Any of the people you work for know what you are?"

"Nope. I kill anyone who learns."

"Good."

Yeah, but not for the ones they killed. Shahara made her way to her seat. Vik, back in his bird form, came over to sit by her.

"What are you doing?" she asked him.

"I'm hanging with you 'cause you seem to be a little more sane."

Syn made a sound of irritation. "Traitor."

"Lunatic," Vik shot back.

Shahara laughed as she put Vik in her lap in preparation of their landing. "It's all right, sweetie. I've got you."

He manifested two arms to give her a hug.

She had no idea why, but his actions touched her. "Thank you, Vik. I needed that."

He walked himself up to sit in the chair beside her before he laid his head on her thigh.

A few minutes later, they docked in the main city on Ritadaria in broad daylight. Syn cursed their luck as he locked down the ship's systems.

She scanned the security that was milling around the bay. "Do you think Merjack's trackers are here?"

Syn shook his head. "Probably not. The prison's on another continent. But considering how well known my father was and how many people still remember him, it'd be easy for someone to ID me based on looks alone—which was how that fucking reporter found me. Her father was being treated in my hospital when she saw me in the hallway. She put two and two together and then came at me. I'd *hate* for that to happen again."

Her, too.

Looking at their *borrowed* uniforms that didn't really fit, she smirked. "And we're not really dressed to blend in here."

He gave a short laugh. "No, we're not. People will definitely notice us."

Nero crossed his arms over his chest. "I can shield you to a safe zone. No one would see you at all."

Syn hesitated at Nero's offer. "How much drain will it cost you?"

"If you don't go far, it won't be bad."

Shahara glanced out the windows at the milling bay

attendants and passersby. As a large port, it was incredibly busy. Aliens and humans bustled about, trying to either board a ship or disembark for the city. There were a large number of customs officials and security guards, baggage handlers and hawkers.

She didn't like the sight of this at all.

"Should we stay on board until dark?"

Syn shook his head. "Too suspicious. We'll have to leave and find a nice cubbyhole until dark."

Not another *cubbyhole*. She'd had just about enough of his questionable *safe* places. "Can I put in a suggestion?"

The men turned to face her with raised brows.

Shahara lifted her hands and started counting off her demands. "Let's find someplace where there aren't *any* dead people, insects, or rodents. For that matter, someplace that's big enough to accommodate both of us without crimping any internal organs."

Syn scoffed. "Picky, picky, picky. If you think it's so easy, why don't you come up with a place to hide?"

"Fine with me."

He grinned. "All right, then, you lead the way."

Nero stood up. "You want cover?"

Syn looked at her before he answered. "Yeah, if you don't mind. Let's play it safe. I'm not in the mood to run right now and I know fighting is suicide. Last thing I want to do is make my enemies happy by dying."

She lifted her pack from the floor. "Are you staying with us?" she asked Nero.

"Just till I get you two parked, then I'm out."

She was a bit surprised by that, but Syn seemed to expect it.

"We've got to get out of here soon or the locals will want to know what the holdup is." Syn took Vik out of the pack. "All right, buddy. I need you on the street to scout. You see the grays coming at us, let me know."

"Yeah, that's nice. Put the poor bot out in the cold to look for local enforcers. You suck, boss." Vik turned into a bird.

Laughing at his surliness, Shahara led the way to the door. Nero and Syn followed after her. She looked back over her shoulder and had a chill go down her spine at their collective intensity. It wasn't often a woman saw one, never mind two men so gorgeous, but their combined auras of raw masculine power was truly impressive.

"So how does this shield thing work?" she asked Nero.

"They'll see you, but no one will pay attention to you. It's like a reflection or an inhibitor. Their focus will be on anything other than the two of you. You'll blend right into the background."

"That's a nice power to have."

"Yes, it is."

She pressed the controls to lower the ramp. "All right, Syn. One cubbyhole coming up. Just remember you have to bear my choice with the same grace and even-tempered temerity I've shown with yours."

He snorted. "Good. I get to whine and bitch. Can't wait."

Shaking her head at him, she left the ship first. Vik took flight and quickly left them behind.

Once they were outside the landing bay and standing on the street, she realized what Syn had meant about daylight. Though it was around noon, it looked more like dusk. She started to suggest they go ahead to the office building until she realized how many people lived and worked here. It literally looked like a sea of bodies.

No doubt the building would be crammed full of

people as well. "How long do we have to wait before we can go after it?"

Syn shrugged. "I don't know how much things have changed, but people used to vacate the prime district after working hours."

Nero nodded in agreement. "You'll have to hold up another six, seven hours to be safe. The streets get completely vacant about two hours after that."

"Then that's our plan." Syn looked at her. "So where do we go?"

Looking up and down the street, she tried to find some place they could stay for that amount of time and not evoke anyone's suspicions. Hundreds of people and aliens walked around them, while busy shuttles, rovers, and transports skidded along the road.

Tons of stores, hotels, and restaurants lined the street. Well, they couldn't very well shop for that amount of time, nor eat.

As for a hotel . . .

Those places always demanded identification, which would prove impossible to provide since they were both wanted dead by the local government.

Maybe the sewer wasn't such a bad idea after all.

"What's the name of this city?" she finally asked Syn.

"Shasra. Why?"

"Just curious." Again she scanned the spindly buildings that spiraled up and sideways all around them in search of a promising destination.

Finally, Syn huffed irritably and moved around her. "You stink at this, you know that? I'd hate to *ever* go shopping with you if it takes you this long to make a decision." He jerked his chin toward Nero. "Don't forget, Scalera can't hold his shield forever."

"Not unless I want a nosebleed and headache. No offense, I'd rather pass on that oh-so-joyful misery."

She glared at them and their combined sarcasm. "Fine, then. What's your brilliant suggestion?"

Without answering her, Syn led her across the street to a hotel. Shahara lifted her brows in surprise. What was he thinking? How could *that* offer them any shelter?

Syn paused at the door and looked at Nero. "I'll take it from here. Thanks for the assist, bro."

Nero held his arm out to him. "You never cease to surprise me."

"How so?"

"You're the only one who knows how to bring me low and yet you never do." He shook Syn's arm and gave him a look of supreme respect. "Stand strong and stay free."

"You, too."

Pulling him in for a quick man hug, Nero stepped back. "And you take care, too, Shahara. Remember the lies we tell ourselves to survive seldom bring peace to our souls."

She scowled as he walked away. "What did he mean by that?"

Syn shrugged. "You must have something guilty on your mind. He can read thoughts and see futures at times, so there's no telling what he knows that you don't."

"And what did he mean about you?"

"I know what weakens him and I've never tried to enslave him with it. I wouldn't do that to him, but he still has a hard time accepting the fact that I know who and what he is and I don't use it against him."

It was a rare thing and Syn was remarkable that way. "So are we really going to stay here?"

"No better place." He opened the door and entered first, then held it open for her as she followed.

Inside the elegant lobby, she became instantly aware of her dirty clothes and lack of sophistication. Wealthy people and aristocrats milled all around, some of them just plain rude as they eyed her dusty uniform with distaste. They were all so impeccably dressed in clothes that would pay her bills for at least six months . . .

Or more.

Gah, Nero, come back and shield me from these people. She hated how, with nothing more than a disdainful look and curled lip, they could make her feel less than nothing and beneath them. Awkwardly, she brushed at her disheveled hair, trying to smooth the frizz.

Syn caught her hand and pulled it down. The fierce look on his face chilled her. "Don't pay any attention to them. They're the ones in the wrong here and you're worth more than all of them put together. Value isn't calculated by a person's net worth or income. It's calculated by integrity and decency. The only people in this room worth a damn are the ones who don't care how we're dressed. If you look, you will see the ones who matter. The rest of them can all go to hell."

She offered him a trembling smile at his wisdom and kindness. That was why she loved him. And he was right. There were wealthy people in the room who didn't pay any attention to them whatsoever and a couple who even offered a friendly smile.

Still, it didn't take away the sting of disdain from the others. The pain they needlessly inflicted on her battered soul as they reminded her that she wasn't good enough to be among them. Even the hotel staff looked at her as if they feared she'd spit on the floor.

Or do something worse.

Tucking her hand into the crook of his arm, Syn strode up to the counter as if he owned the place. His head high and spine straight, he looked at them with a defiance she wished to the gods she possessed.

Then again, he was probably used to such places. Unlike her, he made enough money to be able to pay for such luxuries. For that matter, he probably out-earned most of the snobs they passed and had enough money to buy the hotel outright.

That helped her to forget the others.

And as he moved, she noticed he drew way too many other females' notice. White-hot heat stabbed at her breast and she had the strangest desire to start knocking some wealthy heads together.

Syn didn't acknowledge them in the least as he stopped in front of the main desk.

Lifting a haughty brow, the clerk looked him up and down and appeared extremely put out that she had to wait on them. "May I help you?"

Syn returned her look with an even snottier one. "I'd like a room for the night."

She gave a short laugh as if doubting his ability to pay. "And you are?"

He handed over an ID.

The clerk looked at it, then her demeanor instantly changed. "Lord Cruel, please forgive my rudeness . . . I-I should have recognized you instantly."

Shahara started at the name and had to force herself not to show a single emotion.

He was pretending to be one of the Cruels? Was he nuts? Impersonating royalty was . . .

Shahara, the man is *a wanted criminal.* Not like one more warrant for his arrest would matter one way or another.

The clerk held out a scanner. "I'll just need your imprint, my lord."

Syn placed his hand over the white screen. Shahara held her breath, waiting for the alarm to blare and security to come running for them.

Instead, the white beam scanned his palm, then a small green light beeped.

The clerk's face brightened even more. "We have our king's suite available, my lord. Would that suit your needs?"

He let out an irritated sigh. "I hate to slum so, but if that's the best you have . . . I suppose we can make do for one night." He lifted Shahara's hand and kissed her fingers. "Forgive me, my lady, for not doing better by you, but you know how these plebeian establishments are. Dreadful, really. But tomorrow night I'll have you at my palace and shall make amends for tonight's misery."

Shahara pressed her lips together to keep from laughing at his perfect regal drawl. His acting abilities were impressive. "Well," she said in a bored tone as she joined his mimicry, "I suppose they have beds here, surely. We shall make do and be rewarded by the gods for our suffering."

His dimple flashed as he winked at her.

"We'll make sure and comp your dinner, my lord. Believe me, it's an honor to have you here and we want you to have nothing but the best experience." The clerk looked past them and motioned for a VIP valet. "Please, show Lord Cruel and his guest to his suite."

Syn handed the valet their packs.

He took them without flinching. "Please follow me, my lord."

"It's all right," Syn whispered in her ear as he drew alongside her. "Trust me."

He took her hand. Squeezing it tightly, she let out a shaky breath as they passed by a security guard. There was a part of her terrified that they'd be recognized and stopped at any moment.

What they were doing was extremely dangerous. But Syn seemed oblivious to it as he kept pace with the valet and ignored the rest.

While they waited for the lift, she swept her gaze around the lobby. There were several stores located just beside the lift bay and she watched as people came and went.

Glancing at the various boutiques, her gaze fell to a gorgeous greenish-blue dress displayed in a nearby window. She'd never seen a color so pretty, nor material more delicate. It looked even softer than silk. Maybe a foreign material . . . What was so unusual was that the finely woven strands interlocked around the neck and sleeves to form a spider-web effect. The dress itself was a plain sheath that hugged the mannequin's body.

What she wouldn't give for a single moment of peace to try it on just to see what it'd be like to wear something that wasn't secondhand.

It would be incredible, surely.

But then, what would be the use? She probably couldn't afford the thread used to hem it.

Still, it's beautiful . . .

Syn watched Shahara's face as she stared longingly

at the dress in the window not far from them. She would be breathtaking in it. Come to think of it, he'd never seen her in anything other than work clothes.

She deserved so much better than that. All her life she'd worked and struggled for the sake of her family. And what did she have to show for it?

Tessa was always in trouble and Kasen was down right nasty.

And Caillen . . .

Syn winced. He didn't want to think about Caillen because thinking about Caillen made him all too aware of why he could never again try and settle down.

His past was something that would haunt him forever. Hell, some asshole would probably put it on his tomb—*Here Lies the Last Remains of Idirian Wade's Son. We Forgot His Name, but Hey, Who Cares? He Was a Worthless Filch.*

Yeah, that'd be about right.

The lift pinged open. Tugging gently at her hand, Syn pulled her into it. Still she stared at the dress until the doors closed.

Syn looked away. He'd worn that same hungry look all his life, and all too well he knew what it was like to want something he couldn't have.

Peace. Family.

And most of all, someone to love.

Those three things didn't belong to anyone who bore the Wade surname.

It is what it is . . .

Shahara glanced at the valet, who quickly directed his gaze from her breasts to the wall. Any other time she'd have made him pay for such ogling, but she was still feeling somewhat overwhelmed and intimidated by her posh surroundings.

The doors opened on their floor.

The valet led them out and down the wide yellow corridor to the room at the end of the hall. Syn stepped around her and placed his hand against the door lock that the clerk had programmed to respond to his touch alone. The large wooden doors swung open with a flourish.

Shahara's breath caught in her throat as she looked inside. Never in her life had she seen anything so beautiful. Gold-veined green marble covered the floors, and the walls were painted a vivid, inviting yellow and the trim was all dark wood.

As she entered the suite, a huge vase of fresh flowers greeted her, scenting the air with a wonderful bouquet. The sitting room had overstuffed cream-striped chairs and two large sofas, one of which was set before a fireplace.

Syn tipped the valet and took their packs before he closed and locked the door. He set the packs down and crossed the room to where she stood. "Are you all right?"

"Fine." She took a step down to walk toward the massive windows that looked out over the bustling city.

Whoa . . . It was gorgeous.

She felt like some mythical princess in a fairy tale. Did the people who were born to this kind of life really appreciate it? Or was this as mundane to them as plain flatbread to her?

What a pity if they couldn't understand how lucky they were.

Syn frowned as he followed after her. "I don't know . . . I've never known you to be so quiet. You sure you haven't swallowed your tongue?"

She gave him a nasty glare before turning back to

take in the glorious view. "I suppose you're used to things like this."

He joined her at the window. "Not really. When you grow up without anything at all, you never really get used to things like this. It still awes me that I'm able to be on the inside after all the years I spent looking in windows, aching to be in this world."

"Breaking in windows, don't you mean?"

He smiled and this time there was no defensiveness or anger. "That, too."

She crossed her arms over her chest and eyed him curiously. "So how did we get in here, anyway?"

He handed her the ID, which held his face and Darling's name. "We did this years ago. It allows me to infiltrate areas I'd never be able to access with my own identity."

"You two have a strange relationship."

He returned the ID to his pocket. "Not really. He works with me. Remember? We do a lot of screwed up stuff like this."

"You're not afraid his family will find out?"

"His brother Ryn wouldn't care and I'd pay his uncle to come at me. I want a piece of that bastard so bad I can taste it."

The sincerity in his tone and expression gave her chills. But then she knew why. Darling's uncle abused him. She'd had to pull Caillen back on more than one occasion when her brother was going to head out and kill the man.

"You really are a lot like my brother. You know that?"

"Gah, I hope he's not as attracted to you as I am. 'Cause that's just sick."

She rolled her eyes at him. "You're awful."

He didn't argue as he pushed open the window so that Vik could join them.

Vik landed on the sill, turned into his bot form and slammed the window closed. "I hate this planet. How long we got to stay?"

"Hopefully not long."

"Good, 'cause I'm missing my toaster and need to get out of here."

Syn held his hands up. "I'm not even going to go there."

Scanning the room, she saw the bar. "You want something to drink?"

"Sure, I'd love a glass of wine." He picked up the hotel's link. "I'm also starving. You want anything?"

"I'll take whatever you order."

"When did you get so trusting?" Before she could answer, he laughed evilly.

"What?" she asked, her trust taking a backseat to his humor. Something told her that she was the brunt of his joke.

The smile he gave her was brilliant and gorgeous. "I forgot that you have to eat your own cooking. I guess *anything* else is nirvana."

"Ha, ha," she said, wishing she had something to throw at him.

He sobered as someone came on the line and he ordered food for them. She listened to the sound of his deep voice speaking in his native tongue. It was simply amazing how he could adapt to all these different environments. He could run with outlaws, skim sewers, and quell snotty royalty and unruly clerks.

Most of all, he'd taught a tracer how to trust even when she'd thought herself immune from any man's charms.

How did he do it?

Pouring their drinks, she felt him draw close after he'd finished ordering their food. The heat from his body singed her as he reached around her and picked up his glass. He stood so close his breath tickled her neck, raising a chill the length of her body.

His warm masculine scent wrapped around her like an old comfortable blanket. And her body answered the call with a readiness that astounded her.

How could she still burn for him when she'd just had him only a short time ago?

What was it about this man that made her wanton?

But then she knew. It was everything about him. His humor, his intelligence. That wonderful dimple that peeked at her every time he smiled.

He set his glass aside and turned her around in his arms. "I know an even better way to kill time," he said, his voice deep with need.

Trying to retain her nonchalance, she cocked her brow. "You do?"

That wonderfully wicked smile curved his lips. "Hmm," he said, dipping his head down until his lips met hers.

Shahara parted her lips, welcoming him inside. The warmth of his breath and heat of his body stirred her near to madness and she wondered if she would ever get enough of him. Something inside told her that even if she had him for two hundred years, she'd always appreciate it.

"Uh, people?" Vik rushed over in his bot form to stand at their feet. "I think I'll go patrol for something. Definitely. I'm not into voyeur stuff . . . yeah." He transformed into a bird, then hit the closed window and fell to the floor. "Dammit, Syn. Did you have to do that?"

Syn laughed before he opened the window and helped Vik out. "Don't come back without warning."

"Don't worry. I don't need my circuitry burning out 'cause I saw you naked." He flew off.

Syn shut the window, then returned to her side and pulled her back into his arms.

Suddenly, a laugh bubbled up in her throat.

Syn pulled back, staring at her as if she'd insulted him. "What?"

She smiled. "I can't believe you're ready for another round. Caillen always says he needs a day's rest after he has sex."

He snorted disdainfully. "Caillen's a wuss." He took her hand in his and placed it to the bulge at his groin. "I assure you, I'm well up to the challenge."

Her throat dry, she felt heat creep up her face, to her hairline. Before she could move, he returned to their kiss, leaving her hand trapped between them so that she had no choice but to feel his blood rush through the most intimate part of his anatomy.

Shahara burned with her own need as she shifted her body to fit more snugly with his.

Syn moaned at her surrender. She was spectacular and he couldn't believe that he wanted to make love to her again. Normally, he'd be like Caillen, too, and need a day to rest.

But not with her. Every waking minute he was with her, all he wanted was to feel the security of her arms, feel her breath tickle his neck while he took possession of her body. He got hard every time he looked at her.

She moved her hand from him and wrapped her

arms around his neck. Syn stepped closer, pressing himself against the warmth of her body as he continued to tease her tongue with his own.

"Shouldn't we be plotting our next move?" Her words were ragged in his ear.

"I already did."

"When?"

"While I was in my office. I grabbed my IDs and everything else we needed."

"So you know where the statue is?"

"No. But I'm hoping we can find clues in the office where I stashed it." He put his finger to her lips. "Trust me, Shahara. I'll get the chip and get you out of this. I'm not going to let anything happen to you."

How she wished she could make the same promise to him . . .

Suddenly, a knock intruded. "Room service," a voice called from the other side of the door.

Growling low in his throat, Syn stepped back from her. "Can you get it?"

"Me?" Shahara shook her head. "I don't know how to do this. I've never been in a hotel in my life."

He cleared his throat meaningfully. "C'mon, I can't answer the door like this. It's a guy out there."

Her gaze dipped to the area he indicated and she realized his arousal was more than obvious. Laughing, she crossed her arms over her chest and gave him a playful look of her own. "I think it would make interesting waiter conversation for him and his buddies if you did."

His look turned murderous. "Just open the door, let him bring the food in, and sign the ledger he hands you."

"What about the tip?"

"It's already added to the bill."

Shahara paused for a minute longer, just to annoy him. "All right," she said at last. "I guess you're off the hook."

Before she could blink, he disappeared through a double set of doors to hide.

"You coward!" she called out, mocking him.

"Don't give me no lip, wench. It's all your fault."

Her smile wide, Shahara pressed the release to open the main doors. A young man brought in a huge tray covered with silver and gold dishes. He placed them on the marble-covered table just to the left of the foyer. "Does madam require anything else?" he asked politely.

Wow, no one had ever called her "madam" before. She actually liked it. "I think we're fine."

He handed her a small computer ledger and she started to sign her name an instant before she thought about how stupid that might be. Instead she made up one.

The waiter inclined his head and left her.

"You can come out now," she called out to Syn. "It's safe."

While she waited for him to rejoin her, she starting pulling off lids. Her stomach growled at the wonderful scent of roasted meat and vegetables. Her mouth watering, she took a pinch of the softest roll she'd ever seen before.

It was marvelous.

Syn came up behind her again, silent as a ghost, and pulled her back against his chest so that she could tell the interruption hadn't dampened his mood a bit.

She realized then that he always moved that way. Graceful and quiet like a feral hunting beast. If she didn't know better, she'd swear he had assassin training. But then, given his father, his training had probably been even harsher.

He looked at the food, then back at her. "I don't know which aching I need to quench first. I think I'd rather take a bite out of you."

Catching his chin in her hand, she laughed. "Take care of the food first. I assure you I won't get cold."

His deep laugh joined hers, and he gave her a kiss of promise and a tantalizing stroke between her legs before taking a seat at the table.

Shahara went for their drinks before she joined him.

Sitting down, she stared at all the cutlery the waiter had brought them. There were three different forks—obviously for different foods. Which one should she use? It was a foolish concern, she knew, but after what he'd said about Mara, she didn't want him to find *her* lacking in any way.

As she struggled to put her peas on her fork the same elegant way he did, he reached over and touched her hand. Looking up, she was captivated by the tenderness in his dark eyes.

He took the fork from her grasp and stabbed the peas with it. "I quit caring about such stupid things a long time ago. Manners don't make you decent and it doesn't make you a better human. Trust me. Eat your food in peace and know that you're more of a lady than any noblewoman I've ever met." He handed her the fork.

Swallowing the bite, she watched him from under her lashes, somewhat embarrassed that he'd noticed what she'd been doing. And that she'd failed so miserably at having etiquette.

A painful lump settled in her stomach. "When I was little, I used to sit in the market down the street from where we lived and watch the upper plebs come in to shop. They were always so elegant and beautiful. I used to pretend I was one of them. Did you ever do that?"

"No. I used to pretend I was Vik. I'd send him out to fly, and I'd wear vids so that I could see and hear what he did. I wanted his freedom so badly that I don't think I'd be sane today had I not made him."

She sighed as she remembered her own childhood. While bad, it was nothing compared to his. "Did you move a lot?"

"Constantly. We weren't allowed to keep anything that couldn't fit into a pack that we could grab and go whenever the authorities got too close to my father. I can't even count how many times Digger would wake us up in the middle of the night to run."

She sucked her breath in sharply. "I always hated that feeling of panic most."

He cocked a brow at her words. "You ran, too?"

"From creditors. My dad would wait until the day before eviction and we'd have to flee before they arrested him. I remember when I was ten, my pack got left behind because I was helping Caillen."

Syn paused as he heard the raw hurt in her voice. "What was in it?"

"Stupid girl stuff. A diary, my clothes, but what I missed most was my Agatha doll. She was the only thing new I'd ever gotten." She shook her head. "Ridiculous, right?"

"No. It's not. Objects are the markers of our humanity. Everything we hold onto has meaning for us. Those things are souvenirs that can transport us to that exact moment in time and make us feel that emotion all over again. Take Vik, for example. He reminds me of the need I had to be free, but I also remember the beatings

I took while I worked on him. One in particular was brutal because I was so focused on him that I didn't hear my dad call me."

"Is that why you left him behind?"

"Yeah. I wanted nothing to do with my past. It wasn't until Mara left me that I had Digger send me the picture of me and Talia. It was only then I came to terms with the fact that my past, for better or worse, has made me who and what I am. My father and the anger I will always have for him gave me the ability to kill anyone who ever came at me, but it was my sister and Digger who made me human. Without them, I would be my father's son. And because of them, I can never victimize someone like them, no matter what it costs me."

Shahara took his hand in hers. "You are a good man, Syn."

Syn froze at the only thing no one had ever accused him of before. Coming from her lips, he wanted to believe it.

But he knew better.

"I'm just a piece of shit, Shahara, trying to survive." He pushed his chair back and left her to finish eating in peace. He knew he couldn't stay there anymore and watch her. The pain stabbing his groin was too ferocious. But it was nothing compared to the ache in his chest that wanted things to be different.

That wanted *him* to be different.

Tossing back a deep gulp of wine, he walked over to the music console and chose a soft melody.

Instead of distracting him, it only made him crave her more.

What are you doing, you idiot? Stop the torture. The more you're with her, the harder it's going to be to leave.

It was true, and he was going to have to leave. He was a filch and she was a seax—even if he was dumb enough to think about trying to have a relationship with her, those two things were incompatible. She would have to give up everything she valued to be with him.

Even her brother. Or at least Caillen's respect.

And that was something he could never allow.

Still, he couldn't bring himself to stop this moment of tranquility. This was what he'd always wanted. A beautiful woman who set his blood on fire and a comfortable, lush place to share with her.

Besides, Shahara deserved this. He still felt guilty for taking her on the cold floor of the shuttle. He'd satisfied his lust without any thought to her comfort. That had been wrong of him. He should never have treated her that way.

"What are you thinking?"

He looked up with a frown. "What?"

She set her fork down. "You look so intense. I was just wondering why."

Moving closer to her, he noted that she'd finished her food. He set the empty glass down on the table next to her plate, then held his hand out to her. "Dance with me."

She leaned away from him. "I don't know how."

"C'mon," he nudged. "You can do it."

Shahara bit her lip in indecision. This wasn't her forte, and since she'd never tried to dance before, she didn't want to embarrass herself. "Are you sure?"

He nodded.

Taking a deep breath for courage, she took his hand and allowed him to pull her into his arms.

"Just follow my steps." Leaning down, he kissed her

lightly on the lips while he placed her arms around his neck.

Syn savored the feeling of her holding him. Her steps were awkward and she kept stepping all over his feet. Trying not to grimace or laugh, he whispered quietly in her ear, "Listen to the music and follow the beat."

She improved immediately. Smiling, he reveled at the strange feelings that coursed through him. He wanted to give her this, the one thing she'd never known—a tender moment with a man. She deserved someone to treasure her.

If only it could be him.

"Did you dance with Mara like this?"

He cringed at the mention of his ex-wife's name and shook his head.

"Why?"

"I never wanted to."

She opened her lips to speak again. Syn covered the softness with his fingertip. "Shh, love. I don't want you to ask me any more questions and I don't want you to ever mention her name to me again. She belongs to a part of me that died a long time ago and I don't want to think of her. I just want to be with you."

Shahara bit her lip at his words as a thick warmth spread through her. Her throat tight, she looked up at him and smiled. No one had ever said such a thing to her. "Thank you."

He smiled in response before he reached up and took her right hand from around his neck. Holding it tightly, he brushed her fingertips with a kiss before laying it against his chest.

Shahara placed her head on his chest and stared at their entwined hands. His grip tightened around her waist and he laid his cheek against the top of her head. A thousand emotions tore through her at once and the only one she could name was the love that welled up and filled every part of her.

What she wouldn't give to stay like this forever. To hear his heart beat beneath her cheek while his breath stirred her hair and the music flowed all around. She'd never danced with a man before and she wondered if all men felt this good.

Deep inside she knew the answer. Only Syn would ever stir her emotions like this.

And one day, all too soon, he would hate her. Of that she was certain.

He stopped dancing and pulled the tie from her braid. His look deadly serious, he unbraided the strands of her hair and ran his fingers through it. "I've wanted to do this since the moment I first saw you."

She smiled as her hair spilled around them. "Your turn." She reached up to free his ponytail.

Taking her hand, he led her to the console and pushed a few options. The lights dimmed to a faint glow.

"What are you doing?"

He pulled her to his chest and gave her a tender kiss. "I want to bathe with you," he whispered against her lips.

A tremor of shyness shot through her, but she banished it. She wouldn't let her modesty ruin this. Not when he meant so much to her. "I'd like that, too."

He left her to fill the tub.

Shahara followed him into the bathroom where there was a huge gold and black marble tub that would have probably fit a dozen people. Man, as kids, they could have swam in it.

"You're killing me, woman," he said between clenched teeth. He moved to draw her into a hug.

"No." She pushed him back. "You're mine, remember?"

Clenching his teeth, he returned his hands to the rim and decided that this would definitely kill him.

But if he had to die, he couldn't think of a better way to go.

She started bathing him again. Her fingers sliding over and under him. Just when he thought he'd scream, she finally moved her hands down to his legs.

Syn took a deep breath to steady his nerves. Her boldness amazed him. Especially given the fact that only a few weeks ago, she'd never have touched a man so intimately. Let alone one she'd been sent after.

Once she finished with his bath, he reached for the sponge. "My turn."

"Nope," she said pushing him away with a laugh. "Remember, you're *my* slave. Now be good and return to your station." And with that she began bathing herself.

Fire beat through him as he watched her hands moving over her own body, touching her own soap-laden breasts. Unable to stand it, he reached for his glass and drained it. Refilling it, he tried to keep his eyes off her, but despite his best effort, he couldn't.

She lifted one shapely leg and pulled the sponge over the calf, then up her thigh, and then to her . . .

"That's it," he groaned. "I can't take any more."

She arched a taunting brow and looked at him mischievously. Taking the glass from his hand, she took a sip from the place where he'd been drinking from.

"Lean back," she ordered one more time.

He did as she commanded.

Instead of pulling away again, she straddled him and set his glass aside. The warmth of her body on his stomach scorched him. As he reached up to bury his hands in her wet hair, she lifted herself and came down on him. A deep moan escaped his throat.

Shahara delighted in the tender pain that crossed his handsome face. She'd never felt so powerful, nor so beautiful. Leaning forward, she brushed his wet hair from his face and gave him a fierce kiss.

He felt so good that she couldn't believe it was real.

They'd been through so much in such a short amount of time. Yet it seemed like she'd known him forever. She could barely recall her life before they met. It seemed like some vague, lonely nightmare.

And the last thing she wanted was to return to it.

But what if he didn't feel the same way?

He'd never told her that he loved her, that he cared for her as anything more than . . .

Her heart stopped.

He hadn't even called her a friend. Could it really be that he was only using her for sex?

No. He wasn't like her brother—a manwhore always on the prowl. She couldn't imagine him being like this with anyone else. He was too guarded for that.

Syn scowled at her. "Is something wrong?"

"No." She offered him a smile and refused to think about it anymore. She didn't want to spoil this time with him. And if it was just a moment fate had set aside for her, then the last thing she wanted was for it to end.

If this was all there was for them, then she would enjoy it while it lasted.

He took her right breast into his mouth. Shahara leaned her head back, and moaned at the pleasure of his tongue flicking across her nipple as wave after wave of pleasure crashed through her. She rocked her hips against his, drawing him deep inside.

Suddenly, he leaned her back against the tub, sending waves of water over the rim to splash against the floor.

His strokes became faster as he pressed himself deeper and deeper inside her. Shahara dug her nails into his back, delighting in his intensifying pace. Her body began a needful throb that kept beat with his rhythm. Just as she thought she'd scream out for him to stop torturing her so, her body erupted into waves of blissful release.

"Shahara," he groaned a moment before she felt him shudder as well.

Her breathing labored, she held him against her and stroked the wet strands of his hair. "I love you, Syn," she said before she could stop herself.

He withdrew from her so fast that it left her feeling empty. "What?"

She swallowed in sudden trepidation and anger as she realized he wasn't happy about her stupid declaration.

Why did I say it? I'm such an idiot!

She wanted him to return her words, not look at her with such panic in his eyes. But she wasn't a coward and she would stand by her slip because it was the truth. "I said I love you."

Syn stared at her in disbelief. No one had said those words to him since the night he'd proposed to Mara. Never had he expected them to come from another female.

Especially not a seax.

He wanted to tell her he loved her, too, but the words

lodged themselves painfully in his throat and for the sake of his soul, he couldn't bring them out.

C'mon, say it.

Don't you dare!

His common sense and his heart warred with each other as he saw the expectant look on her face. *I have to say something . . .*

And before he could stop himself, he spoke the first thing that came to his mind. "That's nice."

You lame moron. What a stupid thing to say. She tells you she loves you and you come back with "That's nice?" Gods! You might as well tell her that her ass is fat and go ahead and get the groin kick.

This time you deserve it.

Hurt flickered across her face an instant before rage. "That's nice!" she spat. "That's all you have to say?"

Say it. Tell her you love her.

I can't. I can't love her. It would destroy her career and her family.

Let her go so that she can live.

Bullshit. You're not that altruistic and you know it.

And with that, he knew why he couldn't return the words. He finally understood the truth behind his stupidity.

He was afraid. Shahara had been right when she'd said he was afraid to let people get close to him. Because if he trusted her and she betrayed him, it would kill him. He couldn't go through that again.

I'm so sorry, Shahara . . .

Angrily, she left the tub and grabbed a towel. "You know what *I* think C.I. stands for?" she raged. *"Completely Insensitive!"*

"Shahara, wait." He moved toward her.

"Stay away from me."

He left the tub and pulled her into his arms before she could make it to the door. "Don't be like this. I do care for you."

Her gaze turned even more frigid. "But you don't love me."

"No," he lied.

She clenched her teeth and fought against his hold. Tears welled in her eyes, and Syn damned himself for the bastard he was.

He deserved to live his life alone. Isolated. *I can't believe I'm hurting the only woman I've ever really loved . . .*

Her or you, boy. Her or you.

And he'd been hurt enough in his life. He couldn't let her completely destroy him any more than he could tear her away from her family and career. He cupped her face in his hands. Pain constricted his throat. "I do need you, Shahara. I do. But I can't offer you anything more than that."

Shahara tensed as he pulled her back into his arms and laid his head down on her shoulder. Her first impulse was to drop-kick him right in his exposed testicles, but in spite of her anger, she knew it didn't change her feelings for him.

She still loved him whether he returned her feelings or not. *Gah, I'm pathetic.*

Closing her eyes, she damned fate for its cruelty. She'd finally found a man she could trust and love, and he didn't feel the same way for her.

I could die.

"Please don't be angry," he whispered.

Wrapping her arms around him, she decided that for

now he needed her and, if he needed her, then he might grow to love her as well.

Maybe if she were patient . . .

"I'm not angry." She was more hurt than anything else. And while there was anger, it wasn't at him. It was at Mara and the universe and all the other reasons that had warped Syn to the point he couldn't open himself up to her.

But she wasn't mad at him.

Syn pulled back and stared at her until he was sure she'd spoken honestly. Once the fire faded from her cheeks and eyes, he toweled himself off.

"C'mon." He tossed the towel aside and took her hand. "Let's get some sleep while we can."

She followed him, but he could still feel her sadness. It would be so easy to make her happy, but the scar of his father's sin ran too deep. It had branded him since his birth and it destroyed everything it touched.

Sooner or later, it would destroy if not her, then their relationship. Because sooner or later another curious reporter or official would show up and expose him all over again. They would go after her and it would cost her everything.

She would be guilty by association and that would cause her to hate him.

Sighing, he knew he would die if he faced scorn from her. Better they part now on relatively good terms than he have to live with her turning on him the way Mara had. He never wanted to go through that again.

Shahara pulled the covers up over their bodies as Syn snuggled against her back. Her heart heavy, she listened to his breathing while he positioned one of his legs between hers and draped his arm over her waist.

He rested his hand between her breasts. She sighed at the possessiveness of his hold.

What would it take to gain his love?

And if she did, would he ever admit it?

She started at the sudden realization.

The Syn she knew would never admit it if he felt love. He was too strong for that. Love meant weakness and Syn would never open himself up to that vulnerability again. For all she knew, he *did* love her and he was too defensive to tell her.

I swear, Syn . . . But she couldn't blame him given everything he'd been through.

She heard his breathing even out and felt his hold loosen as he fell asleep. Pressing her lips together, she moved his hand from her breasts and stared down at it. Scars marred his knuckles with one running from the side of his wrist up to his elbow.

So much pain. So much fighting. Would he ever believe that someone could love him?

That someone would stay with him?

She didn't know for sure. But one way or another, she would find the answer to those questions.

"I'm not going to give up without a fight, boy, and as bad as you think you've had it in the past . . . those opponents were nothing compared to me."

Shahara Dagan had never failed a mission in her life and she wasn't about to fail this, the most important one. Somehow, she'd free him.

Most of all, she'd claim him.

CHAPTER 17

When Shahara woke up, the room was completely black. And the space next to her in bed was empty. A slice of fear went through her. Where could he have gone?

"Syn?"

"Right here," he said from her right. The lights came up to a soft glow.

Turning over, she saw him sitting in one of the over-stuffed chairs near the window.

Fully dressed, he stared at her, his face impassive. "We need to get going soon."

"Okay."

He got up and crossed the room. "I'll be waiting outside."

Shahara frowned at the catch in his voice and reached for the clothes he'd folded and placed neatly on the nightstand. What had he been thinking while he watched her sleep?

Whatever it was, it must have been fierce for him to be so cold now.

Sighing, she got up and went to shower and dress.

Syn leaned back against the closed doors, his body aching as he remembered the sight of her sleeping like a child in the bed. Most of all, he remembered the sincerity in her voice as she told him that she loved him.

She loves me . . .

Those words tore him apart. He wanted to rejoice and simultaneously run for cover. How he wished he'd met her when he was a doctor with no past. That was what she deserved. Not some filch with no country, no dignity.

Nothing.

C'mon, boy, heartaches come and they go. You know that better than anyone.

Yeah, they did go eventually. But the pain remained forever. And even if he lived a thousand years, he knew the pain of losing her would haunt him every moment of it.

How do I give up someone who loves me?

The same way you always have. In the end, she'll be just like Paden and will learn to hate you, too. Just a matter of time.

It was true. Closing his eyes, he tried to blot out the image of her peaceful body resting in his arms.

Gods, what had she done to him?

But then he knew. She'd touched him deeper than anyone ever had. Her touch had branded his soul, and no matter how much he might wish otherwise, he'd never be able to let her go. Not without tearing out his heart.

Because in the end, he loved her, too.

What the hell—you'll get used to the pain. Just like you've always gotten used to everything misfortune has tossed your way.

He heard her approach the doors. Moving away from them, he picked up their packs and tried to act as nonchalant as possible.

She was still plaiting her hair as she joined him.

He cleared his throat. "Are you ready for this?"

She wrinkled her nose in distaste, and yet the expression wrung his gut. How could any woman be beautiful while looking so disgusted? "Not really. But if we must go risk our lives and run into more people wanting to kill us . . ."

He didn't respond as he hailed Vik. "What's your status?"

"Annoyed."

In spite of everything, he laughed. "What's going on out there?"

"Street's basically clear. There's a couple on the corner in a rover about to have sex—nasty people doing private things in public, get a room, you no-home-trained plebs. Other than that . . . looks promising."

Syn slung his pack over his shoulder, then held hers out for her. Once she had it in place, he led her out of the building and made sure he ignored the couple in the rover.

Shahara frowned at his continued coldness as she followed after him. What had happened while she slept?

Well, that's the last time I ever fall asleep around you, buddy.

"You always wake up this pissy?"

He arched single brow at her. "Excuse me?"

"You heard me. You were normal when I went to sleep. Now you're like Kasen on a bender. Someone give you a willie while I was out of it?"

"I have no response for that." His tone was completely dry.

She gave him no reprieve. "Yeah, well, if you were a woman, I'd swear you were on your period."

Syn paused to gape at her. "You do know I am my father's son, right? People don't talk to me that way and live."

"Oh, like I fear you. Never. Besides, a fight might dislodge whatever has crawled up your sphincter and bring back the much nicer version of you. No offense, but I miss that Syn."

"Do you talk to your brother like this?"

"All the time."

Syn shook his head. "And he worships you for it? I knew Caillen was a masochistic bastard."

She made a hissing noise at him.

And still he was charmed by her. Even while she insulted him. *I'm the one who's certifiable.*

Shahara let out a sigh as she watched him move up a little to lead the way. Tempted to shoot him, she looked up at Vik, who was keeping pace with them.

She just didn't understand what had happened to him. He'd been so tender at the hotel.

I should never have told him I loved him. It was a mistake of titanic proportions. Now she'd lost her connection to him because he was too stubborn to accept the fact that someone could care about him.

I'm so sorry, baby. He lived in such a harsh place that she wasn't sure anything would ever reach him there.

Trying to push that thought away, she scanned the street, amazed at how empty it'd become in such a short period of time. Absolutely no one was anywhere to be found. It was almost as if someone had dropped a virus bomb, killing all inhabitants and leaving just the buildings behind. If not for the lights twinkling dimly in the thick darkness, she would have really become suspicious. "Where is everyone?"

Syn followed the line of her gaze up to a nearby

building. "They've taken refuge for the night. Shasra is a dangerous place after dark."

"Dangerous? How so?"

"The temperature drops so low that you can freeze to death in minutes if you're not careful."

A twinge of fear skidded up her spine. "We're not dressed for extremely cold weather."

"I know." His blasè tone alarmed her all the more. "Relax, I don't intend for us to be out here all that long."

That was supposed to comfort her?

"Yes, but in case it has escaped your astute attention, Captain Obvious, things keep happening to us that we don't plan on."

He let out an annoyed hiss. His lip was curled, which would have looked fierce had his eyes not been alight with humor. He might not smile, but he was amused. "So what do you suggest? We weigh ourselves down with coats? Encumber our bodies to the point where we can't move our arms or legs in a fight? That'll go over well, won't it?"

So what if he was right? She still didn't like the idea of freezing.

"Well, we better be quick and not become human popsicles. I'm going to be really upset at you if I freeze to death." She reached into her pocket to pull out the map he'd given her inside his flat.

As he took it from her, she realized his clothes were still damp from her earlier dousing. A wave of guilt and dread fear went through her as she realized how cold he would get. "Maybe we should try this another day."

"We don't have time to delay. It's now or never." He headed in the opposite direction of their hotel.

Rolling her eyes at his stubbornness, she followed after him. A freezing wind tore down the street, whistling between buildings. She wrapped her arms around herself and wondered why Syn seemed immune to it. He walked forward as if the dropping temperature was nothing at all.

"Aren't you freezing?"

"I used to sleep outside here on the streets without shoes. Trust me, this isn't cold."

It still didn't make it right. Her throat tightened at the thought of how bad he'd had it in his life.

Who am I to complain to him?

He made her look like a wimp.

Seven blocks later, he stopped. Shahara stared up at the building in front of her and her stomach shrank. Like a hulking ghoul, it stood against the eerie backdrop of three pale moons. No light inside the building could be found, and what few windows were still intact were covered with rotting boards. Weeds obscured the broken walkway and an old faded sign swung over the door.

"It's vacant?"

He went to the boarded-up door without commenting.

With great trepidation, she eyed the sign that threatened to fall on their heads. "This is useless. I'm sure it's gone."

He tore the large board off the door and tossed it to the ground. "Probably, but my research said the building was closed just days after I stashed the chip. There was nothing online to say what office I put it in or who owned it. I'm hoping we either find the chip where I left it or find a clue about what happened to it."

"And if we don't?"

"We're screwed."

Anger tore through her. "You don't really think that after all these years the chip will be where you left it, do you? 'Cause if you do, I have some city property you might be interested in buying."

He gave her a look that would have withered stone. "So what are you saying, we should just give up? After we've come so far?"

"No," she said hesitantly in spite of the voice in her head that urged her to argue with him. She really had no desire to go inside another rundown building and face the unknown.

"Then follow me." He bent over to crawl between the other boards.

This was crazy. Most likely suicide, and yet she followed in after him. *Why do I bother?* Surely there wouldn't be anything left in the building. Well, nothing but dust and scurrying little things she didn't want to bother identifying.

"I just *love* the places you take me."

He didn't acknowledge her comment in any way as he continued down the hallway. Shahara turned around, studying the abandoned office furniture covered by years of dust, debris, and webs. Contrary to her prediction, but for the dust and decay, it looked like people had just picked up and left. There were even cups and dishes left on some of the desks they passed.

It looked like the workers had abandoned everything in one heartbeat.

Why?

Shahara caught herself as she tripped over a half-full trash can. "Don't you find it weird that they left all this stuff behind?"

"Not really. Someone released a virus through the

air ducts that killed fifteen workers in less than an hour. Those who were ill or unaffected ran screaming for the doors. My money says Merjack did it to cover his tracks after he had me in custody. I'm sure he crawled through every office and file here looking for that chip. And since he still wants me, we know he didn't find it. Once the building was vacated, no one wanted to come back for anything since they feared it might be contaminated from what killed the others."

"Should we be scared?"

"Probably."

Shahara couldn't resist goosing him on the bottom.

"Hey!" he snapped, jumping away from her as he rubbed the cheek she'd pinched.

"That's what you get for being such a pessimist. You're lucky I didn't go after something else."

He growled at her as he limped away. "Next time I'm throwing you at my enemies."

She didn't comment.

Syn wanted to be angry at her, but he couldn't quite manage it. In truth, he melted every time he looked at her.

Why?

Because she'd told him she loved him. He couldn't get those words out of his mind. That was the only thing he'd ever wanted in his life. Did he dare believe her?

Why would she lie?

He kept trying to keep her at a distance, and instead she stayed and quipped with sarcastic humor that he actually found entertaining. Shoving that thought away, he continued his search.

Finally he found what he was looking for. A thick metal door sealed off the office he remembered so well from his youth. The last time he'd been here, his breathing had been ragged, his body sweating. Even now he could see the lights dancing from torches in the hall-way, hear the angry voices as they searched for him.

Now he was back . . .

Shahara snorted as he fumbled with the old controls that were rusted out. "Forget it. You'll never get that open."

Ignoring her hostility, he pulled out his charger and studied the lock. True, there was no electricity, but he'd opened far more secure things than this in his time. "One day you will learn not to doubt me." He opened the panel and began crossing wires, connecting some to the hand-held battery.

After several minutes, a spark ignited and the door rasped open.

Shahara gaped at what he'd done. "I'm impressed."

He disconnected the battery. "Once a filch, always a filch."

She frowned. There was an odd note in his voice. Bitterness, maybe. And she realized it must be strange for him to be confronting this part of his past. A part he must have struggled hard to forget.

The last time he'd been here, he'd gone to prison . . .

Her heart ached for him.

Without even glancing at her, he entered the office and began searching it. Taking out a lightstick, she trailed its beam over the scattered debris. "What am I looking for?"

"Something that can tell you who was once assigned to this office."

"I take it the chip isn't here."

He shook his head. "We have to find something per-sonal about the occupant."

She groaned. "That could be anyone. And anything

I find could be from someone who had this office *long* after you stashed the chip."

"No. Look at the furniture and the dust. It's at least twenty years old. Just like it said in my reports. They shut this place down and never returned to it."

"The office still could have changed hands."

He gave her a fierce glower. "Well, we don't have anything else to go on, now do we?"

She held her hands up in surrender. "All right, don't get testy with me." She continued looking through the garbage.

Syn started going through an old desk.

Just as she was about to give up, her light flashed against a stationery pad. Taking three strides, she knelt down and picked it up. "Does the name Merrin Lyche ring a bell?"

He looked over at her. "What did you find?"

"Some old stationery." She held it out to him.

Taking it, he nodded. "At least it's somewhere to start." He tore off the top sheet, folded it, and put it in his pocket. "Thanks. Now let's get out of here before it gets any colder."

Shahara flashed her light up at him and noted the blueness of his lips. "I am *really* sorry I pulled you into the bath."

He smiled before moving the light out of his face. "Don't be. I'm certainly not."

She rolled her eyes at him and his warped reasoning. "Then lead me back before you die of exposure and I have to explain to someone why your clothes are frozen to your body on a clear night."

His laughter warming her, he led her out of the building.

In no time at all, they were back inside the hotel. Shahara paused at the lift area while Syn continued past it.

Frowning, she hurried to trail after him. "Where are we going?"

He didn't answer. Instead, he entered a small boutique.

What in the nine worlds was he doing? Confused, she stopped outside and watched as he sorted through a rack of jackets.

When he found whatever he must have been searching for, he looked up and eyed her. Next, he moved to the back of the store where she couldn't see him.

She debated going in after him. She felt awkward standing outside while passersby eyed her with way too much interest. But one look at the stony-faced clerks inside the store and she decided she had no interest in getting one step closer to them or their disdain. She didn't need them to remind her of her lowly status.

Just as she finally made the decision to go in after him, he took several things up to the cashier. The man handed him a ledger and Syn signed while the man placed his purchases in a bag.

Once Syn rejoined her, he handed the jacket to her. "You wear a small, right?"

"Yes." She scowled down at the warm, soft suede in her hands. Dark brown, it was lined with synthetic fur that felt softer than down.

Syn continued on to the lifts.

Stunned, she hurried to catch up to him. She wanted to ask him about his gift, but the curious stares of the people around them kept her lips sealed.

It wasn't until they were back in their room that she

confronted him. Of course, by then, she was good and angry because she knew why men bought extravagant presents for women. Especially after they had sex . . .

Every time Caillen felt guilty about sleeping with a woman he didn't care about, he would always go out and buy something for her that he couldn't afford to assuage his conscience.

And the more she thought about it, the angrier she became. "Why did you do this?"

He stopped in the foyer. "You were freezing." He placed the bag on the sofa nearest him.

"I won't be tomorrow."

"Maybe, maybe not. We don't know what we'll be doing tomorrow, now do we?"

That was true.

Still . . .

"How much did this cost?"

He looked at her as if the question insulted him. "Why?"

"I don't want you spending this kind of money on me."

His eyes turned blank. "Why?"

She wanted to slap that innocent look off his face. "Why do you think?"

"Woman, I have no idea." He crossed his arms over his chest and eyed her.

Anger burned deep in her belly. "You are a *Complete Idiot!*" she snarled, tossing the jacket in his face. "That's what the C.I. stands for, doesn't it?"

Syn caught the jacket against his chest as he gaped at her. Had she snapped a wheel?

Was *she* PMSing?

He followed her into the bedroom. "What's your deal?"

She stopped and turned back to face him. "I didn't sleep with you for presents. What do you think, I'm some whore you have to pay off?"

He couldn't have been more stunned had she kicked him. Where had *that* come from? "Oh good grief, you can't possibly think that."

"Why not? You said you don't love me. What does that leave?"

It left him feeling like a heel that he'd insulted her with a gift that had been purchased with only the best intentions. "I . . ." He bit his tongue before he blurted out that he did love her, that he'd only bought her the jacket because it pained him to see her uncomfortable. *I would walk through the fires of hell to get you a pair of shoes.*

But he could never tell her that.

"I don't want you to feel obligated to me, Syn. I don't want anything from you."

Tossing the jacket on the bed, he placed his hands on her shoulders. Then he moved them to cup her beautiful face. "I know that," he whispered, fighting the urge to draw her into his arms and squelch her fury with a kiss. "But we can't go out in the city tomorrow dressed like we are."

Shahara felt her heart slide to her feet. His explanation brought an even greater pain to her chest. He was just being practical. Not thoughtful.

Not even remorseful.

She rated so low on his scale that he didn't feel even the tiniest bit of guilt for sleeping with someone he didn't love.

"I bought both of us some clothes that wouldn't stand out."

"Oh," she said, feeling completely ridiculous. *Face it, girl, you don't mean anything to him.*

She tried to convince herself that it was for the best. Especially given what was to come. But her heart didn't listen. It still hurt and wanted more from him than he was able to give.

Syn released her. "Why don't you go and check in with your family. I'm sure they're worried sick about you."

Unable to speak past the lump in her throat, she nodded and went to comply. As she moved to the link, it dawned on her that this had been the longest she'd ever gone without talking to her siblings. She and Caillen kept in almost constant contact.

It wasn't that she didn't love them or that they were further from her thoughts—it was just . . .

She liked being with Syn. She really enjoyed him. Even though their lives were in danger and they were being hunted, she adored his company. Not even his bad mood could push her away.

I am so messed up.

Syn watched her walk away, his chest tight. What he wouldn't give for the freedom to lay his heart at her feet. To stay with her for the rest of his life. But he'd abandoned such dreams years ago. They belonged to his childhood.

And what few he'd managed to keep had been slaughtered on the altar of Mara's apathy and scorn. He wouldn't make that mistake ever again.

Besides, Shahara had a family who loved her. She didn't need his tainted love. And she definitely didn't need his screwed-up life. His best friends were outlaws and assassins.

Yeah . . . just what a seax needed in her life.

Aching at the thought, he joined her in the sitting room.

"Where the hell have you been?" Caillen snarled so loudly over the link that he could hear it from across the room. "I've been trying everything to get ahold of you for days. Don't you ever check your messages? We've been worried to death about you."

"As you can hear, I'm fine," she said testily.

"Are you still with that bastard?"

Syn flinched at the hatred in Caillen's voice.

"That's none of your business."

"Yeah, well, thanks to you and your hormones, Tessa's been taken."

Syn went cold.

"What?" Her voice cracked with obvious fear. "What are you talking about?"

"I got a call two days ago from a man named Merjack saying he has her and, if we want to see her alive again, you'd better turn your *lover* over to him."

She turned so pale Syn thought she might faint.

"Did you hear me?" Caillen demanded.

"I heard you."

"So who do you pick, Trisa? Tessa or a filch?"

Syn put his hand on her shoulder, offering her what comfort he could. He reached over and cut the transmission. "Call Merjack."

She looked up at him and he saw fury glaring back at him. "I'm going to kill that lying bastard." Her tone was low and deadly serious.

"I'm going to help you. But first we have to get your sister back. Make the call."

Shahara nodded even though she could barely see for the raw, unmitigated rage that made her hands shake. How could the bastard have done this? Was he out of his mind?

When I get my hands on you . . .

He would know pain as his primary mistress. But first she had to get control of herself. Passion without control was wasted. She had to funnel it to get him back within her grasp so that she could carve his skin from his body. And by his actions, she knew he was guilty of everything Syn had accused him of.

There was no longer any doubt. Any man who could take her sick and innocent sister hostage when they already had a bargain made . . .

He was going to go down. But first she had to get Tessa back.

Syn took the link from her so that he could talk to Merjack and she could listen. One glance and he could tell she was too mad to be rational right now—not that he blamed her in the least. She was actually doing a lot better than he'd expected. But they needed a negotiator who wasn't as emotionally involved.

She dialed Merjack's extension.

The pathetic worm answered on the third ring. "Well, well, the rat has finally crawled back out of his sewer."

Syn ignored his insults. "Where's Tessa Dagan?"

"She's safe . . . for now."

Like that meant anything. If Syn knew the animal he was talking to, he knew better than to put any trust in Merjack. "I want proof."

"Fine. After we finish, call Warden Traysen at the prison and he'll show her to you."

His fury blinded him as he heard Shahara's sharp intake of breath. Her face blanched.

"You effing bastard," Syn snarled. "You can't keep her there. She's innocent in all this."

What the hell was he thinking? He'd been a lot more innocent and younger when they'd thrown him in jail, and those memories were what tore through him. He knew exactly what they'd do to her if they didn't rescue her immediately.

Merjack laughed. "You forget who my son is. As the father of the president, I can do anything I want to."

And you can die pretty, too, you bastard.

Syn gripped the link, wishing it was Merjack's fat hairy neck he was squeezing.

"You know what I want, rat. Give me the chip, without making a copy, and she's free."

"I don't have it."

"Well, then, I know a few guards and inmates who've been eyeing our new guest . . ."

Syn narrowed his eyes. "If they touch her, I'll rip out your throat."

"The chip, rat, or I'll toss her in with the rape felons. You have thirty hours." Merjack cut the transmission.

He looked at Shahara. Raw panic burned in her golden eyes, and it made him that more determined to kill Merjack. "I won't let them hurt her."

"What if we don't find it?" she asked, her voice cracking.

"We will."

"Oh God, Syn, I'm so afraid."

He drew her into his arms and held her tightly. "It'll be all right. I promise." But he didn't really believe those words any more than she did. He'd given up any hope that karma or justice was fair when his sister had killed herself. Life was nothing but pain, and no matter how much you fought or ran, it always threw you to the ground and beat you to a pulp.

Today would be no different.

Pulling away from her, he reached for the link and called the prison. The warden showed him Tessa in one of the better cells. Though she sat crying on her cot, she didn't look any the worse for her incarceration. They'd left her fully clothed, and a tray of fresh food and drink was set on the table by her cot.

He could sense Shahara's need to speak with her, but he knew they'd never allow it.

"As you can see," Traysen said, "we've taken good care of her. I have a doctor looking in on her and she's been kept isolated from the others. It's the best I can do for now."

Shahara nodded. "Thank you, Warden. But know that if anything happens to her at all, if she even gets a hangnail, I'll be coming for you and I won't stop. Ever."

A chill went down Syn's spine as he saw the ruthless woman who'd broken into his apartment and shot him. After all they'd been through, he'd forgotten this side of her.

The side of her that made grown men piss their pants at the mere mention of her name.

And he saw that fear in Traysen's eyes. The man was staring into the beautiful face of death and in spite of its delicate features, it lacked all mercy. That was a hell unimaginable and he never wanted to be on the receiving end of her hatred and determination. No wonder Caillen wouldn't mess with her.

She cut the transmission. "We need to prepare."

With a subtle nod, he pulled his laptop from the bag and set to work on finding information about the man who'd been assigned to the office where he'd dumped the chip.

Shahara paced the floor while Syn worked, wishing she could do something more productive. A subtle tapping sounded at the window. At first she ignored it.

"Could you let Vik in?"

She popped herself on the forehead. "Sorry. I wasn't thinking." She went over and opened the window.

Vik came inside, cursing them both. "Do you know how painful the cold is on my circuitry?"

"Sorry."

"Yeah, I bet you are."

Syn looked up with a heavy sigh. "Quit bitching and get over here, Vik. I need you to boost my signal. I'm having trouble getting into a couple of servers."

"Yes, oh, great snotty bastard." Vik flew to his side, then extended a limb to plug into the computer. "Nice to know—"

"One more word, Vik, and I'm reprogramming you to remove your voice."

He pressed his metallic lips together and shut up immediately.

Shahara would have been amused had their situation not been so dire. "There's nothing I can do to help, is there?"

"Don't distract me."

And yet she knew she couldn't stay here without bothering him. She wanted to know what he was doing. What he was learning. *Tessa will die if you slow him down* . . .

She picked up the link. "I'm going to leave you alone. Call me when you have something."

He nodded.

Grabbing the new jacket, she left him and Vik and went walkabout so that she could at least try and clear her head. But it was impossible. All she could see was Tessa's face when she'd been a kid, depending on Shahara. Back when she'd been training as a seax, Tessa had learned to cook and would always greet her at the door with some kind of treat.

"One day I want to be just like you."

Only she'd wanted better than that for her sister.

Her heart heavy, she paused in the lobby to stare up at the beautiful dress in the boutique. How she wished she could afford things like that for her and her sisters.

I can't even keep them safe.

Tears of frustration gathered in her eyes as she left the hotel with no destination in mind. It wasn't until she reached a temple at the end of the second block that she stopped again.

Never one for religion, she approached the door slowly. It was Syn's denomination. She still found his religiousness mystifying. How could he have faith after all he'd been through?

But then, maybe that was the beauty of it. There was no faith greater than that that had been tested and survived.

Wanting to find her own peace, she went inside. A young priestess around the age of twenty, and wearing the same robe as Mother Anne, stood in a nearby corner, restocking the supply of tapers. "Good evening, child," she said with a tender smile.

"Good evening, Mother."

"It's a terribly cold night for you to be out. What trouble brings you to our door?"

"I . . . I've come to pray."

The priestess smiled and handed her a candle. "Then I won't disturb you. May you find peace tonight, child, and may the gods keep you and those you love safe."

She didn't know why, but those kind words brought tears to her eyes. "Thank you, Mother."

The priestess inclined her head respectfully to her, then returned to work.

Shahara took the taper and went to light it. As

quietly as she could, she entered the nave and found a quiet spot to kneel on the floor. She glanced around at the statues of the gods and wondered if they really existed. Did they see her or even care what was happening to her?

Neither of her parents had been religious, and she'd never had time for it in her life. But tonight . . .

Tonight she didn't want to feel alone in the universe. She wanted to believe that there was a higher power that had brought her to this pass. That something had a plan, because she certainly didn't.

Don't die, Tess . . .

Tears fell down her cheeks as she faced reality. What was she going to do? To save Tess would mean Syn's life. Merjack wouldn't stop until Syn was dead.

What have I done?

She'd made a pact with the devil for one man's life. And not just any man.

The only man she'd ever loved.

I can't do this. I can't hand him over to die.

But what choice did she have? And as those thoughts chased each other around in her head, she heard one deep, intrinsic male voice above them all.

Trust me.

Syn growled in frustration as he kept searching for information about Merrin Lyche. How could there be nothing on the man?

It was like chasing a ghost.

C'mon, don't do this to me. Most of all, he didn't want it done to Shahara.

Disgusted, he pulled a tiny ring out of his pocket and studied it.

A wedding ring . . .

It'd been a stupid impulse to buy the ring. He'd known it the moment he did it. But as he was buying Shahara her jacket, he'd looked down in the jewelry case and seen its golden diamond stones twinkling. Their fire flashed with the same intensity as her eyes, and he couldn't resist it anymore than he could resist her.

What a tangled, complicated mess they were in.

Of course, he should be used to that by now. Life was a treacherous beast, and every time he thought he had it tamed, it always turned around and bit him on the ass. But he refused to let it humble Shahara. She deserved better than that.

It's hopeless. There's nothing here on the man.

No, he wouldn't give up. He couldn't. Setting the ring aside, he kept looking.

"Hey, boss?"

"Not now, Vik."

Vik extended one arm and shoved him back in his chair. "Dude, listen to the metallic life form."

Just as Syn was about to tear his head off, Vik entered a code and unlocked Lyche's files.

But it was the top file that made every hope he had crumble straight to the ground as he realized one truth.

None of them were going to survive.

CHAPTER 18

Shahara paused as she entered the hotel room and found Syn looking ill. It was obvious he'd received bad news.

Again.

There was also an open half-empty bottle of hard Tondarion Fire next to him—an alcohol so potent, it was banned on most planets. That definitely wasn't a good sign.

"What happened?"

He took a swig of the alcohol straight out of the bottle—impressive and scary. "Lyche is dead."

The news slammed straight into her gut as she neared him. Surely she'd misheard him. "What?"

His eyes mirrored the disgust on his face. "Fate is indeed one serious bitch . . . He died ten years ago, probably from a disease caused by Merjack's gas."

"So what are you saying?"

"Basically, we're screwed." He raked his hand through his hair. "I just unlocked his medical files—"

Vik cleared his throat.

"*Vik* unlocked his files and I found the death certificate."

So glad I was right . . . Weary and upset, she went to

stand by his side so that she could see the report herself.

Sure enough, the man was dead. Not that she doubted Syn, but she was hoping he'd had a concussion that left him unable to read or something.

This can't be happening . . . They needed to find that chip.

"So where does this leave us?"

"I'm working on it. His wife is still alive. I'm doing a search for her contact information. Maybe . . . maybe she still has the statue."

"Statue? Why are you looking for a statue?"

"That's what I put the chip in."

Shahara frowned. "A statue?" she repeated. "How big was this thing?"

He held his hands up to show her about three feet.

"And you chose that again . . . why?"

"It was there and it seemed like a good idea at the time. Besides, it *did* work. No one seems to have found it in all these years."

Holding her hands up, she didn't say anything else as he reached for the link to call Lyche's widow.

He checked his chronometer. "It should be middle afternoon where she is. Keep your hopes up."

They were about the only thing she had up at the moment. *C'mon. Answer the call* . . . She waited, her heart pounding erratically until an old woman answered his call.

"*Fria* Lyche?"

"Yes, yes, this is she. Can I help you?"

"I hope so, ma'am. You don't know me, but I'm looking for a piece of statuary your late husband owned."

"Merrin had several pieces," she said, her voice gentle and kind. "He loved to collect all different types."

"Yes, ma'am. The one I'm interested in looked like an ancient Derridian goddess. Pikra, I think it was."

"Oh yes, the garishly green one with the snake skin and ruby hair. No matter how hard I try, I can't purge that nasty thing out of my mind."

Shahara grimaced at the hideous description. Why would anyone buy such a thing? For that matter, why would anyone hide a valuable chip in it?

Even as a kid, Syn should have known better.

He looked up at her and winked. "That's the one. Do you know what happened to it?"

"Oh my goodness, would you believe the doctors told him not to go back to his office and remove anything at all, and yet he insisted he go back for that monstrosity? He said it had magic-protecting powers instilled in it from ancient times. The only power I ever knew it to have was the ability to make everyone who saw it cringe and curl their lips. I still don't know why he loved it so. He was like a kid with a pet toy. But once he got sick, I made him get rid of that foully hideous thing. It made my skin crawl to be near it. Evil-looking thing, it was."

It was gone? Shahara felt ill at the woman's tirade. *What are we going to do now?*

Syn scowled. "Do you know what he did with it?"

"Gave it over to an auction house. Why are you interested in it, anyway?"

"I remember seeing it in his office a long time ago and I found it . . . intriguing."

"Well, I guess we all have different tastes."

"Yes, ma'am. Um, do you remember which house he turned it over to?"

"Oh, that big one that's so famous on Tondara."

"Berringer's?"

"Yes, that's it."

"Thank you, *Fria* Lyche. I appreciate your help."

She cut the link.

Syn sat back in his chair, put his hands behind his head, and smiled. For some reason that pose made him look mischievous and handsome while the whiskers on his face made him look exceedingly dangerous. "I think we have it."

Shahara wasn't feeling so optimistic. "It's been how many years? There's no telling where it could be now."

"No, but Berringer's keeps detailed catalogs of all its pieces as well as files on all their buyers."

Hope began to well up inside her again. "Are you sure?"

He nodded. "Oh, yeah. I've bought several pieces of art from them."

"Why would you buy from them if they keep detailed—"

"I know someone who works for them who is . . . discreet. I put my bid in through them, and they deliver my purchases to my office."

That made sense. "And how do you know the ugly statue buyer isn't another convict buying through a discreet contact?"

He glowered at her. "I really hate when you call me a convict."

She crossed the room to sidle up to him and touch the tip of his nose. "I mean it lovingly. Really. Because of you, I have a whole new respect for convicts . . . and you haven't answered my question."

"I don't have an answer until I look it up." He kissed her finger before he turned his attention to the laptop.

She stood aside and watched as he effortlessly accessed files and data about auctions and buyers. How

"Why not?"

"Because you've never bro'
building. If you don't know
get killed. Those kinds of facil.
one. Not to mention I know an eas.

"Which is?"

"Donya Arisa."

She frowned. "What is that?"

"The *what* is a *who*. And *she* is easy to man.
Trust me. I'll go see her first thing in the morning.

Shahara wasn't sure she liked the sound of tha
whole manipulation thing. He made it sound like he'd
had a lot of practice doing that with this unknown
woman. The thought caused a huge stab of jealousy to
go through her. "Don't you mean *we*, flyboy?"

"No, me. You're staying here."

"Oh, I definitely don't think so, and you don't take
that tone of voice with me. Ever."

Vik, who'd been completely silent all this time,
perked up. "Oh, I'm out of this." He flew to the window
and let himself out.

"Shahara—"

"Zzzt," she said, holding her hand up. "Wasting time
here. I won't even hear it. You go. I go. It's my sister's
life on the line and I out-shoot and am pretty sure I out-
fight you, too."

"I think we came up pretty even on that score."

"But I am the better shot."

He gave her a grudging glare. "I concede. However,
I think I can take you when I'm sober."

She took the bottle out of his hand. "Good. I'm going to throw this out."

"Uh!" He reached for it.

shed she had his talents. She was only g
ng things and blowing them up.
specially computers and their networks.
After several minutes, he cursed. "Those pa
iveling . . ."

"What?"

He snatched up his bottle and took a drink b
answered. "They don't keep their archived cata
line. They have a private in-house system off-g

"What does that mean?"

"We have to be inside their gallery to find
bought the piece. Which is good that no one
track or trace me through them, but right nov
when I want those files."

She sighed as she stared at the monitor tha
a beautiful emerald necklace she'd love to c
we going to break in?"

He laughed evilly. "Only a brief time arou
I've already turned you into a filch. Can yo
what you'd be like after a year?"

She popped him lightly on the back of th
she used to do with Caillen whenever he'd
with her.

"Hey!"

"It's what you get for that. Besides, \
couldn't straighten you out as easily as yo
me?"

Syn froze at her words as all his hum
truth was, she could straighten him out. Be
it came to her, he was weaker than he'd e
fore.

Diverting his attention before she reali
did to him, he closed down his laptop. "]
breaking in would be the wisest course."

Shahara danced away from him and had the bottle upside down in the sink before he could catch her.

He tried to get it out of her hands, but it was too late. "You are an evil, mean woman."

"And you are drunk."

"I work better that way."

She dropped the bottle and turned to face him. His hair was hanging in his dark eyes that seared her. "No, Syn, you don't. I don't like what the alcohol does to you."

Syn wanted to curse her and tell her it was none of her business. But right then, staring down into her face . . .

He was lost to her.

All he wanted was to have her hold him close and make everything else go away. Yet she couldn't. Not when Tessa's life was on the line.

I have to stay focused. Something that was impossible when she stood so close to him he could see her pupils dilate.

As if she could sense his desire, she reached up and placed her hand on his cheek. "I see you, Syn. I know what kind of man you are, and the only thing I would change is your needless insobriety."

"I don't like to feel."

"And yet you do. No matter how much you drink, it doesn't really go away, does it?"

No, it didn't. But her touch . . .

It chased the pain away. How did she do that? How could she love something like him?

"I will always stand by you, Shay. Always."

Shahara's breath caught at those ragged words that had come straight from his heart. They and the use of her nickname touched her deep inside. And before she could think better of it, she stood on her tiptoes and kissed him.

His hand tightened on her waist as if he wanted to hold on to her forever.

It was then she knew the truth.

He loved her. He might not say it, but she could feel it in his kiss and his touch.

Syn wanted to curse at how good she tasted and felt. There was no one else he'd ever wanted like this. And as her tongue danced with his, his mind tormented him with thoughts of a life with her.

If only they could . . .

He pulled back even though every part of him screamed out in denial of it.

"We need to get going," they said in unison.

Syn stepped back and indicated his stolen uniform. "But we can't go like this."

"Yeah, we'd look a little suspicious. So what kind of clothes did you buy?"

He motioned to the bag on the floor. "Didn't you look before the hissy fit?"

"No. And I didn't throw a hissy fit." She picked up the bag and pulled out a shirt and pair of pants that were definitely cut for Syn. On the bottom was a rust-colored pantsuit for her. It was made of the softest fabric she'd ever touched. "Nice."

"I'm sorry it's not better, but I didn't have time to really look."

His apology stunned her. "Don't be sorry. It's the nicest thing I've ever had."

Syn clenched his teeth at the earnestness of her tone. Gods, how he wanted to rectify that. And as she started taking her shirt off, he realized that he couldn't stay in here. Not if he wanted to stay focused.

"I'm going to the bathroom. I'll be back in a few."

Shahara frowned as Syn all but left a vapor trail in his hurry to leave her. Shaking her head, she pulled her shirt off and dropped it on the desk as she exchanged her uniform for the pantsuit.

As soon as she was dressed, she pulled her shirt back. It caught against the magazine by his laptop and uncovered something that sparkled. Curious, she moved closer to find . . .

A wedding ring.

The sight hit her like a punch in the gut. Was it Mara's?

If it were, it meant only one thing—he'd loved his wife. He'd been lying when he said he didn't. And he must have loved her dearly for him to have kept her ring all these years.

Something inside her shattered at the realization.

Maybe you're wrong. Maybe it's Talia's . . .

But Talia had only been a girl when she'd died. Surely she wouldn't have owned a wedding ring.

His mother's?

No, he hated her too much to have kept hers. There was only one answer and it made her ill.

That's why he didn't tell you he loved you. He's still missing his wife.

She heard him opening the door. Moving away from the ring before he caught her ogling it, she put her uniform in the bag and tried to act as nonchalant as possible. But inside . . .

Inside she was screaming.

He put his old clothes down by the couch.

"Will you finally tell me what the C.I. stands for?" she asked, wondering if he'd share that with her.

"No."

She lifted her brow in surprise. "No snappy comeback? Why, Syn, I think you're losing your touch."

He said nothing. She saw him hesitate at the ring. Then he palmed it so fast that she barely realized he'd moved.

Looking up, he scowled at her. "What? Did I grow a new head?"

She cleared her throat as she hoped her face didn't betray her hurt and anger at him. "No, I was just trying to think what name you might choose that would fit you best."

"How about dead?"

"You're not funny."

"Neither is Merjack."

She rolled her eyes. "So what are we going to do about him?"

"Hope he upholds his end of the bargain and try to stay out of his way."

Shahara clucked her tongue at him. "I *really* think you should come up with a better plan than that."

"Why bother? Life has a way of destroying all plans."

He was such a cynic. Shaking her head at him, she turned to get her weapon out of the pack.

"Shahara?"

"Yes," she answered without turning around.

"If he kills me, would you see to it that I'm buried in the Ilysian Temple on Kildara beside Talia? I have a space already paid for."

His request sliced through her as she realized why he'd chosen to live where he did. His apartment was within walking distance of where his sister was buried. Even all these years later, he wanted to be close to her.

Watch over her.

Wincing for the pain he carried inside him, she wanted to cry. "Yes. I'll make sure that you're . . ."

She couldn't say it. The thought of his death was more than she could cope with.

"Thank you."

Shahara nodded and fought against the pain tearing through her. He really might die.

And then what would she do? How could she live knowing that she'd set all this in motion?

Same way you've lived through every horror. One day at a time. But could she do that knowing she'd hurt him?

Don't think about it. Right now, Tessa was the most important thing. Syn wouldn't get hurt. She'd make sure of it.

Shahara adjusted her suit with a little tug on the gold belt. She knew she should be grateful that they were so close to freeing Tessa, but that just meant she was that much closer to losing Syn, and that tore her apart.

Glancing up at him, she had to smile. He looked stunning in his all-white suit and shirt. The color deepened the tan of his skin.

"Are we ready?"

He gave her that shit-eating grin that was as second nature to him as his sarcasm. "I'm always ready for a fight." He opened the door for her.

As she walked past, he leaned over and whispered in her ear, "You look great, by the way."

She licked her lips as she scanned his tall, sexy body. "So do you."

He actually whimpered. "Why can't we have two more hours in the room?"

She snorted. "Two hours? Honey, you seriously over-estimate your sexual prowess."

He gaped at her retort. "Yeah, right. I am the best when it comes to bedroom play."

"You keep telling yourself that, sweetie. One day you might convince someone else."

Syn wanted to be offended, but he knew she was just teasing him. Strangely, it charmed him.

I am so stupid . . . and in love. Which meant he was basically screwed.

Unwilling to think about that, he led her downstairs and out to a landing bay a few blocks over. He noticed as they walked that she huddled deep in her coat. It was cold, but then he was used to it. Many a night he'd lain on these streets and prayed for a time when he could live indoors and have heat.

Shahara hesitated as they entered the bay. "What are we doing?"

"Nero has a fighter that I'm borrowing."

She cut him a suspicious glare. "Borrowing?"

He tapped his earpiece to open the channel to Vik. "Vik? Foreground. Now." He gave her a droll stare as Vik flew in and landed on his shoulder.

The mecha bristled. "You do know I'm not your girlfriend, right? I don't like that tone of voice and I'd appreciate it if you'd pick a new one. Otherwise, I'll spit invisible poison in your eyeball . . . both of them."

Syn let out an irritated breath, but didn't say anything as he opened his hand. Vik dropped a nav chip in his palm. Holding it up for Shahara's inspection, he smirked. "I called him earlier, then sent Vik to get the key."

She bit her lip as she felt her face grow hot. "Sorry."

"No problem, but just know that no one steals from Nero. He knows who you are and he will hunt you down and make you pay in ways you can't imagine—including this whole brain squeeze thing he does that will leave you with a migraine so bad, you'll wish you could bleed out your eyes to stop the pain. He's nasty that way."

"Duly noted."

Clasping her hands behind her back, she dutifully followed him to Nero's sleek, dark burgundy two-seated fighter. She ascended the boarding ladder first and situated herself in the navigator's chair while Vik tucked himself in between her and Syn.

Syn didn't speak as he ran through the flight checks, but he couldn't help noticing how proud and fierce Shahara looked as she plugged in their coordinates. Her hands were beautiful in their grace and confidence.

The irony of his feelings toward her wasn't lost on him. He'd sworn growing up that he'd never have anything to do with a lowly pleb. Especially not one who could beat him in a fight and out-shoot him.

And as he considered his feelings, he wondered if part of his attraction for well-bred women hadn't been some underlying desire to have his mother accept and approve of him. After all, if an educated, sophisticated woman like Mara could accept him, it only stood to reason his mother would, too.

Now that he was too old to give a shit what anyone thought of him, his true desires came out. He liked the fact that Shahara could stand at his back and protect it. That she knew what she wanted and wasn't afraid to do whatever she had to to get it.

There was a lot to be said for a woman who was as predatorial as he was.

She paused as she realized he was looking at her. "Am I doing something wrong?"

"No. I was just thinking how incredibly beautiful you are."

That didn't seem to please her as her gaze danced around in obvious discomfort. "You're still drunk, aren't you?"

He laughed. "No. The hangover is starting to kick in. Head hammering like a mother."

"Ah, that explains it."

"What does?"

"Your eyesight's screwed up. I could probably take you into a retirement home and you'd be trying to score with Grandma right now."

He should be offended, but instead he laughed again. "You're so wrong." Shaking his head, he launched them.

Shahara didn't say anything else while he concentrated on their launch. Her thoughts were torn between her angry brother, her captured sister, and the man she wanted to love who wouldn't let her.

The bad thing was, she wanted to beat and kill all three of them for basically the same reason. They were all too stubborn to live, and if they'd listen to her, all three of them wouldn't be in their current situations.

Ugh! What was it with her that she surrounded herself with such difficult people? Or even worse, loved them?

I'm sick in the head . . .

Once they cleared orbit, she spoke. "Do you think they'll hurt Tess?"

"You want me to lie?"

Her gut tightened. "You just answered my question."

He reached out and took her hand in his. "Have faith, baby. I won't let them hurt her. I promise. We'll get that chip and I'll make them pay for what they've done."

For the first time in her adult life, she didn't cringe at the use of that particular endearment. It actually warmed her. "I do trust you. It's Merjack I want to rip into pieces."

"We find that chip and you'll have the power to bring him down."

"I hope so."

She stared out at the matte blackness that stretched into infinity. She'd never found space travel particularly comforting. Mostly because she knew the dangers. Yet with Syn . . . while she was worried, she wasn't as brittle as she'd be if she was alone. She knew he'd move mountains to keep Tess safe. She felt like she could actually depend on someone else.

It was a completely different feeling from what she had with her brother. While she knew Caillen would move mountains for her, there was still a part of her that wanted to wipe his chin and cut up his food. A part of her that couldn't allow him to see that she wasn't the big sister who had to take care of him and watch out for him.

With Syn . . .

She could let down her guard and allow him to take care of her. While she could lead, she didn't have to be in charge and stronger than titanium at all times. It was such a nice change to be able to show her insecurities to someone.

With Syn, she felt like a partner.

Vik got up and moved to sit more in her lap.

"What are you doing, Vik?"

He flicked into his bot form and draped over her leg. "I'm getting bored."

"You can't get bored."

"Yes, I can." He stretched out. "How much farther?"

She laughed at his tone that sounded like a five-year-old. "My God, he's like having a child."

Syn snorted. "Yeah. You even have to change his diaper at times."

"Nah. Just my batteries."

Syn arched a brow. "And your attitude."

"Bitch, bitch, bitch. Now leave me alone while I nap."

Shahara didn't know what to make of him as he shut down his power and went into a sleep mode. "You know, Vik really is an impressive invention. You could have easily had a career in robotics and programming."

"You think I didn't try?"

"What happened?"

"Couldn't pass the security checks. They not only investigate you, but your immediate family. While Nykyrian and I were able to fabricate my important files, coming up with records for parents and every known address I would have lived at while growing up, with living references who could give sworn testimony that I went to certain schools and lived in certain places, was something we couldn't do. May the gods bless and hold the computer and robotic companies. They are seriously paranoid bastards."

She touched his necklace that she still wore as her heart broke for him. What a waste of so much talent. "I'm sorry, Syn."

He shrugged. "It's all right. Besides, it took away any guilt I had when I stole info and intel from them. If they'd hired me, I'd have had a vested interest in protecting them."

Well, there was that. Leaning back in her chair, she watched as he worked on the terminal, pulling up info for their coming adventure.

He'd pulled his hair back into a ponytail. His whiskers were dark against his tawny skin and made him look even more dangerous. It pained her to know how much tragedy he'd faced in his life.

"Do you ever think about getting married again?"

Syn froze at her unexpected question. He glanced down as his mind flashed on the wedding ring he had in his pocket that he'd bought for her. Against his best efforts, he imagined what it would be like to live his life with her.

But that was stupid and he knew it.

"No," he lied.

Shahara felt her heart break at his answer. So he did still love Mara. She should have known. And who could blame him? His wife had been beautiful, well-schooled and well-bred. All the things she wasn't.

You're defective. No matter how hard she tried to feel otherwise, she always came back to that one single truth. Life had broken her early and she'd never recovered.

What do you care? You don't need anyone in your life. You're stronger alone. Better. Part of that was true, but she was still human, and being human was about making connections. About feeling a part of something.

You're a part of your family.

Stop whining. You're alive and you have a good life. Granted, it's in poverty, but it could be worse. You don't have to visit your siblings in a tomb.

Like Syn.

That snapped her out of her melancholy. She had no right to complain about anything, and the most important thing for her to focus on was getting Tessa back.

It was midafternoon when they arrived at the gallery. Shahara was starting to feel battered by the constant time zone changes—another serious drawback to space travel. Her body had a hard time making the switch and she no longer remembered what time it was back at her home base.

But Syn didn't look any worse for the wear.

As they approached the posh and hoity gallery that was housed in an all-glass building, the doors, which were flanked by two steel male bodies four stories tall, opened automatically. Suspended from the ceiling was a huge green human eye that focused on them and followed their path in a large circle as they approached the receptionist's desk. The foyer was stark white and as antiseptic as a hospital. If not for the huge red sign over the receptionist's head designating it as Berringer's, she would have gone back outside and rechecked the address.

People bustled all around the lobby. Most of them were buyers holding computer ledgers while the rest were workers trying to make deals and set appointments.

Shahara turned to ask Syn how he thought this would work when a sultry voice laughed, cutting her off.

"Wicked, wicked Syn." The woman's voice cooed at him in a way that made Shahara see red. "Whatever brings you to my little art gallery? I thought you preferred *private* showings?"

How could one woman make such an innocuous word sound so dirty?

Syn flashed her a dazzling grin that highlighted his dimple to perfection. "I was looking for *you*."

Oh yeah, *that* didn't help at all. Now Shahara wanted to slap both of them. It might have helped her jealousy if the woman wasn't quite so gorgeous, or voluptuous.

So incredibly perfect . . .

It was obvious from her meticulous manicure and soft, unblistered hands that this woman had never held a blaster. Never had to lift an eyebrow to do anything other than snap her fingers to have someone else wait on her.

And the more Shahara looked at her, the more she despised the long-legged brunette who stared at Syn as if he were a tasty morsel she was just dying to gobble up. She didn't know why, but an image of the woman licking her fingers while trying to seduce him with her gaze went through her mind.

Keep that up, woman, and you're going home bald . . .

"And just what do you want with *me*?" she purred suggestively, draping a long, shapely arm over his shoulder. She pulled him close, her breasts pressing against his side. Gah, the nerve of her open flirting. Didn't that kind of display get someone fired? "The same as last time, I hope?"

Syn wanted to shove Donya away, but she could be a major bitch, and, if she felt slighted in any way, she'd storm out and he'd never get a chance to look over the catalogs he needed to see. So the best thing was to play along. "If I only had more time, I'd gladly oblige. But I'm afraid I'm in a bit of a hurry."

Her hungry look made him cringe. Yet worse than that was the way she trailed her finger down the low-cut front of her shirt, opening it up until he had a perfect view of her bare breasts and nipples.

"Come now. I can't think of anything I'd rather be than completely *filled* with Syn. If we try hard enough, I'll bet we could get it down to fifteen minutes."

Shahara arched a brow at that and he immediately noticed the raw anger smoldering in her golden eyes. *I'm in deep shit.* If he didn't stop this real soon, Shahara would probably shoot them both. He gave her an apologetic look that he hoped she didn't misinterpret.

Suddenly, she raked Donya with a lust-filled stare, then licked her lips in a sexual invitation that left him instantly hard. "I don't think we could really do that with a threesome, now, could we?" She twirled her hand in her hair with an innocent and yet seductive look that both amazed and aroused him. "Of course, Syn might prefer it if we left him out of it completely. What do you think?"

Syn coughed to cover his laugh. She had spunk. No doubt about it.

Her face horrified, Donya scowled at him. "Syn? Who is this person?"

He wanted to say it was his wife. If for no other reason than to get Donya off him. But he didn't dare alienate her. "She's a friend."

Donya dismissed her immediately. "So what is it I can do for you, gorgeous?"

"First, you can treat my friend with respect—especially given the amount of money I spend here. After that, I need to see the company's archived catalogs."

She pressed her lips into a seductive pout as she ignored the first part of his words. "Wanting to add to your collection?"

"Something like that."

Donya huffed irritably as she finally peeled herself

Syn wanted to be horrified by her actions, but in truth, he found them hysterical. Especially since Donya deserved it, given her rudeness toward Shahara.

What better vengeance without stooping to her level . . .

Once inside Donya's office, she activated the catalog kiosk that stood in the corner.

Shahara stopped by his side and draped her arm possessively over his left shoulder in the same manner Donya had used in the lobby. She folded her hands and rested her chin on top of them as she smiled prettily at Donya, who tried even harder to ignore her.

"How far back do you want to go, Syn?"

"About twenty years."

Donya arched her brows. "Really? It must be some piece. Another Chinergov?"

"No. I don't know the artist. It's an ancient Derridian sculpture that was put on sale by a man named Merrin Lyche."

"Hmm . . ." She punched in the data. "Is this it?"

He froze as he saw it, and that one crystal moment of his childhood slammed into him full force and teleported him back in time. Again, he was fourteen, standing in Lyche's office as he heard them coming for him. And in that panicked chaos of his ragged, terrified panting while sweat trickled down his back with itchy fingers, he'd had one moment of total clarity.

They're going to kill me.

Hide the chip. If they can't find it, they'll torture you for it. So long as you don't break and tell them where it is, you'll live.

Determined to outwit them and survive, he'd looked around until he saw the piece on a bookcase. About thirty inches tall, it was garishly hideous. The skin was off him. "Well, then, follow me." She paused to rake Shahara with a condemning glare. *"You* stay behind us."

Shahara sucked her breath in sharply as if she was getting an absolute thrill from the mere thought of it. "Oh, baby, I can't wait. I love nothing more than a woman with back, and honey, you got a great big one. By all means, lead the way and let me enjoy the sight. I'll have to call all my girls later and let them know exactly how sexy that big ass of yours is." She purred like a prowling feline.

It was all he could do not to laugh out loud. "You are so bad."

She shrugged prettily as she continued to make overt and over-the-top lustful expressions at Donya. "I just know what I like."

And he never wanted to be on the receiving end of her venom—she knew exactly what buttons to push and she was working that into a frenzy.

Donya made a squeak of protest as she covered her butt with her ledger and then proceeded to lead them to her office.

Syn shook his head at Shahara. *Behave,* he mouthed to her over his shoulder.

She pointed angrily at Donya, then made a gesture as if she were choking her.

Donya turned around and Shahara, without missing a single beat, smiled at her and turned her gesture into one that said she was pretending to squeeze Donya's ass while licking her lips as if she could taste her.

Donya shot forward like she'd hit hyperdrive and left them to try and keep up.

Shahara gave a low, evil laugh.

so green, the twisted facial expression so ugly, it was hard to even look at it.

Which meant no one would search it for the chip.

His body quaking from fear, he'd run to it and grabbed it so that he could hide the chip in the base. He'd barely returned it to the shelf and stepped toward the windows before the door crashed open. They'd seized him instantly and it'd taken all of his willpower not to look at the statue to make sure it went undetected. But even as a child he'd known better than that.

So he'd been dragged out . . .

Now he saw the photo of the one thing that had saved his life that day.

"That's it."

Donya frowned at the statue as if it pained her. "Come now, sweet. You've got better taste than that. What? Is this a gift for your *friend*?"

Shahara gave her a sultry smile. "Oh, if only I could be so lucky. I would love to have something like that to remind me of you."

"Of me?"

"Both of you got back, baby. More than that, she's got your hairstyle, too."

Donya's face flushed bright red as her eyes narrowed in fury.

Get control, boy. You can't afford to blow this.

He directed a warning look at Shahara before he turned back to Donya to recapture her attention. "I really need to find this piece, no matter the cost. Do you know who has it?"

It took several minutes before Donya stopped glaring at Shahara and pulled up the information. "We've sold it six times. The last sale was three years ago to a private collector."

"Any chance I can get his name?"

Donya turned the kiosk off. "You know we don't do that, baby. Sorry. But I can make some calls to see if she'd like to sell it."

"Please do so. See what you can arrange."

"My usual commission?"

"Absolutely."

"Then I'll start the calls and let you know what I find."

Syn inclined his head to her. "Look forward to hearing from you." As he started for the door with Shahara, Donya stopped him.

She waited until he'd turned back to her before she spoke again. "Next time you drop by, leave your friend at home."

"Sorry, Donya. Can't do that." He leaned in to kiss Shahara on the cheek. "I love my hot new girlfriend and her wild ways. You really should have taken her up on the threesome. We could have had a lot of fun together."

He left as soon as he saw Donya about to explode. Then he quickly ushered Shahara out of the office and through the building.

"Syn—"

"Shh," he said, not hesitating in their hasty retreat.

Shahara didn't take the hint. "But what about—"

"Shh. I'll explain outside."

Shahara really didn't like being shushed, but it was obvious there was something significant going on that she was missing. So she waited until they were out on the street and Vik was circling above them.

"What's going on, Syn? We have no information."

He flashed her that devilish grin that made her weak

in the knees. "Not true at all." He held up a small hand-held device.

"What's that?"

"Her entire set of secure records, including the current owner's name and address. Let's hear it for the filch, baby. You get me near a computer network and I can drain it dry. But I had to be in the building to get it."

She smiled at his skill, impressed yet again. "You are awesome."

He arched a brow at that as he discreetly took her hand and pressed it up against the bulge in his pants so that she could feel how aroused he was. "Have you any idea of the fire you started in there with what you were doing?"

She licked her lips suggestively, then clamped down hard on his balls as she let her anger at him finally show. "Have you any idea of the fire *you* started?"

Syn's body seized as pain shredded all other emotions. He froze, trying to keep her from hurting him any more. "Careful, love. You might want that to work later."

She twisted her hand, not so much as to incapacitate him, but more as a warning. "You're lucky, given your little performance in there, that I don't rip them off."

"I only did it for you." He held up his palm computer. "I had to have the data."

"Uh-huh." She tightened her hand on his balls, making him raise up on his toes. "You *ever* do something like that again and I'll make you a permanent soprano." She wrenched her hand away.

Syn gasped as he rubbed himself to alleviate the pain she'd caused. "That was just wrong."

"Don't go there. I'm *still* pissed off and you're lucky they're still attached given the way I feel."

He held his hands up in surrender . . . and took two steps back from her. Out of her reach.

Eyeing her warily, he plugged the last owner's number into his link and let it hail her.

After a few seconds, an older woman answered.

"Good afternoon. My name is Chryton Doone, and I'd like to speak with *Fria* Togg about a sculpture she purchased a couple of years ago from Berringer's."

"One moment, please."

The wait this time was a little bit longer. Finally another woman picked up the phone. "Can I help you?"

"I certainly hope so. I'm on a bit of a quest to find an old Derridian sculpture of the goddess Pikra that you purchased."

"Oh, that ugly little thing from Berringer's that I bought to irritate my former husband? God, who would want *that*?"

His stomach hit the floor as he saw the hopeful look on Shahara's face. Since she couldn't hear the woman, she didn't know that their hopes were being dashed. Damn it.

"I take it you don't still have it."

Shahara closed her eyes and winced.

"God, no. I couldn't stand looking at that *thing*."

"May I ask what happened to it?" *Please don't tell me you trashed it.*

"Well, I tried to sell it in the divorce, but no one would touch it. There was a professor at the local university who came over one night to appraise my collection. She had such a historical curiosity over the piece that I gave it to her. I thought it ought to go to someone who could look at it without flinching, and I was able to deduct it as a charitable contribution."

That was at least something. With any luck the professor hadn't looked at it too closely. "Would you happen to remember her name and how I might get in touch with her?"

"Oh, yes. Dr. Whelms. At the University of Eastern Speaks. She's their Art History dean."

"Thank you. I deeply appreciate it."

"No problem. Hope the ugly thing brings you more luck than it did me."

She had no idea. That statue would either set him free or get him killed.

He hung up and looked on Shahara, whose features were now pinched. "Ever get the feeling this is futile?"

She shook her head. "No. Because if it is, my sister is dead, and I'm not about to bury her." She let out a tired sigh. "Gods, Syn. Couldn't you have picked something better than a statue no one wanted?"

"Yeah. I should have known when I stashed the chip that I'd get caught by Merjack, sent to prison, escape prison, live twenty-plus years, and then need to find it again."

"You don't have to be sarcastic about it."

He opened his mouth to respond, but Vik cut him short.

"I have a couple of marks who look a little too interested in you."

"Where?"

"Two o'clock."

Syn turned and saw them instantly. "Shit."

Shahara frowned. "What?"

"Don't be obvious, but we have a couple of tracers on our ass."

He used his gaze to point them out and he had to give her credit—she followed his lead without betraying them. She was good at this.

"What do we do?" she asked.

"I'm thinking."

Her face changed instantly as she feigned laughter over nothing.

"What are you doing?"

She smiled and said in a fake happy tone, "Follow my lead." Wrapping her arm around his, she leaned into him and acted like his silly lover as she walked him toward them.

He wasn't really sure what she intended until she walked him past the tracers. "We have to find a place soon, Syn. I've got to have a taste of you."

His cock twitched at her hungry words and his blood fired to the point where he actually forgot about the tracers.

Until she shoved him into an alley. The moment she did, she pulled out his concealed blaster and whirled.

She nailed the bastards as soon as they came in after them.

He cursed at her actions.

She scowled. "What?"

"You don't just shoot them."

"Why not?"

He rushed to them to verify his suspicions. As soon as he saw their earpieces, he cursed again. "They're company."

"Meaning what?"

He snatched the GPS locator off the lapel of the one he was standing over. "They're tagged, and when they go down, their techs know immediately that they've located their target and been incapacitated. At which point they launch backup. You've just unleashed a thunderstorm on us." He tapped his ear. "Vik. Visuals."

"Uh, yeah. It's ugly. Run north. Now. Fast if you want to live."

He grabbed Shahara's hand and did what Vik told them to do. The moment he cleared the alley, he saw the fugliness Vik had described. There were three bikes and two rovers coming for them.

Shit.

Think, Syn. Think.

If only he had Nero's powers. *You have your own, and they haven't failed you in a long time.*

Yeah, but he was sober, which put him at a significant disadvantage.

Shahara cursed herself for her stupidity. Since convicts as a rule weren't organized, she'd never considered the possibility that their tracers would be.

Syn slowed them down to a walk.

"What are you doing?"

"We run, we stand out. Trust me." He pulled her toward the area where the crowd was the thickest. "We're going to have to separate—"

"No!"

"You don't trust me?"

Shahara swallowed her fear. *He won't betray you.* But *really* believing that was a whole other matter. She looked up into those eyes that were as dark as space. And yet for all their darkness, they weren't empty. In them she saw the man who'd taught her so much in such a short time.

"Where do I meet you?"

"The Miner's Inn on Fifth. It's right off north campus. You can't miss it. I'll see you there in half an hour."

She nodded.

He leaned down and kissed her cheek. "I will be there. But first I have to get rid of them." He touched his ear. "Vik, keep visuals on Shahara to make sure she's not tracked."

"What about you?" she asked.

"A rat knows how to run through a sewer." And with that, he faded into the crowd faster than she could blink. One moment he'd been right in front of her, and in the next, she was utterly alone.

She scanned the crowd around her, looking for other tracers. There was a certain carriage that all those trained in her profession held. Even when they tried to hide it, it stood out to those, like her, who knew what they were looking for.

Dipping her head low, she headed in the opposite direction.

Syn kept his gaze moving as he marked the ones on his ass. Eight . . .

No, nine. There was a female dressed in tan who appeared to be talking to someone.

All well-trained and all tailing him. "Come get some." It was the one thing he always said whenever he was cornered on the street. But what they didn't know was that on the street, he was never really cornered.

He reached under his shirt and pulled out his curlers—titanium blades that wrapped around his hand to form a spiked glove. If he pulled his blaster out and started shooting, the authorities would have him penned down in a heartbeat.

The only way out of this was to meld with the shadows and to take them out one by one.

He flinched as he felt his father's fist slamming against his face repeatedly. *"You want me to stop hitting you? You gotta outsmart me. Think, you little bastard. What do you do when you're out-gunned and overpowered? You outmaneuver them."*

His father's lessons had been brutal, but they'd taught him to survive, and for that he was actually grateful.

Ducking into an alley, he tucked himself into the shadows and waited until two of the tracers went past. He leapt on the one closest to him and brought him into the alley, where he quickly kicked him down and rendered him unconscious.

Syn was rising from the body when the first one doubled back to take him on. He caught the tracer's arm before he could fire his weapon and yanked the link out of his ear so that he couldn't communicate with the others. Even so, the link would let his team know that it'd been removed and was no longer transmitting his biofeed and pinpointing his exact location. Moving fast, Syn slammed his fist into the man's throat, then took him down with short, clean strokes.

He stepped back as he heard the others moving in for him.

Yeah, this was about to get really interesting.

CHAPTER 19

Shahara paused on the street outside the restaurant where they were supposed to meet up.

Syn was three minutes late.

Scanning the crowd, she saw no sign of a tracer and Vik had already confirmed that he saw nothing too. So where was Syn? What was he doing?

Had they captured him?

Or worse, killed him?

Terror went through her so viciously at the mere thought of his death that it almost dropped her to her knees. What if he died because of her? Could she handle it?

She'd never really considered the possibility. But right now it stared her straight in the face and slapped her with cold reality.

He might not make it back. And it would be *her* fault.

She tried to calm herself, but the agony of trying to imagine going back to a life without him was unbearable. *How can I love such a surly asshole?*

Yet she did. And if he died trying to help her . . .

Tears welled in her eyes. She couldn't keep standing here, waiting for him to join her when he might be bleeding and needing her help.

She waved Vik down from the tree where he was perched so that he could keep an eye out. As soon as he was on the nearby fence, she made up her mind. "I'm going back for Syn."

He cocked his bird head. "That's not what he said to do."

"I don't care. He's out there alone and—"

"Can't you *ever* follow instructions?"

Relief tore through her as she heard that deep, sexy baritone. Before she could stop herself, she turned and pulled Syn into a tight hug. Vik shot to the sky with a loud noise of protest at human displays of affection blinding him.

Syn was stunned by her unexpected reception. But what floored him was how tight she held him and the fact that she actually trembled in his arms. Like she'd been afraid something had happened to him.

Gods, it felt good. Too good. Closing his eyes, he took a deep breath and let the scent of her hair shake him to the core of his being. If only he could stay here like this, but he knew better.

They had a job to finish.

"I'm getting blood on you, babe. As much as I'm enjoying this, you might not want to hold me too close."

She pulled back with a gasp. "What?"

He held his hand up to show her where one of the trackers had cut him with a knife. "It needs some sutures, but I'll live. It just hurts like hell."

Shahara was horrified by the way the blood dripped from his hand to the sidewalk. Syn had wrapped a piece of cloth around his hand, but it was already saturated. "Are you sure you didn't open a vein?"

He gave her a droll stare.

"Sorry. I forgot you were a doctor. It just looks bad."

"Well, it's not a scrape. But it's all right. Let's finish this and tend the wounds later."

She pulled him against her again and held him for a minute longer.

He tightened his arm around her and reveled in the heat of her body against his. "You keep this up and I'm going to think you were worried about me or something."

"I was worried about you, asshole. Don't do that again."

He sputtered. "Excuse me, but I didn't do this. You need to leave that blaster in its holster. I mean, damn, woman, I now know where Caillen gets his impulsiveness from."

She tugged at his ear. "I don't like worrying about the people I love. Now do we need to get you to a hospital and tend your wound?"

"No. We don't have time." He dropped his uninjured hand from her face and activated his link. "Vik, eyedog for me. We're going in."

"Will do, boss." He flew higher to get a better vantage point.

Syn took Shahara's hand and led her across the busy street to the university's main campus.

Shahara felt a little uncomfortable as she glanced around at all the students. Some were rushing to class while others sat either alone or in groups on the ground where they studied. A part of her wished that she'd been able to do that. She would have loved to have gone to school like this. Because of her family, she hadn't even finished regular school.

But Syn had. And she couldn't help noticing how many female students paused to stare at him as they passed them. Or worse, nudge each other to show him to their friends. It made her wonder how much of a playboy he'd been as a student, especially since he seemed oblivious to the stir he was causing.

"Did you enjoy school?" she asked him.

"Not really."

"Why not? It looks like it would have been fun."

"I was too afraid of being exposed as Idirian Wade's son—remember, my father hadn't been dead all that long when I started college. His way-too-public trial and execution had been hotly followed and constantly discussed on my campus. Not to mention I didn't really fit in with the kids I went to school with. Most of them came from nice, relatively normal families. Being around them just brought home to me how bad I'd been shafted by my birth and parents. So I avoided them as much as I could."

"I'm sorry."

"It's nothing for you to be sorry over. It is what it is."

Perhaps, but it was still unfair. "You think they know how lucky they are?"

"Some do. Most take it for granted and think their parents owe it to them. They have no idea what the rest of us have to go through just to eat. I remember this one girl I knew in med school had a meltdown over the fact her father wouldn't pay off her debit card after she bought a new wardrobe. When I asked her why she didn't get a job and do it herself, she looked at me like I'd grown another head."

He entered a large white building that looked ancient and oppressive. Too sterile for her tastes, she followed him to the directory kiosk that was fashioned after a real human woman. She was pretty in an emotionless computer-generated kind of way. "May I help you?"

"I'm looking for Dr. Whelms's office."

"Dr. M. Whelms. Art Department, top floor. 516. She's currently receiving. Please check in with her secretary upon your arrival. Have a nice day."

Shahara led the way to the lifts. They entered the lift and he pushed the button for the floor. There were two other students in the lift who eyed them nervously.

Their actions amused her. They had no idea just how dangerous she and Syn really were. And the students bolted out of the lift as soon as they could.

Once the doors opened on the top floor, Shahara hurried to the secretary's desk. They were so close now she could taste it, and she was eager to get that chip and save her sister. For the first time, she was really feeling optimistic.

The secretary, a pretty woman who didn't appear any older than the students here, looked up from her electronic appointment book. "May I help you?"

"Dr. Whelms?"

"Right behind you."

They turned around in unison.

Syn paused as he saw the professor inside her office, leaning over her ledger on her metal desk. He couldn't see her face, but there was something oddly familiar about her mannerisms that nagged at the back of his mind. He knew her, he just couldn't place it.

Don't go in there . . .

He didn't know what caused that feeling, but his body literally seized up in rebellion.

Shahara didn't wait. She headed straight for the professor. "Dr. Whelms?"

When she looked up, Syn could have sworn someone had just knocked him a debilitating blow straight in the gut. No wonder his body had rebelled.

Fate, you are one serious fucking bitch . . .

And so was the woman in front of him.

Her beautiful brow was marked by shock and disdain—a unique combination only Mara could carry off with such consummate skill. "Sheridan?"

Shahara froze as the professor used Syn's real name. How did she know . . .

And then it dawned on her. Though the beauty before her was older, there was no mistaking the eyes and hair of the elegant woman who'd been in the picture with Syn and his son.

This was his ex-wife.

Her stomach drew taut and for a moment, she thought she'd be ill. In person, Mara was even more gorgeous and graceful. Her photos definitely didn't do her justice.

Syn didn't speak as his eyes shot venom at her.

"What are you doing here?" Mara demanded as she shot to her feet.

He motioned to the hideous statue that rested on top of her bookcase. "I need to see that for literally one minute."

Mara rushed around her desk to confront him. Disgust bled from every pore as she raked a disparaging glare over his body. "Get out of here. Now!"

Shahara stood back awkwardly as she watched the woman she would have killed to have been. A woman who had squandered the most precious thing in the universe and thrown it into the face of the man who'd given it to her.

You're not a woman, Mara.

You're a manipulative bitch.

Syn tried to step around her. "Just let me see it for a minute and I'll be gone."

"Why? Are you going to steal it? I should warn you

it's not worth much. Probably about as much as your life."

A tic worked in his jaw. "I don't want to get into this with you, *Dr. Whelms*."

She lifted a haughty brow. "You didn't expect me to keep your *alias,* did you? Or worse, your real name. I wanted a fresh start and so I took it."

"I don't really give a damn what you do or don't do."

While they argued, Shahara stepped around Mara's back and picked up the statue. It was a heavy piece, about thirty inches in height, carved of stone. And so ugly that it defied description. Surely only a blind person could have carved it.

Maybe carving it was what made the person blind.

No wonder the artist had never bothered signing it. She wouldn't have admitted to creating it, either.

As she searched the chiseled crevices, she realized there was no place for anything to be hidden.

Except for . . .

She looked at the black base. Someone had glued felt onto the bottom . . .

It had to be there. It was the only place he could have hidden it. Using her fingernails to pry back the fabric, she hurriedly searched.

"I heard you killed some poor woman. Raped her, too, didn't you?" Mara continued to rant at Syn. "You're just like your pathetic father. Two Wades in a pod."

Shahara looked up and saw the hurt those words caused him.

To his credit, it only showed in his eyes. The rest of him was coiled in fury. "You always knew just what to say to thoroughly piss me off."

"You're nothing but low-bred gutter trash."

Shahara gripped the statue tighter and tried not to listen to any more. Just when she was sure she could fight the urge to bash Mara in the head with it no longer, her finger touched a small round disk about the size of her fingernail.

With a gasp, she pulled back the felt and found it. Relief tore through her with such ferocity, she wanted to shout.

Finally . . .

"Syn?"

He met her gaze.

She held the chip up. "I've got it!"

Mara turned on her with a sour glare. "Got what? What kind of contraband is that?" She reached for her link on the desk.

"You always were a lethal bitch," he snarled, pulling her hand away from the link and shoving her back. "You alert security and I swear on my soul that I'll rip your cold heart out with my bare hands."

"That's what your father would have done, isn't it?"

He penned her between him and the desk as he raked her with a snarl. "You better be glad I'm not my father. He would have cut your throat the day he found out what a lying piece of shit you really are. But lucky for you, I didn't want to deprive my son of his mother."

"He's not your son. Thank the gods. He hates every breath you take."

"You couldn't even let me have that much, could you, you whore?"

Mara slapped him. Hard. "How dare you insult me. Your kind of filth doesn't even deserve to breathe my air. Now get out!"

And in that instant, Shahara saw the truth in Syn's

eyes. Mara truly meant nothing to him at all. He hated her.

His gaze turning dead, he stepped back from Mara and held his hand out to Shahara. "C'mon. Let's go get your sister."

Shahara started to take his hand, then stopped. Syn might have developed breeding by going to school and having money, but she never had.

Before she could rethink her actions, she slugged Mara as hard as she could in her perfect face. And even that was a light punishment for everything she'd done to Syn.

Mara fell to the ground, sobbing.

But she took no pity on her. "Syn may be too much of a gentleman to hit you, but I'm not. I'm not only ashamed to call you human, I'm completely disgusted that we share the same gender. You want to know the truth? The only filth in this room is you, and you're the one who doesn't deserve to breathe our air. Decent's got nothing to do with birthright. It's all about actions, and trust me, you're the lowest form I've ever met and I've taken in the worst scum imaginable. But I'd rather sit at the table with them than you any day."

She turned toward Syn, who stepped back, eyes wide, as if he feared she might hit him next. Grabbing him by the shirt, she pulled him from the room.

Syn was stunned and amazed by what Shahara had done. No one had ever defended him like that. The fact that she had . . .

He could kiss her.

"Damn, Shay . . . damn."

She sighed as the lift's doors closed behind them. "I know. I'm not a lady."

He cupped her cheek in his hand and tilted her face until she looked up at him. "You're more of a lady than any woman I've ever met. And I would take one of you over a thousand Maras any day. Thank you."

She smiled a smile that warmed him. "You're welcome . . . You think she called security?"

"Yes."

"We need to run as soon as the doors open, don't we?"

He laughed. "Always."

Sure enough, the doors opened to show four security guards waiting on them.

Syn let out a tired sigh as he tucked the chip in his pocket. "You kick down two and I've got the others."

"You got it." She headed for the farthest two while he took out the two closest. She caught the first one with a kick to the groin that dropped him and the second with a chop to his throat and a percussion blow to his ears.

An alarm sounded.

Syn left his two vics on the floor and grabbed Shahara's hand to pull her through the building and out to the yard. It was a close escape, but again, they made it off campus and back to the hangar before anyone else found them.

Unfortunately, getting out of the hangar wasn't quite so easy since they had it sealed off and refused to give them flight clearance.

Seated in the fighter while Vik shook in her arms, Shahara looked over at Syn. "What are we going to do?"

"Bet our lives that they don't want to shut this hangar down for a few weeks to do repairs."

Her stomach hit the floor at his tone of voice. She had a sick feeling she knew what he meant. "Don't."

The word had barely left her lips before Syn gunned

the engines. "Open the doors or I'm blasting them out," he told the controller.

"Shut down your engines. Now!"

Syn didn't hesitate.

Shahara bit her lip to keep from crying out in protest as he opened fire on the doors. Vik actually prayed in her lap.

"Syn . . . we're not going to make it."

He didn't back off.

Suddenly, the doors snapped open and he flew through them.

Shahara leaned her head back and groaned out loud as she tried to calm herself. "I really hate it when you do that."

He laughed. "Yeah . . . I prefer to be drunk when I do it. It's easier that way."

"Drunk or sober, you have more balls than any man I've ever known."

"You've never flown with your brother."

He had a good point. Caillen was one step just this side of crazy. And most days it wasn't even a full step.

Raking her hands through her hair, she glanced over at him. "So what's the plan now?"

He cleared orbit before he answered. "Hail Merjack."

She watched as he plugged in the frequency to call him. Merjack answered almost immediately.

Syn's voice was deceptively calm. "I have the chip."

"Good rat." His tone was filled with disdain. "I see you've finally come to your senses about giving me what I want."

Syn's eyes hardened. "Where do we make the exchange?"

"Primer's Point at Ritadaria's Olten Square. Tonight at eight."

"Wait," Shahara said, sitting forward to allow Merjack to see her. "*I'll* bring the chip to you and you better have my sister there."

A slow smile curved his lips as he saw her. "Well, well, the tracer has finally shown herself. Very well. I'll see *you* then." He cut the transmission.

Syn turned his murderous glare to her. "What are you doing?"

If only she knew . . . but her primary focus was to keep him out of jail. "He can't capture you if you're not there."

His features softened. "No, but he *can* take you."

"He won't."

"What makes you so sure?"

"Trust me," she said, hoping she could work out another deal with Merjack before it was too late.

If not, Syn would probably kill her himself.

Shahara checked her chronometer as she waited at the designated time and place. It was almost eight-thirty and still no Merjack.

What could be keeping him?

The old rundown docks were no place to be at this hour. A dreadful cold seeped into every part of her, numbing her hands and face, even her thighs. Her teeth chattering, she rubbed her gloved hands together, trying to bring at least a little sensation back into her fingertips. As she breathed into them, her breath formed a glowing circle around them.

Maybe coming out here hadn't been such a good idea after all.

Could something have happened to Merjack? He'd been so anxious to have the chip that she couldn't believe he hadn't been here the moment she arrived, waiting on her. Indeed, *that* she'd expected.

But this . . . this defied logic.

Frowning, she checked her chronometer again. She'd wait until nine, provided she didn't die of exposure, then she'd head back . . .

Time dragged by as she paced, searching every shadow, hoping it would turn into Merjack. Yet over and over again she was disappointed.

Finally, nine came and went.

Did this mean Tessa was dead?

Or something worse? Had he detected Vik, who was watching for her, and decided not to go through with it?

Terrified of all the scenarios that ended with Tessa or Syn dead, Shahara made her way slowly back to the waiting shuttle and to their hotel room.

It didn't take long to reach it. Vik stayed outside while she went upstairs to find Syn.

He was alone in the room, working on his computer. He stood up as soon as he saw her and crossed the distance between them.

"Well?"

The hopeful look on his face did nothing to improve the lump in her stomach. Frustrated, she sighed. "He didn't show."

His eyes darkened. "What do you mean, he didn't show?"

What had *him* mad? It was her sister in danger and she was the one who'd been freezing her better parts off for the last hour. "Nobody came."

The blood drained from his face. "Dear gods, Shahara . . . tell me you didn't."

Her heart stopped in terror.

Had he guessed her real mission?

"Didn't what?" she asked slowly, the knot in her stomach tightening as she dreaded his answer.

A thunderous knock sounded on the door.

"Lead them back here." Syn rushed for the bedroom.

Shahara started after him, but the doors caved in and a dozen enforcers entered with their weapons aimed straight at her. Targeting lasers danced over her body.

She froze instantly, putting her hands up to keep from getting shot.

Merjack entered the room to glare at her. "Where is the rat?" he sneered.

Before she could answer, Syn emerged from the bedroom and tossed a smoke bomb at them. With a deafening clatter and a white spark, it detonated. Smoke obscured everything and the sounds of ragged coughs filled her ears.

Out of the haze, a hand grabbed her arm. "C'mon," Syn said, hauling her away from the men.

They made it to the hallway. As they rushed for the stairs, an orange blast sizzled just to the left of Syn's face, barely missing him.

Terrified of him getting killed, Shahara pulled him to a stop. If they kept running, Merjack and crew would mow them down in the stairwell. She knew it.

"We have to run."

"No, Syn. They'll kill you. Don't do this. I don't want to watch you die in my arms. Please."

Syn grimaced at her as those words tore him apart. The fact that she cared . . .

He turned around with his arms raised so that they could apprehend him.

Merjack approached them with an evil grin. "Nice move with the smoke cover, rat, but wholly ineffectual." He lowered his blaster until it pointed straight at Shahara's heart. "Now drop your weapon or I'll kill the woman."

Syn complied without hesitation.

Shahara's heart thudded as his blaster clamored to the floor. This was it, her worst nightmare come to light. Syn would be going back to jail.

Please let me wake up . . .

But she didn't, and the closer Merjack got to them, the more she regretted the bargain she'd made.

Merjack sneered at Syn. "Hands behind your head and down on your knees with your ankles crossed."

She heard Syn's angry, ragged breathing as he did what Merjack ordered. She knew how much it galled him to willingly subject himself to their custody. Her heart ached at seeing him in that vulnerable position.

Even so, there was no fear, no submission in his eyes—something she found incredible given how severely he'd been beaten before and how much Merjack wanted him executed.

He was amazing in his defiance.

Merjack turned his gaze to her. "Now the chip, Seax Dagan."

Shahara stepped in front of Syn in an effort to shield him with her body. "You had no right to involve my sister," she snarled, wanting to tear Merjack apart. "Where is she?"

"She's in good health."

"She better be." And Shahara was far from relieved by his assurance. How could she trust a man so ruthless?

"Now give me that damned chip."

Looking over her shoulder, she saw Syn there with his gaze on the floor. The air around him was rife with anger and disgust.

She turned her attention back to Merjack. "Why do you need Syn?"

He raked her with a disparaging lip curl. "You're so naive. Now give me the chip and stand aside, seax, or I'll kill you both."

She laughed darkly. "I don't think you're that brave. Your son may be president of your tiny little planet, but even he can't protect you from my brethren should you kill me without a warrant for my death."

Fear flickered in his eyes a moment before Merjack got control of himself.

Holding to the thought that her threat gave him pause, she considered fighting. But Merjack had them effectively covered. And as she looked past his shoulder, she noted his men kept emerging from the smoke, their blasters aimed straight at them.

No, she couldn't fight against a number that large. Not even Syn was that good.

For now, she had to stay alive. Alive she could do something for him.

Maybe.

"Are you going to give me the chip, seax, or not?"

Syn held his breath, waiting for her to decide. He couldn't understand why she was even bothering to talk to Merjack.

Why hadn't she fought against him before his men had surrounded them?

Shahara took the chip from her pocket and handed it to Merjack.

"No!" Syn shouted, lunging at her as she handed it over. Someone hit him across the back of his head.

Pain exploded, dulling his sight, and he fell forward on all fours.

Shahara didn't so much as flinch.

"Good job," Merjack congratulated the man who'd struck Syn. He turned to face Shahara. "Now to you, seax. I believe we agreed on a million credits for the delivery of Syn and the chip. Should I just credit your account?"

Syn couldn't breathe as he heard those words.

No . . . she wouldn't have done this to him.

She wouldn't. Not his Shahara. Not after all they'd been through and shared.

But looking up at her, he saw the truth. She wouldn't even meet his gaze.

Merjack holstered his blaster. "You'll be happy to know we released your sister this morning, just like I promised. She should be safe and sound at home."

"She better be."

Shocked to the core of his being, Syn stared up at Shahara.

It had all been a trick? Everything they'd shared? Every word she'd uttered?

Every gentle touch?

Disbelief tore through him.

She'd sold him out from the very beginning.

No wonder she'd taken him back to her place that first day. She'd never been in any real danger. Merjack had known she'd taken him. Had planned for her to get him to take her to the chip.

And, like a fool, he'd fallen for it. Every bit of it.

Just like he'd fallen for her. *I am the most pathetic creature ever born.*

And she was worse than Mara. At least his ex-wife hadn't killed him. She'd only threatened to.

Shahara knew that chip was the only way he could ever barter to save his life. Without it, his testimony was worthless. No one would ever believe a filch.

"You bitch!" he snarled, rushing for her throat.

Another soldier clubbed him across the back.

Shahara came forward and stood above him.

He looked up at her through the blood stinging his eyes from the first blow and saw the callousness of her face.

Just for an instant, something flickered in the depths of her gaze that belied the coldness of her voice. Or maybe he just imagined it, like he'd imagined the fact she had a heart.

"What was it you said, Syn? We all use each other." She shrugged. "What can I say? I needed the money."

He glared at her, hating her for everything. So that was the price for his life. One million credits. He supposed he should feel honored. It was a high price for a piece of shit gutter rat.

But it was a bargain for the heart he'd given her—for what he would have given her had she only asked.

One of the guards wrenched his arms behind his back and cuffed them together, then pulled him to his feet. They hauled him out of the room and to the lifts.

Shahara stood, watching them, her face completely cold.

Merjack laughed as he entered the lift with Syn and three guards. "I always love dealing with seaxes, don't you, rat? They're so loyal to the letter of the law."

Syn couldn't speak as he glared at the woman he'd stupidly given his heart to. The one woman he'd deluded himself into believing would stand at his back and protect it.

In the end, she was just like all the others.

When will I learn?

Well, the good news was that he'd never be betrayed again. He wouldn't live long enough for it.

Shahara watched the doors close, then she sank slowly to her knees. This wasn't the way it was supposed to end. She'd hoped to convince Merjack that she'd killed Syn and he would content himself with the chip alone.

She'd never counted on him following her back to the hotel and capturing Syn. Damn him!

What was she going to do? Every part of her screamed in rebellion of what she'd done. Syn was innocent and she'd just given him over to his executioner.

So much for her oaths.

What have I done?

Tears welled in her eyes, but she blinked them back. She couldn't let her emotions rule her. She had only a tiny bit of time before Merjack learned the truth of what she'd really done.

And when he did, he would kill them both.

nd report their findings to the Overseer. Once they found their evidence, the Overseer's court heard the testimony and passed judgment.

It was also the Overseer's prerogative to review any case on any planet that seemed to be a miscarriage of justice and retry the case.

In their world, the Overseer was the most powerful person alive. And even though Shahara had never before met her, she was an integral part of the Overseer's world.

With a confidence she didn't feel, she approached the secretary's desk.

A few years older than her, the man's hair was already turning gray, giving him a distinguished appearance. He looked up from his work. "May I help you?"

Shahara lifted her chin. "I need to see the overseer."

"Your name?"

"Seax Shahara Dagan."

He checked his computer log. "I'm sorry, Seax Dagan. You don't have an appointment, and the Mistress of Justice has a number of meetings this afternoon. I'm afraid I can't squeeze you in today. Would you like to schedule an appointment for next week?"

Next week? Was he kidding?

Syn would be dead by then, and that was the one thing she could never allow.

"No, I wouldn't."

He looked back down, dismissing her.

Fiercely determined, Shahara stepped around his desk and headed straight for the office behind him.

"Wait! You can't go . . ."

The two guards who flanked the door went to grab her. Shahara sidestepped the first one and shoved him into the other, unbalancing them. Sliding herself into the office, she slammed the door shut in their faces.

CHAPTER 20

On trembling legs, Shahara strode into the Overseer's Trigon Court that was located in Central City on Gondara. Here was the highest bastion of law and order in the entire Ichidian Universe. This was where every law in their combined worlds was made and the only place one could be repealed or overturned. The Overseer was the high judge of a five-judge panel and her verdict on any case was final and supreme.

Not even The League could override one of her decisions. She was the voice of the law and she was the last hope Shahara had of freeing Syn from prison.

Centuries after The League had thrown off the chains of the warlord tyrant Emperor Justicale, their leaders had come together to ensure peace and law for everyone—to make sure that no other warlord ever proclaimed himself dictator again. They established the five judges and assigned them the task of seeking out injustice and crime on any planet.

As a seax, she was their soldier who was charged with finding injustices and reporting them, as well as bringing in any criminal wanted by the high court.

All seaxes had sworn to listen for tales of political corruption or human rights violations, investigate it,

She locked it tight while the secretary's muffled voice continued to berate her from the other side.

Her entire body quivering in fear, she turned around slowly.

The office was rather barren given the amount of authority the Overseer was charged with. All it contained was two chairs set before a large, ornately carved desk. Flags from all the organized worlds and empires were set along the left wall, while an electronic map of all the planets, colonies, and outposts took up the opposite side of the room.

The place was huge, no doubt to intimidate all who entered. It certainly had that effect on her.

The Overseer stared at her from over her computer with a puzzled frown. "Excuse me," she said in a gentle, yet haughty tone. "Just who are you and how did you get in here?"

Taking a deep breath for courage, Shahara forced herself to walk the long distance to the overseer's desk. "I'm here to right a gross injustice, Mistress."

Probably in her mid to late sixties, the Overseer still retained a face that could only be described as beautiful and serene.

As a young woman, she must have been stunning. As an older woman, she was dignified. "Everyone who walks through those doors has that claim." She sighed wearily. "And I haven't the time to listen to your story today. Make an appointment with my secretary and come back when it's more convenient."

More convenient? Shahara was aghast at her words. She couldn't believe they came out of the mouth of the very person all the worlds depended on for fairness. "No time for justice?"

The woman laughed as she leaned forward on her

elbows, folded her hands together, and rested her chin on top of them. "To be so shocked by my words, you must be one of my seaxes."

"Yes. I'm Seax Shahara Dagan."

Her smile was patronizing, but contrite. "Well, Seax, justice takes time, and time is one luxury I don't own."

Those familiar words haunted her, tugging at her memory. As the Overseer turned away with a mannerism she was all too familiar with, a strange sense of déjà vu prickled the tiny hairs on the back of her neck.

Now that she thought about it, she knew the exact curve of the Overseer's jaw—a jaw she'd kissed numerous times. She knew the little dimple in the left cheek that had tormented her with devilish taunts and quips.

Drawing closer, Shahara noted that the Overseer's eyes were as dark as space. If she'd had any doubt before that, that threw it out.

"Oh my God," she breathed.

The Overseer looked up, her face impatient. "You're still here?"

Too stunned to think better of it, she blurted out, *"You're his mother . . ."*

The Overseer lifted her brows and stared at her as if she were crazy. "I have no children."

Shahara shook her head, knowing better. "Yes, you do. You have a son named Sheridan Digger Wade and you had a daughter named Talia. And if you don't hear me out, I swear I'll let everyone know exactly who you are and what you did to them."

Panic sparked in the obsidian depths a moment before the Overseer could mask it. "I don't know what you're talking about."

More knocks pounded on the door. It sounded like they were using a battering ram. "Mistress?"

Shahara gave her no reprieve. "Are you sure you want them in here for this?"

The Overseer hesitated a moment longer before she pressed her intercom button. "I'm all right, Briun," she told her secretary. "Just keep the guards outside until you hear from me."

"Yes, Mistress of Justice."

She looked back at Shahara, and this time Shahara noted she finally had the Overseer's full attention. "Now what can I do for you, Seax . . . ?" She paused and closed her eyes. "Forgive me, I forgot your name.

"Dagan. Seax Shahara Dagan. I'm here to get a fair trial for your son."

Disgust and hatred flashed deep in the woman's gaze. She curled her lip. "Like father, like son. I'm sure whatever he's accused of, he's more than guilty of it."

"No," Shahara corrected. "Sheridan is a good, fair man. Nothing at all like his father."

"I don't believe you. Evilness like Indy possessed runs through the genes."

"And half of his genes come from you, Mistress. Believe me. Sheridan has saved my life more than once when other people would have left me to die. He's not his father's son." She hesitated before she added, "But he is yours."

There was something in her gaze . . . like those words had chipped away some of her ice. "What is it you ask for him?"

"I was approached by Seax Traysen on your behalf. He asked me to escort Sheridan"—it was so odd to keep using that name, but she wanted to ram home his identity to the Overseer—"in order to gain proof of assassination and corruption on Ritadaria."

"The Merjack case?"

"Yes, Mistress."

She glanced down at the miniature flags on her desk. "Did you find it?"

"Yes . . . with Sheridan's help."

She nodded. "Very good, Seax. Now, how does this relate to a new trial for a convicted felon? A felon I'm sure more than earned his sentence for treason and theft."

Shahara wanted to choke the woman for the obstinacy she had—for the same obstinacy she'd given her only son. What would it take to make her see she was wrong?

What would it take to make Syn's own mother at least *hear* his case?

Thinking, she scanned the certificates and honors lining the walls behind the Overseer. And as the dates of the Overseer's commissions registered in her mind, she had an epiphany. "How long have you been the Overseer, Mistress of Justice? Twenty years?"

"Twenty-three to be precise. Why?"

Her stomach turned to stone with those words. It was just as she suspected. No wonder Syn had never come forward to clear his name.

It would have meant facing the woman who'd told him that if she ever laid eyes on him again, she'd have him imprisoned. It would have meant facing the woman who'd tried to kill him when he was an infant, and who had twice abandoned him to a world that hated him.

The harsh reality of that made her wince, but at least she finally understood why Syn had preferred to remain a criminal rather than clear his name.

Honestly, she couldn't blame him for the decision.

"Do you realize, Mistress of Justice, that *your* son has been running from tracers and assassins for twenty-three years because he'd rather be killed by them than ask anything from you? Even a fair trial, which is the very least of what he deserves?"

Shahara boldly looked the Overseer up and down, noting that she took her words in stride. "From the outer looks of him, he has far more of your genes in him than his father's. But then, I guess maybe I'm wrong. Unlike you, Sheridan would never allow an innocent man to die without a hearing. He'd at least take the time to listen to the case before he condemned the person to a death he didn't deserve. And he sure wouldn't condemn someone for his own actions that they didn't have any part in. He's remarkably decent that way."

She felt her eyes water as she thought about Syn and the son he continued to claim in spite of everything Mara and Paden had done to him. "You should also know that unlike you, he still provides for his son even though he's not the biological father . . . and his exwife, like you, has tried repeatedly to kill him and arrest him, not for *his* crimes, but for those of his father."

Poor Syn, to have been relegated to such coldblooded bitches in his life.

"As a young man, he crawled out of the sewers you abandoned him in and went to med school on his own. He became a surgeon until a reporter exposed his past. Even then, he didn't become his father. He built a shipping company and was leading a respectable life until I screwed him over."

"What of Kiara Zamir? Did he not rape and murder her?"

"She's alive and well, if you'll bother to check. Sheridan was protecting her when her father threw a fit and, rather than give him the benefit of the doubt, called out for an execution. Syn's only crime was not handing his best friend—the man who is in love with Kiara and who still protects her—over to President Zamir. He would rather die than betray his friend. Again, not the actions of his father—but those of a decent man. And at this point, I have no idea where he learned his decency. It certainly wasn't from his mother."

She turned to leave.

"Wait," the Overseer said, stopping her.

Shahara turned to face her.

"You have proof of his innocence?"

Crossing the floor to stand before the desk, she reached inside her pocket and pulled out the chip. "This proves his innocence conclusively, as well as the guilt of the Merjacks."

"You have reviewed the chip?"

"Yes, Mistress of Justice."

The Overseer took it from her hand and placed it in an airtight container. Positioning it carefully before her, the Overseer studied the tiny chip that contained Syn's entire future.

Shahara held her breath, praying for a miracle.

Finally the Overseer looked up at her. "I can get him a fair trial, but that's all. If our court finds him guilty, then I'll do nothing to stay his execution."

"That's all I ask."

"Very well. Where is he being held?"

"Ritadaria."

She tilted the container so that the chip fell into one corner. "I'll send an escort with you to have him transferred here for incarceration until his trial."

"Thank you, Mistress."

Silence fell between them. Shahara could tell the Overseer wanted to say something more, but doubt hovered in her eyes while she continued to study the chip. "Tell me something, Seax."

"Yes?"

"Really, is he a decent man?"

"Yes, Mistress. I've never known a more noble one. He does you proud every day he lives."

She smiled.

"And may I ask you a harsh question?"

"Why did I leave them?"

Shahara shook her head. "Why did you try to kill him when he was an infant?"

The color faded from her face. "What?"

"Digger told me that you tried to kill him when he was an infant."

Her cheeks darkened with anger. "That's a lie. Talia had wanted to bathe him and I let her. She'd allowed him to fall beneath the water and drown. I was the one who revived him, but Indy wouldn't believe me. I *never* hurt my children."

"But you left them."

Unshed tears glistened in her eyes. "I had no choice. Indy would have killed me had I stayed. I kept hoping that I could convince my parents to take them in. After awhile, it just got easy to live without them."

"And when he came to you when he was twelve?"

"He caught me by surprise and I didn't know what to do. I would have lost everything I had if anyone ever learned that I had been married to Idirian Wade. I panicked when I saw Sheridan and overreacted. By the time I came to my senses, he was gone."

Shahara shook her head. "You see how easy it is to be misjudged when you don't have all the facts?"

"Don't lecture me, child. You have no idea what I've been through over these years."

"And you have no idea what *your* son has had to face alone because of what *you* did."

The Overseer didn't speak as those words hung between them. After a few seconds, she glanced up. "Do you know whatever became of his sister, Talia? Is she all right?"

Shahara swallowed at the desperate longing in the woman's voice. "No, Mistress. Talia killed herself a long time ago to escape her father."

The Overseer took a deep breath. "And what of you, Seax? Why do you defend the son of Idirian Wade with such vigor?"

She answered with the one single truth she couldn't deny. "I love him. Deeply."

"Does he know this?"

"I'm sure he doubts me." Especially given the way she'd been forced to act in the hotel, yet had she shown any weakness, Merjack would have killed them both. "But I intend to make sure he believes in me again."

The Overseer nodded. "We all make mistakes that torture us the whole of our lives. Unfortunately, fate doesn't always allow us a second chance. I hope you get yours, Shahara."

"Thank you, Mistress."

The Overseer smiled sadly. "He must truly be a noble man to inspire the loyalty of a seax."

"He walks with nobility and honor."

She nodded. "Now go, Seax. See to his safety."

Numb to everything except the throbbing pain in his skull, Syn sat huddled in the corner of his icy cell. He swung his chains at one of the rodents that had strayed a little too close for his liking.

At times like this, he really cursed his eyesight. He was able to see every tiny crawling, slithering creature that eyed him as either a meal or a host.

But worse than the insects and rodents was the deadly chill that caused his broken jaw to ache unmercifully. He wasn't exactly sure when it'd been broken. There had been so many blows as he was interrogated by Merjack that he could barely recall which one had caused what injury.

If he didn't hurt so much, he'd have laughed at Merjack's panic as the man had tried to find out what Shahara had done with the real chip.

He really had to give her credit. She'd betrayed them all. First she'd turned him in, then she'd run off with Merjack's money and the chip.

She was some piece of work.

He closed his eyes and let the agony of betrayal ravage his soul.

How could you have done this to me? He would have given her his life had she asked for it. But to have it taken like this . . .

He wanted to kill her.

The door to his cell opened, ushering in another stinging wind. Syn mentally prepared himself for the beating to come. Maybe this time they would finally succeed in killing him.

He listened to the footsteps approach and, though his first instinct was to fight, he didn't move. He just didn't have it in him anymore. His fighting days were over. Now he just wished his life would end, too.

Instead of rough hands seizing him, something incredibly soft and warm was draped over his shoulders. Stunned, he looked up into the golden eyes that had haunted him every moment since Merjack had taken him.

"Hi," she said with a smile.

Rage clouded his sight. He tried to speak, but his

jaw and the cold made it impossible. Disregarding his pain, he reached for her, intending to tear her lying tongue out.

Shahara noted the hatred in his eyes as he sprang at her. "Syn, please don't. You'll only hurt yourself."

As he lunged toward her again, Nero appeared to pull him back. "Easy, buddy. You don't want to do any more damage to yourself."

A man wearing the green and gold uniform of the Overseer's guard stepped between them. "C.I. Syn, born Sheridan Digger Wade?"

His breathing labored from his pain, Syn stopped moving and eyed all of them warily.

When he didn't answer, the man looked to Shahara to confirm his identity before he continued. "C.I. Syn, you are being remanded into Overseer custody pending a full investigation and trial of your case."

Confused, he stared at the guard. How?

"I went to *her*," Shahara explained as if she'd read his thoughts. "She's agreed to hear everything."

Oh, that was fucking great. He'd be lucky if his mother didn't have him offed two seconds after his arrival.

The guard who'd spoken knelt down to release his chains while Nero handed Shahara his clothes.

"We'll wait outside while you get him dressed."

Shahara looked at Syn, who still hadn't moved from his crouched position on the floor. "Thank you."

He appeared so defeated and hurt that it choked her with remorse. His wounds were so much worse this time than they'd been before. It was obvious Merjack had been a *little* ticked off over her subterfuge with the chip.

She couldn't imagine how Syn even managed to breathe, let alone move.

"Here," she said, closing the space between them. "Let me get you dressed and—"

"I don't need your help," he snapped between clenched teeth as he shoved her away with a strength she found shocking given his physical condition.

She wanted to argue but was afraid to try. The last thing he needed was a struggle that would only injure him more. "Here're your clothes."

Syn snatched them from her and tried to dress by himself, but with one broken arm and all the other brutal injuries, he could barely move.

It was useless; he couldn't even raise his arms high enough to pull on his shirt.

This time when she came near, he didn't push her away. Without a word, she dressed him with gentle hands that only seldom hurt his injuries. But that wasn't what really hurt, anyway.

The external injuries he could take. It was the wound she'd given his heart that crippled him. That was the one he couldn't get over.

How could you . . .

When she finished, she took his good arm and placed it over her shoulders. "Just lean on me, Syn, and I'll walk you out of this hell."

"You're the one who put me here. Twice," he snarled through his broken jaw.

Shahara's conscience screamed its own condemnation over his condition. He'd been here less than a day and Merjack had done all but kill him. "I know, baby. I know."

Nero took over once they were outside the cell and helped Syn the rest of the way to the bay.

As soon as they boarded the Overseer's shuttle and launched, one of the escorts brought her a first aid kit while Nero moved up front for the launch. "I don't know how much help this will be. But I think there's some stuff in it to help dull the pain."

"Thank you." Shahara took it from his hands. She dug around until she found the pills. "Do you need water?"

He shook his head before he roughly ground out, "They . . . broke . . . my . . . jaw."

"Oh," she whispered, knowing he'd never be able to open his mouth wide enough take the pills.

No wonder he'd been so silent.

Shahara looked down in shame and replaced the bottle in the kit. Once more she searched the contents for something that might ease his pain.

There was nothing.

"Sorry. There's no injector in here, or anything else to give you."

Syn said nothing. He just laid his head back against the wall of the craft and closed his eyes.

Wanting desperately to help him, Shahara got up, moved around the steel partition that separated her from the pilots and asked the two escorts, "Is there someplace where he can lie down until we get there?"

The man who'd brought her the first aid kit spoke up. "We could make a pallet on the floor with some of our emergency blankets."

At the frown on her face, he turned contrite. "I'm sorry, Seax. This is a prison shuttle, not a luxury class cruiser. It's the best we can offer."

Well, at least the pallet would be better than his trying to sit up. "Where are the blankets?"

He led her and Nero to the storage compartments and helped her pull them out. Together, she and Nero made a semi-soft bed and helped Syn lie down.

Shahara sat beside him while the escort returned to his station. She watched Syn try to swallow and she hated herself for leaving him to Merjack. If only she could go back and change things.

But she couldn't do that.

The least she could do now was try to explain herself, especially given the fact that, for once, he'd no choice but to listen.

"I know you don't believe me." She stroked his bruised cheek. "But I never meant to hurt you."

His glare turned lethal and she could read his thoughts as easily as if they were her own.

"You're right. I did turn you in, twice. But it's not what you think. The first time we met, I thought you were guilty of all those crimes. Then I was approached by another seax, Warden Traysen, from your prison. He'd been investigating Uriah Merjack for years and when he learned about the chip, he decided not to prosecute Merjack for the human rights violations in the prison, but wait until he could prosecute him for murder. The only way he could prove his case was to get your chip."

She brushed her hand across his fevered brow. "He was the one who suggested to Merjack that he contact me, and then Traysen told me what my real duty was. I was afraid to tell you my mission because I didn't think you'd believe me. Now that I know who your mother is, I *know* you wouldn't have trusted me. Ever. You're too stubborn for that and I can't blame you."

She sighed and brushed his dirty hair off his forehead. "You don't know how many times I've regretted my bargain with Merjack."

He looked at her and his eyes were so sad, so tormented that it brought tears to hers. "I know you think I betrayed you, but I really do love you, Syn."

In desperation not to lose him forever, she added quickly, "By the time I saw the real you, it was too late. Everything had been set into motion and I couldn't stop it. That last night, I was going to lie to Merjack and tell him you were dead so that he wouldn't hunt for you anymore. Then I was going to hand you and the real chip into Overseer custody."

The accusation in his eyes spoke loudly: *You think that would have been any better?*

He looked away.

Shahara closed her eyes and wished she could start over with him.

But it was too late.

Sighing in defeat, she put his hand down beside him and went to join the escorts.

Syn watched her leave. His heart begged for him to call her back.

This time he ignored it. He was through with that part of himself. The part of him that was weak and thought it needed someone in his life.

He would listen to it no more.

All he wanted was peace and solitude away from people who lied and deceived him. The only guarantee he'd ever had in this life was that *he* would never betray himself.

Taking as deep a breath as he could, he closed his eyes and vowed to think no more of Shahara.

Nero stepped forward. "She does love you, Syn. If it's any consolation."

He rolled his eyes, then hissed at the pain it caused.

Nero knelt down by his side and used his powers to heal him. Syn cursed as pain swept through him, only to fade. The last part to heal was his jaw.

He met Nero's gaze. "Thanks."

"Anytime. Should I go get Shahara now?"

"No. I don't want her around me."

"Syn—"

"Don't waste your breath, Scalera. I'm tired of being lied to. I don't even know what to believe where she's concerned."

"She can't lie to me. You know that."

"And I'm not you. I don't come with a lie detector. Hell, even yours is defective at times." What they'd had, whatever it was, was over.

He didn't want to live like that. Besides, he wasn't out of trouble yet. They were taking him to his mother for a trial . . .

Yeah, like that was going to go well for him.

Weeks went by slowly as Shahara fought with herself about whether or not she should visit Syn in his new cell. There was no doubt in her mind that he hated her.

Would always hate her.

Even so, she wanted to see how he was doing. See if maybe she could do something to help him.

She missed him so much that it became a terrible physical agony that prevented her from eating or sleeping. From doing anything other than aching for him.

Finally, she could stand no more. Even if he beat her and threw her out of his cell, she had to see him again.

Try one last time.

With that thought, she'd flown to Gondara.

Now she waited outside the minimum-security ward while the guards searched the pack she'd brought for Syn. "Okay, Seax Dagan," the guard said at last. "You may enter."

"Thank you." She took her pack from the guards. "Which cell?"

"LD 204." The guard pressed the release for the series of doors that led down a narrow corridor to the individual cells. It was visiting hours and all the inmates were confined to their rooms.

With a deep breath for courage, Shahara headed down the long line of cells. A two-inch-square window was cut at eye level in each door, but she resisted the urge to look inside. She didn't want to see what misery the inmates felt.

She'd been responsible for putting too many of them in here. And she couldn't help but wonder how many of them she'd wrongfully confined.

As soon as she reached the correct door, the guards buzzed her in. Her hands shaking in fear of her reception, she gently pushed the steel door open.

Syn sat on his cot, his back to her while he gazed out the window onto a courtyard below. His blue prison suit actually looked good against his dark skin and hair, and it made her want to take a bite out of him.

But he wouldn't be receptive to her right now.

He didn't move at all, which made her wonder what he was thinking about that had him so distracted.

She cleared her throat before she spoke. "I heard you'll be out soon."

He jerked around to face her.

For just an instant, she glimpsed his delight, then his face quickly turned stoic. "What are you doing here?"

Ignoring his question, she placed her pack on the small table next to the door.

She'd forgotten just how good he looked when he was freshly shaved and groomed. How absolutely devastating.

Most of all, she'd forgotten how fierce a personality

he possessed. Traveling with him, she'd gotten used to it, but now . . .

Now she was well aware of that deadly undercurrent.

"You look a lot better than the last time I saw you."

He didn't answer.

Sighing at his cold demeanor, she pulled the metal chair back from the table and sat down. "I had the Overseer give you permission to run your business out of here. When I called Nykyrian about it, he was more than happy to turn everything over to me. He also sent a bunch of stuff for you to sign."

She waited, but he never responded.

"Nykyrian also told me to tell you he was sick and tired of running a business he barely understood and that he wished you'd get off your butt and tend to it yourself. He gave me a portable and a bunch of logs and invoice chips from your manager. And in case you haven't heard, Kiara's father has dropped all charges against you and The Sentella."

Again silence answered her.

Well, what did you expect? "Ah, gee, Shahara, how *nice to see you again. I understand completely why you turned me over to be tortured by someone you knew wanted me dead. Thank you, sweetness.*"

She couldn't blame him for his anger.

What was it her mother had always told her? Love was a fragile flower that took a lot of care and hard work to sustain. And just like a flower, it would wither and die if abused or neglected.

Once gone, nothing could ever bring it back.

Still, she couldn't believe it was completely dead. He'd been glad to see her, if only for a second.

Surely he wouldn't have had even that moment of delight if he truly hated her.

She tried again. "The Overseer told me that the judges are ready to release you with amnesty as soon as you testify against Merjack and his son. I guess you'll be going home in a few days . . ."

She waited, and again he said nothing.

Sighing, she realized the futility of trying. He would never forgive her.

So be it. She wasn't one to beg.

"Have a nice life," she said, heading for the door.

With every step that carried her farther and farther from his cell, her heart broke into another piece. It was really over. Syn would never give her another chance. And she couldn't even blame him for it.

Unable to stand what she'd done to them, she started to cry.

Staring at the chair where Shahara had been, Syn pulled out the tiny ring he'd bought for her and looked at the flashing golden stones. He'd had to bribe the hell out of one of the guards to get it.

He should have said something to her. Thanked her at the very least for getting him released—for bringing him his work.

But he'd been afraid to trust himself. If he spoke, he might have forgiven her.

Oh, to hell with forgiveness, anyway. He had his life back and she had hers. He'd known all along that they were incompatible.

What was the use of trying?

With that thought, he went to the pack she'd left on his table. As he reached in for the portable, his hand brushed a large piece of canvas.

Pulling it out, he froze.

It was an enlargement of his picture of Paden. Absolutely stunned, he stared at his son's laughing face.

She must have found someone to repair his photograph and transfer it onto a 10×13 panel. And beneath that was a wallet-sized picture of him and Talia. He'd assumed it'd been destroyed along with his place.

A crushing pressure seized his chest as he held the photographs. Only Shahara would have known how important those pictures were to him.

She was the only person who had ever known him at all.

And he'd let her go.

CHAPTER 21

Syn lay on the couch in his office, staring out at the stars while he did his best to drain another bottle of Tondarion A-Grade Hellfire. He'd tried everything else to forget Shahara and the pain she'd given him.

Only this helped.

He wanted to see her so badly that it caused a physical ache inside him. But he just couldn't bring himself to go crawling back.

Not after she'd turned him in.

True, she'd also freed him. And if she'd handed over the right chip to Merjack, he'd now be dead. It still didn't erase that moment of utter despair when she'd handed him off and had stood over him telling him that she'd used him.

That was what he couldn't forgive. Those words were forever carved in his heart.

Besides, she was a seax. She'd have been stripped of her title had she not taken the chip to the Overseer and seen Merjack punished. That had nothing to do with her feelings, or lack thereof, toward him.

The truth of it cut him like a knife. And even in her endeavor to save him, she'd forced him to spend weeks staring at his mother on a vid screen while he'd been held in a cubicle to testify.

The sight of his mother sitting there so emotionless while she listened to his testimony . . .

Every day had cut him to his soul.

He curled his lip and guzzled more alcohol. That had probably been the worst part of all this—watching his mother sit in judgment of him.

At least she hadn't condemned him—this time. But her refusal to address him had spoken louder than anything else. He had no family.

He would never have a family.

Like I care.

With a deep sigh, he took another swig. He wasn't sure how long he'd been home. His days blurred together, marked only by the empty bottles that he'd strewn across the floor.

A knock sounded on his door.

Was it payroll again? Another week gone by?

Shaking his head to clear it, he decided he'd give Criam the authority to sign the pay forms. He no longer wanted to be bothered with it.

"Come in."

He didn't look around at the door as it opened. But the hair on the back of his neck stood up when he didn't hear anyone walking in.

It wasn't until a shadow fell over him that he knew who it was.

Nykyrian.

The tall blond assassin was dressed all in black, his long hair pulled back into a braid. He leaned heavily against a cane—an injury he'd sustained while saving his wife's life from his enemy. Likewise, one half of his face was still scarred from the crash that had almost ended his life.

"You look like hell, buddy."

Syn saluted him with the bottle. "Funny. I was just thinking the same thing about you."

One corner of Nykyrian's lips quirked up into the closest thing to a smile he'd ever seen from his friend.

Syn took another drink. "What are you doing here? Figured you'd be with your wife living the happily-ever-after bullshit that makes me want to puke."

"You sounded like total shit when I called, so I wanted to see you for myself. I would say I was worried about you, but you might think I've gone soft and hell will freeze before that happens . . . By the way, if my wife goes into labor while I'm here and not at home with her, I will kill you where you lay."

Syn made an obscene gesture at Nykyrian.

"How's he doing?"

Syn tilted his head back to see Kasen in the open doorway. Curling his lip, he snarled at her. "In case you haven't heard, I'm not exactly on good terms with your family right now. So why don't you take your ass out of here before I find enough energy to beat it."

"Ooo," she cooed, crinkling her nose as if he'd just given her some sexual pleasure as she neared his couch, "you promise?"

He rolled his eyes at her. "I should have known that's all you wanted. Well, you're too late. Your sister effectively killed any sex drive I might have for a long time to come. Personally, I'd rather masturbate."

"That's harsh and crude, you pig." She crossed her arms over her chest. "Anyway, that's not why I'm here. You know, me and you *were* friends. And friends are something I don't have a lot of." She moved to stand by his side. "I really was worried about you, Syn. You haven't been exactly seen by anyone since you got out."

Syn took a deep breath. He didn't mean to be such a self-absorbed asshole. It was just that the pain was too raw to deal with right now.

Even so, he hadn't meant to lash out at them.

"I'm sorry. I shouldn't take my anger for your brother and sister out on you."

"It's all right. I'm used to it. I always catch hell because of one of them. Why do you think I'm so surly?"

"Ah, so *that's* the reason."

She took a seat by his feet and eyed the half-empty bottle in his hand, then shifted her gaze to the other three empty bottles on the floor. "Are you drunk?"

"Comfortably Inebriated," he said with a dark laugh, thinking of Shahara and her continuous need to know what C.I. stood for.

Nykyrian scoffed. "Well, if you get any more comfortable, buddy, I'll have to call in a med-tech."

Kasen lifted one of the bottles and read the label. "This stuff can kill you."

"Yeah, but obviously not quick enough." He went to take another swig.

Nykyrian jerked it out of his hand.

"Hey!"

He pulled it away from his grasping hand. "Don't even make that noise at me."

Syn curled his lip. "You and Vik. You're both traitors. You might as well move in with Shahara, too." Vik had gone to live with her and refused to come back until Syn "got over himself." Little wormy betraying mecha bastard.

Kasen shook her head. "I think this is the first time I've ever seen you drink from a bottle."

Nykyrian snorted. "Lucky you. I've seen him tap a keg and funnel it."

"Look," Syn said between clenched teeth, "I don't really want to chit-chat with you two right now. You've seen me, you know I'm alive, now why don't you both just go on home."

Kasen slapped at his feet. "You sound just like Shahara."

His heart stopped at the mention of her name. "So how is old Shahara, anyway? Living high off her million credits she got for having me tortured?"

"No," she said quietly. "She won't touch any of it."

He lifted his brow in surprise.

"She even tried to return it, but the Overseer told her not to. She said Shahara had earned it."

Oh, yeah, she had definitely earned it by screwing him over. Her acting abilities would be worth a thousand times that in the studios. "I'll bet she did."

Kasen clenched her teeth. "Look, I love you like a brother, Syn, and I love Shahara. I can't just stand around and watch the two of you die because you're too damned proud to apologize to each other. She's sorry for what she did. She just mopes around that decrepit hole she calls home, so depressed she hardly moves."

"Do you think I care?"

"I know you do. Look at you." She gestured at him lying on the couch. "You have your freedom and you've cleared your name. Instead of being happy and going about your life, you're sitting here half-dead. Shahara has a million credits and she hasn't even gone shopping for a new pair of shoes. What does that tell you?"

"We're both idiots."

She made a sound of supreme disgust. "And then there's Caillen, who sits around looking like he's lost his best friend, because he *has* lost his best friend."

"Don't even try and defend him to me."

She ground her teeth. "You three are so stubborn. I ought to lock all of you in a room and not let you out until you settle this."

She sat quietly for a little while before she spoke again. "You need to understand something about my family. Me and Tessa are the screw-ups."

He gave her an icy, no-duh stare.

She ignored it. "What you don't know is how it felt to watch your brother and sister drop out of school to support you. Caillen idolizes Shahara. Since the day she got down on her hands and knees and started scrubbing toilets to keep food on the table, he's worshiped everything about her. We all have. No matter how hard things got, it was always Shahara who was strong. Shahara who never complained or scolded. She did what she had to for us, and suffered in silence."

"Yeah, she *is* good at that."

"You don't have to be sarcastic." Kasen rubbed her hands over her pants legs. "Anyway, Caillen was the one who found her after she'd been raped. You don't know what it's like to see someone you love broken like she was that night."

Syn flinched as he thought about Talia. He knew exactly what it was like to watch someone he loved be broken, day by day, until there was nothing left but a fractured shell.

Unaware of how her words affected him, she continued. "She was never the same after that. She quit laughing and smiling and joking around. All she did for weeks afterward was sit in a chair and cry."

"Until she killed him."

She nodded. "That got her out of her chair, but it didn't restore what she'd lost. She would never talk about what had happened. She was so weakened and scared that she even let Caillen drop out of school and help out. Something she would never have allowed before the attack. And since the day he found her half-dead from Gaelin's beating, he wasn't the same, either. He became obsessed with protecting her."

Kasen gave him a hard stare. "When Caillen saw you two together, it killed him. He's always been terrified of losing one of us, especially Shahara. She's the backbone of our entire family. Anytime something goes wrong, it's always Shahara who finds a solution. When we need someone to listen to us, or help us in any way, it's Shahara we run to. He was afraid you'd hurt her, and you have."

She rose and looked down at him. "I can understand why you and Shahara feel the way you do about each other, but don't hold Caillen accountable for what he said. You mean the universe to him. You're the best friend he's ever had."

"Big whoop."

"Fine." She held her hands up in defeat. "Whatever. I don't care what the three of you do anymore. I'm sick of it." She headed for the door. "Maybe I'll see you around sometime."

And with that, she was gone.

But Nykyrian remained.

"What?" Syn snapped at him.

"I know what you feel right now."

"No, Kip, you don't. You have no idea what it feels like to be betrayed like I was."

His expression held its usual stoicism. "After Kiara's

father almost killed me and I barely survived, I went to see her. Like you and Shahara, we were both hurting and we both said things we shouldn't have."

Syn curled his lip in disgust. "What has marriage done to you? Turned you into a woman? In case you missed it, we don't share stuff like this. So can I have my surly, nasty assassin friend back?"

Nykyrian grabbed him by the shirt and jerked him up until their gazes were locked.

Well, the nasty assassin was definitely back.

"All right, asshole. You want to wallow, wallow. It's no sweat off my balls if you crawl inside a bottle and pickle yourself solid. I've got other things to think about now. But let me remind you of something a good friend once said to me when I was being eaten alive by feelings I didn't understand. 'Even when my marriage was bad, it was good.' I had no real idea what you meant that night, but now I do and I'm grateful to the gods I can finally believe in that I took a chance on something that almost killed me. The life I have now . . . no, the *woman* I have now is worth every rotten moment of my worthless existence that led me to her door, and I would relive it all to have one kiss from her lips. You're the one who told me that the right woman was a shelter from the storm."

"And I was drunk at the time."

Nykyrian shoved him back to the couch. "The Syn I know has never been a coward. Don't tell me you're going to let some piece of ass—"

"Don't you dare insult her!"

"Then there's your answer, boy." He handed the bottle back to him. "You have two choices. Put yourself out of all our miseries, or get off this damned couch and live. Really, Syn. This is beneath the ruthless man I call friend."

"Fuck you. You have no idea what she said to me. She told me she was using me."

"And Kiara told me she wished I'd died. I know your pain, Syn. I chugged it down whole and I even tried to wash it away with alcohol. But only one thing cured it."

"And that was?"

"Swallowing my pride. No, it wasn't easy and I choked on it. But I tell you what. Every day I wake up with that one tiny hand touching my skin makes up for whatever manhood I thought I'd lost by apologizing to her. You can sit here and masturbate all you want, but in the end it's not the same thing. Trust me. I do know."

Nykyrian pulled back to glare down at him. "Now, I'm going home to my wife and I'm going to be grateful that I was man enough to fight for her. I dare you to be the man I know you can be." And with that, he left.

Syn lay there while Nykyrian's words tormented him. In the end, he knew his friend was right. The only problem was he didn't have it in him to get up.

Shahara leaned one hip against her kitchen counter, watching Caillen scroll through job listings on her computer.

"I'm never going to find another job," he ground out between clenched teeth.

"That's what you get for being a jerk."

He cast a dirty glare her way. "So when are you going to dive into all that money you were paid? I need a loan."

"Do I look like a bank?" She popped him playfully on the back of his head. "Get a job and then we'll talk."

"Fine, but if I had that much money, I sure wouldn't live in this slime hole."

Shahara looked around at her patched walls. Caillen was right—she did live in a dump. Over the last week, she'd looked at a couple of places to live, but so far she hadn't found any place that seemed like home.

Even if she had, she wouldn't have bought it. No matter how hard she tried, she couldn't bring herself to spend any of the money.

Her guilt over Syn ran too deep.

It'd been six months since they released him. Six incredibly long, lonely months of wondering how he was, what he was doing.

Who he was doing it with.

He wanted nothing to do with her and she wasn't about to go begging again. She might not have much in this world, but she did have her pride.

Sighing, she walked over to her shoddy cooling unit and poured herself a glass of juice. "Surely there has to be someone somewhere who needs a no-account pilot like you."

Caillen made an obscene gesture at her.

Before she could respond, a knock sounded on her door.

Caillen frowned. "You expecting company?"

She shook her head, then went to answer the door.

It was a uniformed delivery man. "Good afternoon, *Fria*. I have a package here for Shahara Dagan."

"I am she."

"Good." He held a ledger out for her. "If you'll just sign—"

"I didn't order anything," she said, interrupting him.

"Ma'am, I'm just the messenger. If you'd like to talk it over with someone who knows something more about it, there's a number on the invoice you can hail." He held the ledger out for her once again.

Signing her name, she took the box from his hands. Caillen looked up. "What is it?"

She shrugged and reached for a knife to open it. Unfolding the box, her frown grew. Layers of gold tissue paper met her hand and she dug through it until she touched something incredibly soft.

Picking it up, her mouth dropped open.

It was the blue-green dress from the hotel lobby that she'd wanted so badly. Not only the dress, but everything that went with it—stockings, shoes, even a shawl.

"Did *he* send you that?"

"Shut up, Caillen," she snapped, reveling in the softness as she held the delicate sleeve up to her cheek. It really did feel as soft as a spider's web. Warmth spread through her.

Why would Syn have sent her this?

Unless . . .

Her heart sped up. Could it be his way of apologizing?

It must be.

And if he were ready to see her again, then maybe, just maybe . . .

Elated, she rushed to the bathroom to try her dress on. Once she had settled it over her body, she ran her hands down the front. Oh, it was magnificent. And it made her feel so beautiful. So feminine.

Needing to share it with someone, she twirled back out to where Caillen sat. "What do you think?"

He glanced over at her and snorted. "You look like some rich guy's mistress. I think it's disgusting."

"You're so mean." Shahara unbraided her hair, then twisted it up into a loose bun. Pulling stray tendrils of it around her face, she glared at Caillen. "It's your own

fault you can't find work. After what you said to Syn, you deserve to starve and go begging in the streets."

For the first time, she saw contrition in his eyes. "I know I shouldn't have said what I did. But you have to understand that there's a special code between guys— you don't bed-rock with your best friend's sister. Ever."

She rolled her eyes at his crudeness.

"You're my big sister, Shay, and I always thought you were above baser emotions."

"Oh, thanks a lot."

Caillen sighed. "I wish I could tell him I'm sorry."

"Why don't you?"

His spine went ramrod stiff. "I'm a man, *Trisa*, not a wimp."

"There's a spice shipment that needs to be delivered to Derridia tonight."

Shahara turned around at the deep baritone voice she'd longed to hear. Like a feral predator watching its target, Syn stood in the shadow of her sheet, just inside her bedroom.

She looked over to Vik, who sat whistling guiltily in the corner. The little booger must have let Syn in while she'd been trying on her dress.

"Why don't you call Criam and tell him I said for you to take it?"

Caillen rose slowly to his feet. "You sure?"

Syn glanced to Shahara. "Good pilots are a *dina* a dozen, but great pilots are hard to replace." He looked back at Caillen. "Now go on before I change my mind."

Caillen shrugged his jacket on and gave Shahara a quick peck on her cheek. "I'll call you later." Then he dashed out the door.

Shahara licked her suddenly dry lips as Syn turned his obsidian gaze back to her.

Gods, he was gorgeous. With his hair down and his cheeks dusted by whiskers, he wore an entirely white outfit that made his skin appear even darker than normal. The white linen outlined every corded muscle, and his pants hugged a rump so prime that it begged to be savored.

In spite of herself, her blood raced.

Feeling suddenly awkward, she searched for something to say. *Tell him you love him.*

No, she couldn't do that.

Not yet.

"Thank you for the dress," she said, deciding that was innocuous enough.

With a sheepish grin, he rubbed his neck. "I thought it would be a nice change to see you in something other than pants and work clothes." A hungry light flickered in the darkness of his eyes. "You look great."

So do you. He'd lost some weight. Not much, just enough to heighten the appearance of his well-developed muscles.

Every piece of her was attuned to him, and all she wanted was to rush to him and pull him into her arms. Run her hands over his muscles and take him . . .

But the thought of his rejection kept her feet riveted to the floor. She wouldn't embarrass herself.

At least not yet.

Silence hung heavy between them. Shahara bit her lip, waiting for him to say something.

Vik turned into a bird. "You know, I'm feeling really awkward, people. Think I'm going to visit with Caillen for a bit." He took off out the window.

At last Syn crossed the distance between them and took her hands in both of his. An emotion she couldn't define creased his brow. "I've missed you, Shahara."

His words gave her so much ecstasy that she felt like singing.

But she couldn't.

Instead she gave him a tender smile. "I've missed you, too."

"No." He cupped her face in his hands while he stared at her with those obsidian eyes. Eyes that mirrored the depth of his emotions, and allowed her to see straight into his soul. "I mean I've *really* missed you."

"And?"

"And what?"

She looked up at him. All she wanted was for him to say it. For him to tell her that he loved her.

Was that so hard?

She saw his devotion, but that wasn't enough. If he couldn't say it . . .

"Never mind."

Syn stared at her in confusion as she pulled away from him. Why was she being so distant?

Fine, then. Two could play that. Folding his arms across his chest, he leaned against the wall. "I heard you quit your job."

"Yeah." She shut down her computer that Caillen had left on. "I surrendered my license as soon as I came home."

"Why?"

She shrugged. "Before I met you, I always thought justice was black and white. Right and wrong. You showed me that it wasn't that simple. And I became terrified when I thought about how many innocent people I might have helped execute. I don't want to be that person anymore."

She looked up at him with those haunting golden

eyes that seared his soul. "I couldn't stand the thought of what I'd done to you."

He pulled her back into his arms. "I need you to be a part of my life."

She tensed. "Yes, you've told me that before and then you refused to speak to me for six months."

"Well, you did hand me over to the man who wanted to kill me."

Sadness shadowed her eyes and she looked down at his chest. "I know."

He lifted her chin so that he could see her expression. "Why didn't you give Merjack the right chip?" He wanted her to tell him it was because she loved him too much to see him die.

"Because I was a seax, sworn to uphold justice and I was on a mission for them."

He winced as she confirmed his fear. He really didn't mean anything to her.

"Oh." He took a step back and released her.

Shahara waited for him to continue.

When he started for the door, she called out, "Why did you think I did it?"

"Nothing. It was stupid." He reached for the latch, then stopped.

She watched as various emotions crossed his face. He closed his eyes and looked like he was battling the devil himself.

Finally he spoke. "I can't do this again," he said in a voice so low she wasn't sure she'd heard him.

Before she could ask him what he meant, he returned to her side. "I love you, Shahara. You showed me what it was like to talk to someone. Really talk. And now . . . I can't live without you."

He knelt before her and took her hand in his.

She stared down at him, awed that a man so strong had humbled himself for *her*.

"Save me, Shahara," he whispered. "Save me from the lonely nights that never end." He reached into his pocket and took out the ring she'd seen that night in the hotel. He slid it on her finger and kissed it. "I want you to marry me, Shahara."

Shocked, she stared at the beautiful ring. "Whose ring is this?"

"Yours."

That destroyed her mood and the tender feelings he'd stirred. "Oh, please," she snapped. "I saw you with it the night you were arrested. How many years have you had it?" She narrowed her gaze. "Who did you buy it for?"

He smiled up at her. "I bought it for you because the color reminded me of your eyes. It was in the store where I bought our clothes. I have the receipt if you want to see it."

She shook her head, her heart pounding. He really did love her. She couldn't believe it. "No, baby. I trust you."

"Then say you'll marry me."

She smiled as joy swept through her and left her breathless. "I will marry you, Sheridan Digger Wade."

His dimple flashed. "Call me Syn."

"As much as I'd like to *give in to Syn*," she said, crinkling her nose playfully at him, "I don't think I can. You're not even willing to share *that* name with me. I still don't know what the C.I. stands for. Besides, Shahara Syn sounds like a disease, or a city."

His warm laugh thrilled her as he stood up in front of her. "Okay, you want to know what C.I. stands for?"

"If you want me to agree to marry you I do."

She watched in amazement as a deep red stain crept over his face.

Could it *really* be that embarrassing?

He rubbed the back of his neck and looked at her from under his lashes. "Do you remember, years ago, that little cartoon vorna cub on the back of *moglas* boxes?"

What did that have to do with anything?

"That cute one who was always getting into trouble?" she asked.

He nodded. "He was named C.I."

Her mouth dropped open as it dawned on her. A laugh bubbled up and before she could squelch it, it burst through, making his face an even brighter shade of red.

"You're kidding. You named yourself after a cartoon?"

"I told you it was embarrassing. I was just a stupid kid, and no one wanted to deal with a kid who didn't have at least a pretense of a real name. I thought it sounded cool."

She shook her head. "In that case, I will definitely be calling you Sheridan."

His eyes twinkled. "I don't think you can do it. You're too used to calling me Syn."

"Oh please, Syn, I . . ."

He flashed his dimple at her. "Told you."

Unwilling to let him have this victory, she tried to think of a name to call him. "How about Syn Wade?"

"How about *you, Gildagard*, kiss me and we go and find a priestess so that I can make an honest woman out of you?"

She stood on her toes and met his lips.

Syn's arms tightened around her waist as he kissed

her senseless. He pulled away from her with a soft moan.

When he spoke, it was with a ragged whisper that set her heart pounding even harder. "How about we find a bed and then a priestess?"

She laughed. "Quit talking, convict, and give me another kiss."

"Yes, ma'am."

And this time when his lips met hers, she knew that it would be forever.

EPILOGUE

Two years later

Syn paused as he saw Shahara brushing her hair while she sat on his bed. He still couldn't believe how lucky he was that he'd taken a chance on her, and it'd paid off in ways he couldn't have imagined.

Thank the gods for Nykyrian. Had his friend not been so harsh with him, he wasn't sure if he'd have ever come to his senses where she was concerned.

Once again, he owed his life to an assassin.

"You know, I was thinking . . ."

Shahara paused to meet his gaze. "About what?"

"We don't have to do this. I can tell Kip that I'm not feeling well."

"Why?"

Because he knew how much it upset her to be around Kiara and Nykyrian's children when they couldn't have their own. She didn't say it, but he always saw the pain in her gaze that she tried so hard to hide.

It was so unfair. He'd never seen a woman more maternal or kinder than her, and yet all she could do was love other people's babies. He hated that for her.

They'd tried everything, including adoption, both infants and older children, but with his past . . .

No one would let him near a child.

She came off the bed and approached him. "I don't mind, Syn."

"You always say that." He pulled her close and held her. "I'm so sorry, Shay."

"There's no need to be sorry, sweetie. Besides, I need to see Kiara and ask her some things."

Pulling back, he frowned. "What kind of things?"

"Parenting advice."

His frown deepened. "Why?"

"Well, I kind of screwed up raising Kasen, Tessa, and Caillen. And you screwed up raising Vik. I'm really hoping that we can do better with our baby."

It took a full minute for those words to sink in.

She flashed a bright smile at him as she went to her top drawer and pulled out a pregnancy test.

It was positive.

"Your treatment worked, Syn. We're going to have a baby."

He couldn't breathe as he stared at the test and then looked at her.

She was pregnant.

His hand shaking, he reached out and touched her stomach. "How far along?"

"You're the doctor. But I think about seven weeks."

Laughing, he picked her up in his arms and swung her around. "I'm going to throw you the biggest baby shower you've ever seen."

"I think Kiara's supposed to do that."

"I don't care." He slid her down his front so that he could cup her face in his hands. "Thank you, Shay."

"For what?"

"For looking into the eyes of nothing and seeing a man you could love."

Shahara wanted to weep at his words that touched her deep inside her heart. "You were never nothing, Syn. And you will always be *everything* to me."

Read on for an excerpt from
the next League book

BORN OF ICE

PROLOGUE

"That right there is the meanest son of a bitch ever born."

Devyn Wade Kell jerked his head up from his paperwork as he heard that deep, familiar voice coming from across the room.

No. It couldn't be . . .

He barely bit back his smile as he instantly saw the newcomer through the group of soldiers who separated them in the mess hall.

Adron Quiakides. Braggart. Womanizer. Lunatic . . . and his best friend since birth.

Only a handful of years older than him, Adron had snow-white hair that fell in a braid down his back. As a League Assassin, Adron wore the uniform well. So black it absorbed light, it was a stark contrast to his hair and molded itself to every muscle the assassin possessed.

His eyes were covered by a pair of opaque shades, but even so, Devyn knew their color better than his own. As a kid, he'd saved the right one from blindness after they'd had a race through a briar patch that had all but ripped it out.

Devyn had won the race. But Adron claimed it was only because he'd almost lost his eye.

As if the loss of a limb could ever slow one of them down . . .

He hadn't seen Adron in almost six months, but he was definitely glad to see him now.

"You mean Kell?" Devyn's commanding officer choked as Adron draped his arm over Quills's shoulders. "Are you high, Commander? He's a friggin' doctor. The only part of me he scares is my tonsils."

Adron tsked at Devyn's CO, who'd done nothing but rag on him for the last two months since he'd been reassigned to this unit. The man really was lucky Devyn had learned to control his temper.

Most days anyway.

Adron clapped the CO on the back so hard, Quills actually staggered from the blow. "Yeah, that's what he *wants* you to think. But trust me. *I* know his skills firsthand. His father was the notorious filch and assassin C.I. Syn. His mother the legendary Seax Shahara Dagan."

Devyn clamped his jaw tight to keep from drawing his blaster and shooting his best friend for letting out a secret he'd done his damnedest to keep. *You asshole.*

Quills gaped at them both. "*He* is their son?"

"Oh, yeah. And I'll do you one better. He was trained from birth to fight by the best assassin The League *ever* created."

Quills scoffed. "You mean there's someone out there better than your father?"

Adron shook his head as he shoved Quills away from him. "No, idiot. My father trained him." He flashed an evil grin at Quills. "Just FYI, my father is also his *god*father. So you want to be real nice to Dev. All of us take it personally when people aren't."

Devyn rose to his feet as Adron closed the distance between them. He held his hand out and let his friend

pull him into a tight man-hug. "It's good to see you again, aridos. But really . . . some discretion would have been nice. Out of character for your rotten ass, but nice."

Adron laughed good-naturedly as he released him. "C'mon, Dev. You need to let these assholes know what you can do. Who you really are. They think you're weak, they'll step all over you."

A true assassin's philosophy, but it wasn't in Devyn's nature to push people around. He was too easygoing for that.

Well . . . again, most days.

Devyn glanced around the room, noting they were the recipients of way too much attention.

Yet true to Adron's words, the soldiers around him held a respect in their gazes that they'd never had before. "Being an arrogant braggart just doesn't work for me."

Adron took his insult in stride. "You should try it. It really does grow on you, trust me."

Devyn laughed at his friend who was much more like an older brother to him. "So what brings you here?"

"People need killing." Adron's tone was completely stoic about his brutal trade. "I was actually on my way back to The League and heard your unit had been dropped here. I just wanted to say hi before I left."

"Who was your target?"

Adron leaned in to whisper so that no one else would know who he'd killed. "Emperor Abenbi."

Devyn was surprised by the name. "The Probekein leader?" Abenbi had once ordered the rape and death of Adron's mother. It was a story they all knew well and it was how Adron's parents, as well as his own, had met. "Was it personal?"

"It was an assignment . . ." A tic worked in Adron's jaw. "And it was personal for what he did to my mother. Too long in coming, in my opinion, but it was legal so my father should be proud."

"He's always proud of you, Adron."

Adron didn't comment. "How long are you here for?"

"We're evacing troops out of a hot zone and have some supplies for the civs. A few days and we're clear."

"Good. I don't want to be taking your body home to your mother."

"Yeah, she'd probably hurt you if you did."

"Probably so." He grinned roguishly. "In all the universe, your mother is the only thing that truly scares me, especially where you're concerned. I don't *ever* want to be on that dark side."

"Ha-ha. And need I remind you my mother wasn't the one screaming at the pool when you got shoved in?"

"Yeah, all right, so we both have screwed-up, irrational mothers. Anyway, I've got to get out of here. I took a little longer on assignment than I should have and if I don't make check-in . . . I don't want to be hunted and have to take out another assassin dumb enough to come at me." He gave Devyn another quick hug. "Take care, little brother."

"You, too, A. I'll see you around."

Adron inclined his head to him before he made his way back toward the doors.

As soon as Adron was gone, Quills stepped forward. "Was he full of total shit, Kell?"

"No, sir."

"Then if your parents are Syn and Dagan, why is your name Kell?"

Because he was the grandson of one of the most ruthless criminals ever born, and his parents had done everything they could to shield him from people who would judge him based on his name alone.

But that was none of Commander Quills's business. "Have to ask my father, sir. I didn't pick my name. He and my mother did." Gods, how he hated being obsequious to these pricks. Why had he joined the military again?

To help people . . .

Yeah, but it was getting harder and harder to take their crap and thank them for ramming it down his throat.

His CO narrowed his gaze at him. "Are you being smart with me, Captain?"

Devyn arched a sardonic brow. How stupid was he that he couldn't tell that was a major affirmative?

Before he could answer, Quills's comlink went off. "Commander? There's an attack on the road twelve miles down. We have orders to move out. Now."

Quills took off and left Devyn alone with the lieutenant who'd joined them. The young man's face was pale and drawn.

Devyn frowned at him. "You all right?"

"I've never been in a battle before."

Poor kid, but he'd learn. "Don't worry, Lieutenant. Your training will kick in and you'll be fine."

"And if not, I'll have you there to patch me back up. Right, Doc?"

"Absolutely."

Inclining his head, the kid took off.

Devyn grabbed his pack and weapon. He didn't like battle any more than the rookie, but this was what he'd signed up for . . .

* * *

This was so not what he'd signed up for.

Devyn was furious as he knelt down on the ground where a boy lay in a bloody mess. No older then ten, his body had been shredded by a mine as the kid and his town had been caught by League troops trying to flush out a group of rebels. One arm was missing and his left leg would never be the same again . . .

Provided he didn't lose it.

"I don't want to die," the boy cried. "I want my mommy."

Unfortunately, Devyn was pretty sure she lay among the bodies that littered the road and village.

His hands shook as he tried to slow the boy's bleeding. "What's your name, kid?"

"Omari."

"How old are you?"

"Nine." He sobbed, trying to rub the blood out of his hazel eyes. His dark brown skin was ragged from his injuries. "My birthday's next month. I'm not going to die before my birthday, am I? My mom said I could finally have a puppy."

Devyn's throat tightened at the boy's panic and fear. He had to get him calmed down. "You go to school, Omari?"

He shook his head. "The League blew it up. I was home that day, but all my friends were killed."

Devyn had to bite back a curse. He'd joined The League to protect people. To keep predators from doing what their own soldiers had done.

Anger burned through him so raw and fetid that he could taste it.

"Kell? What the hell do you think you're doing?"

He looked up at his CO. "Trying to save a life." He

had to force himself to finish the sentence. "Sir." But there was no way to keep the venom and disgust he felt out of his tone.

Quills kicked dirt at them. "He's nothing to us. We have soldiers bleeding. Get your ass moving and tend them."

Devyn glanced to the men who were hurt, but nowhere nearly as bad as the kid in front of him. If he didn't stop the bleeding, the kid didn't stand a chance. "I'll be there in a minute."

"You will do as you are told, soldier. Now move!"

Devyn refused to budge. "In a minute."

Then Quills made the worst mistake of his life.

He pointed his rifle at Devyn. "Move or die."

Devyn laughed bitterly as his mother's wisdom went through his head. He narrowed his gaze at his CO. "Never give a man a choice that doesn't bode well for you."

"What?"

"You want me to move?" Devyn shot to his feet and had the rifle out of Quills's hands faster than he could blink.

"Arrest him!"

League enforcers came at him from all directions. But Devyn didn't care. The only thing that mattered to him was the kid at his feet.

Omari.

He hadn't donned his uniform to slaughter innocents. To cut off town supplies and punish innocent miners who were protesting The League's cruelty to them. This was wrong and he refused to be a part of a system this corrupt.

He slammed the butt of his rifle into the first man to reach him. Another shot at him. He dodged the blast that cut down two other men before he blasted the man aiming for him. He pulled out his knives and went for the next one who tried to kill him.

Turning around, he caught one in his chest and the next in his arm and throat.

One by one, using the skills his parents and uncles had taught him, he brought down every soldier dumb enough to attack him until he stood alone.

His conviction solid steel, he moved back to his commander. "You should have listened to what Adron said. I am the meanest son of a bitch ever born. And you . . ." He shot his commander into unconsciousness. "Are so not."

He paused as he looked over the men he'd wounded. Those who weren't dead anyway. They lay holding their wounds, but made no more moves to attack.

No one else would challenge him. At least not tonight.

Tonight . . .

He growled as he realized what he'd just done. He'd declared war on The League. There would be no going back. They would hunt him like an animal and come for him, night and day.

So be it.

After all, he was a Wade, through and through. And if Wades were anything, they were staunch survivors.

May the gods have mercy on anyone dumb enough to come at him because he wouldn't.

Turning around, he picked Omari up from the ground. "Don't worry, kid. I'll protect you. No one's going to hurt you on my watch."

Hungry for a Midnight Snack?

Sign up for Sherrilyn Kenyon's **Free Short Story**

...and sink your teeth into a brand-new tale

from the world of the Dark-Hunters...

WINTER BORN

Don't Miss The Dark-Hunter Manga Debut!

THE DARK-HUNTERS
VOLUME 1

Story by Sherrilyn Kenyon
Art by Claudia Campos

The first graphic novel in the *New York Times* bestselling world of The Dark-Hunters, illustrated in the traditional Japanese manga format...

Dark-Hunter.com

**They are Darkness. They are Shadows.
They are the Rulers of the Night.**

They Are The Dark-Hunters.®

**Don't miss a single title
from the world of the Dark-Hunters!**

Fantasy Lover

Night Pleasures

Night Embrace

Dance with the Devil

Kiss of the Night

Night Play

Seize the Night

Sins of the Night

Dark Side of the Moon

Devil May Cry

The Dream-Hunter

Upon the Midnight Clear

Dream Chaser

One Silent Night

Acheron

Dream Warrior

Bad Moon Rising

BAD MOON RISING

The War Is On and Time Is Running Out...

Fang Kattalakis isn't just a wolf. He is the brother of two of the most powerful members of the
Omegrion: the ruling council that enforces the
laws of the Were-Hunters. When war erupts
among the lycanthropes, sides must be chosen
and enemies must become allies. But when the
woman Fang loves is accused of betrayal, he
must break the law of his people to save her.

Now in hardcover from St. Martin's Press

SherrilynKenyon.com

The Future Is Coming.

THE LEAGUE IS HERE

Surrender to a brave new world of trained
assassins and lethal lovers, when danger
rules the night, passions are on fire, and
those who dare to defy The League walk
on thin ice…

**Read all of The League novels by #1 bestselling author
SHERRILYN KENYON**

BORN OF NIGHT

ISBN: 978-1-61523-615-2

BORN OF FIRE

ISBN: 978-1-61523-731-9

BORN OF ICE

ISBN: 978-1-61523-608-4